MISSING IN MEXICO

Stuart Gustafson

America's International Travel Expert®

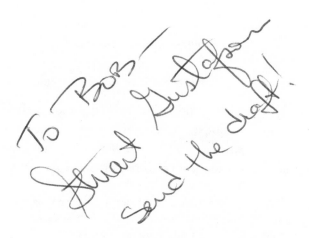

MISSING IN MEXICO

Published by

AITEpublishing
P.O. Box 45091
Boise, ID 83711 U.S.A.

www.AITEpublishing.com

ISBN 978-0-9771727-4-0
Second Printing – April 2012

Cover Design by Greensky + Co.
www.greenskyandco.com

Printed in the United States of America

This book is primarily a work of fiction. Many references to people, places, and events are fictitious, and their resemblance to actual people, places, and events is coincidental or used in a fictional setting. Some content, however, is intended, and is deemed, to be historically accurate.

PREFACE TO THE SECOND PRINTING:

When I started writing this book a few years back, my primary intentions were to write a good mystery novel and to let readers around the world know about San José del Cabo at the tip of Mexico's Baja California peninsula. One thing I didn't expect was for the residents of San José to embrace and adopt the book as "one of their own." During my first return trip to the area, the book had already gained some popularity, and I was invited to do a book signing and talk about the book. I had taken some books with me, but I certainly wasn't planning on that type of warm reception. I should have known better – the locals have always been a warm and inviting group of people.

Some of the people identified with the original cover of the book, the one with the photograph of the church in the city's main square. The book cover has a new look, and the church is still there, albeit a little more mysterious looking. Some readers also liked the way the book's picturesque descriptions made them feel as if they'd been dropped right into the middle of the story and the town. One reader commented that, after reading the book, she felt she already knew her way around town even on her first visit. There have been a few changes in San José del Cabo – some art galleries have moved, and a couple are no longer there. But the good news is that others have opened or expanded, and there's now a blown glass factory in town. The restaurants are just as delicious as before; yes, San José del Cabo is a thriving town!

A distinct pleasure and honor was seeing this book rise to two #1 Amazon ratings in the same category at the same time. It's actually happened twice as of this printing. *Missing in Mexico* has been the #1 Best Seller and the #1 Top Rated Kindle book in the Mexican Travel category – both at the same time! Now, that's exciting. I hope you, too, enjoy reading about a place I thoroughly enjoy going to every year – San José del Cabo, Mexico.

Stuart Gustafson
Boise, Idaho
April 2012

ACKNOWLEDGEMENTS:

A significant part of the pleasure in writing a book is the ability to engage with people who are genuinely interested in your work. They may demonstrate their interest through their encouragement, their organizational skills, and/or their knowledge. This book certainly is much better because of them. Right now, before you begin to read the book, I must tell you about a few of the special people whose contributions are so significant that without them there might never have been a book called *MISSING IN MEXICO*.

My key encourager continues to be my wife, Darlene. She is interested in all that I do, even though she sometimes doesn't see the direction in which I am headed (or she sees it and wonders *why is he headed that way?*). She knows that writing does not follow a "normal" 8-5 routine, and so she gives me the open time and space when I need them. Our two grown children are also very special in that they give me such strong encouragement even when they don't know it. I know they'd be willing to jump on a plane with me anytime I need to go research an area for a new book – they've seen the places I love to go.

There are businesses that help me, and they might not even realize it: hotels; timeshares; airlines; trains; taxis; restaurants; pubs; newsstands; grocery stores, and more. I need all of these when I travel – thank you for making my travels more pleasurable.

A very important person who gave me incredible encouragement and assistance in the early stages of this book is Miroslava Bautista, the former Director of Tourism for Los Cabos in Baja California Sur, Mexico. She didn't know me when I first contacted her, but she was willing to meet with me while I was in Los Cabos for my annual vacation. I showed her the book, and asked her for some input. She was so generous in her time and inputs that I was able to make some great changes – some things that I didn't see on my own. Thank you, Miroslava!

One thing that makes this book special is the inclusion of pieces of the history, the people, the culture, and the language of San José del Cabo. Knowing how to speak some of the language is one thing; writing it down as it is spoken to you in response to a question is something altogether different. I spent some time in Baja California as I researched the history and culture of the area and specifically the town of San José del Cabo. The people – common citizens, government officials, shop owners, ex-patriates who now call Los Cabos their home – all of them were extremely friendly to me. A hearty thank you goes to each and every one of them.

Finally, a really big MUCHAS GRACIAS to my good friend Luis Morales who helped me with translations when my own were not good enough. Thanks, Luis!

There were also many friends who offered to read the book and give me some feedback. I've listened to all of it, and I've tried to incorporate as much of their suggestions as I could and still keep the main themes in the book. To all those who have helped me, "Thank you from the bottom of my heart." [*Gracias desde el fondo de mi corazón.*] Finally, I want to acknowledge and thank you – the readers; for without you, there wouldn't be a need for any of us authors.

Espero que disfruten el libro [I hope you enjoy the book].

Stuart Gustafson

One/Uno
Flight # 1476 from Los Cabos to Seattle
Saturday, January 5th

familia (fă·mĭl'·ē·ă) – family. *Hay cuatro personas en mi familia.* There are four persons in my family.

The voice over the intercom system announced, "Ladies and gentlemen, we trust you had a good time in Los Cabos, but it's now time for us to take you back to the States. The cabin doors have been closed, and Alaska Airlines flight 1476 with nonstop service to Seattle-Tacoma is ready for departure."

"Hey, wait. Sarah's not here; we can't leave without her," the girl in seat 14A yelled in a frightened voice. Mary reached up and pushed the flight attendant call button even as the flight attendant was already headed toward her seat. "We can't leave yet; Sarah's still down there," Mary continued, now reaching the point of hysteria.

"Please calm down, miss. Everyone's already onboard. You can look for yourself," the flight attendant said in a calm voice as she pointed to the window.

"What do you mean everyone's onboard? Sarah's not here; she should be sitting right here!" Mary pulled her tearing eyes away from the empty seat and looked out and saw that the boarding ramps had been pulled away from the airplane, but what she didn't see scared her. How come Sarah's not out there, running in a panic toward the plane? "Where's Sarah? She was just there with me. Where is she? Don't leave; Sarah's missing!" Mary cried out as tears began flowing down her cheeks.

The annoyed passengers felt a jolt as the plane was being pushed back. They were ready for their flight home from Los Cabos. But Sarah wasn't on board; she's missing – Missing in Mexico.

Two/Dos
Seattle-Tacoma International Airport
Monday, January 14th

avión (ă·vē·ōn') – airplane. *Este es un avión muy grande.*
This is a very big airplane.

"Alaska Airlines flight 1745 with non-stop service to Los Cabos, Mexico, is now available for boarding at gate 46. As a reminder to all passengers, you must have a red stamp on your boarding coupon and you must show your passport as you board the plane. Come to the desk here at gate 46 if you don't have that red stamp on your boarding coupon. Once again, Alaska Airlines flight 1745 with non-stop service to Los Cabos, Mexico, is now available for boarding at gate 46."

Stan Walkorski was glad he was able to book a non-stop flight; he wanted to get to Los Cabos and start talking to people down there as soon as possible. He'd been in the nearby airport shop looking for a book to read when he heard the first pre-boarding announcement. He had his passport ready, but he didn't know that he had to have his boarding coupon stamped at the counter. Stan picked up his briefcase and walked over to the gate 46 counter and stood in line behind a man and woman in their matching Hawaiian shirts and khaki shorts. *There are just some sizes of clothes that should be outlawed*, Stan thought to himself.

His mind flashed back to his meeting with the Johnsons, and then to his conversations with Mary and some of the other students on the University of Washington campus. Nothing seemed to fit yet; nothing was falling into place. He knew it was still early, but he also knew that the chances of a happier outcome diminish with each passing day. He unconsciously moved forward in line, keeping pace with the "twins" in front of him. When he was finally at the front of the line, his mind had been so preoccupied that he forgot why he was in line. Shaking his head to snap out of it, he said, "Oh, yeah, I need a red stamp on my boarding coupon, please," as he handed it to the counter agent.

"I'll need to see your passport, sir," the agent replied. As he handed his blue-cover U.S. Passport to the agent, his mind once again tried to sort through all the pieces he had so far. The agent took Stan's passport, compared its photo to Stan as she squinted through her glasses to look at him, and then inserted it into the scanner. The scanner beeped and the agent removed the passport. She then took a large rubber stamp and stamped Stan's boarding coupon with a bold red **SEA**, the code for the departing airport, Seattle-Tacoma International Airport. She said a routine "Enjoy your flight, sir," as she put the now-stamped boarding coupon into the passport and handed them across the counter to Stan.

"Thank you. I'm sure I will," Stan replied as he accepted his passport and boarding coupon from the agent. "Have a good day," he said to her as he was stepping away, but she didn't hear him. She was already engaged with the next passenger. As he walked over to get in line at the boarding gate, he realized that they weren't boarding by zones, even though ZONE 2 was printed in the middle of his boarding coupon. "Why don't we have to board by zones today?" he asked the gate agent as he handed her his boarding coupon and passport.

"Our load," she replied. "We're only about 30% full on the flight today, so it's just as easy to have everyone board at once than to have to turn people back because they aren't boarding when it's their zone number. Have a good flight." The gate agent handed Stan's passport back to him along with the stub from his boarding coupon, and he looked down at it to see that he was seated in 8A.

Walking down the jet-way to the plane, Stan noticed how cold it was. *After all, it is still winter*, he thought to himself. He'd been so busy the past week that the local weather was of no real concern to him. He'd checked online to see what the weather in Los Cabos would be in January, and he was pleased to see the highs in the mid-70s and evening lows around 60. *I can take that over this weather any time.* It was cold in the jet-way, but he saw that it didn't seem to bother the couple in the khaki shorts and Hawaiian shirts up ahead of him. They were just laughing and having a good time. *Oh well, at least they are having fun.*

"Good morning, sir," the flight attendant greeted Stan as he stepped on board the plane – a Boeing 737. A lot of the airlines had been phasing out the 737's for more fuel-efficient aircraft, but it was still nice to fly out of Seattle in a plane that had been built less than thirty miles away.

"Good morning to you, too," Stan replied. "Do you ever get to stay down in Los Cabos or is it just fly down and back in the same day?"

The smirk on her face told him before she could respond – "Down and back, every time. But I've taken a vacation down there – it was a lot of fun. From the looks of your carry-on, I'm guessing this is more of a business trip for you?"

"Yes, that is the bane of the working class, isn't it? Travel to great spots and then just work, work, work." Stan knew that wasn't always the case, but it sounded good. "I'll see you later," he said as he turned right to head down the center aisle. He noticed that First Class was only half full as he continued down the aisle to his row – row 8. *The agent was right; there is hardly anyone on this plane.* There was no one else in row 8.

He had just sat down and buckled his seat belt when he heard the crackle of the PA system come on. "Ladies and gentlemen, welcome to Alaska Airlines flight 1745 with non-stop service to Los Cabos, Mexico. As you can see we have a fairly empty flight today, and we're ready to close the front cabin door. If you would like to move to another seat in your ticketed cabin, please do so now before we close that door. Once we do close the front cabin door, you will need to be seated with your seat belt securely fastened, and all of your portable electronic items must be powered off. This includes your cell phones, your iPods, and even your noise-canceling headphones. Thank you for your attention."

Stan had just unlatched his briefcase and was reviewing his notes about Sarah Johnson when he heard a familiar voice. "Mr. Walkorski – is that close? I hope I didn't butcher your name too much."

Stan looked up and toward the aisle to see the flight attendant who had greeted him as he boarded. "Oh, hi."

"Sir, we have a new seat for you," she whispered as she leaned in from the aisle. "Here is your new boarding stub." The engaging flight attendant handed Stan a boarding stub that had "2A" hand-written on it. As Stan saw it and looked up at her, there was slight smile on her lips.

"Thank you," he said as he unlatched his seat belt, grabbed his briefcase and stepped out into the aisle, following her up into the First Class cabin.

"I think you'll be more comfortable in this seat, sir," she said as she stopped in front of his new row.

"I'm sure I will. Thank you very much," Stan said graciously as he stepped over the legs of the well-dressed woman already seated in seat 2B.

"Excuse me." Stan sat down in his "new" window seat, and he slid his briefcase under seat 1A. As he buckled his seatbelt, he looked to his right to see the new travel companion was not reading anything, so he took the opportunity to say "Good morning."

"Buenos días. I mean, good morning," she replied. "It looks like a pretty day to be flying, doesn't it?" Her distinguished features had a slight Hispanic look, and Stan did pick up just a hint of an accent in her voice. His profession taught him to notice these things, no matter how small they were. Of course, that also made it hard for him to establish close relationships because he was always aware of all the little details. Curses!

"Yes, I guess it is. I hadn't noticed the weather," he said as he paused to look out his window – but his view was partially blocked by the boarding bridge. "I've just been too busy with work I didn't even see if it was clear or not outside." Stan seemed apologetic as this striking woman next to him was doing everything she could in their first minute seated beside each other to be welcoming and conversational.

"Yes, it's supposed to be a nice day today here and, of course, it will be a beautiful day when we land in Los Cabos." Stan's new friend smiled as if she were giving him an invitation to continue the conversation.

Stan was just ready to say something when the PA system came back on. "Ladies and gentlemen, the main cabin door has been closed and secured, and it's now time to make sure that your cell phones and all other electronic equipment have been powered off and put away for our takeoff. At this time, please cease all conversations and give your undivided attention to the flight attendants who are standing in the aisle to give you a brief, but extremely important, safety demonstration of this Boeing 737 aircraft."

Stan looked to his right, smiled at the lady in 2B, and leaned back in his seat and closed his eyes. He'd heard all this many times before.

The announcement continued, but Stan didn't hear it. He was thinking about Sarah Johnson and why she didn't board her flight from Los Cabos on January 5th. Had she been abducted? Did she run away – but why would she? Did she miss the flight and was frightened? But that had been over a week ago, and no one had heard from her.

Stan tried to think about Sarah, but the hum of the two engines along with the late hours he'd been working combined to put him to sleep. He didn't move as the airplane was pushed back from its gate, taxied out to the runway, and then took off on its flight to Los Cabos. Stan was exhausted, and his body responded by allowing him to sleep. The señora in 2B pulled a magazine from her purse and began to flip through the pages. She would have enjoyed continuing the conversation with this man in 2A, but she noticed that there was a sense of relief on his eyes as they closed. *Maybe later*, she thought.

Three/Tres
Hotel El Nuevo – San José del Cabo
Christmas Day, almost three weeks earlier

sorpresa (sōr·prĕ'·să) – surprise. *Tengo una sorpresa para usted.* I have a surprise for you.

José Feliciano's singing of "Feliz Navidad" was blaring in the background as the hotel lobby tried to instill some Christmas spirit for its guests – mostly American tourists. A few of the vacationers who had been enjoying more than their share of the local "cheer" joined in on the chorus:

Feliz Navidad; Feliz Navidad;

Feliz Navidad, prospero año y felicidad.

I want to wish you a Merry Christmas;

I want to wish you a Merry Christmas;

I want to wish you a Merry Christmas from the bottom of my heart.

Christmas in Mexico was enjoyable, but sand on the beach somehow didn't make it seem like a "white Christmas." Sarah Johnson missed going to the cabin in the mountains where they would make a snowman, have snowball fights, and have a "real" Christmas tree – not like the fake one that stood in the center of the lobby of the Hotel El Nuevo. Since "El Nuevo" meant "The New One," Sarah figured that they named the hotel this because it was obviously the "new hotel" when it was built. The Christmas tree had a lot of lights and decorations on it along with empty boxes wrapped to look like presents under the tree. It was a pretty tree, but it was still a fake tree. And the presents were also fake.

As far as Sarah was concerned, there were only two good things about this Christmas trip to Mexico: her friend and college roommate Mary came along with the family, plus the two of them were going to stay for an extra four days after her parents returned home. As a nineteen-year old freshman at the University of Washington where she lived in an on-campus dorm room, Sarah Johnson had a few more freedoms than many of her friends. She deserved her freedoms – she'd always been a good student, and she usually made sensible choices when faced with decisions that other young people might not have handled properly. Sarah was an only child and so her parents typically let her bring a friend whenever they would go on a family trip. That made the trip more bearable for Sarah and definitely more enjoyable for Robert and Tina Johnson, two caring parents who were also very entrenched in Robert's ladder-climbing career and Tina's social activities.

Hotel El Nuevo was situated on Boulevard Antonio Mijares on the eastern edge of the downtown area of San José del Cabo. The locals called the road as Boulevard Mijares, and the street signs – the ones that hadn't been knocked over or defaced with spray paint – said BLVD A. MIJARES. The hotel wasn't the fanciest one in town; the nicer ones – including many of the timeshare resorts – were south of town where Boulevard Mijares intersects with Paseo Malecón San José. Mr. Johnson had originally booked the vacation at the Hotel Presidente Intercontinental, but he changed his mind when he realized that it wouldn't be a convenient walk into town from there. Being close to the town's restaurants and shops was an important selling point to both Sarah and her friend Mary to get them to come on this trip.

"What did you think of Mass last night?" Sarah had to yell over the music.

"It was kind of like watching a foreign film without the subtitles," Mary replied. "I really didn't understand a thing they said. Is there another service we have to go to today?"

"Nope, just the Christmas Eve Mass."

"Did your folks say when they're coming down for brunch? I'm getting hungry. I could do without the music, but the food smells good." Mary raised her eyebrows as she took a big sniff of the aromas that were wafting through the lobby area.

"I thought they said by eleven. Do you have your watch on? I left mine in the room," Sarah replied. "Oh, here they come. Let's go; I'm starving also."

Mr. Johnson was carrying two large boxes that were wrapped in festive Christmas paper. Smiling as he saw the girls approach, he held out the two boxes to Sarah since the top box was hers. "Merry Christmas, honey," he said as she reached for the box. "Merry Christmas, Mary," he said as he handed her the other box.

"Thanks, Dad," Sarah said exuberantly – she was nineteen years old, but still a little girl at heart when it came to presents. "I thought you said we were waiting until after brunch to open presents."

"And since when do I follow the rules?" her dad said as he enjoyed seeing the happy look on her face.

Sarah held the box in her right hand as she reached to give her Dad a hug. She then wrapped her arms, box and all, around her mom. "Merry Christmas, Mom. Is that a new perfume?"

"Yes, your dad gave it to me."

"Thank you, Mr. and Mrs. Johnson," Mary chimed in.

"Do we open them here or at the restaurant?" Sarah wanted to open her present.

"How about if we sit here and have a glass of champagne while you girls open your presents? Let me go get some champagne for us."

As Mr. Johnson turned toward the bar area, the three females sat in the big comfortable chairs that circled a large square wooden table. The table was a highly polished wood, certainly not native to the area. Mr. Johnson returned in a couple minutes with a waiter right on his heels, carrying a tray with four chilled flutes and a bottle of champagne.

"That was fast," Mrs. Johnson said.

"They're not terribly busy right now," Mr. Johnson replied. "Besides, I called down earlier while you were putting on your makeup." His face had a slight smile – he liked to surprise his women.

POP went the cork as the waiter forced it out of the bottle and it went flying up to the ceiling. As the bubbles began to flow out of the bottle, the waiter deftly poured the chilled elixir into the four glasses. He then set the bottle on the table and discreetly left the area.

"Here's to a wonderful vacation, and to three of the prettiest and smartest women I know." As Mr. Johnson raised his glass for a toast, he simply added, "Merry Christmas."

"Oh, Robert," Tina said. "You say the sweetest things. But true." She giggled as she took a sip of the sparkling drink.

"Ooh, it tickles my nose. Thanks, Daddy." Sarah took just a small sip; she didn't drink alcohol, but she also didn't want to cause a disruption in the festive occasion.

"Yes, thank you, Mr. Johnson and you too, Mrs. Johnson." Mary shivered as she took her first sip of the champagne. She was not used to it – the cold, the bubbles, and the alcohol – but she was going to enjoy the experience.

"Mary," Tina began, "I think it's time you start calling us Robert and Tina. 'Mr. and Mrs. Johnson' makes us sound so old. You're a dear. I'm glad you could come." Tina did have a genuine smile on her face as she looked at Mary.

"Thanks," Mary replied. "I'll try, but I know I will forget and then I'll call you Mr. and Mrs. Johnson again. I've had a good time; this has been fun. Thanks for inviting me."

Sarah set her glass on the table and started pulling at the red bow and ribbon on her package. Struggling with it, she said, "Gee, Dad. Did you have to put so much tape on it?"

"You know me," he replied. Robert loved to wrap presents as much as he liked to buy them. But one of his idiosyncrasies was the use of tape. He wasn't satisfied with just one piece to hold something in place. He would tape down the ribbon and the bows so they were absolutely picture perfect and would not move – could not move. Of course, that also meant it usually required a sharp knife or scissors to cut them loose. He reached into his pocket and pulled out a small knife that he handed to Sarah.

"Thanks," Sarah said as she took the knife to cut the ribbon so she could then start tearing off the foil paper that adorned the large box. She tried to grab a loose edge of paper on the end, but it was taped down – of course.

Robert just smiled as his daughter fought with the paper, slicing through the tape so she could find an edge to pull.

Finally she ripped the paper off the box, but knowing that the box top would be taped to the bottom, she instinctively reached for the knife one more time. She turned the box over, sliced the tape, and separated the two halves. Hidden inside the tissue paper were a pair of jeans and two brightly colored tops. As she held up the pink top, she exclaimed, "This is perfect. How did you know?"

"We saw you looking at them in the shop the other day," her mom replied.

"They're great; thanks!" She popped out of her chair, dropping the other top that narrowly missed knocking over her glass. She hugged her parents and then plopped back down in the overstuffed chair. "Here, you'll need this," Sarah said smugly as she slid the knife across the table to Mary.

Mary went through the same routine that Sarah had just completed. She never knew that opening a present would be that much work. But rather than ripping the paper off the box, she slowly sliced the tape connections and then unfolded the foil paper as if the paper itself were a present. Her box also contained a pair of jeans and two brightly colored tops. "Wow – these are awesome!" she exclaimed. "Thanks," she said as she clumsily arose from her chair to give Robert and Tina a hug. Mary was already a little tipsy from the one glass of champagne and her empty stomach.

"Let me run these back to our room while you gals pick a spot to eat," Robert said as he was rising from his seat. He stacked the boxes, the paper, and the ribbon, and then headed down the hallway to the elevator.

"Where do you girls want to go?" Tina asked.

"It smells good right here," Sarah responded.

"Yeah, that's fine with me," Mary chimed in.

"A quick decision. Your dad will like that," Tina commented as she saw Robert step into the elevator. "So, what are you girls going to do next week after we leave?"

"Who knows, Mom. We've only been here a couple days, so we don't know what there is to do. I guess we'll hang out at the pool, maybe go to the beach one day. We'll probably just relax and get ready for school to start back up on the 7th. What do you think?" Sarah aimed the last question over to Mary who was looking totally relaxed.

"Yeah, that's about it. Anything but thinking about school is fine with me. This last term was a real bear, but I couldn't have made it without you." Mary reached for her champagne glass that someone had refilled, fortunately only half-way.

"Right," Sarah said sarcastically. "You're the brightest one I know. You just put too much stress on yourself. You've got to learn to take it easy."

"Well, whatever you girls do, just be careful. There are lots of guys down here, and you two, well, you know what I mean." Tina always found it hard when the conversation got around to 'boys and girls' or 'the birds and the bees.'

"We know, Mom," Sarah replied. "Nothing's going to happen. That's one of the reasons that Mary and I always stick together when we go out – it's safer when it's the two of us."

Mary nodded her head in agreement with Sarah.

Seemingly coming out of nowhere, Robert reappeared. "Well, did you pick a place? I'm starting to get hungry, too."

"Yes, dear. The girls thought we could just eat here. The food does smell really good and we don't have to go walking anywhere. Why don't you finish the champagne so we can go eat?"

"Why don't we just take it with us then?" Robert replied as he reached down to grab the bottle with his left hand while he extended his right hand to help Tina.

The two girls pushed themselves up out of their seats and followed Robert and Tina down the hallway toward the wonderful smells and the sound of a live mariachi band.

Feliz Navidad.

Four/Cuatro
Johnsons' home – Redmond, Washington
Wednesday, January 9th

investigar (ĭn·vĕs'·tē·găr) – investigate. *Es tiempo de investigar el problema.* It's time to investigate the problem.

As he stopped his car alongside the curb in front of 4625 Park Drive in Redmond, Washington, Stan Walkorski observed a well-maintained yard with just the right amount of landscaping. The flowering trees were bare for the season, but everything else was its proper color and shape in spite of the steady winter weather. As a seasoned private investigator, Stan noticed everything – everything was a clue or at least a piece of a clue to him. While most of their neighbors' lawns showed signs of winter neglect, the Johnsons had a beautiful yard. *Appearance is very important to them.*

Pulling his briefcase across from the passenger seat, Stan opened the car door and stepped out into the wind and rain of a "typical Washington winter." He had seriously thought about moving to a warmer area, but the Seattle-metro area was his home – he had family, friends, and lots of business here. He didn't always like the weather, but he had gotten to where he could tolerate it. He was just about ready to push the doorbell when he saw a small statue in the corner. It looked quite new, but he didn't recognize it right away. Stooping down to read the inscription at the base, he saw, "St. Jude – Patron saint of lost causes." He set down his briefcase and rang the bell.

Stan immediately introduced himself when the door opened. "Hello, I'm Stan Walkorski." He was holding out a business card in his right hand and his PI credentials in his left hand.

"I'm Tina Johnson," the lady replied as she took his business card with her left hand and then extended her right hand to shake hands. "Won't you come in, please?"

"Thank you," Stan said as he picked up his briefcase with his left hand, wiped his shoes thoroughly on the WELCOME mat, and then followed her inside.

"This is my husband, Robert," she said as they entered the living room. Robert Johnson was a stocky but well-built and handsome man. His sweater gave him a preppy look, but the fashionable dress shirt underneath it said "high-end professional."

"Hello, Mr. Johnson. I'm Stan Walkorski. It's nice to meet you, although it would be better under different circumstances."

"Thank you. Please call me Robert. Won't you have a seat?"

"And call me Tina," Mrs. Johnson chimed in.

Stan nodded and was about to sit on the sofa when Tina suggested, "Why don't we sit at the table? I think it'll make it easier."

"You're right dear," Robert responded and he motioned for Stan to follow his wife into the dining room. The dining room lights came on automatically as they entered the room. "At the end here, please," Robert said as he touched the back of the chair at the end of the impressive table.

"Thank you," Stan replied as he sat down at the head of the table. He reached down, unlatched his briefcase, and reached inside it to pull out a file folder and a pad of paper. Opening the folder he picked up two sets of stapled pages that each had a bold heading **CONTRACT FOR SERVICES**. Handing one set to each of the Johnsons, he said, "This covers the details of what we talked about on the phone. We'll all sign both copies – one will be for you and the other one will be for me."

As the Johnsons began reading, it struck them both – this is real! The grief, the shock, and the disbelief – it had all hit them before, but it was so very real now that they were doing something about it. Tina sniffled as the beginning of a tear formed in her right eye.

Breaking the silence, Stan said, "Take your time – I know this is difficult for you. I've done this many times, but that doesn't make it any easier for me either. Feel free to ask me any questions that you might have."

"No, it's fine," Robert said as he signed his name on the third page. He slid his set across the table to his wife as she was signing hers. She pushed her set over to Robert and they each then signed the "second set" and handed them to Stan.

"Thank you," Stan said as he accepted the contracts from the grieving parents. He opened each set to the last page and signed his name. He then handed one fully-signed set to Robert who reached inside his sweater and pulled out a check.

As he handed the check to Stan, Robert said, "I hope you can find her." His voice had lost a lot of its confidence and control. He was no longer talking as a senior executive; he was now talking as a dad, Sarah's dad.

"I hope so, too," Stan replied as he looked first at Robert, and then to Tina. "I'll certainly do my best." Stan put the check and his copy of the contract into the file folder, which he then put into his briefcase. Pulling the pad of paper in front of him, he picked up his pen and said, "I know we talked about some of this on the phone, but it's best to start over so all three of us are hearing and saying the same things. Remember, we're not on the clock for my services, so don't be rushed for time."

"Okay. I'll start," Tina said as she sniffled again. She wiped her nose a couple times with a tissue and then began. "We wanted to spend Christmas, I mean this last Christmas, down in Mexico. There were four of us – Robert, myself, our daughter Sarah, and her friend Mary. We flew down to San José del Cabo and we stayed at the Hotel El Nuevo right there in the middle of town. We were there for nine days from the twenty-third to January first. Robert and I flew home on the New Years' Day, and the girls were staying there until Saturday the fifth – sort of an extended semester break for them. They're both going to the University of Washington, and their second semester started on Monday."

Tina was sniffling more now, and Robert took that as a cue for him to take over. "We had talked to them twice while they were on their own, and everything seemed to be fine. We went to SEA-TAC on the fifth to pick them up. We weren't able to meet them at the gate, of course, so we had to wait outside the security area. But only Mary came through Security – Sarah wasn't with her. At first we thought the girls were playing a joke on us, and that Sarah would be the last one through. But no one else came through Security; we looked at Mary and she was crying."

Stan was a little confused – the logic somehow was off. A person gets on a plane but then is not on the plane when it lands. That didn't make any sense to him. "The other day you said it was a non-stop flight from Cabo to Seattle. Once she got on the plane there would be no way for her not to get to Seattle. Right?"

"Mary," Tina started while trying to speak calmly. "Mary said that Sarah never got on the plane in Los Cabos. The plane took off and Sarah wasn't on that flight." That did it – Tina broke out in hysterical sobs.

Robert's face tightened up as he fought to hold back his own emotions. But tears trickled out of both of his eyes. He put his elbows on the table, his chin in his up-turned hands, and sighed. "I don't know. I just don't know."

Stan sat and listened and asked questions for over three hours. He wrote down all the details as Robert and Tina described their Christmas vacation in San José del Cabo; as they talked about Sarah when she was a young girl; as they just rambled on.

Finally, he knew it was time. The parents were now grieving, and while there was nothing wrong with that, he knew there was no new information to be told. Being a private investigator sometimes involved being a grief counselor, and Stan was good at it. But he had also learned through the years how to control the grieving session, and he had to control it now.

Standing up from his chair, Stan said, "I know this has been hard for you – what you've been through in these past few days as well as all that you told me tonight. I'll be going to the campus tomorrow or Friday, and then down to Cabo next week. I'll get in touch with you in a week and a half or so. Try to stay strong."

The Johnsons remained silent. They were emotionally drained as they followed Stan as he headed to the front door.

"Thank you," Stan said as he extended his right hand to them. "Good night," he said as he stepped off the porch to the walkway down to his car.

"Good night," was the faint response from both Robert and Tina that Stan heard when he reached his car. "Thank you" was the tearful pleading from Tina as he closed the car door and headed home.

As he drove home, Stan wondered if there were any clues from the past that might say what could have happened to Sarah. He would just have to ask more questions, although he wasn't certain that he would uncover anything. The only thing he was certain of right now was that she was missing in Mexico. Knowing how the police departments worked in Mexico, Stan was less than optimistic in getting any help from them. *Missing in Mexico* he repeated to himself.

Five/Cinco
University of Washington Campus – Seattle, Washington
Friday, January 11th

estudiante (ĕ·stū'·dē·ăn'·tā) – student. *Él es un buen estudiante.* He is a good student.

As a Seattle native, Stan was more than familiar with the University of Washington. The campus was its own mini-metropolis of hundreds of buildings and with tens of thousands of students criss-crossing the campus on a daily basis. The Johnsons had given Stan the apartment number where Sarah and Mary lived, as well as their room phone number. Most students had their own cell phones, but each room in the campus residence halls still had its own telephone with voicemail service.

Stan called the phone number on Wednesday morning, hoping to reach Mary in the room. Sarah's parents did not know Mary's class schedule, and they didn't have her cell phone number, so Stan just had to try to reach her any way that he could. The phone rang four times and then Stan heard the message. "Hey this is Sarah, and this is Mary," the message started before the two voices were in unison. "We can't take your call, so leave us a brief message. Bye!" The two voices sounded so cheerful – the voices of two best-friend college freshmen. Stan left a message, although it wasn't brief; there was too much he had to say: he had to introduce himself, tell Mary that he had met with the Johnsons, say why he was calling, and ask her to please call him back. He left both his cell phone number and his home number on the message.

Thankfully, Mary had called him that afternoon, and they made arrangements to meet on campus the next day – Friday.

Pulling into the parking lot on NE Pacific Street in the southwest quadrant of the campus, Stan was thankful that he found an open spot. *Gas prices might be high, but they don't seem to stop people from driving.* He dashed across the busy street over to Mercer Hall, one of the few residence halls for first-year students. Stan walked to the fountain in the middle of the two buildings that are each named Mercer Hall. The five-story buildings house a total of about 450 students in single rooms, doubles, and three-person apartments.

Mary said she would be wearing a red hoodie, which she translated for Stan on the phone ("a hooded sweatshirt"), and she was standing there just as she said she would be. "Mary?" he said as he approached.

"Hey," she replied.

"I'm Stan Walkorski. Thanks for meeting with me." He pulled out his ID to show her.

"Sure. Wanna get some coffee?"

"Sure," he replied as he dutifully followed her lead. They walked north past Henderson Hall over to Terry Hall. They went inside and went to the espresso bar in Eleven 01 – an eclectic mix of eating choices on the first floor of the eleven story building. Mary ordered a double espresso, Stan a mocha latte. After he paid for both drinks, she led him to a small table in the corner where it appeared they would have some privacy. "Thanks for meeting with me," he said again as a way to start the conversation.

"Yeah. I've talked to the Johnsons, but I don't know what else to tell them. Plus with the new semester starting up, it's been crazy getting back into the swing of things." Mary was staying somewhat reserved, but he could sense that she did want to talk, hopefully providing some clue to help find Sarah. "What do you think you can do to find her?" Her plaintive question told Stan that she would do anything she could to help.

"I wish I had a simple answer for you, Mary. Sarah's parents asked me the same question Wednesday night. Working a case like this is similar to walking through a maze; you make your decisions about where you are going to go and what you are going to do when you get to the next decision point. If I had all the answers right now, I would tell you and I would tell the Johnsons. They gave me a lot of information, and I'm hoping that you can also give me some information that will lead me to the right clues."

"But I've already told them everything," Mary said, somewhat apologetically.

"I know you have, and I also know this is hard on you. Sarah's parents know that, too. I'm sure that some of my questions will seem like repeats, so I hope you'll just bear with me."

"Sure, anything to help find her." Mary's tired eyes and quivering voice told Stan that she, too, was hurting. Sarah was her best friend – what could have happened to her?

"Thank you," Stan said as he opened his briefcase and pulled out the notes he had taken at the Johnsons. He'd memorized the key points from their meeting, but he wanted to make sure that he didn't miss anything – every little detail was important. "I am going to read some of my notes to you – things that the Johnsons told me. I'll stop occasionally and I want you to tell me if there's anything you remember about it that is a little different, anything at all. Okay?"

Mary nodded her as she sipped the last of her espresso. *She'd need another one soon.*

Most of it was rather routine. Mary had a few things to add about their stay at the Hotel El Nuevo in San José del Cabo, but she agreed with most of what Stan read from his notes. Stan learned nothing new about the first part of the trip – from the twenty-third to the first when the Johnsons flew home. Mary had said that she and Sarah had been to a few bars instead of shopping as they'd told Sarah's parents, but those were things that typical teenagers and young adults do – they weren't of major concern. At least not yet.

"So her parents left on the first, New Years' Day. And then you two had the rest of the week there on your own. I'm not a police officer, and you're not under investigation, so you don't have to tell me anything if you don't want to. I know that some teens will do things in Mexico that they won't even tell their best friends about, and especially not their parents or some other adults. I know that. But I swear that whatever you tell me will never be told to anyone else. I promise. All I'm trying to do is to help the Johnsons find out what happened to Sarah. Okay?"

"I know," Mary said rather hesitatingly as she arose to go get a caffeine refill.

"I'll get it," Stan said as she was heading over toward the espresso machine.

"That's okay. I've got a card," she replied.

While waiting for Mary to return, Stan looked out the windows at the bare trees. *I feel like one of those trees, barren.* Just then Mary returned with another cup of steaming hot espresso. He waited for her to look re-engaged before he started again. "Did you do anything different after her parents left that you hadn't done while they were there? Did you go to different restaurants or bars? Did you go out with any new people? Any dates?"

"No, there wasn't anything really different after they left. It was more like just a vacation for the two of us. Sure, there were a couple of guys we hung out with, but we'd seen them even while her parents were there. But we always stayed together. If you're asking if Sarah went home with any of them, the answer's 'No.' We've known each other long enough that we know there's safety in numbers. And in our case, that number is two. The two of us stay together all the time – or at least we used to. That way no one would ever get into any trouble."

"Did you two talk about school, what you were taking this term?"

"No way. First term was over and we'd already gotten our grades. We managed to get some awesome schedules for this term – lots of classes together, but there was no reason to talk about any of it down there. Those days by ourselves were a break for us – no school, no parents, no restrictions." Mary paused a little before continuing. "Yeah, we both talked about how neat it would be to live down there all the time. Nothing to do but hang out, go to the beach, hit the parties. But Sarah was the practical one; she always wanted to know what we were going to do for a living. It was a fun thought, though." Mary stared out the windows, most likely <u>not</u> looking at the trees that had no leaves.

Stan asked a few more questions about what the two girls did on those four days after the Johnsons had left. The answers were ordinary answers, not revealing anything of major value to Stan. The girls had gone shopping along Boulevard Mijares and on some of the side streets. They went to "Ladies Night" at Shooters, an upstairs bar just two blocks from their hotel. They spent a couple days lounging around the pool, and one day at the beach working on their tans. Stan felt that Mary was telling him everything that she could; there just wasn't that much else to tell.

"Tell me about Saturday the fifth. Did you have any breakfast? When did you pack your bags? When did you check out of the hotel?"

"That Saturday was just like any other day there, except that we had to leave. We didn't have a wakeup call so we slept in. We kinda needed it 'cause we were out late on Friday night. I called down and ordered a bowl of fresh fruit, some toast, and lots of coffee." Mary was more methodical now as if she were reading entries from journal. "We sat in the room as we ate breakfast, then Sarah took her shower, and then I took mine. We packed our clothes, but she didn't have much to pack. She'd sent her big suitcase home with her parents."

They didn't tell me that.

"Wait a minute. Sarah's parents took one of her suitcases home with them when they came home on the first?" Stan asked the question that Mary had just answered, but he still had to ask it.

"Yeah, why not? She said it would be easier for her if she didn't have to lug that big one around at the airport. Her dad thought it was a good idea, and I sent mine with them also. So all Sarah and I had left were one smaller suitcase and a backpack each. Anyway, after we packed we went downstairs and checked out. Mr. Johnson had arranged to have everything else there charged to his credit card, so all we had to do was to sign the bill. We got on the shuttle and went to the airport."

"What time was your flight?"

"Two o'clock or close to that, I guess" Mary answered.

"And what time did the shuttle pick you up?"

"It was supposed to pick us up at eleven fifteen but it was late, maybe like fifteen minutes or so."

"You're lucky it was only fifteen minutes," Stan offered. "What about when you got to the airport? Anything unusual happen there?"

"No," Mary started. "The driver took our suitcases out of the back of the van and he carried them inside the terminal as we got in the line for Alaska Airlines. It took about twenty minutes to get to the front where they put our bags on a table and opened them to check for stuff. We then went to the counter where they took our bags and gave us our boarding passes. They said the flight was on time and so we should go on through Security to the gate. That's what we did."

"Then what?"

"We went over to the security line, put our backpacks on the belt and we went through the thing without any problems. We got our backpacks and found our gate. I saved Sarah's seat while she went to look in the Duty Free stores; I don't know if she bought anything or not. She came back, and then I went to look. Perfume, cigarettes, and tequila – people were buying it, but it wasn't anything I wanted."

"Did it seem like it was crowded inside? Did you notice anyone watching you or talking to Sarah while she was in the stores?"

"No, it wasn't too crowded; certainly nothing like SEA-TAC on a holiday weekend. Sarah's cute, so guys are always looking at her. But I didn't see anyone following her or anything like that. Do you think that maybe someone nabbed her?" Mary had perked up; perhaps it was the espressos.

"I don't know," Stan replied. "But it would be pretty hard to nab someone inside an airport with all those people standing around. She would've yelled, which would've drawn attention to her. It's hard to imagine something like that, but I'm not ruling it out – I'm not ruling out anything. What about when you boarded the plane? Weren't you two together? Her parents said you told them that Sarah never got on the plane."

"They called our flight but we couldn't get on right away because we were in zone 2 or zone 3; anyway we had to wait until we could board. When it was our time, we went over to the gate and got in line. They were trying to rush people through so they could take off before a storm came in. We were at the front of the line when Sarah said she had to go back to one of the stores to get something for her parents. I said I'd wait, and she said, 'No, go on. I'll be right there.' She turned around and walked back to one of the stores that she'd already been in. So I kept going. They took my boarding pass and checked the stuff in my backpack. As I walked out the door I looked back and I saw Sarah still in the store looking at things."

Mary paused. She was doing well up to this point. Her composure had held up, but she was now getting to the more emotional part – the part she didn't want to re-live.

"That's okay," Stan said noticing it was getting harder for her. "Take your time. I'm going to get another; you want one?"

"Sure," Mary replied.

"The restrooms?"

"Out that door and to your left."

"Thanks. I'll be right back," Stan said as he headed away from the windows. It felt good to stand up and stretch his legs.

As he returned a couple minutes later, Stan got in line to get them each a refill. He noticed that Mary was talking to someone on her cell phone. He couldn't hear what she was saying, but the animated gestures showed a happier Mary than the one he'd just been talking with. He ordered his latte, her espresso, paid for them, and dropped the change into the tip jar. He walked slowly over to their table, wanting to give her some time and space to regroup from their conversation. He set her cup on the table and stepped away to give her some privacy.

"Thanks," she said as she closed her cell phone and pick up her third double espresso of the morning.

"You're welcome," he replied. "Is it always this busy in here?"

"No, sometimes it gets <u>really</u> crowded and there's no place to sit down."

"Wow," was all Stan could say. He was mentally trying to calculate how much money this place made off the students' addictions to caffeine. "We're just about done, I think. So you walked out the door and went to the plane and got on it. But Sarah never got on the plane?"

"No. I kept looking out my window to see her, but she never showed up. I told the flight attendants about her, but they said there was nothing they could do. I said, 'But her bag's on board. Certainly we can't take off without her.' I think that got their attention as they asked me her name again, and then picked up their phone."

"What did they say after that? Did they tell you that they took her bag off the plane?"

"No, they never told me anything else. Not much time went by and they started with their instructions to fasten our seat belts 'cause we were going to be taking off. I rang my flight attendant call button, which really ticked them off. I asked them again about Sarah, and they just said, 'There's no problem, we have to take off now.'" Mary started crying quietly as the emotion that she had been holding inside finally surfaced.

Stan took a sip of his latte and leaned back in his chair, letting Mary cry. As she regained her composure, Stan offered his handkerchief to her, but she declined, using one of her napkins instead.

"So the flight took off, and Sarah wasn't on it." It was a statement, but Stan intended it as a question; and Mary answered it.

"Right."

"What happened when you landed at SEA-TAC?"

"I asked them one more time about Sarah. They were frustrated with me, and they said there was nothing they could do. Sarah's name was on the flight list, but she never boarded the plane and she didn't have any luggage onboard either. There was nothing else I could do, so I just got off the plane, and walked out through Security where I met the Johnsons."

"And you've never heard from her? No phone calls or emails?"

"Nothing."

"Did she say anything to you while you were down in Cabo? Was she unhappy with anything, or was there anything that worried her?"

"No, everything was fine. She had good grades and was really happy. She'd been dating this one guy, but they'd broken up right around Thanksgiving. Something bad has happened to her. I just know it. What else could it be?"

"I don't know what it could be, Mary, but I am going to do my best to find out what happened, and to find her." Stan tried his hardest to sound confident, but even he knew that the prospects of finding Mary dwindled as each additional day went by.

A sudden thought came to Stan. "Mary, you said that you and Sarah each checked one bag in Cabo and that you each had a backpack, right?"

"Yeah."

"And the flight attendants said that Mary's bag wasn't on the plane, right?"

"Right."

"So how could she check it in at Cabo but somehow it wasn't on the plane?" Stan asked this question, although it wasn't asked to anyone in particular.

"But it was," Mary said emphatically. "Her bag was on the carousel at SEA-TAC just like mine was. I recognized it because of the big purple and gold bows on it – our school colors." All of a sudden Mary was more engaged as she realized for the first time that Sarah's bag _had_ been on that flight.

"Her bag was on the carousel?" Stan repeated.

"Yes, it came off the belt right after mine did. Sarah's parents took it home with them."

That's something else they didn't tell me.

"You mean to tell me that Sarah's bag came off the carousel, and that her parents took it home with them?" Stan was starting to talk more rapidly now.

"Yeah, they recognized it also and they took it."

Stan tried to put the pieces of the puzzle together. Here's what he knew:

> Mary checked in at Los Cabos; she checked in one bag, received her boarding pass, and boarded the flight to Seattle.

> Sarah also checked in at Los Cabos; she checked in one bag, received her boarding pass, but didn't board the flight to Seattle.

> The airlines aren't supposed to fly with luggage from a customer who has not boarded the airplane.

> Mary arrives on the plane in Seattle, and her luggage is there of course.

> Sarah was not on the plane to Seattle, but her luggage <u>did</u> arrive.

Something didn't make sense. Even though the plane was taking off from Mexico, the airline still had to follow the FAA regulations of not transporting luggage from a customer who's not on the plane. Stan had been on flights that were delayed as the ground crew had to find and remove a piece of luggage. So how could Sarah's suitcase still be on the plane to Seattle?

"Excuse me, just a minute," Stan said to Mary as he pulled out his cell phone. He punched in the 10 digits for the Johnson family home, hoping that one of them was there. He was getting discouraged, but then the phone was finally answered.

"Hello," the female voice said as she answered the phone.

"Hello, Tina. This is Stan Walkorski."

"Oh. Hi, Stan. How are you?"

"I'm fine, thank you. I'm here on campus talking with Mary."

"How is she doing? She's such a nice girl." Tina Johnson asked about Mary in a caring, motherly voice.

"Yes she is, and she misses Sarah, too. Tina, Mary said Sarah's suitcase was on the flight from Cabo and that you and Robert took it home from the airport. Is that right?"

"Yes, we just thought that perhaps she missed her flight, so we took it home." Then in a tone of expressive curiosity, Tina asked, "Well, why would the airline say her suitcase wasn't on the plane when it was?"

"Right, I don't know why they would say that, but I have a hunch. Would you do me a favor and get the suitcase so I can ask you to look at something?"

"Sure; can you wait for a minute?" Tina's voice was suddenly filled with anticipation.

"Yes, I'll wait," Stan replied as Tina had already set the phone down and was leaving the room to retrieve Sarah's suitcase.

Not more than a minute passed before Tina returned to the phone. "Are you still there, Stan? I have the suitcase here."

"Yes, I'm still here. Is the baggage claim tag still on it?"

"Let's see. Yes, it is."

"It is?"

"Yes, I just said it was."

"Good. Whose name is on it? Is it Sarah's name?"

"It should be; it's her suitcase." There was a short pause, and then Tina continued. "No; it says Mary Raymond. Why would Sarah's bag have Mary's name on it?"

"I'm not sure right yet, but I have an idea I need to check into. Thanks, Tina. Tell Robert I said hello. Okay?"

"Okay, Stan. Does this help you?"

"I think it might. I'll talk to you later, Tina. Bye for now."

"Bye, Stan. Let us know."

"I will. Bye, Tina," Stan said as he closed his cell phone.

Mary looked a little puzzled as Stan was looking happy. He wasn't smiling, but she could still tell that he was happy.

Stan began, "The baggage claim tag on Sarah's suitcase has your name on it. That's why the flight attendants said her suitcase wasn't on the plane. As far as the airline knew, you had checked two suitcases on that flight, but Sarah hadn't checked any."

Mary's eyes opened very wide – not from the espresso, but from the information she had just heard.

Six/Seis
Approaching San José del Cabo
Monday, January 14th

conversacíon (cōn·vĕr·să'·sē·ōn) – conversation. *¿Le gustaría tener una conversacíon?.* Would you like to have a conversation?

"Excuse me, sir. You have to complete the immigration forms before we land in Los Cabos." Stan heard the words being said, but they didn't register. He was, as the saying goes, "Dead to the world." "Excuse me, sir." This time he felt the hand on his right shoulder that was nudging him to awaken. "Mr. Walkorski?"

That did it. He knew his name, and someone touching him and saying his name meant that alertness was required of him. Blinking his eyes a few times and shaking his head quickly to the right and to the left a few more times, he finally rejoined the conscious world of Alaska Airlines flight 1745. He instinctively looked to the right because the touching he felt was on his right shoulder. "Hi," was all he could come up with.

"Sir, we'll be landing in Los Cabos within the hour, and you must complete your immigration forms before we land. May I offer you a snack or a drink?" The same flight attendant who'd moved him from seat 8A in Economy Class to seat 2A in First Class wanted to complete her cabin duties, but she also wanted to accord him First Class service.

"Thank you, uh, Margie," he said as he looked at her name tag. "Sorry, I guess I was out of it for a while. Just a Coke will be fine; thanks."

As Margie handed the two forms to him, she headed to the front galley to pour him a glass of Coca-Cola. "You must have been really tired," Stan's neighbor in 2B said.

"Wow, I guess so," he replied. "I'm sorry to have been so rude. My name is Stan Walkorski," he said as he extended his right hand to her.

"That's okay," she replied. "I've also slept on many long flights. It is nice to make your acquaintance, Mr Wal…"

"Walkorski," Stan interjected. "Think of being in the mountains in winter. You can either walk or ski. My name is Walk-or-ski; Walkorski. It's not an easy name, is it?"

"My apologies, Mr. Stan Walkorski." She said his name somewhat hesitantly this time, but with skill.

"No apologies necessary. It's a tough name, not like Smith or Jones."

The lady in 2B smiled in response. "My name is Carmelita Sanchez. I am pleased to meet you, Mr. Stan." She giggled a little as she called him by his first name, something that she would not normally do. "My name is a common name, as many of our names are in *México*. And," she paused, "we do not have many mountains where we can ski in the snow."

Stan noticed that she said *México*, not Mexico. She is a lady of class; *I wonder what she does living in Cabo.* Stan stole a quick glance at her left hand and saw that she wore a beautiful white gold ring with a stunning diamond perched on top. "I am pleased to meet you, Señora Sanchez. I wish that I had not fallen asleep so we could have talked on the flight." Realizing he'd been asleep for a couple hours, he continued, "I hope I wasn't snoring. I guess I was just really tired."

"No, you did not snore."

"Thank goodness," Stan replied just as the flight attendant was bringing him a glass of Coca-Cola. "Thank you, Margie," he said with a slight smile. He took a small sip and let the flavor and the bubbles of the Coke rest in his mouth before swallowing.

"Business or pleasure?" Señora Sanchez asked.

"Business of course; I'm not lucky enough to come down here for pleasure. And you – do you live in Los Cabos?"

"Not any more. My family lived in San José for many years, but I moved to Seattle to live near my daughter after my husband passed way." She paused for a moment and then continued in a softer voice as she made the sign of the cross. "May he rest in peace," she said softly.

Stan saw her expression change and he decided he should allow her some personal space and time.

She sensed Stan's reluctance to continue the conversation. "That's okay; thank you. It has been many years, but it's still hard to believe. My brother Roberto and his family still live in San José del Cabo."

"Su hermano Roberto y familia?" Stan said to try out his rusty Spanish.

"Sí, my hermano Roberto y su familia viven allí. ¿Hablas Español?" she answered with a pleased look on her face. She was no longer talking with a man sitting in seat 2A; she was now conversing *con un amigo* (with a friend).

"Not very much," Stan replied. "My Spanish is not very good. I know some phrases and how to put a few sentences together. But beyond that, I can't really carry on a conversation. If I try I usually end up misunderstanding what they said, or I'll say the wrong thing – and that can be really embarrassing."

"At least you tried." The glow on Señora Sanchez's face brightened as she was feeling more comfortable – more comfortable in fact than she had felt in years in being around a man who was not a member of her family.

"Thank you. I mean gracias," Stan replied. He took another sip of his Coke. Now he was the one starting to feel uncomfortable. *What's going on here?* Was he flirting with her, or was she flirting with him? This was a strange feeling for him; he wasn't sure what to do.

That issue was solved for him when she started, "Señor Stan, is it okay if I call you that?"

"Sure, that's fine. Walkorski's a hard name even for most of my friends who've known me for many years."

"Yes. Señor Stan, if it does not seem too forward of me – I think that is how you say it – I would be happy to show you around my town if you have time. Or are you going to Cabo San Lucas?"

"No, I'm not going to Cabo San Lucas. I will be in San José del Cabo staying at," he had to pause as he pulled a piece of paper from his shirt pocket. "I'll be staying at the Hotel El Nuevo."

"Oh yes, that is a very nice hotel. And it's very new, as its name says."

"Sure, I would love a tour of the town. I've never been there, so I don't even know where the hotel is. I was just told that's where I should stay."

"Is there a business meeting there? It is a popular hotel for the tourists and for business meetings."

"No," he replied as he lowered his voice so he wouldn't be broadcasting to everyone else in the First Class cabin. "I'm a private investigator, and I'm trying to locate someone who didn't go home after a family vacation there." Stan's face took on a serious look as he wondered if he should've told her why he was going to Los Cabos.

"Oh, that's too bad. If there is anything I can do, or my brother Roberto, please let me know." She reached down to her purse and pulled out a small but elegant wallet. Opening it she pulled out a small card, a business card. She turned it over and wrote something on the back. "Here is my brother's address and his phone number where I will be." She then handed the card over to Stan who graciously accepted it.

"Thank you," he said as he pulled a business card from his pocket and wrote "Hotel El Nuevo" on it. He handed his card to her outstretched left hand and smiled.

"Your forms," she said. "The immigration forms. You must fill them out before we land."

"Oh, yes. I forgot about them. Thank you."

"Some more Coke, or something different?" the flight attendant asked as she stood dutifully in the aisle.

Stan first looked at the flight attendant, and then he lowered his eyes to look at the lady in 2B. "Señora Sanchez, would you like to have a glass of wine with me? Or perhaps something else?"

"Sí, a glass of wine would be excellent, thank you."

"Blanco o rojo [*white or red*]?" he asked.

"Blanco, gracias," she replied.

"Two white wines, please." As the flight attendant walked to the forward galley, Stan switched his look back down to the lady who had just become his traveling companion. Her face revealed a very slight girlish grin. *She's happy. I wonder what that means.*

Moments later, the flight attendant reappeared. "Here you are," she said as she put a wine glass on Señora Sanchez's tray. "I thought you might like some cheese and crackers to go with the Piñot Grigio," she added as she set the plate down on the platform between the two seats.

After both wine glasses had been set on the trays, Stan raised his glass as he looked to Señora Sanchez. He didn't know what to say in Spanish, so he just held his glass up, hoping that she would recognize the gesture.

She did, and she gently touched her glass to his. Even though the clink of the two glasses was slight, it did still catch the attention of the passenger across the aisle in 2C; he smiled.

"Thank you for making this flight enjoyable; I would truly like to take you up on your offer to show me around the area." Stan paused as she gave him a slight smile, nodded her head, and put the glass to her lips to take a sip.

As he took his first sip of the chilled wine, she said, "I would enjoy it also."

"Thank you," Stan replied. He then picked up one of the crackers with the cheese on it, took a bite, and then followed that bite with another sip of the wine. "Oh, the forms – do I have to fill out both of them?"

"Yes," Señora Sanchez replied. "The bigger one is for the entire family, but that's just you on this trip. The smaller one is for each person to complete. When you go through Customs, they will tear off the top part of the bigger form and give you the bottom part back. You have to hold on to it and bring it back with you when you are ready to leave the country. If you lose it or forget it, the Customs Officials can make it very hard on you, and you will probably have to pay a fine."

"Well there's an incentive to keep it." Just as Stan started writing on the first form, the airplane shook as it started to descend into Los Cabos International Airport. The wine sloshed in his glass, but none spilled out as there was only a small amount left in the glass. He hurriedly completed both forms and put them in his ticket case just as he could feel the landing gear begin to lower. The extra drag on the aircraft once again caused a shaking motion that made him instinctively reach to hold the glass.

"Would you like a last refill before we land?" the flight attendant asked as she came back into the First Class cabin after collecting the plastic cups and other debris from the economy cabin.

"No, thank you," Señora Sanchez replied as she handed her empty glass to the flight attendant. "And thank you for the crackers and the cheese; they were very nice."

Stan took the last sip of his wine, and even though he would have liked another glass, he declined. "Yes, thank you, Margie. It was all very nice," he said as he smiled and handed his glass to her. As Stan sat back in the leather seat, he let out a big sigh as he was now truly relaxed; but he knew this relaxation would last for only a few more minutes. He had just closed his eyes to fully enjoy those last few moments of peace when he heard that familiar crackle of the PA system.

"Ladies and Gentlemen, as you can tell we are now on our final approach into Los Cabos International Airport. Please make sure that your seat belt is fastened securely across your lap, and that your seatbacks and tables are in their upright and locked positions." Stan relaxed as he closed his eyes and tried to think once again what could have happened to Sarah. Not only is she missing, she's missing in Mexico. Is there any hope of finding her, and finding her alive?

Stan's eyes opened and he looked to his right and said, "What's this I heard about a red light and a green light when you go through Customs?"

"Oh," Señora Sanchez began. "When you get your luggage you have to put it on the belt to go through the X-Ray machine. Once it comes out you push a button, like the button on the street light that you push to cross the street. If the light turns green, then you are done and you leave. If the light turns red, then they will make you open your bags and they will search them."

"That's it?" he asked somewhat incredulously. "What's the logic behind whether the light turns green or red? Is it based on the X-Ray scanning?"

"No; it's just how they do it to decide whose luggage to check."

"Oh, okay." Stan still didn't understand the logic, but he realized that perhaps there really wasn't any logic to understand. Gazing out the window, he said, "Is it always this green? I thought this was a desert."

"Oh, yes. It is a desert area. But we receive most of our rain in December and January, and with the cooler weather, the plants turn green. It is a pretty sight, isn't it?"

"Yes it is. I just didn't expect to see so much vegetation." Stan continued to look outside as the plane finally settled down on runway 16. "Welcome home," he said as he glanced back to Señora Sanchez.

"Gracias, Señor Stan. It is nice to be here so I can see my family. Don't forget to call me so I can show you around San José."

"I will, thank you. But please stop calling me 'Señor Stan.' Please just call me Stan."

"Thank you, Stan. And you must call me Carmelita."

"Thank you, Carmelita," Stan replied as he extended his right hand as a gesture of a new level of friendship.

Carmelita swiveled her torso counter-clockwise so she could shake hands with Stan.

Two new friends.

The Boeing 737 reached the end of the runway and made a U-turn heading back to Terminal 3 as it taxied on the runway itself. As the pilots finally maneuvered their way to the area on the tarmac where they would temporarily park the plane (turnaround time was just a little over an hour), they tapped the brakes several times as they eased to the final spot. "From the flight deck, we'd like to add our welcome to you here in Los Cabos. Hope you have a great time, and we look forward to seeing you on your return trip."

Looking out his window, Stan could see the ground crew rolling the tall stairway into its place at the forward door on his side. He saw the young man climb the stairs and then there was a tap-tap on the cabin door – the universal sign that everything was ready on that side of the door. Margie turned the big door handle to the right and the door swung open for the ground crew to finish opening the door.

Even though Carmelita had given him an implicit okay to be friendly, Stan knew that the traditions and customs in Mexico meant that he shouldn't display any outward signs of friendship at this point. Once inside the terminal, a uniformed young lady was asking to see everyone's forms. Carmelita and Stan showed theirs and the young guard nodded for them to continue.

As they moved past the first hall Stan looked to his right to see two big signs for the "Mexican Nationals" and the "Foreign Visitors." Both signs were in Spanish and in English, no doubt due to the large amount of English-speaking visitors to the area. As he moved to the right he was surprised to see that Carmelita was staying on the left side, for the Mexican Nationals. He waved to her as he didn't know if he would see her once he passed through the Customs line. As he approached the Customs Officer he handed him his passport and the two completed forms.

"Business or pleasure?" the Customs Officer asked.

"Business," Stan replied.

"What type of business?" was the response.

"I am a private investigator."

"What are you investigating?"

"I am looking for information on a missing person." Stan suddenly realized that perhaps he should've just said that he was there on vacation. But it was too late to change now.

"If you find this missing person, are you planning to take him or her back to the States?"

Stan paused briefly as he remembered that Mexico does not like to extradite people; perhaps the "missing person" did not want to be found. "No, I am just looking for information to tell her parents."

"How old is she and how long has she been missing?" The Customs Official was not showing any signs of ending the interrogation.

"She's 19 and she's been missing for about two weeks."

"Where are you staying?" The Official continued his questioning and Stan knew that he had to satisfy the Customs Official so he could have his passport stamped and get through the line.

"Hotel El Nuevo in San José del Cabo," Stan replied. He knew that the locals referred to the town as simply San José, but at this point he didn't want to sound like a local or someone more knowledgeable – he wanted to sound like a first-timer, which he was.

"Are you a police officer?"

"No, señor. I am not a police officer."

"Are you going to ask our police for their assistance in helping you find this person?"

"No, sir. There's no reason that your police would need to be involved. I don't even know that she's here, or even in Mexico." Stan knew he had to do something quick, or this could go on for a very long time. He lowered his voice and continued. "Her parents are very wealthy and they gave her money to come down here for Christmas break. Why they would do something like that, I don't know. I'm guessing she changed her ticket and went to Cancun, but her parents insisted I come down here to look for her. They're paying for this trip, so I have to pretend I'm looking for her. They have the money so I'll do what they want." Stan gave the Customs Official a 'you know what I mean?' look.

"Sí, I know what you mean. Okay," he said as he stamped Stan's passport and the white form. He tore off the top part and handed the bottom part back to Stan along with his passport and the other form. "Just don't go asking too many questions; it makes some people uneasy."

"Yes, sir. Thank you," Stan said as he picked up his items and walked toward the baggage carousel that held the luggage from his flight. Somewhat paranoid now, Stan kept his focus in his own world, not making eye contact with anyone else. He saw his suitcases approaching from the right and he reached out to pull them from the belt. The line was not very long to go through the X-Ray machine – some of his fellow passengers had already gone through while he was being grilled by the Customs Official. He placed his suitcases and his briefcase on the belt as he saw the matching shorts and shirts couple pushing the button and a green light appeared. He retrieved his items from the X-Ray machine belt, pushed the button and he, too, got a green light.

Stepping into the next hall, Stan was greeted by several people wanting to show him their resorts – it would turn out that they were trying to get him to visit timeshare properties – but he said, "I already have a reservation with Cape Travel. Do you know where I'd find them?"

"Sí, just go through those double doors, and someone will be out there with a Cape Travel sign."

"Okay, thank you very much," Stan replied as he headed toward the glass doors. Stan encountered his second pleasant surprise on this trip when the 70-degree weather warmly greeted him to Mexico. *This sure beats Seattle right now.*

Seven/Siete

San José del Cabo

That same afternoon – January 14th

comer (cō·mĕr') – to eat. *Quiero comer tacos.* I want to eat tacos.

Once the last couple had climbed into the van and the driver had slammed the rear doors shut, the eight passengers were about to begin an adventurous ride into town. There were more seats than eight in the van, but Stan didn't see how it could accommodate any more luggage. The suitcases were stacked so high in the back that any sudden stop would send one or two of them hurtling onto the passengers in the very back seat. "I'm glad I'm not sitting in the back," Stan whispered to the passenger on his left as the driver pulled on the gear shift lever and the van lurched forward.

Within one minute the van was leaving the airport. There was a large green sign over the road that said, *'Bienvenidos a Los Cabos'* [Welcome to Los Cabos]. The driver veered to the right and turned onto Highway 1. Stan peered out the window as a way of passing the time. There were empty lots, some lots with half-built homes, and several small buildings with hand-painted "TAQUERIA" signs announcing they were taco stands. At the first stop light, Stan saw a couple street vendors selling T-shirts under their canopies. He knew they were still several miles from town. *Who would be buying T-shirts out here? Probably the tourists who rented a car at the airport, he thought.*

The asphalt covering on Highway 1 was anything but smooth. It was constantly bumpy with an occasional pot hole just to keep you alert. Not knowing where he might have to go in search of Sarah, Stan paid attention at the stop lights even though he wasn't writing down the names of the streets. The next one was Calle Ernesto Aramburo, and then Calle Baja California. He saw a Pemex station on the left side of the road, making a mental note of it in case he had a rental car and had to fill it up with gas. As the road went up a slight rise and to the right, Stan was focusing on the brightly colored buildings (the ones that had paint, that is) and he missed the next stop light as the driver drove through the green. Then there was Avenida La Paz that went to the right, and another Pemex station on the left.

"What's that building?" Stan asked out of natural curiosity.

"That's Soriana," one of the passengers replied. "It's a big grocery store with a good selection and decent prices."

"Thanks," Stan said as he filed away that information for future use. *Won't need a grocery store on this trip, but maybe on another one.* The next light was for another street that only went to the right – Colonia Chamizal. Another Pemex station, and then one more right-only street – Pescador. Stan knew that *pescador* had something to do with fish, but he wasn't going to ask another question and be labeled a "tourista." A couple lights later the green sign had a left arrow and said 'San José Centro.' Stan later found out that *centro* typically means the center of the town. So if you got on a bus that said Centro, you could guess that it was going to the center of the town – well, most of the time anyway.

The driver turned left at that light, and headed down the hill along Valerio González Canseco. A half block down that road was the bus station. *Now that's something to remember; I wonder if the buses run on a regular schedule.* The driver turned left into the bus parking lot and let out a couple who were taking the bus north to La Paz. Pulling back out onto the street, the driver narrowly missed a taxi. Even though it was a close call, Stan noticed the absence of car horns; in fact, he hadn't heard any since he arrived. The drivers seemed to be much more courteous than the ones in the States.

A few stop signs later, and a left turn onto Boulevard Mijares brought Stan to his stop – Hotel El Nuevo. He had to excuse himself as he climbed over the legs of the passenger to his right, and he was able to climb out of the van without stepping on anyone's toes or tripping on the steps as he got out. The hotel bellman was quickly out to the van and grabbed Stan's luggage as quickly as the shuttle driver pulled them down from the towering stack. Stan handed the driver a couple dollars since he hadn't yet exchanged any money for pesos. "Gracias, señor," the driver said as he was re-closing the back doors; he didn't have to slam them this time.

"Welcome to Hotel El Nuevo, señor," the bellman said as he extended the handles on Stan's suitcases and pulled them into the hotel.

"Gracias," Stan replied – now the hard work was about to set in. Sarah's missing, and his job was to find her.

Eight/Ocho
Waikiki Beach – Oahu, Hawaii
June, 10½ years earlier

curioso (kyoor'·ē·ō'·sō) – curious. *Caminé cerca un gato curioso.* I walked near a curious cat.

"It's cold!" Sarah Johnson shrieked as the first wave slammed into her, almost knocking her over. She was knee-deep in the water and chatting with her friend Beth when the wave surprised and hit them both.

"Brrrr!" exclaimed Beth as she shook her body to try to warm up.

In reality the water wasn't that cold. The two girls, best friends for the past three years at Lakeview Elementary School, had been sunning themselves on their towels and then ran into the surf because, as Sarah said, "I'm hot. Let's go in the water and cool off."

Robert and Tina Johnson hadn't even looked up as the two girls jumped up from their towels and ran toward the water, kicking up sand with each step they took. Robert was absorbed in reading the latest business book, while Tina was going through one of the many magazines that she had in her beach bag. Both of them were lathered with sunscreen, and they made sure the girls' arms, legs, and faces were also covered with sunscreen.

Going to Hawaii that summer was a special vacation, but it was also a typical vacation in that daughter Sarah was able to take a friend with her. Her parents felt that bringing along a friend made the vacation more enjoyable for Sarah, and for them, too, of course – Sarah had someone to keep her busy. Beth's parents were happy to let Beth go with the Johnsons because Beth was also a single child and it gave her a chance for a nice vacation with a friend. Beth went with the Johnsons the previous year when they'd gone camping along the coast of southern Washington; she was almost like a second daughter to Robert and Tina.

Sarah and Beth were jumping up and down as another wave approached them. They were ready for it this time although it was still a little bigger than they expected. The water splashed up in their faces as the wave crested on its journey to the shore. "Yuck," Sarah said as she spit out a mouthful of saltwater. "How can the fishes like this stuff?"

That caused Beth to giggle, and just as she did, she was yanked down by the pulling action of the wave as it moved back from the shore toward the open ocean. She used all fours to get up off the sandy bottom and also spit out a mouthful of water. "Let's go back," she hollered to Sarah who was pulling the open palm of her right hand across the top of the water like a gliding bird.

"Okay," Sarah replied. "I'll race you," she said as she turned toward the beach and tried to run. She wasn't prepared to run in the waist-deep water, and she fell forward as the tidal action inhibited her stride. "Hey, wait for me," she yelled out to Beth who was almost to the water's edge.

"No way," Beth yelled as she looked back at her friend who was getting back on her feet. "You're the one who wanted to race." Beth continued running but once she was completely out of the water she had to look around to find the Johnsons. She and Sarah had drifted in the water as the currents gently pushed them south. Finally seeing Mrs. Johnson waving to her, she turned a little to her left and ran through the soft sand back to her towel. Sarah, the faster runner and being able to see where Beth was going, got there shortly after Beth. The two girls flopped down on their towels and started giggling.

"Did you two leave any sand on the beach?" Tina asked. The girls' legs were covered with sand, as they had once again kicked up lots of sand with each step as they ran across the beach.

"Don't be silly, Mom," Sarah replied.

"How was the water?" Robert asked as he put a bookmark in his book and set it down. "Is it warm?"

"It was cold when we first got in," Beth said. "Then it was okay, but then the waves that hit us were cold. And the water tastes yucky!" she added.

"Yeah," Sarah chimed in. "How can the fishes drink and live in that water?"

Neither Robert nor Tina had an answer for that question. Tina looked at her husband with a look that said *Answer the question*. "Maybe they're used to it, just like we're used to breathing air." It was a feeble attempt and he knew it.

"Oh, yuck," was the response from both girls. Apparently "yuck" was the popular word for second-graders going into third grade.

"Do you girls want a sandwich and some chips?" Tina asked as she reached for her beach bag. The large bag seemed as magical as Mary Poppins' bag because Tina could pull all kinds of things out, and there seemed to be no end to it.

"Yeah," they both screamed.

"Okay, but let's remember that there are other people out here. So we shouldn't be so loud. All right?"

"Yes, Mom," Sarah answered.

"Yes, Mrs. Johnson," came the reply from Beth.

"Thank you, girls. Now – who wants a cheese sandwich and who wants peanut butter and jelly?" Tina asked as she pulled out a brightly flowered zipper bag. The thermal bag held four sandwiches plus four small cartons of milk.

"Cheese, please," Sarah said with a wide grin, amused at her own rhyming.

"It doesn't matter to me," Beth replied, displaying her excellent manners – just one of the many reasons why the Johnsons liked taking Beth on trips with them.

"We have both," Tina said. "Your choice – cheese or peanut butter and jelly."

"Peanut butter and jelly, then. Thank you, Mrs. Johnson," Beth answered.

Tina handed each girl her sandwich plus a carton of chilled milk. "Are you hungry, Robert?"

"Yes, dear. Any one is fine with me," he said without looking up from the book he'd started reading again.

Tina handed a sandwich and a carton of milk to Robert and then took the last ones for herself. She opened a large bag of potato chips and put some in two bowls – one for the girls to share, and the other for Robert and her.

For once, there was silence, except for the sandwich chewing and the milk slurping, in their small piece of paradise. The rest of the beach area around them continued in its varied regimen of talk, laughter, reading, playing cards, and even a little snoring. How could you argue with catching a nap on Waikiki Beach?

After the girls ate their sandwiches, some chips, and the milk, they were eager to run back to the water, but Tina imposed the 30-minute rule: You have to wait thirty minutes after eating before going back into the water. Sarah knew it was a house rule, but she pouted nevertheless.

Finally, they were allowed to go back to the water, and Tina went with them this time. Robert was not a big ocean water fan, so he was extremely content to stay on the sand and read his book. But realizing that he'd probably already had too much sun, Robert didn't want to stay much longer; getting a sunburn was not his idea of a good time.

After about twenty more minutes, Robert closed his book and put it back into his beach bag. He then stood up, picked up his towel, and tried to gently shake the sand off of it without sending sand flying onto other people. It took him a minute before he was able to catch Tina's attention. He waved at her and she waved back. Tina then turned toward the girls once again. "Darn it," he muttered. He was hoping that she would realize that he wanted to leave.

He kept looking out to the water, but no one was looking back at him. He didn't want to leave their towels and beach bags alone there on the sand, but he looked around and saw that other towels were devoid of people. Still slightly uncomfortable at the thought of leaving their things alone on the beach, although he had his wallet and room key with him, he set his towel and bag on Tina's towel and headed down toward the water.

As he was nearing the end of the "dry zone" – the area not yet touched by the waves – Tina happened to look over and see him. "You're not coming in?" she asked even though she saw that he still had his shorts and shirt on.

"No, you know I don't like the ocean. Besides, I think we've been out in the sun enough for today. Any more and we might get burned. How about if we go back to the hotel and the girls can play at the pool if they want?"

"Okay," was Tina's less than enthusiastic response. Robert was not always the "most fun" on a vacation. But she knew he was right; getting a sunburn would definitely make the rest of the vacation miserable. Turning back to the frolicking girls, she hollered over the noise of the waves, "Let's go girls. We need to head back to the hotel."

"Aw, Mom. Do we have to?" Sarah whined.

"Yes, Sarah. We do have to. But you two can play in the pool if you want. And we have Cokes back in the room."

"Okay, Mom. Come on, Beth. Maybe there's some kids we can play Marco Polo with back at the hotel." With that said, Sarah started running back to the beach and their towels; Beth followed shortly behind.

After they had gathered up all their towels, bags, and trash, they meandered through the maze of people, beach towels, and chairs, finally reaching the sidewalk that ran parallel to the beach. The sidewalk served a dual purpose: a walkway from the hotels to the beach areas, and a dividing line with flowers, trees, and buildings on one side, and the beach on the other. The builders of the sidewalk envisioned it being a well-traveled walkway – which it was – and so it had been built double-wide to accommodate a lot of walkers and bicyclists.

The four of them stomped their feet on the sidewalk as they attempted to dislodge all the sand from their feet and their sandals. As they went to the right on the sidewalk, the imposing sight of Diamond Head was in the distance in front of them. The extinct crater had long been one of the world's most famous natural landmarks. The sidewalk was fairly empty so the four of them were able to walk side-by-side. The girls walked in step with each other so the sound of their sandals hitting the sidewalk was a steady beat.

Approaching the Johnson group was a pair of nuns in their black habits. Sarah and Beth looked at each other and giggled. They thought they looked funny in their long black robes, especially in summertime.

Nodding his head toward the nuns, Robert said, "Good afternoon, Sisters" as they were close enough to make eye contact and speak to each other.

"Good afternoon," one of the nuns replied. "Hello girls," she continued as she looked down at Beth and Sarah.

The girls just giggled again. It's amazing what can amuse eight year-old girls.

"Girls," Tina said in a reprimanding voice. "That was not nice."

"What are they doing wearing black robes at the beach?" Sarah asked, unaware of her mother's rebuke.

"Those aren't robes the same way we think of robes," Robert replied. "They are Catholic nuns, and that robe is what they wear – it's like their uniform."

"But you called her 'Sister,'" Sarah replied.

"Well," he started. "That's what they are called. It would be like calling you two 'Sister Sarah' and 'Sister Beth.' If someone saw you, but didn't know your name, they could just call you 'Sister.'" Robert hoped that answer would suffice because he didn't know how much more he could explain it so it made sense to the girls.

"If that's their uniform, where do they work?" queried Sarah as the four of them continued to walk toward their hotel.

"Um," Robert started.

Tina decided to take over because she had gone to an all-girls Catholic School and could do a better job of explaining. "Nuns work in many places, but it isn't always the same way we think of work. You see, a nun devotes her life to God and so she might do many things. She might live in a convent where many nuns live together, or she might even teach school. I went to a school where we had nuns for teachers." Tina's eyes turned serious as she said, "Sister Frances was very strict. If you talked in her class, she would hit the back of your hand with a wooden ruler. And it would hurt."

"Did she ever hit your hand, Mrs. Johnson?" Beth was starting to get curious now.

"Oh, yes. I don't think there was a single girl who got out of her class without being hit by that ruler." Tina chuckled to herself as she thought about those times in school and how often she and her friends were caught even though they thought they had been quite sneaky.

"But what's a convent?" Sarah asked.

"Well," Tina started to answer as they reached the connecting sidewalk for their hotel. "A convent is a place where nuns live. They spend a lot of time praying, and they also have gardens where they grow their food. They might take in sick people to help them get better. Not every convent is the same." Tina was starting to realize that it was going to be very difficult for her to give a complete explanation to an eight-year-old.

"But what about their kids, where do they go to school?" Sarah asked.

"The nuns aren't married," Tina continued. "They live their lives for God, and so they don't have any children."

"You mean it's like if there were only girls at our school and there were no boys around to bug us?" This idea of being a nun was starting to sound good to Sarah – even in her own eight-year-old world.

"Yes, that's right," Robert chimed in. "No boys to bug you."

Sarah turned to Beth and giggled. "No boys to bug us." She giggled again. *I like that,* she thought to herself.

Nine/Nueve
Hotel El Nuevo – San José del Cabo
Tuesday morning, January 15th

desayuno (dĕ·sā'·yū'·nō) – breakfast. *El desayuno empieza
a las siete.* The breakfast begins at seven.

Room 304 at Hotel El Nuevo was like most of the other rooms at the
hotel. It was like most other rooms except that it was the room that Sarah
and Mary had stayed in while they were in San José. That made it special,
and that's why Stan had specifically requested it when he made his
reservations the previous week. He'd said that the friend who recommended
the hotel to him had stayed in that room, and it was a very quiet room. So he
would like to stay in that room if possible. That was a lie, of course, but he
really wanted to stay in Sarah's and Mary's room; he needed to.

Stan spent most of the previous afternoon and evening scouring the
room for clues. Even though he wasn't a forensic expert, he had a small kit
that he used to look for blood spots, fingerprints, etc. Perhaps Sarah had
taped a note to the bottom of one of the drawers. Had there been some
struggle that Mary didn't tell him about, either because she didn't want him
to know about it or it happened when she wasn't there? Were there any fresh
signs of the doors or windows being pried open? What about the air
conditioning vents – was there anything behind them or could they be
accessed from someplace else? What could be seen from the room through
the windows? Who could see in through the windows? Could someone get
on the patio from the roof or from another room's patio? Stan wanted to do
all of this checking before he started asking the locals any questions, or let
them know why he was here.

All his digging and searching were in vain. The bedding had been
thoroughly washed, including the bedspreads and blankets. The couch and
pillows had been sprayed with a cleansing solution, also yielding no clues.
He looked everywhere he could think of, but he couldn't find anything that
would give him a hint of Sarah's disappearance. Even though the hotel was
only few years old, there were many grown trees that did a good job of
blocking the views to and from room 304 at Hotel El Nuevo. Stan was
frustrated, but not discouraged. His many years as a PI had taught him the

value of perseverance; now he was going to need some extra patience to go along with that perseverance. *Not that many are easy to solve; this one is elusive and it's going to be extremely difficult.*

In addition to taking some mental notes, Stan jotted down a few items in his small pocket notebook in case there was something he wanted to talk with Mary or the Johnsons about. He decided to take the stairs rather than the elevator down to the hotel restaurant for breakfast. He noted that the hallway was rather dim, surprising given the newness of the hotel. The stairs were in an open area, so there was nothing to worry about with them. Upon reaching the main floor, he didn't know where the restaurant was, but his nose told him which direction to go. "Buenos días, señor. How was your first night here in San José?" The assistant manager who checked him in yesterday was now serving as host at the restaurant. *I hope everyone else in town has as good a memory as his.*

"Buenos días. It was a very good night. I slept well, thank you. And now I am ready for the best breakfast in town," Stan said with a slight grin back to Miguel.

"Then you picked the right place, señor. Follow me, please." Miguel led Stan to a small table near the back of the restaurant, the kind of location that would allow Stan to observe people without really being watched himself. "Some coffee, señor?"

"Yes, with cream, please." Stan normally was not extremely fond of overly effusive people, but he developed a way to use it to his advantage when it was necessary. Since Miguel had remembered that Stan had just arrived yesterday, perhaps he would also remember something about Sarah Johnson that would help him. Stan took out his little notebook and wrote Miguel's name in it. *No rush, I'll talk to him later.* Looking up, Stan saw a waiter coming his way with a pot of coffee, so he picked up the menu and look for a hearty breakfast because today was going to be a very busy day.

"Are you ready to order, señor, or do you need some more time?" The waiter, just like everyone else he had encountered so far, spoke pretty good English. He poured the coffee into Stan's cup, and placed a chilled cream pitcher next to it.

"I'm ready, thank you. I'll have the Huevos Rancheros and a large glass of, uh, orange juice, please." Stan said as he looked at the waiter; Stan sneaked a look at his name badge also. His name was Pepé. "Thank you," he said as he handed his menu to Pepé.

"Gracias, señor. Do you want the salsa on your eggs to be Mexican style or American style? Mexican is hotter than American."

"The American salsa will be fine. Thank you, Pepé." As he took the first sip of the coffee, he savored its robust flavor. *It's not Starbucks, but it's pretty good.* Stan worked his way through that cup of coffee without realizing that he was drinking it faster than normal.

"Your breakfast will be out soon, señor."

"Thank you," Stan replied. Pouring some cream into his second cup, Stan started planning his day. He hoped to talk with some of the locals today to see if any of them remembered Sarah and anything that might have gone on with her. Stan was deep in thought when Pepé brought the large steaming plate of Huevos Rancheros.

"Be careful, señor. The plate is very hot. Do you need ketchup or anything else?"

"No thanks." The large plate consisted of two fried eggs on top of corn tortillas, hash brown potatoes, and refried beans, all covered with a red salsa. Instead of a fruit garnish, there were three slices of avocado, a lime wedge, and a two stems of cilantro. Stan was used to having three regular meals at somewhat regular times, and yesterday's travel interfered with that. He was hungry, and he devoured the breakfast, washing it down with the orange juice.

"Anything else, señor?" Pepé asked as he refilled Stan's coffee cup.

"No, thank you. This was all very good."

"Charge it to your room; number three-o-four?"

"Yes. Thank you, Pepé."

"Are you off to do some souvenir shopping? I can tell you the best place to get silver and opals for your lady friend."

"Not today, thanks. I'm just going to walk around for a little bit. Do I need to sign anything?" Stan would want to talk with the hotel staff, but not right away. He wanted to stroll through town first.

"Nothing to sign, señor. Have a good day," Pepé said as he cleared away the plate and utensils, and then left Stan to enjoy his third cup of coffee.

Ten/Diez
San José del Cabo
That same morning – January 15th

tienda (tē·ĭn'·dŭ) – store. *Quiero ir a la tienda nueva.* I want to go to the new store.

Stepping out onto the sidewalk from the hotel lobby, Stan was immediately met with the warmth of the day. It wasn't hot; it felt like it was about 70 degrees. That would be considered a heat wave at this time of year in Seattle, but it was actually cool for San José, and the locals displayed that by wearing long sleeves or sweatshirts. He was comfortable in his short sleeve shirt, slacks, and his Rockport shoes. He had tried many brands but he found that the Rockports were the most comfortable for a lot of standing and walking, and he did a lot of both in his line of work.

Hotel El Nuevo was located at the northeast corner of Boulevard Mijares and Calle Coronado. The main plaza, or town square, was two blocks north, and it appeared that there were enough little shops along the nearby streets to keep most tourists busy and happy. Stan turned right toward the square, figuring he had to start somewhere to get acquainted with the layout of the town and to get his orientation. The sidewalk was an interesting mix of walking space, trees, and businesses that had expanded their reach out on to the sidewalk area. There's no real sidewalk, per se, just mostly six-sided pavers that were probably made in a local factory. Adjacent to the hotel was a *farmacia* [pharmacy] that sold all kinds of prescription drugs over the counter. *Is that Albuterol really the same as what you get in the States?* Next to the pharmacy were a jewelry store and a Tequila store.

As he reached the southeast corner of Boulevard Mijares and Calle Manuel Doblado, Stan saw The Palm Tree, an interesting looking eclectic restaurant. A sign that hung over the sidewalk said "Shooters Sports Bar" with a sign pointing down the narrow street or alleyway. *Mary said she and Sarah had gone to Shooters for a beer; I'll have to check that out later in the evening when there's some action.* Stan decided to see exactly where Shooters was so he headed down the road. The road itself was actually stamped concrete made to look like various size rocks. About one hundred feet down the road was a squared archway in the stucco wall with an interesting sign above it:

Shooters Sports Bar – San José del Cabo, Mexico

What happens at Shooters
Never really happened!

Stan stepped inside the archway just to get his bearings. He saw another Shooters sign on the wall to the right with a few steps up and then more steps angled up to the left. "Go on up, señor. The bar is open," a man to his left said to Stan.

"Thanks. I was just trying to find out where it was. I'll be back tonight," Stan replied as he looked back to his left. But the man was gone. Stepping back through the archway Stan headed to the main street where he saw that the road to his right, Boulevard Mijares leading up to the plaza, had various items blocking the road to discourage drivers from entering the area. There were various sizes and shapes of concrete planter boxes with palm trees; there were some two-foot high concrete balls, and then the road and sidewalk became one. City Hall, with its square bell tower, was off to the left. Farther up was a large fountain with jumping waters, just like at some of the Las Vegas hotels. Behind the fountain was a 90-degree curving wall with four arches cut out of the wall and a half-arch at each end. High on the wall was an inscription that Stan strained his eyes to read. Seven perched busts were on pedestals behind a short chained off area in front of the arched wall. Those seven must have been important in the development of San José del Cabo. The center bust, the tallest one, was Mijares. The fountain wall also had an inscription: Plaza Publica "José Antonio Mijares." *This Mijares fellow must definitely be a central figure for San José.*

Stan was just about ready to stroll into some of the shops surrounding the town square when he heard a bell ringing. He had seen a bell in the City Hall tower so he thought that was where it came from. As the bell continued to ring he determined that the sound was coming from someplace west of the town square. Looking in that direction he saw a twin-towered church set up above street level, and he counted a total of ten rings. He looked at his watch; it was about three minutes past ten o'clock. Stan would later find out that the church was the town's mission, although it wasn't the original building and that was not the original location.

Seeing that some of the shop owners were unlocking doors and changing their window sign from *Cerrado* [Closed] to *Abierto* [Open], Stan figured he would start with the shops that would have the most appeal to nineteen-year-old college girls. He saw a señora open the door to her store and roll out a hanging rack of blouses and skirts. The colors were amazing – reds, pinks, greens, blues; what a kaleidoscope of artfully matched colors and designs. "Buenos días, señora," Stan began as he entered her small store. He understood only the first three words of her reply and decided he better take a different approach. *"¿Hablas Inglés?"*

"Sí, I speak some English," the women said with a pronounced accent. "Looking for something for your lady?"

"No, thank you. I am looking for some information on two young girls who were in San José two weeks ago. Do you recognize them?" he asked as he pulled two pictures out of his shirt pocket.

"Did they do something wrong?" she asked.

"No, nothing like that. One of them is missing, and I'm trying to help her parents find some information that might help them locate her. They were staying at the Hotel El Nuevo, and I thought your store might appeal to them." Stan didn't have any idea if her store would be one that the girls would have gone into, but he said this as he touched one of the cotton dresses.

"Oh, that's too bad. They are pretty girls. I have a lot of tourists come into my store, so it's not possible for me to remember all of them. But I think I remember these two; this one has a pretty smile," the shopkeeper said as she pointed to Sarah's picture. "Yes, they were in here. They were looking at some long dresses, just like these," she said as she pointed to the rack of dresses right by Stan. "They tried some on, but they didn't buy any of them."

Buoyed by this recognition, Stan's hopes began to climb. But his experience had told him not to get too excited too early. "Did you notice anything particular? Had they been drinking? Was anyone watching them? Was there anything a parent should worry about?" Stan knew he was throwing a lot of questions at her, but he knew he had to give her some leads on things to think about.

"No, there was nothing. They were talking and just having a good time. If someone was following them, I didn't see him."

"Would there be anything that would help you narrow down what day they came into your store? Perhaps a certain person was working and that person only works on a Thursday or a Friday for example." Stan was trying to get as much information as he could from the lady who truly wanted to help.

"I was here alone, so it would not have been a Saturday. That's all I can think of; I'm sorry I wasn't much help," she said

"You were a big help, señora. Muchas gracias," Stan said as he turned to walk out of her store. Stan already knew it wasn't a Saturday because Saturday January fifth was the day of the girls' return flight. If it had been Saturday during the previous week when the Johnsons were still here, that wouldn't add anything. *Not great help, but at least it wasn't bad news.*

The next shop was a jewelry store with a big MEXICAN OPALS sign in the window. Perhaps this was the store that Pepé was talking about. He pushed on the door but it wouldn't open. He saw a sign in the window next to the door that said *Horario* [Hours]. He wasn't sure that he knew the Spanish days of the week, but most of them were 1100 – 2000, so he took that to mean the store was open from 11:00 AM to 8:00 PM. Since it was just past 10:00, he'd have to come back to this store.

Next was a small grocery store that appeared to cater to kids or tourists; it was mostly snacks, ice creams, and soft drinks. Being adjacent to the town square meant that most of the tourists would pass by the store on the way to the fountain or to the church. Stan was thirsty so he decided to buy a bottle of water here. "Ten pesos or one dollar, señor," the man behind the counter said. Stan pulled out his wallet and realized that he hadn't exchanged any dollars for pesos. He handed the man a one dollar bill. "Gracias," was the man's reply.

"You're welcome," Stan replied. He then continued, "I was wondering if you could help me; I'm trying to find someone. *¿Hablas Inglés?*"

"Yes, I speak English. Are you looking for a local person or for a certain type of store?" The man's English was pretty good, Stan noticed.

As he pulled the two pictures out of his shirt pocket again, he showed them to the man and he said, "Do you know if you saw these two girls about ten days to two weeks ago? One of them is missing and I am trying to help her parents find her."

The man's eyes squinted as he looked at the pictures. "Yes, they were in here, but I don't know the exact date."

"You sound pretty confident; how can you be so sure?" Stan asked.

"Most of my customers," the shopkeeper began, "are locals or old tourists, usually with a group. There are not very many young Americans who come into my store, so it is easy for me to remember the few who do. They bought bottles of water, just like you did. And they also bought a bag of chips."

"Was there anything particular about them that you recall? Is there anything they said that you can remember?" Stan continued his line of questions.

"No. They just came in here, looked around and got what they wanted. As you can see, the store is not very big, so it wouldn't take them very long to look at everything in here." The man was acknowledging what Stan was aware of – the store was small.

"Did you notice if anyone else was paying attention to them, or did anyone come into the store after them and ask anything or say anything about them?"

"No. By the way that they acted, you would've thought they lived right around the corner, and that coming in here was something they did every day. The only thing that made them different was the color of their skin, hair, and eyes. Sorry I can't give you any more help than that. Has something bad happened to the girl? I have a niece about the same age, and I know I would feel really bad if something happened to her."

"I don't know yet. I'm still trying to find her. I'm staying at the Hotel El Nuevo; I'll check back with you before I leave in case you remember anything else. Is that okay?"

"Sure, that's fine." The man diverted his attention to another customer who'd come into the store.

"Thanks again," Stan said as he walked out of the small place. But the man did not hear him; he had engaged in conversation with the new customer in his store. Stan wasn't paying attention as he stepped out of the store, and he almost stepped on a small dog that was being taken for a walk on a leash by his owner. "Excuse me," Stan apologized to the old man who had an unlit cigarette hanging out of his mouth. The old man mumbled something and kept on walking; the dog hadn't even noticed the peril that almost befell him.

The next shop was still closed for the day, and the one after that looked closed for good. After that was "Die Trying," a clothing store that advertised itself as "Born and bred in Cabo San Lucas, and living large since 1992." Its posted motto was "Don't Die Watching, Die Trying." Stan walked into the store and it was obvious that the clothing in here was not for him. But he could see that Sarah and Mary might have been attracted to it – shirts, shorts, sandals, and swimming suits.

"Hey," was the greeting from the twenty-something clerk in the store, a young man with an earring dangling from each ear and one through his right nostril. Stan didn't even want to guess how many other piercings he might have, or where they were.

"Hi," Stan responded. Saying "Hey" as a greeting just didn't work for Stan. "I was wondering if you recall seeing these two girls," he said as he pulled the two pictures out of his pocket. "It would have been almost two weeks ago on January second, third, or fourth."

"I might have; what's the deal?"

Stan took that response to mean "Maybe." "One of the girls is missing and her parents have asked me to locate some information on where she might be. They were visiting from the States. Anything you recall?" After asking that last question, Stan actually wondered if this guy could even recall what he did last night.

"Yeah, I remember them. Who wouldn't remember a couple of babes like that? They were talking about going to the beach for a day of rays. One bought a two-piece, and the other bought shorts and a halter top." *Mary didn't tell me about that.*

"Did they say what beach they were going to?"

"No. I told them they should go up to Cabo Pulmo. When I told them where it was, they said they didn't have a car. So I told them to just take a taxi to Playa Azul." The young clerk was actually being more helpful than Stan thought he could be.

"Where's that?" Stan asked.

The clerk pointed to his right as he said, "Just go down this street, Boulevard Mijares, until it hits the end. Turn right and that's where the timeshares begin. You can go to any of the beaches along there – that area is Playa Azul."

"Okay, thanks. One last question. Did anything seem odd or out of place when they were in here?" Stan knew that was probably a strange question to ask this guy; "odd or out of place" could be his nickname.

"Nah, they were cool. Just two young chicks hangin' out. They seemed like good friends. Nothing odd there."

"Thanks a lot, man. You're a big help." Stan actually meant that; this was the first real help he'd gotten.

"No problem, man. Good luck."

"Yeah," Stan replied as he was heading out the door. Stan's gait was a little stronger now as he mentally reviewed what he'd learned so far:

> Sarah's and Mary's pictures had been recognized by three shop owners so far (one advantage of their standing out from the crowd).

> They bought beach outfits in a store close to their hotel.

> They were given a recommendation of a close beach to go to, although he didn't know if they actually went to that one. Mary said they went to the beach, but she didn't specify which one.

> None of the people recognizing them felt there was anything wrong or that they were being followed.

> Stan found nothing that appeared to be amiss in room 304 at the hotel.

He had more work to do, but he was feeling good about what he'd learned so far. He still wanted to talk to more merchants; he needed to go to Shooters Sports Bar, and then there was the beach to go to (although he didn't know if Playa Azul was the right one). Good progress so far, although he didn't have much tangible to tell the Johnsons. The walking around was making him hungry. *Where's a place the girls would go to eat?*

Eleven/Once
Misíon San José del Cabo Añuití – San José del Cabo
That evening – January 15th

oracíon (ō·rǎ'·cē·ōn') – prayer. *¿Va a decir una oracíon por mí?* Will you say a prayer for me?

After some time off his feet and then a quick dinner across from the hotel, Stan walked north on Boulevard Mijares to the plaza, and then left toward the church, San José del Cabo Añuití – the central Catholic church in San José. The setting sun lit up the twin towers as if they were rocket ships sitting on a darkened platform. Stan walked up the steps from Calle Hidalgo and was approaching the entrance to the church when he saw a Padre over to the right. Hoping it might be the parish priest he walked over to him. "Excuse me, Padre. Are you the parish priest? I don't speak much Spanish."

"God understands all languages my son, and even when we don't speak He still hears us. Yes, I am the parish priest. How may I help you?"

"Gracias, Padre. I'm here from the States trying to find information for some grieving parents whose daughter was visiting here, but never returned home. I will be at Mass tonight, and I was hoping that you might say a special prayer for the girl; her name is Sarah."

"Of course, my son. Please come by during the day and perhaps someone can give you some information that will help." The priest then put his right hand on Stan's shoulder as he said a quiet prayer.

As the 7:00 Mass started, there were about thirty people inside. After a few intonations in Spanish that Stan didn't understand, the priest then said, "Tonight we will include a special short mass for one of God's children who is lost and whose parents are seeking guidance. The child's name is Sarah. Please turn to page 27 and follow me in the words of the Missa Brevis." Stan didn't understand much, but he was thankful for their prayers for Sarah.

Not an overly religious man, Stan was still drawn to stay in his pew after the Mass had ended. He'd felt a connection and that he would be able to find Sarah. He finally got up to leave, and on his way out he dropped a 100 pesos bill in both the mission collection box and in the poor box. He'd be back.

Twelve/Doce
Shooters Sports Bar – San José del Cabo
Later that evening – January 15th

útil (ū'·tĭl) – helpful. *Ese hombre es muy útil.* That man is very helpful.

Stan felt re-energized as he walked down the steps from the church to cross the street to the plaza. The fountains were flowing, just as his tears had flowed during the short mass for Sarah. The water was jumping but there was no music for it to be in rhythm with. The plaza was mostly empty; there were a few people out strolling, and they had jackets or sweatshirts on – January was still cool for the locals. Turning right on Boulevard Mijares, Stan could already hear the music spilling over the rooftop from Shooters. It did seem a little strange that he was heading up to a bar right after going to Mass, but he wasn't going up there to party – this was work. He stopped to read a plaque at the front of City Hall, but all he could understand were the dates; without understanding the Spanish words, they were meaningless to him.

He crossed the plaza and walked down the road to the square archway where he had been before. He stepped into the open patio area, turned right and went up three steps before turning left to go up another twenty or thirty. As he got to the top of those steps, there was a hand-written *BAÑOS* [bathrooms] painted on the stucco wall. He turned right went up three more steps and figured he would use the *baños* later. Right now it was time to see if anyone remembered Sarah and Mary. One more right turn and he was in Shooters Sports Bar. There were some tables and chairs in front of him along the half-height wall; they were empty – it was still early.

A few steps forward into that area and a left turn took him to the western wall of the bar/patio; it too had tables and chairs lined up against the wall. The bar was in the center area and there was a covered area at the far (southern) end of the patio. There were half a dozen tables and chairs in that area, an area that was situated two steps up. The bar area (i.e., all of Shooters) was not very big; patrons would either have to see other people or choose to not see them. With only about thirty tables, they would all be taken quickly, but not everyone took a table; some were at the bar, and others by the rooftop edge. Stan didn't want to stand at the bar; his feet were tired, plus he could better engage with the staff by sitting at a table.

The plastic tables were all the same size, about the size of a card table. They were blue and they sported beer ads, just like the matching blue chairs and umbrellas. A big banner stretched across the back of the patio facing Boulevard Mijares said, "Shooters Sports Bar – Home of the $10 pesos Beer." As Stan was selecting a table, he noticed the shirt on one of the servers. He'd seen the slogan before: "What Happens at Shooters Never Really Happened!" *Seems they've one-upped the Las Vegas ad.*

Stan picked a table close to the bar, but then most of the tables were close to the bar. His back was to the 'upstairs' area, but he preferred to be able to see the entrance way and the bar. A waiter approached. "Hello señor. It's happy hour; you want a dollar beer?"

The exchange rate for converting dollars to pesos had been fairly constant around ten to one for several years. So it was common for ten pesos to be considered the same as one dollar. Stan had gotten a slightly better exchange rate when he cashed in some dollars earlier in the day, so he would be paying in pesos. "Sure. What kinds?"

"You can have Pacifico, Tecate, or Corona for a dollar. We have other brands for just a little more, plus we have a full bar if you want, señor."

"Pacifico, por favor," Stan replied. Corona was the most popular Mexican beer in the U.S., but he wanted to try something different. As he looked at the ads on the tables, chairs, and umbrellas, Stan saw that Corona was on most of them.

It took less than a minute for the waiter to deliver the Pacifico with a small lime wedge perched on top of the opened bottle. As he set it on the table, he asked, "Would you like to see a menu for snacks or for dinner?"

Stan wasn't really hungry; he'd eaten earlier, but he figured that the waiter would be more willing to engage in conversation with him if he were ordering something else besides just a beer. "The snacks menu would be great; thank you." The waiter was back with the single-sided open-faced SNACKS menu even before Stan had time to squeeze the lime into the bottle. "Gracias, señor," he said as the waiter set the menu on the table.

"Oh, you speak Spanish?" the engaged waiter asked.

"No, not really. I know a few words, but if I try to say too much it's usually wrong. Sorry."

"Don't be sorry, señor. I wouldn't know English but most of our customers speak English, so I had to learn. If I didn't learn, I wouldn't be able to wait on them, which means I wouldn't make any money. Now that's not good, right?" The waiter had a good sense of humor.

"Sí, that's not good. Thank you for understanding."

"You're welcome," the waiter replied.

With a slight rapport now established, Stan thought he would try to expand it a little more. He extended his right hand toward the man and said, "My name is Stan."

Reciprocating the gesture, which Stan knew almost everyone would do, the waiter grasped Stan's hand said, "My name is José; nice to meet you Stan."

"Gracias, José. Nice to meet you, too. Give me a minute or two on the snacks, okay?"

"Okay, Señor Stan." José turned around and walked to a nearby table to see if they wanted a refill of their "dollar" beers. They did. So did the next table. José picked up the empty bottles by the necks and carried them to the bar where he put them in cartons that were quickly filling with empties. *At least it looks like they recycle the bottles here; that's nice.*

The speakers for the music, unfortunately not too far from him, were blaring American rock and roll oldies. Stan had nothing against The Rolling Stones (*Jumpin' Jack Flash*), Bachman Turner Overdrive (*Takin' Care of Business*), or Lynyrd Skynyrd (*Sweet Home Alabama*) – he just didn't want his eardrums ruined. Taking a sip of his beer as he looked over the top of the short stucco wall, he had a good view of the front of the City Hall and of the plaza. He saw that the local buses made a left turn on Calle Manuel Doblado rather than making a U-turn, and they couldn't go straight because that was the start of the pedestrian-only part of Plaza Mijares. It's a good view from the bar, a distinct advantage of being at the second story level. And it helped being in an open-air area. You didn't draw any attention to yourself if you looked out there, unlike if you had to lean to look out a window.

Stan watched José as he chatted with all the customers; he certainly knew the locals as well as the tourists who frequented the place. He was very friendly, an important trait in his line of business. He looked to be about 60; very short trimmed hair (could be buzzed at home); pretty good shape except for a slight 'beer belly,' and he seemed to favor his left leg just a little bit. His engaging smile said he liked his work. *He'll remember the girls if he was working that night.* A couple more sips on the bottle and the beer was gone. *Hmmm; that did hit the spot.*

Seeing that José was coming toward his table, Stan took a quick glance at the menu. "Well, Stan. Find something you like?"

"Yes, I'll have the Buffalo Wings, not very spicy, please."

"Another Pacifico?"

"Sí, una mas, por favor." Stan was feeling quite confidant in the little bit of Spanish that he knew. But he also knew this was a safe place to at least give it a try.

"Gracias, señor," José replied as he grabbed Stan's empty bottle and headed to the bar. As soon as José stepped down to the serving area, another Pacifico was on the bar waiting for him. José added the lime wedge on top and turned in Stan's direction. "Your wings will be here in just a couple minutes," José said as he set the bottle down. "But those minutes might be Mexican minutes," he said as he flashed a broad smile. "Do you know about Mexican minutes?"

"Yes, I do. The watch runs just a little slower for them, right?"

"That's one way to look at it. We say that the Mexican minutes take a siesta so that's why it takes them a little longer."

"Yes, the siesta. That's a good idea. Maybe I will try one tomorrow." Stan was serious when he said that – maybe he <u>would</u> take one tomorrow.

Apparently having some spare time, José asked, "Here on vacation, señor?"

"A little bit of vacation," Stan started. Then realizing the opening that the waiter had just given him, he thought this would be his best chance. He pulled the pictures of Sarah and Mary out of his pocket, showed them to José, and then continued, "I'm looking for some information on these girls. Do you remember them coming in here?"

José immediately changed his demeanor and he stiffened a little. "Are you police? Are they in trouble?"

"I'm not a police officer, and the girls are not in trouble with the law. One of the girls is missing, and her parents asked me to try to find some information about her. That's all. I know they came up here, maybe ten days to two weeks ago; it would have been a Tuesday, Wednesday, or Thursday night. Anything you can tell me would be a big help."

"I'm not sure if I saw them or not. I'll think about it."

"Please do. I have extra tip money for some good information." Stan was surprised that the mention of extra tip money didn't immediately sway José. He put the pictures back into his pocket. He'd put the request out to José, and now it was up to José to respond or not. José's face had a concerned look on it as he walked away; his carefree look was gone.

Stan wasn't much of a beer drinker. He took a sip of the second beer, and realized that he already had to go to the bathroom. Remembering the painted sign at the top of the steps, at least he knew where it was. He got out of his chair and carefully walked a wide U-turn as he re-traced his way from coming into the bar. He saw a pennant hoisted on a small flagpole: HAPPY HOUR. When he got to the BAÑOS sign he turned right because that's where the arrow pointed. A few steps later and he made another right turn and up one step. The swinging door on the left said *'Damas'* and the one on the right said *'Hombres.'* He opened that door and stepped into the three foot by four foot area that had one toilet in it. *I can't imagine that the Ladies is much different than this.*

Returning to his table, Stan saw that José was walking his way with a plate of Buffalo Wings. It was a lot more than he'd expected. As he set them on the table, José said, "I'm on my break so I can talk to you for a couple minutes. But that's all."

"Do you have time to get a beer for you – on my tab?"

"No, that's okay. I shouldn't drink beer anyway. My wife reminds me of that all the time. The two girls – I remember them. It was a Wednesday night; I know that because I was off on Tuesday night and it was my first night back. They were nice girls; they had a couple beers and that was it." José was speaking in a low confidential tone so no one could overhear their conversation.

Stan could barely hear José with the loud music blaring away, so he doubted that anyone else could either. "Do you remember anything particular? Did any guys hit on them? Or did they leave with anyone?" Stan was ignoring his wings and beer now; he was now full swing into PI mode.

"Girls like that always get hit on," José started. "But we watch out for the singles up here. We let the guys make an approach, but we can also tell when the girls have had enough, and we let the guys know to stop. Any more than that and they're banned from here forever. And we mean it. We want people to have fun, but also feel safe up here."

"So the girls were hit on? Anything particular about the guys who were hitting on them?"

"No, but yes. They were a couple of guys from Cabo San Lucas who come up here occasionally. They've never caused any problems, at least not that I know of. They score once in a while, but they're just young guys whose blood tells them to hit on pretty girls."

"So what went on?" Stan asked.

"Nothing really," José began. "They offered to buy them a beer, but one of the girls said, 'That's okay, big spender. I think we can afford the dollar ourselves.' They hung around for a few more minutes talking with them, but eventually they got the hint. So they left your two girls and went after a couple of the local San José girls who come in here specifically to get the free beers from guys like them."

"What about when the girls left? Did anyone go with them, or follow them later?"

"No. I watched them just to make sure. One of them went to the bathroom, but she was back out quickly. I guess it wasn't to her liking. Anyway, they went down the steps, and I kept my eye on them by looking over the edge. When they got up to the corner here, they turned this way and walked down the sidewalk and went straight to the hotel and went in."

"Which hotel? Do you mean Hotel El Nuevo down there at the corner?" Stan asked.

"That's the one. I watched for a couple minutes more; no one else went that way, and I didn't see them come back out. I never saw them again. I wish I could tell you more, but that's it. I hope that's some help."

"José, yes that is a lot of help. Thank you, very much," Stan said as he handed him a folded 100 pesos bill as they shook hands.

"Gracias, señor," José said as he accepted the money. "Where are you staying in case I find out any more information?"

"Hotel El Nuevo for a couple more days."

"I'll do a little asking around. I'll be quiet though. Those were nice girls."

"Yes, they are," Stan replied in a very serious voice. José got out of his chair and went back to waiting tables; his "break" was over. Meanwhile,

Stan's cold beer had warmed up, and his hot Buffalo Wings had cooled down. He nibbled on the wings; he was still full from dinner so nibbling was all he could manage. And the beer was not that appealing to him, but he managed to make an attempt to consume some of each.

He was done. He couldn't eat one more wing, take one more sip of warming beer, or have his eardrums bombarded by one more loud 1970's song. When he saw José looking in his direction, Stan raised his hand to get his attention. As José approached, Stan said, "The check, please. How do you say that in Spanish?"

"*La cuenta*; or you just make a writing motion with your hand as if you are holding a pen. Can you say it, *la cuenta*?"

"La cuenta, por favor," Stan said with confidence.

"Excellent, señor. I'll be right back with your check."

Stan tried one more sip of the beer. He'd had enough. The bill was 99 pesos; Stan put down two 100 pesos bills and handed it to José as he looked him directly in the eye. "Gracias, José."

"De nada, señor. Good luck."

"Thanks." Stan wiped his face with the sauce-soaked napkin and got up to leave. Even though he had to walk down a dimly lit set of steps, he managed it without any problems. As he exited the squared archway, he decided to turn right instead of left just to see what was down that road besides a small parking lot. Even though it was night time, he knew his directions back to the hotel from there – it was only a block away.

Thirteen/Trece
Camp Lookout, near Mt. Rainier National Park
Summer, 7½ years earlier

modales (mō·dăl'·ĕs) – manners. *Ella tiene modales muy agradables.* She has very nice manners.

Going to camp was part of the normal routine for students going into the sixth grade at Lakeview Elementary School in Redmond, Washington. Long-time residents who had other children in school were aware of the program, and many of the parents even looked forward to the two-week "vacation" they had while the kids were at camp. Information was sent home with the fifth grade students in March, and the deadline to apply for camp was the first of May.

There were two camp options: "Hobbies for Life" and "Outdoors Can be Your Friend." The arts and crafts camp didn't really appeal to Robert, to Tina, or to Sarah. Although the family didn't do a lot of camping, the second choice was more exciting, and they all agreed that Sarah would attend that camp. Beth's family had moved the previous year – her dad had accepted a promotion to move to Huntsville, Alabama. Sarah's new best friend now was Maggie, someone Sarah had known for two years, but had gotten close to only during this past year. Maggie was also going to Camp Lookout. The two may have planned it that way.

Leading up to departure for camp was an anxious time as Robert was being quite overprotective of his daughter. Her body had started the normal female changes, and he was just being "typical Dad." Sarah was used to it, so she didn't let it bother her. Robert was more bothered by the fact that Sarah was not fazed by his behavior; Tina just kept out of it. He attempted to have several "Watch out for this" and "Be careful of that" conversations with his suddenly growing up daughter, but she would just reply with "I know, Dad." She wasn't being snotty about it, she <u>did</u> know. And she knew how to take care of herself. Maybe that was what bothered Robert the most – his daughter was growing up and didn't require her dad to safeguard her anymore.

The school had chartered tour buses rather than use the city's standard school buses, a decision that was undoubtedly influenced by a bus breakdown last summer on the way back from camp. A subsequent investigation into the bus records revealed a pattern of inadequate maintenance, unsafe brakes, plus the transmissions were not intended for use on steep mountain grades. Several parents banded together in a lawsuit against the school district; the case was still tied up in the courts. The kids didn't care about all that; they were just excited that they were going on the big buses that had air conditioning and seats that reclined.

Sarah and Maggie were somewhat quiet as they waited with their parents. Finally, the camp counselors started calling paired names of students to board the bus. Each student was paired with another student as part of the buddy system; that way no student was ever on his own or her own. While the two-week outing was intended to teach some survival skills, safety was a key element and it was built in from the very beginning. As Sarah's and Maggie's names were called, each girl hugged her parents who were both reluctant yet happy to see her head off to camp. Sarah had never been away from home for even a few days, let alone two weeks in the mountains.

The girls grabbed their backpacks and ran toward the front of the bus, and then they slowed to a walk as they approached their counselor, Mrs. Ames. Mrs. Ames was strict; she was not tolerant of a lot of things, and running at school was one of them. She had a soft heart deep down inside, which is why she thoroughly enjoyed being an elementary school teacher. But she knew that she had to maintain that tough exterior so she could properly teach and develop these young minds. She loved being a teacher, and she viewed being a camp counselor as an extension of that teaching role.

"Good morning, Mrs. Ames," the girls said in unison as they reached the opened bus door.

"Good morning, Maggie. Good morning, Sarah. Are you two ready for camp?"

"Yes, ma'am," Maggie replied.

"Yes, ma'am," Sarah echoed.

"Well, good. Go find some seats and let's have fun." Mrs. Ames actually showed a sign of friendliness, something she rarely did during the school year.

Sarah climbed up the steep steps into the bus, using the handrail to help pull herself up; the bus was designed for adults, not for sixth graders.

Maggie followed her, helped along with a gentle push on the backpack by Mrs. Ames. The girls chose seats near the back of the bus, put their backpacks under the seats in front of them, and settled in as the rest of the bus filled two-by-two. *Two-by-two; just like Noah's Ark.*

This bus was the girls' bus. There was another bus for the boys and their counselor, Mr. Roberts. There was some gender separation for the camp, primarily on the bus trips, and in the sleeping accommodations. Unlike some other summer camps, Camp Lookout stressed respect for each other, including the other gender, as part of its program. Thus, most of the camp activities were gender neutral and everyone took part in them.

The 115-mile trip took a little over two hours; it would have been three to four hours in their school buses. As the bus pulled into camp and slowed to a stop, some of the girls hopped up from their seats.

Mrs. Ames, however, had something else in mind for them. She stood up, turned around to face the girls, and took the microphone that the bus driver handed her as he was getting out of the bus to unload the sleeping bags and suitcases. "Young ladies," she began. "Please sit down; we have plenty of time." The counselor paused. "You will notice that I have called you 'young ladies.' You are entering the sixth grade, and your bodies have begun to show the signs of becoming a woman." This elicited a slight giggle from many of the girls. "Because you are growing up and you are becoming a woman, you are no longer a girl, and I want you to think of yourselves as young ladies. I will call you young ladies, and I expect you to act like young ladies. You are no longer a fifth grader, and I don't want to see you acting like a fifth grader."

The counselor continued. "Girls run; young ladies walk. Girls giggle when someone says something nice to them; young ladies say 'Thank you.' Girls whisper things about someone else; young ladies keep those thoughts to themselves. Do you get what I'm saying? This camp is not just about camping and outdoors and survival. It's also your time to develop and return home as a young lady. Oh, one more thing. You've all been to the sex education classes. So have the boys, but unfortunately half of them still don't understand it. Now there might be one boy, or maybe more than one, who wants to try out his new-found knowledge here at camp. If anyone tries any of that on you, you know how to protect yourself and what to do. I also want you to come to me right away. I'll handle it from there, and you won't have to worry about it. Are there any questions?"

A girl in the second row raised her hand. "Yes, Annie. What's your question?"

"Is Mr. Roberts giving the same talk to the boys in their bus?" This caused a few more giggles from the girls who were not yet ready for the transformation to young ladies.

"A little bit, but not exactly. He'll tell them that if any of the boys try anything sexually with any of the young ladies – and that is how he is referring to all of you – then that boy is expelled from camp and his parents are called to come up here to get him right away." Mrs. Ames insisted on being straight-forward; girls were growing up much faster than the previous generation. Honesty with them was the best approach. "That was a good question, Annie. Are there any others?"

"Have any boys been expelled before?" was blurted out from the fifth row.

"Jane, young ladies raise their hand when they have a question to ask. I won't answer that question because the most important thing for you to know is that you are in control of yourself, and that includes your body. Do any other young ladies have a question?"

No more hands were raised.

"All right. Remember that you _are_ young ladies. I will treat you that way, and so will Mr. Roberts and the rest of the camp staff. As you quietly and orderly get off the bus, I will hand each one of you a packet that has a list of who is in which cabin. There is also a map of the camp so you know where your cabin is. Pick up your suitcase and sleeping bag and take them to your cabin. Once you get there, put your sleeping bag on your assigned bunk, and put your clothes into your locker. We will all meet in the auditorium at 11:00, so you have about thirty minutes. I will see you then." She hooked the microphone in its cradle, and started to leave the bus. She noticed that the girls, the young ladies, were all still seated. She stepped back up to the top step and, with a small smile on her face, said, "Thank you, young ladies. You may leave the bus."

An instant transformation from a girl to a young lady is not easy to do. Most of the girls on the bus _were_ still girls. They giggled as they jumped up out of their seats, grabbed their backpacks and shoved in a fruitless effort to rush the process of getting out of the bus. Sarah calmly remained in her seat, as did Maggie. There was no rush; they had assigned bunks; they were near the back of the bus, and they didn't have to be at the auditorium until 11:00. Besides, once everyone else was out, their sleeping bags and suitcases would be the only ones left and they wouldn't have to search for them.

The 11:00 auditorium talk was the standard introduction with a review of the camp rules, safety and first aid instructions, and an overview of what they would be doing in the next two weeks. Some slides were shown, including photos of scraped knees, bandaged heads, and a few arms in slings. "Accidents happen, but safety is the best prevention." That ended the talk, and all the campers headed to the cafeteria for lunch, which was immediately followed by the first real activity of the day – knot tying.

Most of the sixth-grade campers thought that the knot tying lesson was merely something to fill up the time, including Maggie. "What's the point of learning how to tie a bunch of knots?" she asked Sarah.

"You never know if you're going to be in a situation where one of them can possibly save your life," Sarah said. "If you have two short pieces, you can make one longer piece by tying the two of them together with a square knot. And the bowline knot won't come undone no matter how hard you pull on it. In fact, it gets tighter the more you pull on it. Come on, Maggie. Just get into it." Sarah had read about some of the knots when she did a school project on "Surviving in the Woods." She carried a length of line with a carabineer in her backpack – just in case she needed it. She'd never needed it, but she always knew that she had it with her – just in case.

After the instructor taught them how to tie the knots, he showed them which knot to use in certain situations, similar to what Sarah had just told Maggie about the square knot and the bowline. "Okay, we're going to take a short break now, and I mean short. Use the restrooms if you want to, but be right outside at the campfire pit in fifteen minutes. You'll get instructions there on which group you will be in for practicing tying knots and how to use the knots when you're out in the woods. Thank you." With that dismissal, most of the boys jumped up and hurried out of the auditorium while the young ladies – that group now consisted of almost all the sixth-grade girls – calmly rose and left in an orderly manner. Mrs. Ames would've been proud of them.

"Do you think we'll ever have to tie some knots in the woods?" Maggie asked Sarah as they were walking outside.

"I don't know, Mags," Sarah started. "Even if you never have to use them, just knowing how can give you confidence in other things you do." Sarah was definitely sounding older and wiser than her eleven years and ten months.

"Oh, okay," Maggie replied in her typical easy-going manner.

At the campfire pit, the two girls found out that they were in group C, which was meeting by a tall pine tree that marked the beginning of one of the many trails. It was a mixed group, six boys and six girls. They practiced tying several different knots for about thirty minutes, and then they were given a sheet of instructions for uses of the knots. They were to pair up, same gender pairing was okay for the first few activities, and work on the applications. They were given some materials and told what to do; it was up to them to determine which knots to use to complete the exercises.

Sarah and Maggie flew through the first few applications, having troubles only with the last one – lashing branches together to make a floating raft. Their instructor, seeing how quickly and deftly they had moved through the first few ones, came over and gave them a small hint on how to finish their raft. He was impressed with the skill and ease in which Sarah and Maggie had completed their tasks; the three groups of boys were still fumbling around with their first two tasks.

The rest of the day flew by; the girls actually enjoyed the first dinner at camp, and then they grabbed their jackets and went to the campfire pit. The campfires were always a big hit; they sang songs, and took turns roasting marshmallows over the raging fire. While the campfire time appeared to be just a fun time, several lessons were also being taught to the youngsters. One of them was safety around fire; one of the instructors rolled up his sleeve to show them a severe third-degree burn he received through no fault of his own. His right arm did not look much like an arm at all.

They were also told how to thoroughly extinguish a campfire: spread the burning materials (but not outside the fire pit); gently and repeatedly pour water over <u>everything</u> in the pit; cover everything with dirt (no twigs or other materials that could catch fire), and look for traces of smoke. "Even the smallest amount of smoke coming up from the pit tells you that there is still something burning. Start over and repeat the four steps until there is no more smoke and the dirt is not warm. Boys and girls," *Did he just call us 'girls'? We're young ladies.* "Failure to completely extinguish your fire could be the start of the next major forest fire. Let's not let that happen."

Sleep came easy for Sarah and Maggie – and all the other young campers – that night.

The days flew by as hikes were taken, personal safety lessons were taught, and ravished appetites were filled by hearty meals. They were all encouraged to send postcards home (postcards and stamps were provided by the camp); most of the young ladies did, while only a few of the boys did.

At the beginning of the second week, the campers had the option of a hike and overnight campout, or they could stay at the main camp and work on a project. This year's project was clearing the debris caused by a huge storm on one of the trails. The camp provided the tents, and the campers took their own sleeping bags and other gear. Sarah was thoroughly excited about the hike and campout; Maggie was neutral, but she said she would go so she could be with her best friend.

On the day of the hike, Maggie was sick and so Sarah was the only one without a partner. The counselors suggested that Sarah either stay at camp or join another group of girls to make it a three-some. She said "No" to the first suggestion, and "No" to the second. She could make it okay on her own. After all, she and Maggie had been receiving top scores in all the activities so far. A single camper was against the camp rules, but Mrs. Ames convinced the hike leaders to make a one-time exception for Sarah.

The hike proceeded without incident, and Sarah was fine on her own that evening. She even helped out two other girls who were having trouble setting up their tent. Sarah put hers up just fine, even though it usually took two people; she was quite self-sufficient. There were the usual sixth-grade boys' tricks and noises that night, but Sarah kept them away from her by setting a low rope trap that tripped two of them who were trying to sneak near the girls' tents. The boys' yelping evoked the wrath of the counselors who told the boys in no uncertain terms to stay in their own tents. Sarah slept fine that night; she didn't need anyone else around to make her feel comfortable. She was up early in the morning and helped to get the fire started. After breakfast, she was the first one to take her tent down, clean off the dirt and debris, and fold it properly so it would fit into its bag. She then helped two neighboring girls, and then the two boys whom she had tripped the night before. The hike back was uneventful.

Sarah was happy to see that Maggie was feeling much better when she got back to her cabin. They hugged, and Maggie begged Sarah to tell her all about the hike. Maggie couldn't stop laughing when Sarah told her about setting the trip line for the boys. "They deserved it," Maggie said. "Too bad you couldn't have done something worse."

"I could've," Sarah replied. "I could've," she said with a devilish grin on her face.

Camp finally came to an end, and there were no major injuries – at least no major bodily injuries. A few boys had their pride hurt, something they would probably experience later again in life. Most of the campers slept on the comfortable bus during the ride back home. A few sang songs, but most of them slept.

Sarah and Maggie were once again the last to get off the bus, much to the distress of their parents who thought that maybe they weren't on the bus. As they got off quietly and confidently, Sarah and Maggie picked up their sleeping bags and suitcases and strolled over to their parents.

"Well, how was it?" Tina Johnson blurted out as she was so happy her daughter was back home.

"It was fine, Mom," Sarah replied quite calmly. "Mags and I had a good time."

The two young ladies hugged each other and turned back to their parents.

Sarah had learned a lot at camp. Camp Lookout taught her how to look out for herself.

Fourteen/Catorce
San José del Cabo
Thursday, January 17th

conducir (cōn'·dū·cĭr) – to drive. *¿Quieres conducir el coche?* Do you want to drive the car?

"Hola," was the greeting from the man on the other end of the line as he answered the phone.

"Buenos días," Stan started, knowing he might not get too far with his Spanish. *"Mi nombre es Stan. Esta allí Señora Carmelita Sanchez, por favor?"* [My name is Stan. Is Mrs. Carmelita Sanchez there, please?]

"Sí. Un momento, por favor," was the reply.

I guess my Spanish wasn't too bad.

"Buenos días, Señor Stan. Cómo está?" The pleasant and familiar voice on the other end of the phone sounded <u>so</u> <u>good</u> to Stan. That's one of the hardest parts about traveling on an investigation – you typically don't know anyone and you are on your own.

"Muy bien, y tú?" [Very good, and you?]

"Muy bien, gracias. It's nice to hear your voice again, Señor Stan. And your Spanish is very good. Have you been taking lessons down here?" Stan could hear the smile in her voice. Most people didn't know that your voice actually sounded different if you smiled while talking.

"No lessons. But that's about all I can say in Spanish, except maybe to order another beer. But it's a little early in the day for that, though."

"Yes, for me it is too early for a cerveza. But I'll let you order it when it's the right time. How is your investigation going? Any good leads, as they say on TV?"

"Some people remember seeing her. And I'll take you up on the cerveza. I know just the place where I can buy you a beer and it won't cost a whole lot. I was at Shooters the other night. Ten pesos for a beer, not a bad deal."

"Shooters?" Carmelita said with surprise. "I didn't know that place was still open. That's where I learned the words to the American rock and roll songs. Are they still as loud as I remember?"

"Just as loud, if not louder," Stan replied. He was pleased that the conversation had a casual tone. He was afraid that things might get more formal once she was back in her own country. "I was hoping to take you up on your offer to show me around town. Is the offer still open?"

"Of course it's still open. What are you doing today?" Carmelita's voice was excited as she did want to spend more time with Stan, and she wasn't sure if he would call her or not. "Today is an excellent day because more shops are open as we get closer to the weekend. How about if I pick you up at your hotel in one hour?"

"One hour here at the hotel?" Stan asked just to make sure. He was actually surprised that she took the lead in getting together. He was surprised, and he certainly wasn't disappointed.

"Yes," she answered. "One hour American time. Not one hour Mexican time."

"I've set my watch; I'll see you in 59 minutes and 40 seconds. What kind of car will you be driving?"

"I don't know yet. I'll have to ask my brother Roberto. But I will be the only one pulling over to pick up a strange American man. Or at least I hope I'm the only one."

"Hey, I'm not that strange. Okay; see you in 59 minutes."

"Okay. *Hasta luego."* [See you later]

"Bye for now," Stan replied as he set the phone down. Carmelita sounded really happy to be able to see him. *Is this going too fast?*

Stan left his room and bounded down the steps forty-five minutes later. *She might not be late, but I want to be there in case she is a little early*

"Buenos días, señor," said assistant manager Miguel as Stan stepped into the main lobby. "It's another beautiful day here in San José; are you going out to see more of the city?"

"Yes, I am, Miguel. I've left a small bag of laundry on the bed. Would you ask housekeeping to take care of it, please?"

"Of course, señor. Room 304, sí?"

"Yes, that's right. Gracias, Miguel." Stan appreciated it when the hotel staff remembered him. "Have a good day," he added as he walked through the wood and glass double doors out to Boulevard Mijares.

"You, too, señor. Remember, you can drink the water." Miguel chuckled a little as he said that. Most first-time tourists to San José and

Cabo San Lucas bought lots of bottled water because they had been told to not drink the water. But it was actually quite safe to drink the water in the restaurants and hotels in most resort areas.

Stan was focusing on nothing in particular when his attention was awakened by the honking of a small white car that stopped in the traffic lane. He looked at it as did many others. It was only when he saw Carmelita reaching her left arm out of the window, extending it upward and waving her hand at him – that was when he recognized her and realized that she was not going to pull over for him. There were no parking spots available, so she had no other choice. Stan had no other choice, either, so he quickly stepped out into the street, opened the passenger side door, and hopped in.

"Hello," he said to her in a hurried voice. He was a little out of breath from the quick movements. And from the excitement of the day so far.

"Hello. Sorry, but there were no places to park and I didn't know how else to let you know it was me." Carmelita Sanchez sounded apologetic for the way she got Stan's attention.

"That's okay," he replied. "You're early," he said as he looked down at his watch.

She laughed. "Yes, I am a little early. I think I learned that living in the States. But I didn't want to be late because someone else may have come by and honked at the American tourist, and he might have gotten in that car by mistake."

"If he did get in the wrong car, then yes that <u>would</u> have been a mistake. A mistake on his part."

"So where do you want to go?" she said as she started moving slowly north on Boulevard Mijares. At the next intersection was the beginning of Plaza Mijares, so she would have to turn left or make a U-turn.

"You're the tour guide. Where do you want to take me?"

"Let's drive around this main area a little bit, then we can have some lunch, and then maybe visit our Art District; it's very nice."

"All of that sounds great to me," Stan answered.

As she reached the barricaded entrance to the plaza, Carmelita turned left on Manuel Doblado. The windy narrow street was made even narrower with the cars parked on the left side of it. "If you are in *Centro*, or downtown, this is the main road that will take you to Federal Highway 1, the road you took to come in from the airport. This doesn't look like much of a main road, but this is it. There are a couple other roads on the left toward the beach that also go straight through from Boulevard Mijares to Highway 1. The first one is Coronado, and the next one is Valerio González Canseco, but unfortunately that one is one-way from the highway to downtown."

"I think that's the one we came down on the way from the airport. Is that the one with the bus station?" Stan asked.

"Yes, the main bus station is there on Valerio González; that's what it's called. We typically drop the other name Canseco from it. It's complicated; I'll explain it sometime to you. That's where you would go if you want to take the bus to Todos Santos, to La Paz, or even up to Mexicali or Tijuana. I see you are already learning some of the town," Carmelita said as she looked over at Stan. "How about if I take you to a real Mexican hangout? It's called The Hangman."

"Do I have to do anything crazy or stupid? I've heard there are a few of those places," Stan said somewhat hesitantly.

"Oh, no. Not here in San José. That's the Giggling Marlin down in Cabo San Lucas. The Hangman is just a good place to eat. Mostly locals, plus a few tourists who've been here before; but it's not in a place where most tourists would even think of going."

"All right; I'm up for it." Stan was relieved that he didn't have to embarrass himself just to have lunch.

The traffic on Manuel Doblado wasn't moving very fast. The tourist drivers were looking to the left and to the right to see all the shops. Even when they saw one they liked, they then faced the issue of finding a parking space – a rare commodity. When there was an open spot, that's when the fun began, especially if the open spot was on the left side of the road. Most Americans are used to large, marked off spaces; those didn't exist in San José.

Carmelita maintained her slow pace as Stan checked out the shops on both sides of the road. The colorful fronts and doorways to some of the shops presented an intriguing invitation. *Maybe I'll come down here and do some looking around. Maybe.* The pair finally reached the stoplight at Federal Highway 1. Stan looked around and saw a familiar sign, Pescador. He had seen that sign on his way in from the airport. "I saw this on the way in. I know that *pescado* means fish. What does *pescador* mean?" Stan hadn't asked on the shuttle, but he could find out now.

"Think of English," Carmelita began. "When you add an 'er' or an 'or' to the end of a word, it turns that noun into the person who does that thing. So if you take 'fish,' and add 'er' to it, you get 'fisher' – one who fishes. Since you like some words to be gender-specific, you add 'man' to it to get 'fisherman.'" *She certainly knows the rules of the English language better than many Americans.* "So if you start with pescado, which means fish, and add an r, you get pescador, which means one who fishes, a fisher, a fisherman. There's your first Spanish lesson."

Carmelita continued as they crossed the highway and made a right turn. "This area is known as Pescador because this is where many of the fishermen lived back when San José was a small town. That's the way we call these sections of town, by the people who lived there; or by the ones who lived there when it was getting settled. That's a decent local sports bar if you ever get tired of Shooters," she said as they passed Dante's Bar & Grill on the right side of the road.

Looking straight ahead it would have been hard to miss the next restaurant on the left. With the man hanging from a noose, it could be only one restaurant – The Hangman. It was still early enough that Carmelita was able to find a close parking spot. Stan hopped out of his side, pushed down the door lock, and walked around to the other side of the car. As he carefully opened the door, making sure he didn't bang it into the curb, he graciously extended his hand to Carmelita. She took his hand, swung her feet around to the left, and stepped out of the car. Seeing that she did have the car keys in her other hand, Stan pushed down the door lock and then shut the door.

"Does this look okay to you?" she asked as she stepped up on the curb.

"If it's okay with you, it's okay with me," Stan replied as he continued to gently hold her hand as they walked together up the steps to the restaurant.

"*Buenas tardes. Bienvenidos a 'The Hangman,'*" was their greeting as they entered the open air restaurant. [Good afternoon. Welcome to 'The Hangman.']

Carmelita rattled off a response so fast that Stan didn't even try to pick out a word that he might understand. She and the waiter had a brief exchange, and then he showed them to a quiet table – as quiet as it can be in that type of a restaurant. As they were seated, the waiter handed each of them a menu and then once again said something to Carmelita.

Fifteen/Quince
San José del Cabo
Later that afternoon – January 17th

árbol (ăr·bōl') – tree. *Este es un árbol alto.* This is a tall tree.

Stan paid the bill after lunch, and he and Carmelita walked down to the car. She unlocked the driver's door, Stan opened it for her, and then he went to the passenger's side, which Carmelita had reached over to unlock. "What do you think? Did you like it?" she asked as she looked over her right shoulder before pulling out into the road.

"Now I see why a siesta is so popular. I could use one right now," Stan replied. "Yes, it was very good; the flavors were outstanding. Thank you for selecting it. What's next?"

"I have to go up here a little way to get back on Highway 1. Then we'll come back this direction and head into the north part of downtown. I'll show you a few restaurants that you might want to try, and then we can stroll through the art district. Is that okay? Or do you need to do some of your work?"

"Everything is part of my work; I never know when some information will come up that leads to something else." Stan wanted to let her know that he didn't consider this an interruption, and that he planned to enjoy whatever time he had with her today. "I always like to know of good restaurants to go to. And even though classy art is not my thing, I'd like to see more of what San José has to offer. So, lead on, my awesome tour guide," Stan said as he rolled his window down only part way.

Carmelita continued north on the windy road and finally reached the place where she wanted to make a right turn to get over to Federal Highway 1. She eased onto the highway and accelerated into the traffic flow. Moving over into the left lane, she pulled into a break in the center divider that allowed cars to stop before making a left turn. As she turned left, Stan remembered seeing that Pemex station – the last one before getting into town. She turned left after the station. A little farther down she made another left and then a right on Comonfort, and went a couple blocks before finding a shady spot on the right side of the road.

"That's a prime spot, parking under a shady tree," Stan said as he eased his door open, being careful not to hit it against the curb.

"Yes," Carmelita replied. "You don't always find the right spot to park in. During the week, these streets are a little busier than on the weekend." She closed her door and joined Stan on the sidewalk. "The area we're entering now is our art district."

"So this is it," Stan said as they walked toward the corner where Calle Guerrero intersected with Comonfort. "I'd seen it highlighted on the map, and I was hoping to walk through it."

"Oh, I forgot to tell you. After I told my brother Roberto about you and why you were down here in San José, he said that he'd read in the paper about a young hitchhiker's body being found up north a little ways. It was just last week, and of course it didn't mean anything to him at the time. It was up near Santiago, right by the Tropic of Cancer Monument." As Carmelita turned to Stan, she saw a look of astonishment on his face.

"I wouldn't imagine that he still has the newspaper," Stan said although he knew it was highly unlikely. At the time of the article, it wouldn't have meant anything to her brother.

"No," she said apologetically. "I asked him, but he'd already thrown it away. The newspaper is called *Tribuna de los Cabos*, and its main office is just over on the main road – Boulevard Mauricio Castro. I could take you over there later if you would like."

"That would be nice. But I haven't heard of that road, Mauricio Castro. And you said it's the main road?" Stan was a little confused because he thought the *main road* was Highway 1 that came in from the airport.

"I'm sorry," Carmelita replied. "Boulevard Mauricio Castro is the actual name of what is also called Highway 1. Most locals call it Boulevard Castro."

"Sure, a quick stop there later would be good to see if they still have a copy of that article. Thanks." The two of them continued their walk into San José's Art District.

Sixteen/Dieciséis
Art District – San José del Cabo
Present day

caminar (kă'·mē·năr) – walk. *¿Quieres caminar a la ciudad?* Do you want to walk to town?

The Art District in San José del Cabo is not at all like Fifth Avenue or the Tribeca in Manhattan. Nor is it like Geary Street in San Francisco. What it is, however, is a marvelous little area carved out of the city's Historic District. The area is essentially four square blocks, although a few galleries lie on the opposite sides of the streets from those blocks.

Being a compact, almost self-contained area that sits adjacent to Plaza Mijares, San José's Art District [*Distrito del Arte*] is easily accessible. Most tour buses stop right outside the square on Calle Hidalgo, plus the city's main church sits in the southeast corner of the district. The area is roughly bounded by Vicente Guerrero on the west, Miguel Hidalgo on the east, Ignacio Zaragoza on the south, and Comonfort on the north. Morelos runs south to north in the middle of the district, and Alvaro Obregón runs west to east. There are plenty of one way streets in San José, but you won't see any "One Way" signs; you just have to know which way to go.

You don't find painted velvet canvases here; these classy galleries are not the "tourist traps" that you might normally think of for border towns. Well, the only things that border this area are the Pacific Ocean and the Sea of Cortez. San José del Cabo is a long way from the U.S./Mexican border. Most of these galleries shutter their doors at the end of May, and then re-open in November – timed to coincide with the primary tourist season. As with any business, some of the galleries and shops that were open in May might not re-open in November. The art business is a tough business, whether in Mexico, the United States, or any other place in the world.

There are two regular weekly events designed to attract people to the District. The Tuesday morning Art Walk (from 9 AM to Noon) includes free coffee, and there's Art Night on Thursday evenings (from 5:00 – 9 PM). Rumor has it that some of the galleries provide a complimentary glass of wine that night. A bonus to these two events is that the visitors to the galleries typically feel more comfortable because they are not alone – the weekly events draw more people in at the same time. The Art Night is also nice because it allows people to do some other activities during the day, and then go browse through the galleries in the evening. The annual Art District brochure describes the galleries as well and highlights some of their works.

It would be a mistake to try to say that there is one "best" gallery in the Art District. Each one is different, which means that unlike many U.S. galleries, you won't find the same pieces in more than one gallery in San José. The galleries typically represent certain artists, and a gallery owner could even be one of those represented artists. As you stroll through the Art District on the Thursday Art Night, you might even have a chance to talk with some of the featured artists in the galleries.

One of the cutest little art galleries (not just in San José, but anywhere) is El Armario at the corner of Morelos and Obregón. You would never be able to tell from the outside or from the inside that this was the site of the city's first gas station in the 1970's. Gallery owner Cinthya Castro has a middle name that is not known by very many people – Tatiana. When she was born her mom wanted to name her Cynthia, but her dad wanted the name Tatiana. When her parents went to fill out the paperwork to record her birth, the clerk was confused and so she spelled her name "Cinthya." (But her dad still calls her Tatiana) El Armario is a combination of a folk art gallery and a coffee patio. The palette of colors displayed in the art is very wide. Cinthya carries a unique selection of Mexican folk art of ceramic pottery, candles, clay figurines, jewelry boxes, landscapes, and portraits.

Among the newer galleries in San José that not only features great works but that also contributes to humanitarian causes is Muvezi – Fine African Art. The gallery is located on the north side of Obregón between Hidalgo and Morelos. Muvezi is a Shona word for "carver of stone," and the gallery slogan or byline is "Trading Art for Health." The gallery features Shona Art, which is sculpted stone that has been fired to give it its color and beauty. The sculptures come from Zimbabwe where the average income is one dollar per day, which has the world's highest inflation rate, and which has an 80% unemployment rate. It also has an infant mortality rate of 50% and a life expectancy of 37 years. By ensuring quality stones for the sculptors to use, paying them a fair rate for their work, and then by returning a share of the sales of their work in the form of health solutions to combat malaria, Muvezi and its foundation have helped regenerate an art form that was dying.

Undoubtedly the most impressive gallery in San José is Galeria de Ida Victoria, owned and operated by Ida Victoria Gustavson. The local press has called it "the finest gallery south of Los Angeles," and *The Wall Street Journal* said, "The soaring Galeria de Ida Victoria has an impressive collection of original paintings." Those quotes place an enormous pressure on the gallery owner to deliver, and Ida has done that. The gallery is on the western edge of the Art District, on Vicente Guerrero between Zaragoza and Obregon. Entering the spacious gallery leaves one with the impression of being in one of the major art houses in the U.S. or in Europe. Ida and her husband Pete Signorelli have developed a unique and artistic way of displaying the art without ruining the walls. With its multiple levels and open-air quality, the gallery is able to present works of all scales and allow them to fit naturally in their settings. Ida herself is an artist and she has had her works published in many forms, but her true love is displayed in Galeria de Ida Victoria where she is able to showcase original works of art by exceptionally talented artists from around the world.

Sitting next to Galeria de Ida Victoria is Casa Don Pablo. Carlos Ignacio is the owner of this small gallery located in one of the original historical homes in the area. As such, it is a small gallery. The house itself had about five rooms, and that is all the space that was available for Carlos and his gallery. Guests coming through the front door today are greeted with an amazing collection of original Mexican art, wood carvings, local historic photographs, and fine silver. The house originally belonged to, and the gallery is named after Pablo L. Martinez, the first historian in Baja California. Born in 1898 in a little area called Santa Anita just north of San José, Pablo Martinez also founded the first newspaper in the area. Don Pablo never married and so he didn't have any direct descendants. His sister thus inherited his house upon his death. Her name was Doña Lapa, and she was the first OB/GYN in the area. She was also the grandmother of Carlos Ignacio, and so that is how he obtained the house, which he's transformed into a charming gallery. Seeing some of the works in Casa Don Pablo makes you think of the well-known Spanish Pablo – Pablo Picasso. There are "rocks" made of papier mâché with embedded fossil drawings. Some of the hand-thrown plates look as if they are right out of Picasso's ceramic collection. When Carlos is not explaining the details of the art, he'll show you some old books containing historic information of the area. The gallery is a definite must-see.

The other galleries and shops in San José's Art District are also worth going into. Wandering through the district on the Tuesday morning Art Walk or the Thursday evening Art Night adds to the pleasure of seeing the amazing displays. The Art District's in the middle of the city's Historic District, so there's history all around. Ask any of the gallery owners a single question about the area, and be prepared for a marvelous description of the history and charm of San José and Los Cabos.

Seventeen/Diecisiete
Tropic of Cancer Monument –
50 kilometers north of San José del Cabo
Friday, January 18th

vacía (vă'·cē·ă) – empty. *La botella azul está vacía.* The blue bottle is empty.

Stan had a copy of the small article from *Tribuna de Los Cabos* covering the discovery of a hitchhiker's body near the Tropic of Cancer Monument. Carmelita had read the article to him, and then he carefully wrote down her translation of it:

January 11 - The body of a young female was found in an arroyo near the Tropic of Cancer Monument just south of Santiago along Federal Highway 1. Two couples traveling from San José to La Paz had stopped to take photographs of the 2-meter sphere on Thursday January 10th. One of the men, Jim Lee, walked down into the arroyo just north of the Monument for personal reasons when he saw the body.

Mr. Lee called back to Mrs. Lee and the other couple, who thought that Mr. Lee was in harm. When they arrived there to see why Mr. Lee was calling for them, Mrs. Lee dialed 080 for Emergency Services on her cell phone. Two officers from Santiago drove to see what Mr. Lee and the others had found. After talking to the four tourists for about twenty minutes, the officers told them they could leave and continue on their trip.

The body was still fully clothed in jeans with a sweatshirt covering a shirt with "Cabo San Lucas" on it. The officers did not find a purse or wallet near the body, but there was a copy of a U.S. Passport in one of the pockets. Officials have not yet confirmed the identity of the victim, but the Passport copy had a photograph matching the victim's face, an 18-year old from Toledo, Ohio. No more information is available at this time.

Carmelita had offered to drive Stan up to the Monument, but he wanted solitude as he re-read her translation and reflected on the parents who wondered where their daughter was. He was relieved that the young female wasn't Sarah, but his eyes still filled with tears as he thought about the girl and her family. Why was she down here? Was she by herself? Was she with friends? How did she end up dead in that arroyo? Where did she meet the person who did that to her? Was she trying to escape from something? When did her parents realize that she was missing in Mexico? Stan knew he would never know the answers to those and all the other questions that her family would have. Could the same fate have happened to Sarah? He didn't want to think about <u>that</u> possibility.

"Thank you, again," Stan said as he and Carmelita both arose from the plush chairs in the hotel lobby. Even though he would have preferred a more private meeting in his room, he also knew the appearance that could make, and he didn't want to create any issues for Carmelita or her family.

"You're welcome, Señor Stan," she said as she firmly grasped his helping hand. I wish I could do more to help you, but you know how to reach me."

"You don't know how much you've helped already. And even though it wasn't Sarah, I need to go check out the area as if it were her. I don't know if there are any clues that could help me find her. I'll be calling soon." Stan was sincere when he said he would be calling her again soon – he enjoyed being with her.

"Are you sure you don't want to use my brother's car? He doesn't mind; it has full insurance; you'd be okay in it."

"Thank you, but no. If anything happened, I'd feel really bad. It's just as easy for me to rent a car down the street. I talked to them last week, and they have cars available all the time. This way I can go and come on my own schedule, and there's no inconvenience for you or for Roberto." Stan was having a hard time convincing even himself why he shouldn't use the car that was offered to him. But he just knew that he shouldn't.

"It's not an inconvenience, but I understand. Don't stay up there too long, and try to come back before it gets dark," Carmelita said in a voice that displayed true caring and concern.

"I will," Stan said as he instinctively embraced her shoulders and gave her a slight kiss on her right cheek. Realizing what he had just done, he instantly removed his hands, stepped back, and had a slight look of shock in his wide-opened eyes.

Knowing what he was feeling, Carmelita reassured him. "That's okay. We Mexicans give hugs all the time." After a short pause she added, "And we kiss both cheeks." With a slight smile that spread across her face, she said "So long" with her eyes as she turned around and walked out of the hotel.

Stan longingly watched her as she walked to the car.

"She's a special lady," assistant manager Miguel said as Stan reached down to pick up his briefcase.

"Yes, she is," Stan replied as the smile that was just on Carmelita's face was now duplicated on his. He walked out of the hotel, seemingly tracing her steps with his. By instinct he turned right before he realized that the car rental agency was to the left. He laughed to himself when he realized his mistake and turned around to head south on Boulevard Mijares. As he slowly walked the block and a half to the Quality Rent-a-Car office, he was unaware of anyone else on the sidewalk, or the cars and buses on the road. His mind was elsewhere.

The agent was holding his cell phone to his right ear and talking quite animatedly when Stan walked through the open door. The man quickly lowered his voice and said something that Stan interpreted as, "I can't talk any more now. I'll call you later" because the man quickly ceased the conversation and closed his phone.

"Good morning, señor. I'm glad to see you back. Did you want a car today?" All of a sudden the agent was talking to Stan as if he were a long-lost friend.

Staying quite businesslike, Stan replied, "Yes, I would."

"Very good, señor. Have a seat while we fill out the paperwork very quick."

Quickly, Stan said to himself.

After the paperwork was completed, and Stan saw where the agent had checked the 'Full Insurance' box, Stan followed the agent out to the street to inspect the car for any damages. Stan was quite amused when the agent was checking items such as Steering Wheel, Spare Tire, Windshield Wipers, and Floor Mats. The agent sensed Stan's surprise and said, "If I don't check that you have a spare tire, you could sell it and make a few dollars. I know that you would not do that, señor, but some people have."

"That would not surprise me, Alfredo." Stan didn't mind making some small talk, but what he really wanted to do right now was to get on the road and head up to the Tropic of Cancer Monument. But he had to remember that he was in Mexico, and many things moved at a slower pace here.

"Okay, señor. I think we're okay now," the agent said as he headed back to the door. Once he got inside, he went behind his desk, sat down, and opened a drawer to pull out one more form. "This form, señor, says that you are not allowed to drive this car on the dirt road that leads out of San José along the coast up toward Cabo Pulmo. That road is a very bad road for cars. If you drive on that road, then you are 100% responsible for any damages to the car even though you have purchased insurance. Is that clear, señor?"

"Yes, that's quite clear, Alfredo," Stan said as his patience was beginning to get a little thin. "The only place I am going is up toward Santiago to the Tropic of Cancer Monument."

"Oh, if you are going up there, let me give you brochures of a few places you might want to go to along the way." Alfredo started digging through another drawer to find some brochures for Stan. Although the agent was truly attempting to be helpful, Stan didn't <u>want</u> any more help – he was sorry he'd said anything.

"Here you go, señor. While you are up at Santiago, you will want to visit *Las Cascadas* [The Waterfalls]; they are very nice at this time of the year. On the way back, stop at Miraflores; it's on the right side as you're coming back. There you can visit some hot springs and see some old fossils."

Aren't all fossils old? Stan thought. But at this point he wasn't about to say anything.

"All right, señor. Your total is $66.00, sixty-six U.S. American dollars. Remember that you must return the car with a full tank of gasoline just like it has in it right now. Any questions, señor?"

"No, I don't have any questions. Thank you." Stan was now trying to keep his conversation to the bare minimum. He just wanted to GO!

The agent finally handed the keys to Stan who got up and walked out to the car. Silence was going to be nice. *Wouldn't it have been nice to have reserved a car with Hertz, and then just show up, get in your car, show your license and drive off?* Yes, that would have been nice. But this wasn't Hertz!

Stan opened the driver's door and slipped into the seat. *Yes, this is not a Hertz car.* The car was clean inside, but the seat seemed quite small, and there was a definite cigarette odor despite being a 'No Smoking car.' As he set his briefcase on the passenger seat, he reached a little farther and pushed down the door lock, fastened the seat belt, adjusted the mirrors, and he was finally ready to go. He was glad he'd paid the extra five dollars for a car with automatic transmission; shifting gears was one more thing he didn't want to have to worry about.

After starting the engine, he backed up carefully because he couldn't see past the van that was parked next to him. Slowly he eased the car back onto Boulevard Mijares when all of a sudden a noisy Urbano bus (one of the local ones) went by just barely missing the car's rear bumper. Stan sighed a heavy sigh, and then continued pulling the car out onto the street. Making it safely out, he moved the gear shift lever to **D** and started forward. He followed the white bus a block and a half where it turned left onto Calle Manuel Doblado, the road he'd taken with Carmelita to head out of downtown. The bus didn't go all the way to the main highway, but Stan kept going straight until he came to some cars stopped at the light at Federal Highway 1. He turned right heading north and was now on his way to the Tropic of Cancer Monument.

Fifty kilometers was not very far to drive, but Stan knew that he had to give his full attention to everything on the road or on the side of the road on this trip. Some of the road was familiar to Stan from both his trip in from the airport and also from his drive the other day when he and Carmelita had lunch at The Hangman. Once he saw Pemex and Soriana on the right, he knew that was about the end of the familiar territory until he reached the airport. Passing the airport exit made it seem that he was now moving into the unknown.

As the divided road passed over a large ravine, Arroyo San Lázaro, he saw a wide barren wash that appeared to be swept clean by the once-a-year rushing waters that came down from the mountains. A quick glance to the right showed a small green brushy area that probably still had some water in it. *That must be where the arroyo flows into Rio San José.* Another blink of the eye and the divided road became a two-lane road. The casitas and the ranchos were farther apart now, and the area was certainly not like the drive from San José to Cabo San Lucas. *No large hotels or condo projects around here, and I don't think there ever will be.*

The area had more rolling hills than Stan thought it would. As the road angled slightly toward the Sierra de La Laguna mountain range, the natural landscape of undulations, small river washes, and rough-looking little bushes took over. Even though the climate was dry and arid, the area was not a desert. Stan didn't see any large Saguaro or Prickly Pear cactus that most people think of when they envision a desert area. He did see some large birds gently circling overhead looking for rodents or other potential food sources.

A small animal darted across the road startling Stan. He realized that his full attention wasn't on his driving, something that he should be doing. He shook his head back and forth a few times and he blinked his eyes so he could give 100% concentration to his driving and to the road ahead. *This is not a time or a place to be daydreaming.* Stan was not concerned about highway robbers or anything like that. But inattention along an unknown narrow road could cause him to lose control or have other problems.

Stan first saw the sign for Caduaño, and then the road became quite windy for a few kilometers before he saw the signs for Miraflores. One of the signs said FOSÍLS with an arrow to the left. The next sign, a Pemex sign, was apparently a favorite target for shooting practice as people drove by it. But it was nice to know that there was – *hopefully still is* – a gas station out there. The other sign was just a directional sign pointing to the road to Miraflores on the west side of Highway 1. As he looked at his map, Stan saw that he had about twelve more kilometers until he reached his destination. The time had passed much faster than he thought it would. He'd forgotten that the distances he was traveling were in kilometers and not in miles. Because one kilometer was only about five-eighths of a mile, the fifty kilometers he was going was only about thirty-two miles.

Those next twelve kilometers passed quickly as Stan reached his destination. He was a little surprised that there was only one small road sign to let travelers know about the Tropic of Cancer Monument; the sign simply said, "Tropico de Cancer." If he were not specifically coming to the monument, he probably would have missed the sign and kept on going. He slowed the car and turned on his left turn signal far in advance of his turn.

The loud *blink-blink-blink* of the turn signal was obnoxious, but at least he knew the turn signal was working.

As he turned left into the paved area for the monument, a truck carrying a load of used tires roared past him heading north. The truck driver honked his horn as if Stan's slowing down to turn had been a major inconvenience for him. Stan didn't even bother to look back; he was sure that there was a hand gesture associated with the honking. As Stan pulled into the gravely area, Stan saw that there were no other cars in the area; it would be hard to call it a 'parking lot.' The Tropic of Cancer Monument was a concrete sphere about six feet high sitting on a platform of concrete and painted white rocks. *Slightly unimpressive*, Stan thought to himself since there was no one else to talk to in the area. *No, actually it's even less than slightly unimpressive – whatever that makes it.* The Monument had a makeshift fence around it – *to protect it from what?* There were some cacti inside the fence, but even the fence had an opening that you could walk through.

Stan took a notebook and camera out of his briefcase, got out of the car and locked it. No one else was around – that he could tell – but habit and common sense told him to lock the car anyway. He walked around the monument, noticing that there had been a solid line on it, apparently tracing the Tropic of Cancer latitude. That line had worn away from weather and neglect. He walked north to the arroyo where the young female's body had been found last week. He still had so many nagging questions about that tragedy, but he knew that he would never know the answers. It was just his nature to <u>want</u> to know the answers, regardless of that impossibility.

The arroyo was as unimpressive as the monument. It was just a dirt wash that occasionally had a flash flood or rain runoff run through it. As he looked in both directions, it didn't appear to start anywhere, and he couldn't see where it ended. It was formed by nature, and it was also formless in its nature.

The banks were not steep, so Stan decided to venture down into the arroyo. He saw an area that looked as if it could have been where the body was. There were a lot of footprints, some of them looking like boot prints. He didn't see any signs of a body being dragged down there, so the body could have been carried down there by one or two people. Or, the female could have walked down there with someone else who then killed her. *So many mysteries, so many unknowns.*

Stan saw what he had come there for; it was a good thing he didn't have great expectations of finding anything in particular – there was nothing. There were no major clues for what happened there last week, and there were no clues for finding Sarah. As he climbed back out of the arroyo, his shoes sank in the silty dirt making it seem more like climbing up a sand dune. Once he was back on the firm surface, he stomped his shoes to clean them off. As he did, he apparently startled a large lizard that went running from its resting area over to one of the few small bushes that managed to live in this environment. The lizard's sudden movement also startled Stan, making him once again aware of his surroundings.

Maybe he wasn't the only one out here. He quickly scanned the area, even looking under the car at a distance for a shadow in case someone was hiding over there. No, he was the only one there.

Driving back south toward San José, Stan's mind was focused on the next steps. What had he found out down here; how did that fit in with what he already knew; what did all it add up to; what was he going to tell the Johnsons? *A lot of questions without many answers.*

He welcomed the idea of being back in town; he felt more comfortable being in San José than he did out at the Tropic of Cancer Monument. Seeing the big CENTRO sign overhead, Stan turned left on Valerio González, passed the bus station, and then came to the stop sign at Boulevard Mijares, his most familiar street in town. He made a left turn, drove a block and a half and pulled back into the same spot in front of Quality Rent-a-Car. As he was pulling in he saw that the curb was painted Solo Rent-a-car, *solo* meaning 'only.' He was actually a little surprised that people obeyed that curb marking. What he didn't know was that cars would be towed and the drivers heavily fined for parking in those marked spots. It was just another one of those customs that you knew only by living here for a long time.

"Hello, señor. Is there something wrong with the car?" The familiar voice of Alfredo the agent greeted Stan as he walked through the agency door.

"No, there's nothing wrong with it. I'm just returning it."

"But, señor, you have rented the car until tomorrow. You can't return it now."

"What do you mean I can't return it? I'm done with it; I don't need it any more. I'm bringing it back. Here are the keys." Stan did not quite understand why he couldn't return the car.

"But you have paid to rent the car until tomorrow," the agent replied. "I can't give you a refund just because you come back so early. I'm sorry, señor."

"I didn't ask for a refund. I've paid for the car; I've used the car. Now I'm returning the car. Rent it back out again; I don't care. I'm not looking for any money back." Stan was getting a little exasperated with Alfredo; how much clearer could he be?

Finally, the agent understood what Stan was saying and he picked up Stan's paperwork that was still sitting on the desk. "Okay, señor. Let's go check the car and make sure it still has all the tires and the steering wheel." The joke fell far short of amusing Stan. In fact, Stan was not sure if he could ever enjoy Fettuccini Alfredo again without thinking of his encounters with Alfredo the agent.

With the paperwork all completed – *Oh, to have been able to rent from Hertz* – Stan walked out of the office, turned right and headed back to the solitude of his hotel room.

Eighteen/Dieciocho
San José del Cabo
Saturday, January 19th

recordar (rā·kwĕr·dǎr') – to remember. *¿Recuerdas el camino hacia el restaurante?* Do you remember the road to the restaurant?

Waking from his most restful sleep since he'd left home, Stan briefly enjoyed the peace he felt. A little bit of the morning light made its way through the window shades, but it wasn't too much that it made it a blinding light. He didn't hear anyone else rustling about, and the outside noise was almost non-existent. *"Buenos días, mundo,"* [Good morning, world] Stan said to no one in particular as he got up to take his shower, shave, and get dressed for the day. It was indeed a good morning, and he just felt that he needed to say it.

He called room service to order breakfast so he could stay in his room and concentrate on his plan for the day. He'd been here for almost a week, and he knew he had to tell the Johnsons something, and it needed to be soon. But what was he going to tell them? A few people had seen Sarah and Mary, but that was pretty much it. He knew he hadn't overlooked anything; he just needed to do some more digging.

After breakfast, Stan got into a focused frame of mind. He set his breakfast tray outside his room so he would not be distracted by the aromas from the wonderful *desayuno* [breakfast] or from the coffee carafe. Stan was set in his ways, and he knew it. But he also knew that he liked to work in a certain way, and that way had always been successful in the past for him and his clients.

Ready to begin, Stan sat down at the desk and pulled out a pad of paper. He took the pen from his shirt pocket and he began to write down the things he knew at this point:

- Sarah and Mary stayed in the same room he's currently in, room 304.
    o He checked out the room; it seemed clean with no signs of forced entry or any other problems.
    o Hotel management saw no problems with the girls.

- The girls were seen by a few people in town who remembered them, but no one recalled anything out of the normal, their being followed or picked up by anyone.
- Their shuttle trip to the airport was normal, although it was a little late picking them up (but maybe that was normal). Regardless, they made it to the airport on time.
- They each had one suitcase to check on the plane when they left, which they did.
  - It turns out that both bags were checked in under Mary's name – was that intentional on Sarah's part, or did the airline just put both tags on Mary's ticket because hers was the first one they were processing?
  - NOTE: Go to the airport to see if anyone remembers the girls (highly unlikely), and ask about putting both bags on one ticket, etc.
  - QUESTION: Did Sarah know that her suitcase was checked on Mary's ticket?
- Both girls went through the main Security with no problems. Mary doesn't recall anyone in particular watching or following them.
- Their flight was called, and then their Zone number was called for them to board.
  - They got out of their seats in the waiting area and stood in line; Mary was in front of Sarah. *(Was that intentional on Sarah's part?)*
  - Each of them had her own backpack.
  - As they were at Gate Security, Mary's boarding pass and her backpack were checked, and she was told to go on through. Just as Security started to check Sarah's backpack, she grabbed it from the table and headed back to one of the Duty Free stores. Mary called to her, but Sarah said she'd be right there.
- Sarah never boarded the non-stop flight from Los Cabos to Seattle.
- No one has heard from Sarah since then.
- NEW QUESTIONS:
  - Has anyone used Sarah's internet account?
  - How much money did Sarah have with her?
  - Has Sarah used her credit card or her debit card?
  - Have any 'Jane Does' shown up any at hospitals or morgues in Los Cabos?

- o Have there been any police reports for unidentified females in Los Cabos?
- o What about in Santiago, in La Paz, or in Todos Santos?
- o Could she have just disappeared? But to where? And why??

Stan was a little discouraged as he realized that he now had more questions than the answers he'd gotten in San José. He knew it wasn't going to be easy to pick up on the trail if Sarah didn't want to be found. He <u>had</u> to get the answers to his questions. *I wish I hadn't checked in that rental car; I could really use it now.* Stan weighed his options: rental car; taxis; his friend Carmelita. As much as he didn't want to make it seem like he was just wanting to use her as a driver, he knew that he would need some help inquiring at the police stations, hospitals, and morgues. He would need a local person to do the asking, and the local person would also know how to start the conversation to lead up to the tricky questions. He decided to ask Carmelita for help, and maybe even her brother Roberto since he was a San José local.

Stan was about to call Carmelita when he remembered that she'd told him that most of the art galleries opened early on Saturday morning. Maybe now would be a good time that he could inquire about the girls. Even if he spent only five to ten minutes at each gallery, plus a few minutes to walk to the next one, it would still take him about three hours to visit all of them.

He hung the "Do Not Disturb" sign on the door as he hurriedly left the room. *I'll make my own bed when I get back.*

Exhausted – more mentally than physically – after his hasty venture through the Art District, Stan slowed to a lazy stroll as he walked through the plaza on the way back to the hotel. Turning right from Zaragoza onto Boulevard Mijares, Stan remembered seeing Tequila Restaurant on the next block down – on Manuel Doblado just west of Boulevard Mijares. Stan had heard good things about the restaurant, and it wasn't just a tequila bar; that just happened to be its name.

As he enjoyed the savory flavors of the Enchiladas Rojas along with the frosty blended margarita, Stan pondered what he had learned that morning. The gallery owners tried to be as helpful as they could be, but none of them recalled seeing the girls. Even though he hadn't gotten any new information, he still felt it was productive; it was productive in the sense that there wasn't anything so far that he was overlooking. After he finished his meal, he moved the plate aside, and then spread out his notes on the table. He put the pictures of Sarah and Mary on the notes just to help him focus his thoughts.

He asked for his check, paid it, and then left a good tip for the waiter. He was gathering his items together to leave when his waiter stopped at his table. "Señor, if you don't mind," the waiter said in a soft voice. "The pictures of those girls." He paused to see if it was acceptable for him to continue. "I remember seeing them. They came in here for dinner, but it was a few weeks ago. It was right after New Years. Are they okay?" The waiter's voiced expressed concern and sincerity – *he's probably a dad himself.*

"You saw them?" Stan asked the obvious question.

"Sí, señor. But as I said, it was over two weeks ago – a day or two after New Years. Are they okay?" he asked again.

"I don't know," Stan sighed. "One of them is fine, but the other one is missing. Do you have time to talk some more right now?"

"I can't stop working to talk right now. But if you sit back down, I'll stop by when I can." The waiter put a menu back on the table as a hint for him to sit down. Stan sat down, opened the menu, and appeared to be looking at it. But even though his eyes saw the words, he wasn't really looking at them.

With his hopes renewed Stan wondered what this waiter would be able to tell him. He took the pictures back out of his pocket and discretely sat them on the side of the table near where the waiter would approach him. There was the normal lunch-crowd noise that's in any restaurant, but Stan didn't hear any of it. He was so intently focused on gathering any tidbit of knowledge that would help him to find Sarah.

A couple of minutes later – although it seemed more like half an hour to Stan – the waiter came back by Stan's table and stood as if he were waiting to taking Stan's order. Instead he was deftly looking down at the pictures on the table. "Sí, I remember those two girls. One of the reasons I remember them is that they were so quiet. Most American girls who come in here alone seem to be in a big party mood. These two were quiet, just talking among themselves. They didn't even have anything to drink besides some sparkling water. That's the other thing that made me remember them. You said one of them is missing. What happened?"

"That's what I am trying to figure out. This one," Stan continued as he pointed to Sarah, "did not get on the plane to fly home. She went back into the terminal – to one of the Duty Free shops – just as her friend boarded the plane." Stan pointed to Mary in reference to Sarah's friend.

"I'll be right back, señor," the waiter said as he stepped back out to help his customers at another table. He was back sooner than Stan expected. "Señor, this one you said did not get on the plane, has any one heard from her?"

"No, there's been no contact. Her parents have asked me to try to find her. That's why I'm here in town."

"Wait a minute, señor. This one," the waiter said as he pointed at Sarah. "I've seen her again." He squinted his eyes to look at the picture again. Stan saw his look, and he picked up the picture and handed it to the waiter for a better look. Stan's eyes were as wide open as they could be. Could this be the first real clue to finding Sarah?

"Sí, señor. This is the young American I saw. She is a very pretty girl and once you see her face, it is not one that you forget very easily. It was last Saturday night – there was a festival in the plaza celebrating our elected officials here in San José. We have this festival every year on the second Saturday in January. I was in the plaza listening to the speeches, watching the dancing, and enjoying the music, when I saw her walk by. Do you know how the fountain curves? I was standing right there and she walked that way in front of me," the waiter said as he made a left to right crossing gesture with his right hand. "She looked in my direction, but I don't think she recognized me. There are a lot of Mexican men who look like me, but there are not many girls who look like her down here."

His hopes buoyed by this sudden information, Stan could hardly contain himself. "Did you see where she went?"

"She was headed in the direction of the church, but I didn't think to watch where she was going. The plaza was crowded anyway, and as you see, I am not very tall, so I wouldn't have been able to see her for very far."

"Thank you very much. That is very helpful. I know her parents will be very happy to hear that." As he reached back with his right hand to get his wallet, he said, "What is your name, señor?"

"My name is Juan, señor. I am happy that what I have told you can help you."

"Yes, I am happy also," Stan said as he pulled a green 200 pesos bill out of his wallet along with one of his business cards. "I am staying at Hotel El Nuevo. If you see her again, or think of anything else, please call me." He handed him the card along with the extra tip.

"Gracias, señor, but you have already given me a nice tip. I know a lot of people think you have to pay everyone in Mexico for information, but that's not true." Juan took Stan's business card and put it into his pocket, but he handed the 200 pesos back to Stan.

"I'm sorry if it looked that way. I meant it as a way to thank you for your help, Juan."

"That's okay, señor. I am happy to help you if I can. I have a daughter, and I know how I would feel if I could not find her."

I was right; he is a dad. "Juan, please. Buy something for your daughter, or something for your wife. My gift to them. Okay?" Stan gently handed the note back to Juan who reluctantly accepted it.

"Thank you, señor. I will stop at the church and light a candle for your friend. What is her name?"

"Her name is Sarah. Thank you, Juan." Stan was overcome with both joy and sadness at the same time.

"De nada, señor. If I see her again, I will call you at the hotel." Juan then picked up the menu and headed toward the bar area. He was happy that he could help the American.

Stan couldn't wait to call Carmelita with the news. He also wanted to call the Johnsons, but he knew he had to wait until evening hours when both Robert and Tina would be home. On his way back to the hotel, Stan was thinking of the things he still had to do – but were they still as important now that someone had seen Sarah here in town? It was a week ago, but that was also one week after she was supposed to be on a plane to Seattle. He still needed to get the answers to a few of the questions: her internet account; how much cash did she have; had anyone used her credit card or her debit card? *Only the Johnsons can answer those questions. I'll just have to call them later tonight.*

Back at the hotel he called for Carmelita but she was not at the house. "No message; gracias," Stan said as he didn't know how to say *message* in Spanish (*mensaje*).

Feeling like a hunting hound that finally picked up a scent, Stan didn't want to let any more time pass. He knew he really needed someone to help him translate, but he also knew that time was precious – he would worry about translations later if necessary. The Padre at the church had told him to stop by during the day to see if anyone could help; that had to be the next place to go.

On the way out of the hotel, he stopped at the front desk. "Ah, Miguel. If there are any messages for me, please let them know I will be back in maybe an hour, maybe less. If the señora calls, please ask her to come here and wait for me. I have some very important news that I must go check on right now. Okay?"

"Si, señor. I will take any messages that come for you. Is this news good news?"

"I hope so, Miguel. Gracias," Stan said as he walked briskly out of the lobby. After he was already out on Boulevard Mijares, it was only then that he realized he had not been very polite to Miguel. Sure he was in a hurry, but it wouldn't have taken much time to start with "Hello. How are you?" He would apologize to him later. He was in a rush now.

As he approached the fountain in the plaza, he imagined where Juan might have been standing on last Saturday night when he saw Sarah. Stan tried to imagine where Sarah would've been coming from to then go from his left to his right. As he looked left, Shooters came into view. Could she have been at Shooters that night? If so, where was she going? The church is to the right, but perhaps she was going someplace else. José, the waiter at Shooters Sports Bar, said he hadn't seen her since "Wednesday night" – that would have been January 2nd. But perhaps José wasn't working at Shooters last Saturday, or even if he were maybe he just didn't see her or recognize her. Add that to the list – *go back to Shooters and ask some more questions.*

Stan pulled out of his thinking mode and got back into his action mode. He turned right and walked across the plaza to Calle Hidalgo. As he crossed the street and walked up the steps to the church – actually called a *misíon* – he started looking around for something that would resemble an office. None of the doors in the building on the right looked like doors to an office. And he didn't feel comfortable walking under the archway to the open area in the back. He'd seen children playing out here before, so he decided to just sit on the bench and wait.

The swaying palm branches overhead made interesting patterns as their shadows moved back and forth on the ground in front of him. He was beginning to get mesmerized by the interleaving of the shadows when he heard a group of young children come running out to play. He was highly reluctant to talk to any of the children, so he looked around for an adult. Finally, a nun slowly walked out to where the children were playing. Stan stood up, made eye contact with her and slowly walked over to her.

"Disculpe," he started slowly. *"¿Dónde está la oficina?"* [Excuse me. Where is the office?]

Stan's Spanish was apparently very good (or very bad) because the nun replied with a flurry of words that he didn't understand. He stood there bewildered for a moment, and then he asked, *"¿Hablas Inglés?"* [Do you speak English?]

"No Inglés, señor," she replied.

Just then one of the young girls who had overheard the conversation ran over by the nun and looked up at Stan. "Señor, she said that the office is that way, and then to the right. There is a sign over the door that says 'Oficina.' I can show you if it's okay with the Sister." The young girl had been pointing through the archway, where Stan had originally thought it might be.

"Thank you for your help, but I'm sure I can find it. Muchas gracias," Stan said with a smile to the young girl. And as he stepped away from the nun, he also said "Muchas gracias" to her as he nodded his head in respect to her.

"De nada, señor," the nun replied. The young girl ran back to her group of friends and got right back into the game they were playing.

As Stan went down the two steps to the walkway/driveway, he wondered what was connected by the archway overhead. It was obviously built after the church was constructed; it just seemed strange to him. The enclosed plaza area was quite large, and Stan saw several cars parked back there. He turned to the right and saw several doors and windows. The fourth door had a small metal sign over it that said 'Oficina.' Striding with confidence he headed for the door. He didn't know what he would say or ask once he was inside, but he would face that when he got there.

He ascended the two steps and saw a sign on the door: 'Empuje.' He remembered that *empuje* meant 'push,' so he turned the worn brass knob and pushed the door open. The office was quiet; three women were working at desks spread around the room, and they seemed to be focused on what they were doing.

Not knowing exactly how to begin, he stopped instead of approaching one of them. "Buenas tardes, señoras."

"Buenas tardes, señor," was their unanimous reply. *Now what?* he thought.

"¿Hablas Inglés?" he started with because he certainly didn't know what else to say in Spanish.

"No Inglés, señor," replied the woman at the desk on the right.

This was his first real impasse; everyone else he'd encountered spoke at least a little English. Hmmm. *"¿El Padre; está aquí?"* [The Padre; is he here?]

"No, señor. El Padre no está aquí," the same woman replied. Then as an afterthought, she added, *"Mas tarde."* [Later.]

Stan looked at his watch; it was now 1:45. He wondered how <u>much</u> later. Was he due back at a specific time, or did he just show up when he wanted to – later? *"¿Mas tarde?"* he asked pointing to his watch hoping she would interpret his asking "Later?" as a way of asking what time he would be back.

"Sí, señor. Mas tarde. A las quatro y media."

"Four thirty?" he said mostly to himself. He looked at his watch again. *Four thirty – is that my watch time or is it Mexican time?* It didn't really matter because he couldn't affect it one way or the other. "Gracias, señoras," Stan said as he turned toward the door and pulled it open. As he descended the steps back into the open courtyard, he hoped that Carmelita would be able to come back with him. Now he would need a translator.

Nineteen/Diecinueve
San José del Cabo
Later that afternoon – January 19th

reunión (rā·ū'·nē·ōn) – meeting. *Tengo una reunión en dos horas.* I have a meeting in two hours.

Stan was sitting in his hotel room, watching the seconds go by on his watch, hoping that Carmelita would call soon. He was eager to go back to the *misíon* to talk with the Padre because perhaps he could reveal some information about Sarah. It wasn't for sure that she was headed to the church that evening that Juan said he saw her, but he had nothing else to work on. He had talked with all the gallery owners in the Art District, which covered the area adjacent to the church, and none of them reported seeing her. He knew he couldn't go door-to-door asking people if they had seen her. He barely spoke enough Spanish to get by in restaurants; he would be lost trying to talk with everyday residents, especially on their home turf.

Siesta. That's what Stan needed, a siesta. He took his shoes off – *oh, that feels good* – sat on the bed and let his head gently fall back to be cradled by the plush pillow. As he closed his eyes, he tried to visualize Juan standing in the plaza and seeing Sarah walk by. He would have reason to notice her: she stood out as a pretty American girl, plus he remembered serving her at the restaurant. But he wouldn't have any particular reason to keep watching her to see where she was going. That would be rude, plus he really had no reason to. Stan tried to replay that video again and again.

Where did she come from? Had she been back at Shooters that night? If not, where had she been? Did it seem like she was in a rush to get somewhere? Or was she just strolling? What time was it? Does that even matter? Questions. Questions! QUESTIONS!!! It seemed that getting one answer was a curse, because all that one answer did was to present a lot more questions. *And I need answers, not questions!*

Stan's fatigue – as much mental as physical – took over, and he fell asleep. The softness of the bed, the way the pillow held his head, the gentle hum of the A/C unit – those factors and more allowed Stan to doze off.

Ring-Ring. Ring-Ring. Ring-Ring. The rudeness of the phone's insistent peal startled Stan more than it woke him. His head was still cradled in the pillow when the phone beckoned him again. *Ring-Ring. Ring-Ring. Ring-Ring.* This time he knew what it was and he swung his feet off the bed, sat up, and picked up the phone from the desk set sitting on the nightstand next to the bed.

"Hello, I mean *Hola*," he slowly said, still half-asleep.

"Stan, is that you?" the somewhat familiar voice asked.

"Yes," he said groggily. "Hi, Carmelita." He recognized her voice but he was still having a hard time coming back to reality. "I was lying on the bed," he continued in a much clearer voice. "I guess I really fell asleep."

"Just like on the airplane, right?" Carmelita said to tease him.

"Right, just like on the airplane. I had forgotten about that. But obviously you didn't. How are you?"

"I'm fine, thank you. Roberto said you called. How was your trip to the Tropic of Cancer Monument? Did you find out anything?"

"I'd forgotten all about that trip, and that was only yesterday." Stan looked at his watch and saw that it was 4:00. "I can tell you about that later. I know this is short notice – no, it's extremely short notice. Can you come down here to the hotel? I found someone who saw Sarah just last week here in town, and I'm going back to the church to talk with the Padre at 4:30. Can you come and be my translator? I'll buy you dinner afterwards." Stan's voice was racing as he so anxious to find out more information about Sarah.

"Well, Stan. You know a lady just can't accept a date that fast." Carmelita cut her voice short.

Stan's mind was blank; had he offended her? Did he say something wrong? Did it appear that he was being too forward or taking advantage of her?

"Carmelita," he began slowly. "I'm sorry. I didn't mean it that way. I'm just so excited because I finally found a piece of information that might help me find her. Please forgive me." Stan's voice and expressions had gone from exuberance to condolence in about twenty seconds flat.

"Okay, Stan. I forgive you," Carmelita said with a laugh in her voice. "I was just kidding you. You're too serious and you take things the wrong way. I'll park on Manuel Doblado. It's easier to find a spot there, and then I'll walk to the hotel. See you in front in fifteen minutes. Okay?" she said with a lilt in her voice.

"Okay," Stan said somewhat robotically. He didn't mind that she was teasing him, but her initial reaction had really taken him down. *Women!*

He went into the bathroom to wash up, refreshing his face with the cold wash cloth. He quickly changed clothes to something that would be more suitable for dinner, including a different pair of shoes. Grabbing his sport coat from the closet, he put his notes and pictures into his shirt pocket and left the room. It was 4:10. He went down the stairs with an additional bounce in his step, but he slowed down as he neared the last few steps to the lobby. "Hola, Miguel," he said to the assistant manager as he walked toward the front desk.

"Hola, señor. Did you get your call?" Miguel had to have known that Stan got the call, or it would have gone into the voice messaging system. Maybe he was just trying to build up his tip.

"Yes, I did, Miguel. Gracias. I'll be out for a while this evening; please take any messages for me."

"Of course, señor. Have a nice evening."

"Gracias, Miguel," Stan said as he left the lobby. As he stood outside the hotel's doorway, Stan saw that the traffic was moving quietly along Boulevard Mijares, and the sun was still high enough up in the sky to cause him to squint his eyes in the sunlight. He was tempted to look at his watch, but he knew that wouldn't get Carmelita there any faster. Besides, the Padre might not get there until five o'clock or later. *Relax.*

Knowing there wasn't any benefit to just staring across the street and waiting for Carmelita to arrive, Stan turned left and slowly walked about a hundred feet to the next-door jewelry store. He had nothing in mind as he looked at the items in the display window; it was something to do to pass the time. He had been in front of the window no more than fifteen to twenty seconds when an attractive young lady walked out the front door.

"Hello, señor. Why don't you come inside; it is air conditioned inside plus there are some very nice things for your special lady." She was convincing, but Stan wasn't convinced.

"No thanks. I'm just waiting for someone to come by," Stan said as he continued to look at the items in the window display. He could just walk away toward another store or back to the hotel, but he was going to outlast her.

"She must be very special to be with you, señor. Come on in, I have some nice rings and bracelets at very good prices just for you today. I can give you a special discount, but the store closes soon. So you must come in right away. What's her favorite color?" The sales lady tried a different approach because she saw that Stan was not budging from his spot outside.

"Thank you, but no thanks," Stan replied as he was trying to be polite. He knew sales people had a hard job, but that wasn't his problem. He saw Carmelita's reflection in the window, and he didn't want any more discussion at the jewelry store with her around. "Thank you," he said politely to the sales lady as he turned to his left and started walking toward the hotel. He knew it might appear that he was walking away from Carmelita, but he also knew he could explain that to her. He continued walking, but walking slowly, back to the front of the hotel.

As he reached the hotel's covered entrance, he turned around and started walking slowly back down the street toward Carmelita. She was walking a little faster, so she closed the gap faster than he did. He stretched his arms out toward her when she was about ten feet from him. "Hi. It's good to see you," he said as they embraced each other.

"I saw you at the jewelry store, but then you started walking away from it," Carmelita said almost as a question.

"I needed to get away from that sales lady, and I saw you in the window reflection, so that was a good time to escape from her. How are you?"

"I'm fine. So you have some good news?" she asked with excitement.

"Yes, one of the waiters at Tequila Restaurant recognized Sarah from when she and Mary were in there right after New Years. Then he said he saw her last Saturday night while he was attending a festival in the plaza. He seemed quite confident that it was Sarah. Do you mind if we talk as we walk?"

"No, that's fine," she replied.

"Okay, thanks," he said as he looped his left arm in through her right arm. Walking this way was a comfortable feeling, both for Stan and for Carmelita. They walked without saying anything up the first block and then the second block as they reached the plaza.

"Thanks for coming," Stan started. "I probably don't need a translator with the Padre, but just in case. Okay," he started and then he paused. "How about just an excuse to see you. Is that okay?"

"Yes, Stan. That's okay. Or maybe even more than okay. I know this has been a difficult time for you. If my daughter were missing, I would want someone looking for her who is as committed and as passionate as you are. Sarah's parents are lucky to have you working for them." With that said, Carmelita tightened her right arm around Stan's. She looked over at Stan, her eyes locking with his. Even though she did not know Sarah, Carmelita was feeling a special bond to her because of Stan.

"Thank you. I hope nothing ever happens to your daughter or to anyone in your family, or your brother's family. I don't really like what I have to do sometimes, but it's my job." They were angling across the plaza toward the church when Stan decided to take Carmelita to where he thought Juan was when he'd seen Sarah. "Juan said he was standing about in this area when he saw Sarah walking from over there to over there." Stan used his extended right arm to show the general direction from left to right, just as Juan had shown him. "He didn't know where she'd been or where she was going, but he's very sure it was her. He said that recognizing her was that much easier because he'd waited on Mary and her in the restaurant. What do you think?"

"I think that Juan is telling you as much truth as he can. There wouldn't be any reason for him to tell you something that's not true. If he has a family, then I am very certain that he told you what he saw. Now what's this about meeting with the Padre?"

"I spoke with him earlier in the week," Stan began. "It was right before Mass on Tuesday night. He told me to come by during the day and perhaps he might be able to help. Now that Juan said he'd seen Sarah just last week, and she was headed toward the church, ..." Stan stopped talking as he was a little choked with emotion. "If she were headed toward the church, then maybe someone there would recognize her picture. I hadn't thought of that before; only now that Juan said he'd seen her."

Without saying anything more, they started walking across the plaza away from the fountain. When they reached Calle Hidalgo, rather than going up the steps to the 40' x 80' open area in front of the church, they walked north on the sidewalk to the roadway that almost seemed like an alley. As they made the right turn on the sidewalk, Carmelita used her right hand to make the sign of the cross on her head, chest and shoulders. Stan had seen some drivers and passengers do the same thing when they drove in front of the church – not all of them, just some of them. They turned left and walked up the incline of the driveway, under the archway, and into the back plaza.

"Wow, it's been a long time since I was back here," Carmelita said. She stopped and just looked around. "It looks a lot different when you're little than it does now."

"I never thought of that," Stan replied. "Does it seem a lot smaller now than it did when you were little?" *Well, there's an obvious question,* Stan thought after he'd already asked it.

"Not as much smaller in the size of the plaza here, but the buildings seem shorter than they were. Of course I was a lot shorter back then. Is the office still over here?" she asked as she turned to the right. "Oh, it is. That was a door that you never wanted to have to go through as a kid."

"I can imagine," Stan said as they walked over toward the *Oficina* sign. "I was sent to the Principal's office more times than I want to remember. That was definitely not a place you wanted to be sent. Did you go to school here?"

"Not really school, but we went to church here. And I started going to my catechism classes here before we moved to a different house."

Stan walked up the steps, opened the office door, and held it open for Carmelita to enter. He closed the door and then said, "Buenas tardes, señoras."

In near unison, the ladies replied, "Buenas tardes."

Carmelita then said something, and the women responded with some laughter. Of course, he didn't understand any of it – too many words being exchanged too quickly. Stan knew to just stand there quietly. He finally heard Carmelita say something he did understand, "Muchas gracias, señora." She then turned to Stan and said, "We can go down the hallway here to his office."

"Good," Stan said to Carmelita. As he turned to follow her, he looked back and said, "Muchas gracias, señoras."

"De nada, señor," was the singular reply.

The meeting with the Padre went well, and even though his English was pretty good, Carmelita did most of the talking because it was easier for the two of them to converse in Spanish. Stan trusted her, and he could tell from some of her motions that she was relaying all the information to him that Stan would have said. Carmelita asked Stan for Sarah's picture, and the Padre took it and made a photocopy of it. The meeting ended with a prayer, and then the Padre spoke in English. "I remember you from earlier this week, my son, and I will ask if anyone has seen this Sarah. Please understand that there are some vows that can't be broken, but I will tell you all that I am allowed to. I know that time is important; I will call you if I hear something. If you do not hear from me in one week, please stop back by. Know that God is also looking for her and watching over her."

I wish I <u>could</u> know that, but I'm just not sure. She's missing in Mexico, and her parents want to find her.

"Gracias, Padre," Stan said as he stood and shook the Padre's hand.

Carmelita and the Padre shared a brief exchange and then she followed Stan back out the hallway to the front office. Two of the ladies were gone; only the one at the center desk was still there. Stan looked at her and smiled as he said, "Gracias, señora. Adios."

"Adios, señor. *Vaya con Dios*," [Go with God] she replied.

As he and Carmelita closed the door and walked down the steps into the plaza, Stan looked at her and said, "Not very promising, is it?"

"It's very difficult to tell right now. I told him where you are staying and he said he would call you if he gets information he can tell you. You must understand that people in my country are not very anxious to give information to Americans if it means that person might have to go back to the States against their will. Perhaps if I continue to do the talking with him, we might learn more about Sarah. What do you think?"

"I think you're right. I'm sure there is a lot I don't know about your customs, especially when it involves the church. And, yes, I would very much appreciate your help. So if that's an offer to help, I'll take it."

"Okay," she said. Then she put out her right hand and said, "It's a deal." As they shook hands, she said, "Now what about that dinner you promised me?"

Twenty/Veinte
San José del Cabo
That evening – January 19th

rompecabezas (rōm·pā'·kă·bā'·săs) – puzzle. *Me gusta armar rompecabezas.* I like to work on a puzzle.

As they slowly walked out of the restaurant, both Stan and Carmelita were sure that they wouldn't be able to eat again for at least three more days. "I can't remember the last time I ate like that," Carmelita said. She had indeed eaten a lot, as had Stan.

"The food was great; that's for sure. But I think we could've just split the dessert. Each one of those could feed a party of four." After a slight pause, Stan continued, "But they were definitely good, weren't they?"

"Yes, they were. I've never had a chocolate dessert prepared liked that. I didn't know you could combine so many types and flavors of chocolate and still be able to taste each and every one of them. If we go back there, all we need is the coffee and a dessert."

"I'll remember that. But the shrimp were pretty good, too," Stan added as they made their way up Calle Hidalgo toward the plaza. They could hear voices of young people once they crossed Obregón and were nearing Plaza Mijares. They were half way up the block when they started to cross the street to the plaza. Stan heard a sudden burst of laughter behind him and he looked back; it was coming from the alleyway by the church – the one that led back to the office where he and Carmelita had been earlier that day.

He looked at his watch, 7:20. Mass would not be out yet. "Why are the girls in those uniforms? They aren't like the ones I've seen there during the day." The girls were wearing a yellow skirt and a green blouse and sweater; it wasn't the white blouse and plaid skirt that Stan had seen before. The sun had set but the lights were bright enough to see the colors of their uniforms.

"Oh," Carmelita began. "Those girls are learning about becoming a nun. Not many of them will continue, but they teach them about life in a convent, serving as a Sister at a school or a church. It is intense, I think you would call it. Many start out, but not many finish."

"Sounds like an advanced boot camp for soldiers – it sounds good at the beginning, but once you find out how tough it is, it loses its appeal."

"Yes, but just like your military, the service to God is not meant to be easy. But it has its own rewards."

Plaza Mijares was rather empty, which was surprising for a Saturday evening. As they meandered toward the fountain, their hands brushed against each other, and Stan hesitated a moment before he clasped her hand in his. They walked for a few more steps, and then he stopped, forcing Carmelita to also stop since they were holding hands.

"What's wrong" she asked, concerned that he might think that holding hands was not allowed.

"Those uniforms," he started. "Does anyone else wear them?"

"No, well yes," she replied. "The colors are for the Holy Order of Saint Christine; that is the group of Sisters who are leading the classes there tonight."

"I couldn't really tell the ages of the girls, uhm, the young ladies, who were there. What ages would be there?"

"The young ladies, as you called them, must be at least fifteen years old. There is no upper age limit except that they can never have been married."

"Without making it sound too personal, what about chastity?" Stan felt a little uncomfortable asking this question, but he was trying to find out as much information as he could.

"The Holy Order of Saint Christine prefers that all the women be chaste. The church is a little more modern in its thinking now, and it knows that some women will have lost their virginity before they come to realize their calling. No questions are asked about prior life or behavior, only that they intend to follow a pure and chaste life once they belong."

Sensing a new track to follow, Stan asked, "Do the young ladies live together in a special place?"

"No, they all live at their homes with their families."

"What about ones who don't have a family? Where would they live?"

"With another family or on their own. It is only when they graduate and accept the full vows of the Order – that is when they join with others in a convent, in a school, or in a church." Carmelita knew a lot about the process that these women were going through.

"Do you think that Sarah could have gotten involved with them?" Stan was trying to piece together some very loose fragments.

"It's possible, of course. If she's a young woman who's trying to either find herself or escape to something different – that's always a possibility. What do you think?"

"The pieces of the puzzle look like they could fall that way. But I don't want to force what I know into a pattern that's not real." He let go of Carmelita's hand as he raised both hands to his temples. He closed his eyes in thought, then he opened them and became quite expressive with his hands. "Listen to this and let me know what you think." Stan started to list what he considered the pieces of the puzzle that he currently had. He began:

- Sarah missed her plane back to Seattle, apparently on purpose. We don't know that yet because no one's heard from her or talked with her. But for now, we just have to assume that she did miss it on purpose.
- If she missed the plane on purpose, she must have had a reason. And that reason would have included a plan as to what she was going to do.
- One week after she misses her plane, she's seen here in the plaza walking in the direction of the church, where you say they teach classes for becoming a nun, joining a convent, etc.
- We've shown the Padre a picture of Sarah; he didn't recognize her, and we'll have to wait to see if anyone else does.

"That's about all I know," Stan said in a concessionary tone. "It's hard to believe that she could be living on her own if she hasn't used a credit card or her debit card. I'll have to ask her parents about that." Stan looked into Carmelita's eyes and saw a look that showed how much she wanted to be able to help Stan.

"I wish I knew what to do to help you, Stan. This Sarah seems like a very smart girl. And a very smart girl who doesn't want to be found will know how to not be found. Does that make sense?"

"Yes. Unfortunately, it makes way too much sense. You're right. If Sarah doesn't want anyone to find her, she can probably do that. At least being an American, she does stand out a little in Mexico – if that's where she is." Stan had to accept the fact that Sarah might <u>not</u> be in Mexico any more.

Grabbing Carmelita's hand once more, Stan started heading south. "Do you want to go to Shooters with me?"

"Are you still hungry?" she asked.

"Not at all, and I definitely don't need a beer. I just want to see if anyone remembers seeing Sarah on the same night that Juan says he saw her crossing the plaza. He indicated that she was coming from that direction, and since she had been there before, maybe she was there that night."

It was still early enough on Saturday night that Stan and Carmelita had no trouble finding an open table – away from the booming speakers. Stan looked around for José, but he didn't see him. "Welcome, amigos. Welcome to Shooters. Do you want a beer, a margarita, perhaps a special drink for the two of you?" The waiter was definitely outgoing as he greeted them.

"We're not sure yet," Stan said. "Is José here tonight?"

"No, he's with his family at a funeral in Puerto Vallarta," the waiter replied, not as cheerful as before.

Stan knew he would feel more comfortable talking with José, but José wasn't there. He pulled Sarah's picture out of his pocket and showed it to the waiter. "I am trying to find this girl, and I'm wondering if you saw her in here last Saturday night – the night they had the big fiesta in the plaza?"

The waiter looked at the picture, but it was just a glance. "No, señor. I don't remember seeing that girl. Do you need another minute to decide on your drinks?"

"No, thanks. We're not that thirsty," Stan said as he worked his way out of the blue plastic chair and then helped Carmelita up. Stan grabbed her hand as they walked toward the narrowly lit stairs leading down to the main floor. Once they were outside on the narrow street, Stan said, "I'll have to go back when José is there; he'll be more willing to talk to me than that guy was."

"Don't get frustrated, Stan. People in Mexico are very protective of women. He doesn't know that you are trying to help her, or at least help her parents. As far as he knows, you could be a pimp and she owes you money."

"I'd never thought of it that way. But I see your point."

They walked in silence, ignoring the music spilling over the wall from Shooters, as they made their way back toward Hotel El Nuevo. They crossed the street and Stan continued walking with Carmelita until they reached her car.

"Thanks for your help, and thanks for being a friend. I'm not sure how I would do it without knowing you are there."

"You would do just fine, Stan. But thank you for saying it. And thanks for dinner; now I won't have to eat for a few more days." They both chuckled, and then they both stood there by her car, in awkward silence. They were holding hands, but neither knew what to do, or what to say.

"Will you," she started just as he began to say something.

"Go ahead," he said.

"Will you call me tomorrow?" she asked. Her voice indicated that she was hoping he would.

"Yes, I'll call you. In fact, I was thinking of going into Cabo San Lucas just to look around. Would you like to go with me?"

"Sure, but only if you let me drive. The drivers down here can be a little crazy at times, and I know a little more how they think. It would be better if we went down there on Monday because more places will be open and we can ask more people about Sarah. How about if I pick you up in front of the hotel Monday at 2:30? By the time we get down there, shops will be open and I know a great little restaurant to take you to."

"More food?"

"Sí, more food. Don't worry, you'll be hungry again by then."

"Okay. Monday at 2:30 in front of the hotel. See you then. Thanks again for your help."

They were still standing there, holding hands, when Carmelita leaned forward and kissed Stan on the cheek. Instinctively, he returned the kiss. A brief smile and then he turned and started to walk away. Stan turned back to her and said, "Good night."

"Buenas noches," Carmelita said as she unlocked the car door.

As Stan crossed Boulevard Mijares and turned to head to his hotel, he heard her car drive past him. He didn't look; he just wanted to savor the memory of those last few moments together.

He walked into the hotel lobby oblivious to the sounds and movement around him. He was tired and drained of energy, yet re-charged by the excitement of finally having something positive to tell the Johnsons. He went up the steps to his room, sat on his bed, and took off his shoes. *I'll call the Johnsons at 8:00 their time*, he said to himself as he laid his head on the pillow. It was now 7:50 Mountain Time.

Twenty-one/Veintiuno
Cabo San Lucas/Redmond, WA
That same evening – January 19th

confundido (cōn·fūn·dē'·dō) – confused. *Estoy confundido por el clima.* I am confused by the weather.

The phone rang three times before it was answered. "Hello, Tina. This is Stan Walkorski calling."

"Oh, hi, Stan. I almost didn't answer the phone because the Caller ID had a really strange number on it." Tina Johnson's voice was filled with anxiety, but also with anticipation. "Please tell me you have some good news for us." She wanted to hear something that would give her hope.

"Is Robert also there? I'd like you both to be on the phone to hear what I have," Stan replied.

"Oh, no!" she exclaimed. Stan could hear the tears in her voice. Had the worst been realized?

"Tina, it's not bad news. I just want to talk with both of you at the same time."

"Oh, thank God," she replied. "Yes, he's here. Just a minute," she said as she set the phone down. "Robert, it's Stan calling; pick up the other phone," Stan heard her calling in the background as she was talking away from the phone.

"Hi, Stan. You have some good news for us I hope," Robert blurted into the phone as he picked it up.

"Hi, Robert. Tina, are you there?"

"Yes, I'm back on," she answered.

"Okay, here is what I've found so far. The most important thing is that Sarah was seen recently in San José del Cabo. So as of last week, she appeared to be fine. So take a deep breath and relax."

"Do you know where she is now?" Tina pleaded.

"Tina, relax. He'll tell us everything he has so far. Let's just take a minute and be thankful that she's been seen, and so maybe she's still okay." Robert wanted to know all the details just as much as his wife, but he knew that Stan would tell them.

"Yes, Robert. I'll give you all the details. I just thought that knowing she's been seen was the most important thing to let you know right away." Stan's voice was calm, and a calming influence was needed at a time like this. "Here is what I've been able to find out so far." Stan then told them everything he had learned: being seen with Mary at Shooters, but not being followed back to the hotel; their dinner at Tequila Restaurant, a fortuitous event in itself; shopping at the Die Trying store across from the hotel; the sighting in the plaza a week after she missed her flight home. He omitted the details from his meeting with Mary – he had already told them all of that.

"I've made an acquaintance here who has introduced me to many locals where I've asked for help. There's been no sign of any kind of foul play, at least none that's been reported to the police down here." Stan didn't feel there would be any value in telling them about the female hitchhiker whose body was found at the Tropic of Cancer Monument; that would have just thrown Tina into a further frenzy.

Stan continued. "The one big question that remains open is money. How has Sarah paid for things down here? Has there been any activity on her credit card or her debit card?"

"Robert, have you seen anything on her accounts?" Tina asked.

"I don't know," Robert started. "Don't you remember that she changed the address on her accounts to her dorm room? We'll have to get in touch with Mary and either go get the statements or have her open them for us."

"Do you have any idea of about how much cash she had with her when the four of you came down here?"

"Not really," Robert answered. "She keeps all her own accounts, but I know she never asked me for any money while we were there. I did give her some before we went down, and then I gave her some more for when she and Mary were going to be there on their own."

"Do you mind telling me how much?" Stan asked.

"I gave her five hundred dollars each time," Robert replied.

"From what I've heard from people who saw her, she wasn't spending money extravagantly. But even so, that won't keep her going for long unless she has other plans. You're right, Robert. You'll need to contact Mary and find out about her accounts. That won't give us all the answers, but it'll help some. When do you think you can get a hold of Mary?"

"I'll try to call her tonight," he answered. Robert then continued, "What other leads do you have? If we find out that she has withdrawn money, what will that tell us?"

"Any credit card activity," Stan started, "will tell us where she's been and when. It could also tell us the types of things she's been buying. If she's pulled money out on her debit card, that will also tell us where she's been. The frequency and quantity of her withdrawals will give us an indication of how much she's spending. Certainly if she pulled out a large amount before you went down there, then that could mean that this was planned. None of that matters as much as finding her, which is what I'm focused on. I've shown her picture to all the art gallery owners in the area; I've been to all the restaurants and the little shops around the hotel; the one possibility right now is the church. You remember the one right off the plaza?"

"Yes," Tina replied. "We walked over there for Mass on Christmas Eve."

"What connection could the church have with her disappearance?" Robert asked.

"I'm not exactly sure," Stan started. "But the waiter in Tequila Restaurant who recalls waiting on Mary and her says that he saw Sarah a last week in the plaza. Remember I told you that? Well, he said that he saw Sarah walking across the plaza toward the church. He's sure it was Sarah, but it was a crowded plaza; they were holding an annual festival there, so he wasn't able to see exactly where she was going. He just knows it was in the direction of the church. I've talked with the Padre at the church, and he's also going to ask around. And then just tonight I saw a group of girls, young women, whatever you want to call them. They were all in a uniform that means that they are all studying to become nuns or join a convent." Stan paused.

"Join a convent?" Robert asked. "Why would Sarah want to join a convent? She's in school and doing very well." Robert was being a father now – trying to convince himself that there would be no valid reason for his daughter to do something like <u>that</u>.

"I don't know for sure about it," Stan continued. "It is just another lead I'm working on. I'm going in to Cabo San Lucas on Monday to do some checking around there. There's a lot more partying that goes on in Cabo San

Lucas, but the people here in San José say that she and Mary didn't seem like the partying type."

"Well, no. They're only nineteen," Tina added.

"The drinking age is eighteen in Mexico, dear," Robert began. "Besides, pretty girls like Sarah and Mary could probably get anything they wanted down there – regardless of age." Robert was right; girls like them did have access to <u>anything</u> they wanted.

"As I said, I don't think I'll find that they did any partying in Cabo San Lucas, but I do need to check it out. It will also give me a chance to see if anyone there has seen Sarah recently. Certainly if I hear anything from the Padre at the church, I'll let you know right away. I'm encouraged that Sarah was seen recently, so I want you to keep your hopes up." Stan was trying to sound reassuring to them – to parents whose only daughter was missing. He <u>didn't</u> want to tell them that the news he'd just given them was better than he honestly could've hoped for. He knew that if he were looking for her in the States that the odds of finding her alive would be less than five out of one hundred. The odds in Mexico had to be much smaller than that. He couldn't tell these hurting parents that there was a one percent, maybe a two percent, chance of their ever seeing Sarah again. There were some parts of his work that Stan really hated – this was one of them. He was encouraged because of the sighting, but he was also discouraged because it also seemed like Sarah knew what to do to make sure she was <u>not</u> found.

"Thanks for calling, Stan," Robert began. "I'll call Mary and I'll let you know as soon as I can what we find out about her accounts. Thanks for the good news so far." Robert also knew that he had to sound encouraging – Tina needed it. He did too, but he couldn't let her know that.

"Yes, thank you, Stan," Tina said as she was holding back tears. She missed her baby – her only daughter. *What mother wouldn't?* "I say a prayer every night for her. Please find her." Tina was crying at this point.

"Thanks again, Stan," Robert interjected. He knew that Stan <u>was</u> trying to find Sarah, but he also understood his wife's pleading.

"You're welcome. I'll keep you informed." Stan was staying positive and focused. There wasn't anything else he could do. He heard one phone click, some sniffles, and then the other phone was returned to its cradle.

It's difficult even when you have <u>some</u> good news to deliver.

Twenty-two/Veintidos
Cabo San Lucas to San José del Cabo
Monday, January 21st

aeropuerto (ĕr'·ō·pwĕr'·tō) – airport. *¿Dónde está el aeropuerto?* Where is the airport?

Pulling back onto Avenida Lázaro Cárdenas in Cabo San Lucas, Carmelita had to dodge not only the oncoming cars but also the tourists on foot whose brains had been numbed by too many cocktails. She and Stan had been to numerous restaurants and bars in their search for information about Sarah, and they were both happy to be on their way back to San José. It was a Monday night; *what's this place like on the weekend?*

Carmelita had taken Stan to the most likely places where Sarah and Mary might have gone, or where Sarah could have gone on her own. Most of those places were right along the main road into town, Avenida Lázaro Cárdenas, or at least quite close to it. Carmelita had suggested that they park the car in a central location and then walk. She pulled into the lot at Plaza Arámburo, diagonally across the street from the Hard Rock Café – but that would not be the first stop.

Their first stop was the Cabo Wabo Cantina, a night club made quite popular by its owner Sammy Hagar, a self-professed professional rock and roller, nightclub owner, and Tequila connoisseur. "I told you it was going to be loud inside," Carmelita was almost yelling to Stan as they walked out of the second-story entrance. "Just wait until a live band starts playing; it gets even louder in there!"

"I listened to rock and roll when I was younger, but never that loud," Stan remarked. "No wonder so many kids are going deaf."

"What was that?" she asked.

"I said that it's no wonder." Stan stopped mid-sentence when he saw Carmelita smiling. He was caught at one of his own jokes. "Funny."

Winding their way through the T-shirt shops, they crossed the street to The Giggling Marlin Bar & Grille, whose motto was "If our food, drinks, and service aren't up to your standards, please lower your standards." It didn't take too long being there before Stan saw what they meant by that. He saw young Americans, both male and female, doing all sorts of stupid things just to "win" a free pitcher of beer for their table. He saw some locals in there, but he didn't see any of them participating in the "How stupid can you be" activities. One of the more popular items was to hang someone upside down by their feet and have them drink shots of tequila. *I sure hope they know where the bathrooms are.* No luck there either finding anyone who had seen Sarah, but at least it was a lot quieter.

They crossed Marina Boulevard and cut through the hotel lobby to get to the restaurants sitting right on the marina. Part of walking along the marina meant facing numerous vendors selling hats and silver, or wanting you to go on a fishing trip; there were even young children wanting you to buy things. "I know they're cute, but just say 'No,'" Carmelita said. "If you buy anything from them, it just reinforces a life of begging." They worked their way through the busy marina, stopping in some of the establishments along the way.

Once they were almost back to where they started, they continued along the second part of the marina, stopping at the restaurants as they headed down to Puerto Paraiso, the largest shopping mall in Cabo San Lucas. Aside from being the largest, it also was home to the Harley-Davidson store, a Ruth's Chris restaurant, a hamburger joint and a great ice cream store. There were other stores, but those were the only four that Carmelita felt were of interest. No one they talked to there had seen Sarah or Mary.

Stan was beginning to wonder how much more they were going to walk when Carmelita said, "Here is the restaurant I was talking about. Let's stop in for a bite and something to drink."

"Excellent idea," Stan said without trying to sound as if he were mocking her.

After they finished eating, Stan remarked, "You have certainly had a lot more luck asking about Sarah than I have."

"They're not afraid of me because I'm a local. I can strike up a little conversation and let them know how frightened you are that your daughter is missing. They trust me, so it's just that much easier."

"So that's what you've been saying – that she's my daughter?" Stan asked.

"Of course. No one likes a daughter to be missing. Especially down here."

"But no one has seen her," Stan said. "I hate to say it, but I guess that's a good thing."

"Yes," Carmelita replied. "I think it is a good thing that no one has seen her. And I believe them. I was watching their eyes when they said 'No.' They were looking at me, and not looking away as most people do when they're not telling the truth."

"Hey, I'm supposed to be the investigator here. But you're right – the eyes are usually the first thing that tells me when someone's lying to me. You said we still have a couple more places to go to? I hope they're on our way back to the car."

"Yes, just two more," she said. "Sure there are more places all over town, but it's hard for me to believe that Sarah alone, or Sarah and Mary together, would have gone somewhere else on their very first time to Cabo. Let's go to the Hard Rock Café and then to El Squid Roe. If we strike out there, they didn't come down here." The confidence in Carmelita's voice was now sounding very reassuring to Stan – the one who was supposed to provide the reassurance.

Stan paid the check and they headed back toward the car, saying "Hi" again to the fellow at the Harley shop. The response was the same at the Hard Rock Café and then at El Squid Roe – no one had seen the girls. At least they were now on the right side of the road as they headed back to the car.

They had certainly done a lot of walking, but they were now headed back to San José. "Thanks for driving down here, and for asking about Sarah. I know I couldn't have done it without you."

"You're welcome, Stan. As much as it would have been good to have someone say they had seen her, I feel so much better that she wasn't down here. And I'm sure she wasn't."

"I agree with you. I would imagine that every young kid coming down here for the first time would have gone to several of those places we went to. We didn't find out anything positive, and so we can cross Cabo San Lucas off the list. If Sarah's still down here, she's in San José."

As Carmelita let the car slow down for the red light, Stan asked, "What's that over there?" He was looking across the intersection to the lighted area.

"Oh, that's the bull fighting ring. As you can see, it's not too big, so they have them only on Tuesday nights. I don't really like to see them kill the bull."

"I don't like it either," Stan agreed.

"Up that road about a half-mile, however, is one of the best glass factories in the region. They'll put on demonstrations for you; I even have some Christmas ornaments from them."

"How do you say 'glass factory' in Spanish?" Stan asked.

"We call it *el vidrio*," Carmelita began. "*Vidrio* also means glass, but when you refer to a business or a factory as *el vidrio*, we know that you mean a glass factory and not just a glass."

"Hmmm," Stan started. "I think I would like to come back to it when we have some extra time."

"Sure," Carmelita replied.

The light changed, and they were now headed out of Cabo San Lucas. Stan saw the markers beside the road – *we call them mile markers at home* – clicking off the kilometers from the center of Cabo San Lucas. He remembered seeing them go by quickly on his drive up to the Tropic of Cancer Monument. "It's amazing how much faster the kilometers go by than counting the miles."

"I know," Carmelita said. "I remember when I first moved to the States and how far apart the markers there seemed to be. Of course a kilometer is only about six-tenths of a mile. But it still seemed strange."

Just then a cell phone rang.

"That's not mine, Stan," Carmelita said.

"Oh, I'd forgotten I even had it with me. I didn't even know it was going to work down here." He fumbled with getting it out of his pocket; the seat belt made it more difficult.

"Hello, this is Stan," he said as he rolled up his window to cut down on the noise.

"Oh, yes. Hi, Robert. How did it go with Mary today?"

Stan listened again before replying, "Oh really?" Then a pause on both ends.

"Well, when did she say that Sarah had stopped her mail? So where is it going? If it's not going to your house, where is her mail? Where are her bank statements?"

"Uh-huh." Pause. "Yes." Pause. "Okay, I agree, Robert. I'll call the airline tonight and see if I can switch my flight to tomorrow. What time can I call you on Wednesday?"

"Okay. I'll call you then. And I'll call you before then if I can't get out of here tomorrow. But I should be able to." Stan looked over at Carmelita who was nodding her head up and down to tell Stan that the flights shouldn't be full.

"Thanks for calling, Robert. I found out a little more today, but it can wait."

"Right. The first thing you do tomorrow is to call the Campus Police and report Sarah missing; tell them that you will need an affidavit to file with the Campus Post Office. Then contact the Campus Post Office and see if they are holding her mail; if so, find out where you can get it – let them know you have an affidavit from the Campus Police. Get the mail and then we'll get together on Wednesday. See you then." Stan closed his cell phone, put it in his pocket, rolled the window back down, and then took a deep breath.

"Sarah stopped her mail at school?" Carmelita asked.

"Yes. They were hoping that her bank statements were there so they could check on her cash situation. It certainly sounds like she planned this before she left. She did some pretty good planning for a nineteen-year-old. They want me back there to help them. Of course, I think they really just need some moral support right now, but they're paying me. So I have to fly back there tomorrow."

"I'd offer to take you to the airport right now to check on tomorrow's flights, but there wouldn't be anyone there. Once the last plane leaves, everyone goes home. I'll help you call back at your hotel."

"Okay, thanks."

They rode in contemplative silence the rest of the way back to San José. As she pulled up to the hotel, Carmelita said, "I'll call the airline for you. I doubt that you'd get an English speaking person at this time of day.

As they got out of the car, they didn't even notice how much quieter it was in San José compared to Cabo San Lucas. They walked into the lobby and headed toward the stairs when Stan stopped. "Thanks again for your help." He grabbed her hand and they walked up the stairs to his floor. He didn't care what anybody thought if they saw them.

Ten minutes later they came back down the stairs – she had managed to get him on a noon non-stop flight to Seattle. They walked out to her car. "I'll pick you up at 9:45 in the morning," she said. "There won't be much traffic at that time of the morning so you'll be there in plenty of time."

"Maybe I'll have you make all my travel arrangements from now on. Thanks. I'll be out here with suitcases in hand." Stan continued to hold her hand; he didn't want to let go. And he didn't want to let her go.

"Go," she said. "You have a lot of packing to do. I'll see you in the morning."

"Okay; I'll see you tomorrow." He was still holding her hand as he leaned forward and gave her a kiss on the cheek.

She also gave him a kiss on the cheek before getting in the car.

Stan stood on the sidewalk and watched as the car turned left and was gone. He walked back into the lobby; Miguel was at the front desk. "Hello, Miguel. I have to check out tomorrow morning, and fly back home. It just came up. Is that a problem?"

"No, señor. That is not a problem."

Stan just stood there as if he had not heard him.

"Is there anything else, señor?" Miguel asked.

"Yes! Can you get me some roses in the morning?"

"Are they for the lady, señor?" Miguel asked with a smile.

"Yes, they are, Miguel."

"What time is she picking you up, señor?"

"How did you know she was picking me up?"

"Because you did not ask me to call a taxi for you."

"You're very smart, Miguel. She's picking me up at 9:45." Stan was impressed with the logic that Miguel had used.

"I will have some nice roses for you in the morning. Do you think you will be coming back, or are you done with your work here in San José?"

"I think I'll be coming back; I sure hope so. I just don't know when."

"You just call me, and I will make sure we always have a room for you. You better go pack now, señor."

"Thank you, Miguel. Hasta mañana."

"Hasta mañana, señor. Buenas noches."

"Buenas noches," Stan replied. Good night. *Yes, overall it <u>had</u> been a good night!*

Twenty-three/Veintitres
Los Cabos International Airport
Tuesday, January 22nd

decepción (dā·cĕp'·cē·ōn') – disappointment. *Su ausencia causó cierta decepción.* Her absence caused some disappointment.

"Miguel at the front desk got them for me," Stan began to answer Carmelita's question about the roses as she turned left on Calle Manuel Doblado heading toward Federal Highway 1. "I wanted to take you out for dinner tonight, but I hope the roses will do instead." The short drive up the narrow road turned quiet as both of them were disappointed that Stan had to return to Seattle so quickly. A possible blossoming friendship was suddenly cut short.

Carmelita was about to turn right onto the highway as the light turned green when a large black SUV accelerated through the red light into what should have been her lane. "I thought they didn't run through the red lights down here. Don't the police hit them with a stiff fine?" Stan asked.

"Fortunately, most people do obey the lights. That driver probably keeps a large bill with his Driver's License so he can hand both of them to the *policia* if he gets stopped."

"I'm sorry that I won't be here to take you out to dinner tonight, but I'll be thinking of you while I'm microwaving whatever I can find in my freezer." Stan was glad that the SUV driver caused a slight break in their conversation because that little distraction helped to ease the tension in the car.

"And I will also be thinking of you while I am eating with my brother and his family," she replied.

The two rode along in silence as Carmelita continued to drive north on Highway 1 to the airport. As they left the main part of town they went through some little areas known as Santa Rosa and San José el Viejo. Stan recognized a few of the buildings from his trip to the Tropic of Cancer Monument just a few days earlier. Even before he could see the airport tower, Stan knew they were getting close because he could see the large Corona warehouse just south of the airport.

As they reached the airport exit at Kilometer 43, Carmelita asked, "Do you think you're coming back?"

Stan didn't know how to answer that question. It was the type of question that you'd like to have a lot of time to think about so you could say what you mean and mean what you say. He also would have liked to have more time so they could talk about it; *why is she asking this just as we get to the airport?* "I don't know for absolute sure, but I think I will. There is still more to do down here, but it really depends on what the Johnsons say." As soon as he said it, he knew he didn't say the "right" thing; he knew that because he could see her face flinch. "But regardless of whether the Johnsons want me back down here or not, I would like to come down here for a little while to see you; that is, unless you are also going back to Seattle soon." He saw her face relax.

"I think I'll be down here for a couple of months to stay with my brother. It's been too long since I spent time with him and his family, so I need to be here for a little while. Maybe I can work on my Spanish while I'm here; what do you think?" She chuckled a little as she said this.

"I think that your Spanish is fine. Your English certainly is very good. You know, it's a shame that Americans are not required to learn a second language, and not just a year or two of it. I think they should start learning a language in the early grades and continue it through high school. After all, the world is almost becoming a singular global economy, and we need to be able to communicate with people in their language, and not just in English."

"I agree. We didn't learn English when we were young here in San José, but now they are teaching it to the children at the same time they are learning our own language. I don't know what formal name they have for it, but essentially it's teaching them the English word the same time that they learn the Spanish word for something. So when they are learning their colors, they will learn *azul* and blue at the same time; *rojo* and red; *negro* and black; *blanco* and white. As they repeat them, the children begin to have two words stored in their brains for the same thing. That is also sometimes why you will hear people use English words and Spanish words in the same sentence – to them they are interchangeable. I wonder what it would be like learning three or four languages at the same time as you learn your own language. Now that could be confusing."

"That's for sure," Stan replied. "I know a lot of people who have a hard time making a complete sentence out of just one language. If they had to speak using two or three languages at the same time, they would never be able to say anything." He paused for a few seconds and then he continued. "Hmmm, maybe that wouldn't be so bad after all."

Carmelita looked at the sign at the airport entrance to see which terminal was for Alaska Airlines. "You're at Terminal 3," she said as she turned left rather than going into the lot for Terminal 1.

"Thanks. I certainly didn't pay any attention to it when we landed," he said. "You can just drop me off at the curb if you want. That way you don't have to look for a parking space." Stan was trying to not impose on her, but it sounded as if he were trying to cut things short, and he realized it. *I'm not doing very well here.* "What I meant was that if you have something else you need to do, I'm okay with just sitting around and waiting for my flight. I don't know how long it will take to go through Security."

"Your flight's at noon, right?"

"Yes, at 12:05 to be more exact," he replied.

"I know this is hard to believe, but the planes here in Los Cabos usually take off ahead of schedule. So you don't want to be late."

"Why do they take off ahead of schedule?"

"When it's time to board the plane, they usually board the passengers using the doors in the front and in the back of the plane. It's a more orderly process than having everyone go through just one door. So once everyone who has checked in is on the plane, they close the doors and take off. It's actually a pretty good system they have. Each plane that comes in here just turns around and flies right back to the same place. And because of where we are at the tip of Baja, people don't fly through here to get to someplace else."

"That's a good way of doing it," Stan acknowledged.

"We are pretty early," Carmelita said as she looked at her watch. How about if I park and we go in and you check in? We can then sit and talk until it's time that you have to go through Security and to the gate. Is that okay?"

"Sure, that's okay." Stan was actually glad that she wanted to "talk" some more. He didn't know where this relationship was going to go, or if it was a relationship at all.

"Okay, then. We'll have to park over here and walk up to the terminal. The planes have a good system for flying in and out of here, but no one did a good job of planning when they built the terminals. There isn't any space close to the terminals for people to park and go inside."

"That's okay. I thought I read in one of the magazines that they were going to build a parking garage that would connect to all three terminals."

"That's been talked about for a long time; I'll believe it when I see it. And not just started but finished, too," She said in a more forceful voice.

"I don't know if you have heard this saying, but we sometimes say 'When pigs begin to fly' to refer to something like that. There's a lot of talk, but it doesn't seem like it will ever really happen."

"Yes, I've heard that saying in Seattle," Carmelita said. She then continued, "We have one that's like it, and it's from the everyday people. It is *'Eso será el día cuando los pollos corten sus propias cabezas y salten en las ollas hirvientes.'* It translates to 'That will be the day when the chickens cut off their own heads and jump into the boiling pots.'"

"Yes, that would be an interesting sight, headless chickens right along with the flying pigs." Stan laughed at the thought of the headless chickens jumping into the pot of boiling water to be cooked. "Actually it could be a little messy, couldn't it?"

Just then Carmelita found a parking place and pulled into it. She shifted the transmission into Park and turned off the engine. She didn't take the keys out of the ignition, instead she first looked over at Stan, and then she reached into the back seat for the roses; but it was too awkward of a position for her to be able to reach them.

Sensing that she wanted the roses, Stan reached toward the back seat and brought the roses to the front and gave them to Carmelita. "Here you go. We can sit and smell them because I don't have to go in there yet."

"They do smell nice, Stan. Thank you again." Carmelita now paused as she was about to ask something that she really didn't want to hear the answer to, but she knew she had to ask. "Do you want to take these, or even just one of them, back to Seattle? Perhaps you have someone to give them to?"

"No, no, and no," Stan responded sternly. "I got them for you; there is no one in Seattle, and even if there was someone I wouldn't take one of your roses. I'm not married and I am not seeing anyone there. As you've probably noticed, my line of work doesn't lend itself to establishing close relationships." Stan exhaled and then started to get a little nostalgic. But he felt the need to explain.

"I was dating a lady for a long time. We were very serious and I thought we were in love. We'd talked about marriage; we hadn't set a date, but we were talking about it. I was working on several cases at the time, and my hours were crazy, unpredictable, and there were just too many of them in a day. Plus I was working seven days a week. We hadn't seen each other in a few days, and I was close to her apartment late one night. I stopped and knocked on her door. She didn't answer, so I knocked again. Finally she came to the door and asked, 'Who's there?' I told her, and she opened the door, but not all the way. It was if I was a stranger that she didn't want to let into her apartment. I was just about to say something when I saw someone else sitting on her couch. I demanded to know who it was, and she said he was just a friend. I know the neighbors got an earful that night because I sure yelled at her and her 'friend.' Well, anyway, that was the end of our relationship, and I haven't gotten into another one since then."

"That must've really hurt. You were talking about marriage but she had other men over to her apartment. Even if he was just a friend and nothing was going on, I can understand how you must've felt. I'm sorry."

"Thanks. I've gotten over it. My solution after that was to just work so much so I never had any time to spend with someone else." *Uh, oh. There I go again.* "But it's been different with you. I just feel comfortable with you and I really like being with you."

"Thank you, Stan. I like being with you." She leaned over to her right and gave him a kiss on his left cheek.

Stan placed his hands on the back of her neck and then leaned forward, angled his head to the right, and kissed her on the lips. It was a bold move, but one he wanted to do. At first Carmelita flinched, but then she relaxed and enjoyed the kiss. It had been a long time for her, too.

When their lips parted, Carmelita said, "Thank you. That kiss told me everything I need to know about you." She continued softly. "You're a warm, caring, and gentle person. You have not wanted to start any new relationships for fear of not being there when the other person wants or needs you. You've been hurt, but you are not a person who wants to hurt others. I wish I were coming back with you, Stan." She then leaned forward and initiated their next kiss; this one was stronger and more passionate.

"I wish you were coming back, too. I know it's too late for this flight, but could you fly back tomorrow?" Stan was now talking with his heart.

"No, I can't." She sighed before continuing, "My brother needs me here. Besides if I flew back to Seattle you would probably come right back down here. And what good would that do?" She tried to add some levity to the serious conversation because she was afraid that otherwise she might cry.

Stan reached his left hand over to her lap, clasped her right hand, and allowed their intertwined hands to dangle together between the seats. "You're right. I know you're right, but I didn't want that as the answer." Stan was finally allowing himself to show pure emotion; it was a strange feeling, but it did feel good.

"I know," she replied as she squeezed her hand to tighten their grip.

Stan responded to her by extending his right hand across to gently caress her left cheek, and then he gave her a soft kiss on the lips. "I know, too," he said quietly in resignation.

"Will you call me?"

"Yes," Stan replied. "I _will_ call you."

"Here, write this down. You'll need to know how to call down to San José." She didn't want to let go of his hand, but she knew she had to. Once Stan had his pocket notebook out and a pen in his hand, she continued: "Dial 011 for international long distance; then 52 for Mexico; 624 for Los Cabos, and then my brother's number. The same seven digits you dialed from down here."

"I've got it. I'm supposed to meet with the Johnsons tomorrow. I don't know how long it will be or what they will have found out today about Sarah's mail as well as her bank accounts. If I don't call you tomorrow night, I'll call on Thursday. Okay?"

"Okay," she replied reluctantly. Carmelita had not been looking for romance or any type of a relationship after her husband passed away. But the feeling that was burning inside her made her feel good. It made her feel that she could enjoy being with a man once again. She didn't think she would ever be able to feel that way; but she did. And she liked it.

Stan put his notebook back into his shirt pocket, and he reached back down to hold her hand. He leaned his head back into the headrest, closed his eyes, and smiled. *This is good.* He then opened his eyes and he looked over at Carmelita. "Thank you for being more than a friend. You have helped me on the case; you've shown me around, but you have also shown me that it's okay to have feelings for another person. I didn't think I would ever feel that way again. But you've changed all that. Thanks."

Carmelita squeezed his hand again. She couldn't speak; her throat was tight, and a tear began to run down her cheek. Stan took his index finger and wiped the tear from her jaw up to the corner of her eye. He brought that moist fingertip to his own lips and he kissed it. "I know," he said. "I know." The second time was in a softer voice as he was also starting to feel his chest tighten.

They sat there in silence for ten minutes, for fifteen minutes, for twenty minutes. Not saying a thing, just holding hands and occasionally glancing at each other. She sniffled and tried to hold back the tears, but the inner emotions were too strong. Stan used his free hand to pull a handkerchief from his briefcase and hand it to her. She wiped her eyes and then brushed the cloth back and forth along the bottom of her nose. Stan reached for it, but she pulled it back saying, "I'll wash it, and then that way you have to come back down here to get it."

"I'll let you wash it if you want. I just need to use it also." Stan repeated the same motions with the handkerchief that Carmelita had done. "Until we meet again," he said as he re-folded it and handed it back to her. And then to lighten the mood he added, "I thought hotels were expensive when they charged $2.00 to wash a handkerchief. This one is going to cost me a plane ticket to get it back."

Carmelita laughed, and it was a laugh of mixed emotion.

"I'd better get in there," Stan said. It was getting close to the time when he did need to check in, but he also knew that their emotions were peaking.

"Okay," she said.

Stan opened his door and stepped out. He grabbed his briefcase and went to the back of the car where Carmelita had popped open the trunk from her set of keys. He pulled his suitcases out of the trunk, set them on the ground, pulled up the handles, and then he shut the trunk.

"Follow me," she said as she got out of the driver's side.

"Not so fast," Stan replied. He walked over to her, grabbed both of her hands, and looked her right in the eyes. "I wouldn't feel right doing this inside the terminal with all those people around, so …" He let his voice trail off as he released her hands and wrapped his arms around her while he pulled her closer to him. They kissed, and it was a kiss that he didn't want to end. He knew that meant he would have to come back here.

She didn't want it to end either. And she knew that she would find an excuse to return to Seattle if he didn't come back down here soon.

"You're special," Stan said as he reluctantly let the kiss end. "I know we've only known each other for a week."

"Eight days," she corrected him.

"You're right; eight days. But I feel so comfortable around you. I can say things without feeling vulnerable. And you make me feel good." He then gave her a quick kiss. "And you're a great kisser."

"And how many women have you been kissing for your test?"

"Not many, and none in a long time. But if there are any women who kiss better than you, then their men are extremely lucky."

This time she leaned forward and kissed him. "Follow me," she said again. But this time he did. He picked up his briefcase, grabbed the suitcase handles, and walked behind her as she went down the row of cars. The parking lots at Los Cabos International Airport were not laid out in the same orderly fashion as most U.S. airports; there was no marked walkway for pedestrians. Actually, there was one, but people parked in it anyway.

They finally made it to the terminal, and the double glass doors opened automatically for them. Stan scanned the far walls looking for Alaska Airlines. It was to the right. As they slowly walked over to get in line, Stan heard Carmelita sniffle once more. He didn't look over even though he wanted to. Once they reached the front of the line, an inspector opened his suitcases as an initial security check. The uniformed man then closed them and carried the bags to the check-in counter. Stan and Carmelita followed him.

"Two bags to check, sir?" the counter agent asked.

"Yes, two bags," Stan replied. "Is there a later flight to Seattle today?"

"Yes, there is, but it stops in Los Angeles and the connection to Seattle has not always been that reliable."

Stan paused for a moment. "Okay, thanks. I guess it's better to stay on this non-stop."

"Yes, sir. At least on this flight, you know that when you take off, you're going to get to Seattle," the agent offered.

"Oh, I have one more question," Stan started. "Let's say someone else was traveling with me and we each had just one bag to check. Would you automatically put both bags under my name for example? Or do you make sure you put my bag under my name and the other person's bag under their name?" Stan was hoping to find out why Sarah's suitcase had been checked under Mary's name for their flight back to Seattle.

"If it's husband and wife traveling together, we just put them under the first name on the ticket; that makes it easier. If two travelers are not related, then we tag each bag to its owner. That way, if one of them doesn't get on the plane or something like that, then we are able to identify that person and take the bag off the plane. Even though we're in Mexico, we abide by the FAA rules because our flights are going to the United States."

Stan continued with his questions. "So if another fellow and I were traveling together on the same flight, you wouldn't check my bag in under his name?"

"Not unless you said that both bags were his or unless he said both bags were his."

"Okay, thanks. Sorry to have taken so much of your time."

"No problem," the agent replied. "Here is your boarding pass. Have a nice flight."

"Thank you," Stan replied as he picked up his briefcase, turned around and began walking back to the center of the terminal.

Carmelita had not been standing right next to Stan so she didn't hear all of his conversation with the counter agent. "Was there something wrong with your flight or your seat assignment?" she asked as she walked along side.

"No, I was asking about two people traveling together and each of them had one bag to check. You see, Sarah's suitcase was checked in under Mary's name, and so either Mary said they were both her bags, or Sarah did. In either case, it was intentional. Mary didn't tell me anything about it, but then she didn't even know that Sarah's bag had her name on it. So the only way that could have happened is if Sarah said that both bags were Mary's."

With one free hand now, Stan was able to hold Carmelita's hand. They slowly walked hand-in-hand toward the Security checkpoint. His plane was going out of Gate 4, and so he headed over to the sign that said "Gates 1 – 5." He stepped out of the way so others could get in line; he wanted a few more minutes with her.

"You'll find her, Stan. I know you will." Carmelita's voice was soft and measured as she spoke. She was now calm, accepting the fact that he did have to leave. But she also knew in her heart that he would return to Los Cabos, and to her.

"Thanks. I just hope her parents have that same confidence in me."

"They hired the best; where would they go now?" she asked.

"Keep that up, and I'll have you writing ads for me." Stan then switched to a lower, more somber voice. "I'll be back. I need to find Sarah; I need to see you again, and I need to get my handkerchief back. Take good care of it while I'm gone." Stan didn't want to get too emotional, so he held on to his briefcase as he leaned forward to kiss her.

She thrust both arms around him while still holding her purse in the left hand. She squeezed him and she kissed him back.

"*Hasta luego,*" he said [See you later]. "I <u>will</u> be back."

"Bye," she said through a stream of tears. She quietly prayed that he <u>would</u> be back. And soon.

Twenty-four/Veintiquatro
Johnsons' home – Redmond, Washington
Wednesday, January 23rd

planear (plă·nē'·ăr) – to plan. *Le gusta planear las cosas.*
He likes to plan things.

The neighborhood on Park Drive in Redmond, Washington didn't look any different – at least as far as Stan could tell – from when he was last there two weeks ago. There were a few houses that still had Christmas lights going back then, but in the daylight it's harder to tell if they had taken them down. Stan didn't think this area had any homeowner's association restrictions, so that meant that there probably was one house that left the lights up all year long. At least all the front yard displays had been taken down.

The yard at 4625 Park Drive was as immaculate as the last time he'd been there. He did admire people who maintained their yards all year long, whether they did it or hired someone to do it. *I'm sure the Johnsons wish more of the neighbors felt the same way.* It still took a conscious effort to keep it looking nice, especially when the weather was unpleasant. Stan parked alongside the curb even though the driveway was vacant and Robert had said that both he and Tina would be home. One of them could be late arriving at home, and he could be in their way to pull into the garage. It was just more professional to ensure that they had access to their driveway and garage.

After shifting the car into Park and turning off the engine, Stan pulled the keys from the ignition and put them into his coat pocket. He then reached over, grabbed his briefcase, and hoisted it to the mid-seat console. He'd reviewed the papers last night after he got in from Los Cabos, but he wanted to make sure everything was there that he thought should be there. He was ready organizationally.

But he wasn't 100% sure that he was ready emotionally. Robert had called early in the morning and set this one o'clock appointment; Stan wasn't really sure what to expect. He knew from experience that this first follow-up meeting was typically the roughest. The parents would expect solid answers that weren't always available. Regardless of the situation, he was working for the Johnsons, and their satisfaction was important. Fortunately, he'd been in this situation before, so he was able to anticipate some of their questions, or at least to think quickly enough to have a good answer for those other questions.

As he was pushing the "Sarah Johnson" folder back into his briefcase, Stan slid the top of his right index finger along the top of one of the sheets of paper. "Ouch," he said as he withdrew his hand and saw the small cut on the finger. There wasn't much blood but he grimaced from the pain, and he knew it would bleed every time that he hit it against something for the next week. Instinctively, he put the finger in his mouth and sucked gently on it. He didn't know why; it was just instinct.

Grabbing the briefcase handles carefully now he opened the car door and stepped out into the street. Midday Wednesday in Suburbia – nice and quiet, the way it should be. He closed the car door and walked around the back of the car to the walkway leading up to the front porch. The St. Jude statue was still there. *It's a shame they think this is a lost cause.* He held the briefcase in his left hand as he used the middle finger on his right hand to push the door bell.

"Hi, Stan," Robert said as he opened the door and extended his right hand.

"I'll shake hands later, Robert. Got a paper cut; do you have a bandage?"

"Sure. Come on in. How'd you do that?

"I was putting a file back into my briefcase and I slid my finger along a piece of paper."

Robert cringed as Stan described what happened – just the description was enough to send chills down his spine thinking about it. "Let's go sit in the dining room, and I'll get one for you. I knew your job had its dangers, but really!"

"Thanks," Stan replied somewhat sarcastically as he knew that Robert was only kidding.

"Hi, Stan," Tina said as she entered the room. "What happened?" she asked.

"You know, it's a tough job out there," Stan said in his rough PI voice.

Tina's eyes opened wider. "Really?" she said.

"No," Stan said. "It's just a paper cut I got in the car. Robert's getting a bandage for me."

"Would you like a cup of coffee?" she offered.

"Yes, thanks. Warm coffee is really nice on a day like this."

"Cream or sugar?" she asked.

"Cream or milk, whatever you have is fine. Thanks, Tina." Stan wanted to show his appreciation for her kindness.

Just then, Robert re-appeared with a wet cloth, a towel, and an antiseptic bandage. "Here, wipe your finger on this," he said as he held out the wet cloth and then the dry towel and the bandage.

"Are you sure?" Stan asked hesitantly as he wasn't comfortable wiping the blood on one of their wash cloths.

"It's fine," Robert replied. "I'll just go run it under some cold water and then toss it into the laundry. It'll be fine."

"Okay," Stan said as he used the wet cloth to wipe the blood from the tip. "I don't need a towel," he said as he blew on the finger tip to dry it – he didn't want to use one of their good towels. Robert was certainly being gracious; there was no question about that. Stan then took the bandage, peeled off the protective papers, and wrapped it on his finger. All was good again.

Tina re-entered the dining room with a tray of coffees and set the tray on the large table. She then proceeded to serve Stan and Robert, and the last cup was hers. "I hope you like the flavor," she began. "It's a special mocha blend from our local shop."

"Thanks," Stan said. "I'm sure I'll like it." Stan liked *coffee*, just not coffee that had to be flavored with all sorts of things. Looking at Robert, he asked, "Were you able to get Sarah's mail at the Campus Post Office today?"

"I did," he started, "but there weren't any bank statements. So I called the bank, and they said that Sarah had called and asked them to hold all statements there at the branch and not mail them to her."

"What?" Tina exclaimed. This was obviously the first time she'd heard that.

"Did they say when she called?" Stan asked.

"I didn't think to ask that," Robert replied. "But I was able to get the last statement from them at the branch office. "

"And?" Stan asked in anticipation.

"She withdrew $5,000 from her savings account two days before we went down there." Robert appeared upset, but that was not going to accomplish anything.

"And there haven't been any withdrawals since then?" Stan asked.

"No, and there haven't been any charges on her credit card," Robert answered.

Stan thought about it for a minute, and then he said, "Interesting. It looks as if she was planning to do something big while she was down there. Whether it was a major purchase or just a wild spending spree is anyone's guess right now. So how much is left in that account?"

"Um," Robert mumbled as he rummaged through the papers in front of him to find that statement. "There's still over seven thousand dollars in that account."

"Did you ask them at the bank if there had been any withdrawals this moth?" Stan asked.

"I didn't ask them that," Robert began. "But I did ask them what the current balance was, and it's the same as the end of the December statement."

"Good. So that means that she hasn't taken any more out." Stan really didn't want to ask the next question. "Did you instruct the bank to freeze the account?"

"I did," Robert said, "and they said they would."

"Okay. What about her checking account and her credit card? Has there been any activity on those accounts?"

"No," Robert replied. "Nothing."

"That's not terribly surprising," Stan said. "Credit card charges can be traced to the exact location where the charge occurred. So if someone doesn't want anyone else to be able to know where they are, or where they were, they won't use a credit card."

"Stan, are you saying that Sarah intentionally planned to just run away in Mexico?" Tina asked in a mother's frantic voice.

Stan slowly responded in a measured tone, "I don't think she was planning to run away when the four of you went down there. But based on this new information that Robert got today, and from what I learned while I was there, those things would lead me to state that her disappearance could be an intentional disappearance by her. I still don't know that for sure, but the indications are pointing more to that than to an abduction or something even worse than that." Stan never liked to refer to 'something worse' when talking to a client whose child is missing, but he had to take control of this.

"What do you mean by that?" Robert asked.

"What I mean is that the indications so far – the one big withdrawal before the trip plus what I want to tell you from what I learned down there – are that she is alive, safe, and in control." Stan knew this might be a stretch, but it was important that Robert and Tina felt that she was okay. And Sarah's being in control would convey that thought.

"What did you find out down there?" Robert asked.

"I'll tell you in just a minute. You said you told the bank to freeze the savings account; what about the others? I know she hasn't used them, but did you put a stop on them also?"

"Yes, I did," Robert answered.

"Okay. So how much did you say was left in her savings account?" Stan asked.

Robert shuffled through the papers again to find the right one. He extracted it from the pile and said, "Just a little over seven thousand."

"Here's my suggestion: call the bank and remove the freeze from the savings account. Lock out the checking account and the credit card, but leave the savings account open. She's used it before. If she needs money, this would probably be the account she would try first."

"But," Robert started.

"She's your daughter, Robert. If she really needs the money, would you rather she be able to get it from this account, or would you rather she have to do something else to get it?" Stan was starting to play hardball here, something he didn't like to do, but it was something that he sensed that he had to do.

"You said you found out some things down there; what are they?" Tina asked.

"First of all," Stan started, "I think she is alive and okay. That's just my own thinking, but I'm usually right. I talked to several merchants who recall seeing Sarah and Mary in the vicinity of the hotel right after New Years. There didn't seem to be anything out of the ordinary from what they saw. It was just two friends in Mexico enjoying the sun and being by themselves.

One of the people who had seen them, a restaurant waiter, says he saw Sarah about a week and a half ago in the main plaza, the one that's to the right of the hotel. I asked him how certain he was, and he was quite sure that it was Sarah that he saw."

"Come on; how would he know?" Robert asked negatively.

"That's a fair question. The plaza was crowded – it was a festive Saturday night – but he recognized her from when she and Mary had been in the restaurant just one week earlier. As he said, 'There are not a lot of young blondes who live there.' I'm encouraged by that, and I was following up on it when you called Monday night." Stan threw that last bit in because he wanted Robert to know that he <u>was</u> working while he was down in Los Cabos; it wasn't party time that the Johnsons were paying for.

"Are you saying that you think she intentionally stayed in Los Cabos, but that she hadn't planned it before we went down there?" Tina was still trying to understand the whole situation.

"Yes, that's exactly what I'm saying," Stan began. "Put yourself in her shoes. If you were planning to run away, wouldn't you pull everything out of your savings account and your checking account before you left? She took $5,000 out before the trip, certainly more than most people would typically need. That leads me to believe that something happened down there that made her act on a certain feeling or thought or idea that had been inside her for a long time. Whatever she did might seem like a rash decision to you, but in her mind it was a logical one, something that was necessary to do. Does that make sense? You might not like it, but if you can accept it for what it is – and it's just a hypothesis – then we can continue to work to find her using that as a starting point."

"That's it?" Robert asked. "That's all you've come up with in the week or so you were down there? What else have you been doing?" Robert's voice was getting heated.

Stan knew he had to show some restraint in responding to Robert. He would do that by not directly answering his question, a trick he learned from watching politicians being interviewed. "I talked with the airline about Sarah's bag being checked in on Mary's ticket. They said for couples traveling together, like you and Tina, that they might just put the two bags on one of your tickets. But when it's two individuals such as Sarah and Mary, then they ask whose bag or bags. For Sarah's bag to be tagged as

Mary's means that either Mary or Sarah told them that both bags were Mary's. I need to talk with Mary again anyway, and I'll ask her if she said that both of the bags were hers. I doubt that she did because she was surprised when Sarah's bag showed up at SEA-TAC."

Stan continued. "Finding someone who does not want to be found is a slow and meticulous process. Sometimes you don't even know what you don't know. And what you do know isn't much. You hired me to find Sarah, and I'm working hard to find her."

"You found one person who'd seen her recently, and the airline told you that one of the girls said to mark both bags as Mary's. That sure doesn't seem like you've had to work too hard for just that!" Robert had raised his voice as he was mocking Stan's statement that he had been working hard to find Sarah.

"Honey," Tina interceded in a softer voice. "I'm sure Stan knows what he's doing; that's why we hired him."

"YES, WE HIRED HIM AND WE CAN FIRE HIM, TOO!" Robert screamed.

A tense calm settled over the room as if it would take a little longer for the sound to dissipate throughout the house.

"Robert," Stan began gently. "You are right. I work for you on a 'for hire' basis. You may terminate our relationship at anytime you want, and I'll turn over my findings to you. All that's in the contract we signed and I'll certainly abide by it. I think there's something deeper here that's bothering you. I told you it would take time to find any information at all, and then even longer to follow the leads. That's what's happening right now. I was going to follow up with a possible lead yesterday but you called and wanted me back here. There's not a whole lot more I can do here in the States to find Sarah."

Stan paused so the sound of silence could help to engage some logical thinking rather than emotional thinking.

Stan continued, "Why don't you and Tina discuss this just between the two of you. You might think that this is just a business arrangement for me, and it partly is, but I'm also emotionally involved here. I want to find Sarah; but whether or not I continue is up to you. I'll stop the meter right now; you decide what you want to do. Just keep this in mind – the more time that goes by makes it that much harder to track down leads that might take us to her.

You have my number; call me with your decision. I'll refund your balance; don't worry about that." Stan closed his folder – without using the bandaged finger – and put it into his briefcase. His actions clearly indicated that he was leaving and that he considered himself no longer working for the Johnsons.

As Stan was starting to get out of the chair, Tina was shaking her head back and forth, and her lips were pursed in a sign of frustration and confusion. "Robert, no. Stan's working hard to find our baby; don't do this." Tears began to flow as she felt all hope of finding Sarah slipping away. She knew that if Stan left they might never hear from Sarah again. "Robert, please," she pleaded.

Stan was just standing at his chair, not because he was hoping that Robert would ask him or tell him to stay on the case. Instead Stan was staying put out of respect for Tina and her show of care and concern. This was their only child that they're talking about, and Robert was acting as if it were just some normal business decision he would make at work.

Robert's elbow was on the table and he was resting his chin in the open palm of his hand. He took a big breath in and slowly let it out. "Stan," he began in a softer and more civil tone. "Would you mind staying so we can talk about this? I'm frustrated, but I don't need to take it out on you." Robert was used to being in control and it was difficult for him to accept this situation. "Please?" he added.

"Yes, I'll stay," Stan said as he sat down. "I know you're frustrated, and you have every right to be. This is a frustrating experience as well as a gut-wrenching one. Think of working on a thousand-piece jigsaw puzzle, except this one has no picture on it; it's a solid color. You have nothing to refer to as help in putting it together. That's what we're doing to find Sarah. We didn't have anything solid to begin with, and now we're slowly developing our own sections of the puzzle, if you want to think of it that way. It's going to take longer unless we're able to somehow find a lead that takes us right to her. It can happen, but we don't know which lead that is, or even what we have to do to uncover that particular lead. There are no assembly instructions for us to follow; we're building it as we go." Stan paused in case one of them wanted to say something; Tina did.

"Stan, do you really think you can find her?" she asked, hoping to hear the right answer.

"I do," Stan answered. "But as I've said before, there isn't a specific formula to say how much longer it will take. And," he hesitated before continuing, "there's always the possibility that we won't find her. I don't like to say that, but it's a fact. I think she's alive; I just don't know if she's still in Los Cabos or not. But the longer we wait, the more time she has to leave and go somewhere else." He didn't add *'if she hasn't already left the area.'*

"Stan, if you'll accept my apology, I would like, I mean we would like, you to stay on the case," Robert said in a matter-of-fact manner.

"Yes," Stan began. "I accept your apology and I'll certainly stay on and try to find Sarah for you." Stan stood up and extended his right hand to Robert, but keeping the index finger just a little bit away.

Robert also stood and shook Stan's hand. Tina walked over to Stan and put her arms around him. "Thank you," she said. "Thank you." Her voice was softer as she unsuccessfully fought to hold back the tears that were natural for any mother desperately wanting to do anything to find her child – her only child.

A peaceful calm had come over the room; all the previous tension had melted away.

"Does anyone want more coffee? I'll put on another pot," Tina said.

Is coffee the cure for everything here in Seattle?

Robert nodded his head up and down, and Stan said, "Yes."

As the smell of the freshly ground and brewing coffee began to drift in from the kitchen, Stan started to outline his plan to move forward:

- Could he look at the bag that Sarah sent home on Mary's flight? Would there be any clues in what she sent home and what she might have kept?
- Robert would need to remove the freeze on Sarah's savings account.
- He'd call Mary later today to see if he could meet with her Thursday or Friday at the latest.
- He would book a flight for Sunday to go back to Los Cabos.
- Once down in Los Cabos, he would follow up with the Padre at church; check with the waiter again to see if he remembered anything more about seeing Sarah; has anyone else seen her?

Robert agreed with what Stan said he would be doing, and he also said he would tell Tina. "Look, Stan. I'm sorry I acted the way I did. I know you can understand the pressure we feel; please don't take it personally."

"I understand, Robert, and of course I don't take it personally. Actually," he continued, "I'd be surprised if you weren't upset at the progress because I'd want to know more if I were the parent. You know I'll do what I can to find Sarah."

"I know," Robert replied as he nodded his head up and down in agreement. "And I won't question anything else that you do."

Twenty-five/Veinticinco
San José del Cabo
Monday, January 28th

otra vez (ō'·tră·vēs) – again. *Quiero ir allá otra vez.* I want
to go there again.

It had been five days since he'd met with the Johnsons, and Stan felt slightly frustrated that he hadn't really made much progress in that time. Of course, being in Seattle didn't allow him to do anything down in Los Cabos. But it was the Johnsons who called him back to Seattle. *They're paying for it all, so I have to do what they want.* And then to top it off, he couldn't get a non-stop flight from Seattle; he had to connect through Los Angeles. That added over three hours to his journey, arriving late the previous evening.

He'd tried to call Carmelita at her brother's house the day before to tell her of his plans to return, but she wasn't there. Stan's message was short; it had to be because Roberto didn't speak much English. It was *"Stan en Cabo Lunes, mismo hotel."* [Stan in Cabo Monday, same hotel.]

Mary was out of town on a school trip for most of the previous week, so she didn't even call him until Saturday. She said that she didn't recall anything at the airport check-in counter about saying that both of the bags were hers; *so perhaps Sarah did check them both in under Mary's name.* When asked about the clothes that Sarah had in Los Cabos, Mary couldn't remember. That ruled out trying to compare what she had versus what came home. *There's no telling what she kept with her.*

Stan knew that most of an investigation was out of his control, but that didn't make it any easier. He knew, however, that to have any peace of mind, he would have to just do what he could because there really wasn't much else that he could do. He didn't like that answer, but it was the answer. He never liked that answer, no matter how many times he'd come to the same conclusion.

He was pleased, however, that he was able to get his same room at Hotel El Nuevo – room 304. It certainly wasn't the fanciest or the biggest room at the hotel, but at least he knew its nuances as well as the normal sounds from the hallway and from the street. It felt good sleeping in that bed again.

"Good morning, señor," Miguel boomed from across the lobby as Stan descended the stairs and started walking toward the restaurant for breakfast. "Did you sleep well?"

"I certainly did, Miguel. It's nice to be back here. By the way, I forgot to ask when I checked in last night if there were any messages for me."

"Let me look for you. I'll come find you at breakfast," Miguel replied.

"Gracias, Miguel," Stan said as he continued through the lobby area. The smell coming from the restaurant was just like it was before – that was a good thing. He'd slept late so he didn't have much competition for tables in the restaurant.

Just as Stan sat down, a waiter came by to bring coffee. "Hello, señor. Welcome back."

"Gracias," Stan said, not recognizing the waiter who'd obviously remembered him. "How are you?"

"Muy bien, señor. And you?"

"I'm very well, thank you." Without looking at the menu, Stan ordered his breakfast – Huevos Rancheros.

"Would you like any juice with that, señor?"

"Orange juice, please."

"Of course, señor," the waiter said as he walked away from Stan's table.

Stan was savoring the first sip of the rich Mexican coffee when Miguel appeared. "I'm sorry, señor. There are no messages for you. Is there anything I can do for you today?"

"No thank you, Miguel." Stan offered up a slight smile but it was a struggle to do so. Miguel understood the body motion and he quietly left the table and walked back to the front desk.

Why hadn't Carmelita called to leave a message for him? Maybe it was better that way; he could now focus 100% on Sarah. Or at least he could focus on Sarah 100% of the time that he wasn't thinking about Carmelita. *Maybe she didn't get the message.*

Pepé brought a large glass of orange juice along with the steaming plate of Huevos Rancheros. "Enjoy, señor," he said as he set the plate in front of Stan.

"Thank you, Pepé," Stan said as he now remembered the waiter's name. It was also on his name tag, but Stan <u>did</u> recognize him once he saw the name tag. So much was going through Stan's mind; he wanted to block it all out so he could just enjoy his breakfast. The juice tasted freshly squeezed. *There really is a difference between this and frozen.* And the Huevos Rancheros were just as he remembered from before, deliciously tasty.

After breakfast Stan decided to take a short walk to reacquaint himself with the area, plus it was nice to be able to go outside without long sleeves and a jacket.

"Will you be gone long, señor? In case someone calls for you," Miguel added that last bit to give a reason for his question.

"Probably not, Miguel. Thanks."

The warmth of the day felt so good as Stan stepped out to the sidewalk. It was a little cool when he'd come in from the airport, although it was still much nicer than in Seattle during the daytime! He made his customary right turn to go north along the street up to the plaza. He knew nothing would've changed in the short time he'd been gone, but it was important for him to do this – he was resetting his bearings so he could re-immerse himself into the area. There wasn't much activity yet as the shops were just starting to open, and there weren't many tourists out this early.

As Stan walked toward the fountain he was drawn to look at the church on his left. He wasn't a terribly religious man, so he wasn't sure why he was compelled to look over there. As he did, however, he heard the laughter of the children playing. Stan didn't have any children, but those sounds always made him stop and smile. One of the amazing things about children is how they can always have fun and be happy. Stan walked toward the church and sat on one of the benches that formed a triangle around a small grouping of trees and bushes. He was able to do two things here: think, and soak up the sun. He wasn't sure which one was more important, but he also didn't really care.

The sound of the children subsided as they went back to wherever they'd come from. Stan looked but he didn't see anyone over there. Then he remembered that he was supposed to meet with the Padre again to see if anyone had recognized Sarah's picture. He arose from the bench and headed to the church.

Walking up the narrow road leading under the archway, Stan could hear a few more voices in the courtyard that lay ahead of him. But these were not the voices of children playing; they were adult voices engaged in normal conversation. He continued into the courtyard and turned right, toward the office door. When he opened the door to the office he noticed that there was only one lady there; there'd been three the last time he was here. "Buenos días," he said.

"Buenos días, señor," the lady responded.

"*¿Padre aquí?*" he asked.

"Wednesday" was her simple reply. Clear and concise, no extra words were necessary.

"Gracias," was Stan's equally simple reply, and he turned back around and walked out of the office. As he was walking back through the archway out to the street, Stan remembered that he wanted to talk with Juan at Tequila Restaurant. How certain was he that it <u>was</u> Sarah that he'd seen in the plaza on that Saturday night? Stan had brought along a few more pictures of Sarah to show him. Stan didn't want to dissuade Juan; he just wanted to feel quite confident that it was indeed Sarah.

Reaching Calle Hidalgo, he knew he needed to turn right but he wasn't exactly sure how many blocks he needed to go before turning left; he'd left his downtown map in the room. *Rats!* The restaurant wasn't far from the hotel, so if he couldn't find it on his own he would just go back to the hotel and get the map. The first street he came to, the one on the south side of the church, was Calle Zaragoza. Stan was pleasantly surprised when he reached the next road, Manuel Doblado. He looked left and saw the sign for Tequila Restaurant hanging out from the wall. He knew it couldn't have been too far, but it was still nice to find it without having to use the map. He was starting to feel a little more like a local, or at least like a frequent visitor to San José. He didn't mind using a map when necessary, but it was also nice to be able to walk around without one.

Walking against traffic on the narrow street was a challenge, especially when the local buses roared by. He decided that staying on the sidewalk was indeed a smart plan. As he reached the overhead sign for the restaurant, he noticed that the door was closed. *Well, maybe they open early for lunch.* As he looked at the sign on the door, he saw that they didn't open until 6 PM. *Strike two.*

Without anything else in mind on where to go or whom to contact, Stan headed back to the hotel. It had been a good walk, but he wanted to accomplish more than just have a pleasant walk in the fresh air. But that's all it was going to be for now. Oh well, at least he was close to the hotel.

Entering the hotel lobby, Stan saw Miguel and had a thought. Carmelita had made a phone call for him; perhaps Miguel would also make a call for him. Miguel of course said 'Sí.' A few minutes later, Miguel came over to where Stan was sitting. "Her brother says that she's gone to Mexico City to visit her aunt, and she won't be back for two weeks."

"Gracias, Miguel," Stan said somewhat dejectedly as he got out of his chair and headed to the stairway. *Today's a shot day.*

Twenty-six/Veintiséis
San José del Cabo
Wednesday, January 30th

huevos (hwā'·vōs) – eggs. *Me gustaría huevos con jamón para el desayuno.* I would like ham and eggs for breakfast.

The road traffic outside his bedroom window sounded just like every other day's traffic, except it seemed to have started a little earlier. But it wasn't the traffic that awakened Stan; he was used to that. He'd slept well, and it was just time to get up.

While he was showering he thought about the previous day. There weren't many shops open on Tuesday, except for the stores that primarily targeted the tourists. He stopped in a few of them, but none of them recognized Sarah – not a surprise considering how many tourists they saw each week. Also, Tequila Restaurant waiter Juan was gone until today. His niece was getting married in Acapulco so he was out of town for that. His only other hope had been stopping in at Shooter's to talk with José, but he didn't work on Tuesdays. Stan was starting to wonder whether it was even worth it to come back down here. *At least the weather's better here than in Seattle.*

The pulsating water pounding down on his back helped to relieve a little of the tension that Stan was feeling. He knew it didn't do any good to get frustrated about how the investigation was progressing, assuming that it was even progressing. He'd investigated many cases of a missing person, but this one really got to him. Getting emotionally involved in any case was not good, especially when few leads were going anywhere. He was here to work, to do what he could to find Sarah. *It's not my fault that she's missing.* That thought reverberated in his head as the hot water continued its rhythmic assault on his body. It wasn't his fault, but it was frustrating nonetheless.

Stan got dressed, put his cell phone in his pants pocket, and the small notebook and pen in his shirt pocket. *Positive attitude.* He knew that he needed to have a positive attitude today as he headed out. Stan decided to have breakfast in a little café behind Plaza Mijares as it would be quieter than at the hotel, plus it would afford him the opportunity to map out his plans. The café he had in mind was also a small place where Sarah might have been; it was not in the normal flow of activities in San José. Today's breakfast was going to be later than when he typically had breakfast, but the town didn't seem to wake up until ten anyway, so there was no use in getting an early start on the day.

Stan made his customary right turn as he stepped out of the hotel. It was a weekday, a work day, but the sidewalks were still empty, as it was too early for there to be many tourists out and about. He had walked this way so many times that he could now recognize a few of the shop owners. He hadn't talked with many of them, so he didn't know their names, or vice versa. But their faces were becoming familiar.

Stan really enjoyed walking through the plaza itself because of its expanse; it would take a gathering of at least a thousand people to make it seem crowded. Stan liked people, but he also liked to have some space so he could think. And thinking was something he was trying hard to do right now. He was trying to think about all the possibilities of what Sarah could be doing and where she could be. He didn't want to focus on the "why" because that was irrelevant to his job – his job was to find Sarah.

The fountains weren't shooting out any water yet; *they don't start those until about ten o'clock*. Stan glanced to his left toward the church; going there would definitely be on his plan for today. He didn't see any activity over there, but he knew it was going on inside the buildings. He wondered if he would ever see more than just the two rooms in the office that he'd been in. It didn't really matter, but he was just curious what some of the other rooms looked like and what went on inside them. He was starting to lose focus; his focus right now was to go to Lupita's for *desayuno* and plan out his day. Just thinking about breakfast made his stomach growl. Nine thirty was late for him, and his stomach was reminding him that it was ready to be replenished.

He walked around the fountains, past a few more shops on his right until he reached Calle Alvaro Obregón. He turned left and walked a half block to Lupita's Café. He hadn't been inside before, but he'd seen it when he was just wandering around after going through the Art District. As he entered, he saw that there were only about eight tables that would seat four people each. Some of the tables only had two chairs; there were only about twenty chairs total. *I doubt they rely on the tourists, so the food must be good if the locals eat here.* Stan smiled as his nostrils caught a whiff of delightful aromas.

"Hola! Buenos días," was the greeting that was yelled out to him from the kitchen.

"Buenos días," Stan replied as he looked to see who it was. He continued walking toward one of the three open tables when a short plump woman, an apron tied around her waist, came out of the kitchen door toward him.

"Just one for breakfast, señor?" she asked. She didn't seem to be re-directing Stan, so he continued to the table in the corner.

"Yes, just one, gracias," he replied as he sat down so he could face the front of the café and see out of the windows.

"Coffee?" she asked as she set a menu on the table.

"Sí," Stan replied enthusiastically. He missed having coffee in the room as most U.S. hotels had a coffee pot in the rooms. *Oh well, this isn't the U.S.; yes!* He waited until she walked to get the coffee before he opened the menu. Everything was in Spanish, further telling him that the restaurant's customers were primarily locals, or visitors to the area who could speak Spanish. Stan noticed that everyone in the café seemed to know her; she <u>must</u> be Lupita.

"I'm sorry we don't have an English menu, señor," she said as she poured the cup of coffee for Stan.

"That's okay," Stan replied as he noticed that her English was pretty good. "What should I have?" Stan had found that the best way to develop an immediate relationship with a restaurant owner is to eat what they recommend. It had worked for him in the past; why not give it a try now?

"Our Huevos Rancheros are the best in town," she replied with a big grin that showed a missing tooth on the upper right side.

"If that's what I smell, then that's what I'd like," Stan said. He was actually hoping to have something different this morning – he'd had Huevos Rancheros every morning at the hotel. But there was a good reason for eating what she suggested. He would eat a bowl of Rice Krispies if she had recommended that for breakfast.

"Sí, señor," she said as she picked up the menu and headed toward the kitchen. "Gracias, Ramón. Hasta mañana," she said as one of the older men left some money on the table and got up to leave. She didn't rush over to the table; patrons of this type of a restaurant don't cheat on paying the bill. Ramón waved over his shoulder as he walked out the door.

Stan took a sip of the steaming coffee; the coffee was very good! He pulled the notebook out of his pocket to begin his planning for the day. The top two items were to visit the Padre and then stop by Tequila Restaurant to talk with Juan, but he didn't know if this was one of the days that it didn't open until later. He'd decided earlier that he needed to do a mass canvassing of the area; that is unless he was extremely lucky to strike it rich with a hot tip on Sarah. What he had to do now was to plan out the canvassing – to divide the area into sections that he could walk through in a day. He would do this every day until he'd covered the entire area, at least the reasonable area to cover. Once he mapped it out, he would then know how long it would take him to cover the area.

"Gracias, Pancho," Lupita said as she was approaching Stan's table with a huge plate of food.

"Gracias, Lupita. Hasta mañana," was the man's reply.

"Here you are, señor," Lupita said as she placed the plate in front of Stan. Not only did it smell delicious, it looked great – Stan was hungry!

"Gracias, Lupita," Stan said. She looked a little surprised that he knew her name.

"De nada, señor," she replied.

Stan inhaled deeply so he could take in all the aromas at once. It smelled better than the hotel's Huevos Rancheros, and he was certain that it was also going to taste better. That was confirmed after he had taken a few bites. It had taken a little longer to prepare, but it was certainly worth it. It was absolutely delicious. He savored each bite and each flavor that he discovered. The fresh oranges on the plate added a distinctive touch and their juicy sections provided a nice complementary taste. *I think I've found a new breakfast place!*

The restaurant was slowly clearing out while Stan ate his breakfast. "Do you have a minute?" he asked Lupita as she refilled his coffee cup.

"Of course, señor," she said.

"Oh, please sit down," Stan said as she had remained standing.

"Gracias." Lupita's face registered a look of concern. Had she recommended something that he did not like?

"The Huevos Rancheros were great; thanks for suggesting them," Stan started. Lupita's face relaxed. Stan pulled Sarah's picture out of his shirt pocket. "I'm looking for this girl," he continued as he showed the picture to Lupita. "I'm not a police officer, and she hasn't done anything wrong. Her parents from the States have asked me to help find her." Stan then took a business card from his pocket to show her that he was a private investigator. "She was here in San José with a friend for a few days after New Years; the friend says she didn't get on the plane with her to go back home. Have you seen her at all?"

Stan sat quietly as Lupita stared at the picture of Sarah. He saw a look of concern develop on her face. Did she recognize Sarah and she wasn't sure what she should say? Did she have a daughter herself and the thought of her daughter's possible disappearance bothered her?

"I don't know, señor."

"You don't know if you've seen her, or you don't know if you should tell me anything? I understand that. I'm an American who came into your restaurant for the first time today, and I'm asking you to make a hard decision. But I'm doing it for the parents who really want to see their daughter again."

"I understand that, señor," Lupita said as a tear began to form in her eyes. "I have three daughters, so I know how her parents feel." She took another long look at the picture. "I don't have a lot of Americans who come in here. So I usually do remember the ones who do come in. It might seem funny, but I actually can remember an American who comes in, but not a Mexican – except for my locals."

"That makes sense to me," Stan said as he was trying to engage on a personal rather than just on a business level. "Also, it's possible that she's still here, or was here just a week or two ago." Stan added that last part realizing that it was more likely that Sarah would have been in here recently by herself rather than around New Years when Mary was still here with her.

"Okay. I remember that she was in here one, maybe two, weeks ago. I think she walked by before that, but I'm not sure." Lupita's voice sounded confident, something that Stan used to help him determine whether or not to believe what he was hearing. He believed Lupita. "But she was in here only one time, and I don't think I've seen her since then. I wish I could help you more," she said as she picked up Sarah's picture one more time. A tear fell from her eye and splattered on the table; she quickly wiped it with her apron.

"That helps me, Lupita. Just one more question. As you said, you don't get a lot of Americans in here, and your menus are all in Spanish. Do you remember anything else about her? Did she order in Spanish? Did she seem to interact with anyone else in here?"

"She did order in Spanish, and her Spanish was pretty good, but she didn't talk to anyone else. She just kept to herself; she ate, she paid, and she left. That's all; I'm sorry."

"There's nothing to be sorry about. You've been very helpful. Thank you," Stan concluded as he extended his right hand to her. As she accepted it, he could tell she was a 'working woman' by the feel of her hand – an honest working woman. Lupita got up and went over to one of the other tables and began chatting with the occupants there. Stan wasn't worried that she was talking about Sarah or the reason that Stan wanted to talk with her. Lupita was a mother herself; Sarah's disappearance was not something to be talked about in idle chit-chat.

Lupita brought coffee over to Stan and refilled his cup as he was looking at his map and figuring out what area he would cover today. "Gracias," he said as she poured the coffee. Stan wasn't at all surprised that Sarah hadn't been back to the restaurant. As the only American she would have distinctively stood out from everyone else, not something that a 'hiding' person would want to do. It would be safer for her to eat at Shooters or some other place that is frequented mostly by American tourists. But her sighting at Lupita's was one more piece of the puzzle, and every new piece that got placed was one step closer to completing it. *It would be much better if I knew how many total pieces are in the puzzle.*

"La cuenta, por favor," Stan said after he finished the last cup of coffee. Any more coffee and he would explode. As Lupita brought the check to his table, Stan thanked her again for the great food and for her help. The total bill was seventy-seven pesos; Stan left one hundred fifty pesos on the table as he stood up and headed toward the door.

"Gracias, Lupita. Hasta mañana," Stan said as he walked by the kitchen door.

"Hasta mañana," she replied.

Stan's cell phone began to vibrate in his pocket as he closed the door on his way out of the restaurant. He fished it out of his pocket and saw that it was a Roaming number he didn't recognize. "Hello, this is Stan." He squinted as he attempted to hear the other person.

"I'm sorry; who is this?" he had to ask.

A shorter pause. "Oh, hi. How are you?" he exclaimed.

"Yes, I asked Miguel at the hotel to call your brother, and he said you wouldn't be back for two more weeks."

"Well, I'll be here at least all of this week," Stan continued. "And probably some of next week; it all depends on what I'm able to find out this week. I did just come out of a little café – it's called Lupita's – right behind the plaza, and" – Stan was cut off by Carmelita at that point.

"Oh, you've heard of Lupita's? Well, anyway, Lupita said Sarah came in for breakfast a week or two ago. But she's been in there only once. That's not surprising for someone who's trying to hide."

"Uh huh. How's your aunt?"

"That's good. What's it like getting around in Mexico City? I hear it's so large that traffic is quite a problem."

"No? I guess that makes sense; if you know where you're going, it's a lot easier than when you are there as a tourist."

"Yes, I'm starting to feel more comfortable here in San José."

"Right. Any chance you'll be coming back to San José earlier, or will you be there for at least two more weeks?"

"Oh, okay. Well, if you can get back any earlier, I'd love to see you again before I head back to Seattle."

"No, that's okay. I understand. Can you give me a call on Saturday or Sunday? I should know by then how much longer I'll be down here."

"All right, thanks."

"Yea; great talking to you, too."

"Okay, bye." Stan closed his phone wondering if he would see Carmelita again before he had to go back to Washington. She'd been so much of a help to him, but that wasn't the only reason he wanted to see her again.

He looked at his map, and figured he would first stop at the church to talk with the Padre, then cover the streets he'd outlined for the day, and finally finish up at Tequila Restaurant to talk with Juan. He would wait until later in the week to stop by Shooters to see José one more time.

Twenty-seven/Veintisiete
Los Cabos International Airport
Friday, February 8th

posibilidad (pō'·sē bǐl'·ē dǎd) – possibility. *Hay una posibilidad que volveré el año próximo.* There is a possibility that I will return the next year.

"Thank you, Miguel, for everything you've done for me. Here's a stack of my cards in case anyone comes looking for me. I've told a lot of people down here where I was staying, so it's possible that someone might come asking for me." Stan was checking out of Hotel El Nuevo and headed back to Seattle, Washington.

"Señor Stan, please call me if you're going to come back to San José. I will make sure that you always have a nice room. Are you sure I should tell people your address if they ask about you?"

"Of course. Maybe only give out the phone number if it's someone you already know, one of the shop owners or someone like that. But you can give my address to anyone. You never know; there might be someone out there who knows something about Sarah but it takes them time before they can say anything about her." Stan hated to leave San José but he'd gone to all the shops, and he'd talked with everyone who'd previously said they'd seen Sarah; there was nothing more for him to do. Anything else he did at this point would just be wasting his time and the Johnsons' money in hopes that something lucky would happen. Some luck is always needed in an investigation like this, but he'd be relying 100% on luck at this point. He couldn't do that; it would be unethical and it would be unprofessional.

"We'll miss having you here, señor," Miguel started. And then he heard the sound of the taxi's horn. "Oh, there's the taxi. Let me go with you to talk to him in Spanish just to make sure there's no problem."

"Thank you, Miguel." The two of them headed out to the taxi, and Miguel spoke to the driver in Spanish; it was a short conversation.

"The driver knows the fare is two hundred pesos and he is to take you directly to the airport without picking up anyone else. I have his number so if there's any problem, you let me know, and he will never drive a taxi in Los Cabos again." Miguel was quite matter of fact and feeling proud that he was able to make sure that Stan would not be ripped off by the taxi driver. Most of the taxi drivers were honest in Los Cabos, but it was just good sense to make sure that his hotel patrons didn't get cheated.

"Miguel," Stan started as he handed him a one thousand pesos bill. "Thank you again for all you've done. I hope I come back down here, whether it's for business or for pleasure. And I will call you and stay at your hotel."

"Muchas gracias, señor," Miguel replied. He placed the folded note into his pocket without looking at it. There would be plenty of time after he was back inside to look to see how much Stan gave him.

"De nada," Stan replied as he stepped into the taxi.

Traffic was very light, as it was on most mornings. Stan knew the route by heart so he knew when the driver would be slowing down, where he would be turning, and about how long it would take to get to the airport.

As the taxi slowed near a spot where he and Carmelita had been, Stan thought about her. She had called on Sunday, and it was a pleasant conversation. Stan said he would be heading back to Seattle later in the week. Carmelita said that her aunt still needed her there in Mexico City, and that she would be there for at least two more weeks. Stan asked her to call him when she got back to Washington because he didn't know when or if he would be going back to San José. Of course, he would like to go back down, but there wasn't anything in the investigation right now to justify it. *I probably could have worded that part a little better.* She said she would call him when she got back to Washington in a couple of months. He said that would be nice. They exchanged good-byes, and that was it.

That was it. What Stan thought might turn into a longer relationship somehow evaporated quickly. He knew it was essentially his fault. He was there on business, and he was also on a leash that was controlled by the Johnsons. He had to go back to Seattle when they called him a few weeks back. And then he didn't know he was coming back to San José until it was too late to call Carmelita. Now he has to go back to Seattle just a week or two before she returns to San José. *Talk about timing!*

Stan wasn't paying much attention to the trip; he knew the driver would get him promptly to the airport. He felt the car jerk to a stop.

"Here we are señor, Alaska Airlines."

Twenty-eight/Veintiocho
Johnson's home – Redmond, Washington
Saturday, February 9th

esperanza (ĕs·pĕ rŏn' ză) – hope. *Nosotros nunca perderemos la esperanza.* We will never give up hope.

The flight from Los Cabos to Seattle was uneventful. The plane took off on time and it landed on time. The bonus was that the plane was not full, allowing Stan to have all three seats on his side of the aisle to himself. The extra space was nice, but so were the additional quiet and the ability to concentrate. He had all of his "notes" in his brain, all the things that he would be telling the Johnsons, but he hadn't been able to put them on paper while he was still in San José. He had to be separated from the area – both mentally and physically – before he would able to commit them to writing. The long flight, combined with the two open seats, allowed him the chance to organize his thoughts and write them down in a form that he hoped would make sense to the Johnsons.

The basic summary was that he'd not found Sarah, but he couldn't just give them that one-line summary. He needed to tell them what he did, what contacts he made, what he found out, what his current thoughts were – all of these things so they knew what he'd done to determine what had happened to her and hopefully to locate her. That justification was necessary for two reasons: Sarah's parents had every right to know that he did everything he could to find her, and that the extensive efforts justified his expenses. He wrote out all of this on the flight, but he wasn't prepared to give them a copy of his notes. He'd done that early in his career and it had ended up causing a lot of grief to the parents to see it writing. They would read and re-read it over and over again, causing further pain and anguish. No, he would talk them through it. If they requested a written report, he would oblige them and send them a copy of his notes.

Stan didn't sleep well that night after he got home. He went through his stack of mail and had his first home-cooked meal in almost two weeks. The one glass of red wine did help him to relax, but there were so many thoughts running around inside his head. Was there something else he could've done to find Sarah? Was there anything that the Johnsons didn't think to tell Stan about Sarah? Was she still in San José? Where could she have gone? What's she doing? Was she okay? Why'd she leave? When did she plan it? Did anyone else know about her plans? Would she ever contact her parents? Questions, questions, and even more questions. All these questions running around in his head made it hard for Stan to sleep. He knew he'd done his best to find Sarah; it appeared that she was very smart and that she'd planned it all very well.

He had to stop beating himself up; none of this was his fault – it was time to move on. Not that the Johnsons would.

The overcast sky seemed to set the mood for the day as Stan turned onto Park Drive. He had his headlights on, not that he needed them to see, but so others could see him. Just as he went around the curve in the road two young boys darted across in front of him. Stan hit the brakes; the boys kept running – they were impervious to danger.

Stan slowed as he approached the Johnsons' house; the yard looked as nice as ever. He'd had some clients in the past who essentially went into seclusion when Stan wasn't able to find their missing children, or the worst possible scenario had occurred. Their normally neat and clean yards were neglected; trash cans were left at the curb for weeks; the blinds stayed closed – those people had given up on life. Something precious had been taken from them and they withdrew into their cocoons. But the Johnsons maintained the neatness of the exterior – it was the interior that was crumbling for them.

Stan took a sip of his bottled water and grabbed his briefcase. Stalling wouldn't change anything, and the Johnsons would see his car out front anyway. He gathered his composure so he could portray confidence, and he walked up to the door. Some early spring bulbs were peeking out of the ground; *I wonder what color they'll be*. He noticed the St. Jude statue on the porch as he rang the doorbell.

"Hi Tina," he said as the door was opened.

"Hi Stan. Come on in," she replied as she stepped aside so he could enter their home. "Robert just called and he'll be back in a few minutes."

"Thanks," Stan said as he walked in to the smell of freshly-brewed coffee.

"Have a seat," she said as she led him into the dining room – their standard meeting place. "Some coffee?"

"Sure," he replied. He didn't really care if he had coffee or not, but it seemed to be the thing they always did. "Thanks," he said as she brought two cups in from the kitchen.

"How was your flight home?"

"It was good," he began. Stan knew that he had to be careful in his choice of words. Tina was in a fragile state, and he didn't want to say the wrong thing, or say something in the wrong way that would further upset her. "I don't think I've ever seen any other airport where the flights always leave on time." He was trying to fill the time with small talk until Robert got home.

"Well, we don't travel that much. Why do you think that is?" Tina asked the typical follow-up question.

"The weather's usually very good, so they don't have the weather delays that we have here at SEA-TAC or they have down in San Francisco. So once the planes get there, they're able to go right back out. Also most of the airlines have flights that just go back and forth between one airport and Los Cabos; so it's kind of like a shuttle between the two airports. That way they're not waiting for passengers to come in from another flight before they can take off. I think it's a pretty good system." *When is Robert going to get here?* "Oh, I saw you have some bulbs starting to come up out front. What are they?"

"There's some grape hyacinths and a few crocuses. They just seem to come up every year; it makes the gardening a little bit easier," Tina answered.

"I'm sure it does. I've thought of moving into a condo so I don't have any yard work to do at all. But I do think I'd miss the green grass; I actually like the smell of a yard when it's just been mowed. There's something about it that appeals to me." Stan was quickly running out of things to say that didn't relate to the case. He sat back in the chair and picked up his coffee cup. He raised it slowly to his mouth and took a long sip.

The sound of the closing door from the garage told them both that Robert was home.

Stan took one more sip of his coffee, and then stood up as Robert came into the dining room. "Hello, Robert."

"Hi Stan," he responded as the two men shook hands. "How's that cut finger of yours?"

"Oh, it's fine thanks. I'd forgotten about it," Stan said as he then looked at the faint scar on his index finger.

"Hello, dear," Robert said as he kissed Tina. "The coffee smells good."

"I'll get some for you. Go ahead and have a seat," she said as she went into the kitchen.

"Thanks," her husband replied as he sat down in the chair opposite where Tina had been sitting. The three of them had somehow developed a pattern of who sat where. "Good flight back?" he asked.

"Yes," Stan began. "I was telling Tina earlier how it was nice that the planes were always on time in Los Cabos – they certainly don't have the same weather delays as we have at SEA-TAC."

"You're right. That unpredictability in winter makes travel a lot more precarious. It really wreaks havoc on conducting business when you don't know if you're going to be able to get out or not." Robert was still in his business mode.

"Here you go," Tina said as she returned from the kitchen. "Would you like some more, Stan?"

"No, thanks. Actually a glass of water would be great. Thank you."

"So, no major breakthroughs while you were back down there?" Robert jumped right into it.

"Nothing major, but if it's okay, can we wait until Tina comes back? I want you both to hear it all." Stan was polite but stern.

"Sure, that's okay," Robert replied. He was used to being the one to set the tone and the pace of the discussion. It was hard for him to concede that role to anyone else.

They both sat there in silence waiting for Tina to return. Stan was comfortable in silence; Robert wasn't. Fortunately for her husband, Tina soon reappeared with Stan's glass of water.

"Thank you," he said as she handed the glass to him. Robert and Tina looked at Stan, waiting for him to begin. He took a sip of the water because he knew this was going to be a long and difficult discussion.

"As you know," he began, "I haven't been able to find Sarah." He paused to let that sink in. Robert's jaw tightened upon hearing those words, and tears started down Tina's cheeks. Stan took another sip of water. "That doesn't mean, however, that I think it's a lost cause. I feel she's still alive, and that something will turn up to give us the break we need." He intentionally used the plural pronoun to indicate that all three of them were a team in this search.

"There's quite a bit of evidence – at least it's evidence in <u>my</u> mind – that her disappearance was intentional, meaning that she wasn't abducted against her will." He paused again. The Johnsons' emotions continued. Robert got out of his chair, went into the kitchen, and returned with a box of tissues. He used one for himself and then set the box in front of Tina who immediately pulled out a handful.

"I'm sorry," Tina struggled to say through the tears and the sniffles.

"There's nothing to be sorry about, Tina." Stan tried to reassure her, but he knew that the only words that would comfort her now were, 'I've found Sarah and she's fine.' But he couldn't say those words; he wished he could, but he couldn't.

"I don't think she went to Mexico with a solid plan of running away. She would've done things a little differently if she'd planned it all completely before of you went down there."

"Why do you say that?" Robert asked.

"I think she would've taken more money out of her accounts than what she did. Yes, she withdrew five thousand dollars, but she could've taken more. If she had been absolutely certain that she wasn't coming back, she would've pulled more money out and possibly put it into Travelers Checks. She might've even taken all of it, something that would've forced her to go through with it. That's the first thing."

Stan continued. "The people I talked with down there who remembered seeing both Sarah and Mary together said that nothing seemed out of the ordinary. They were just two college girls enjoying the sun and being on their own. They didn't do any wild partying; they didn't go out with any guys, although there were some who tried to pick them up. All indications were that everything was fine." Stan paused as he didn't want to pour too much information on them all at once – there was plenty more to come.

"The third thing is that in my talks with Mary, she said there were never any signs from Sarah that she wasn't happy here or at school. She did fine in her classes; she was looking forward to second semester; they were even talking about what they would do on Spring Break next month. If I had to place a bet, I would put all my money that running away – and that's what I think it is – was only slightly on her mind as the four of you went down there. The only negative thing I've found out is that Mary said Sarah had been dating a fellow on campus, but that they broke up right around Thanksgiving."

"Oh," Robert seemed surprised. "She'd never told us she was dating anyone. So what would've caused her to do run away?" Robert asked. "She wasn't an impulsive person."

"That's a good question," Stan started. "Just because she wasn't planning to run away – or stay in Mexico for some other reason – at the time you went to Los Cabos doesn't mean that the seed hadn't been already planted. In fact, I would have to say that the thought had already been there in her mind."

"You mean that she'd been thinking about running away before this?" Tina asked.

"I wouldn't necessarily put it that way," Stan began. He paused to make sure he had the right words to use. "I think that there was something in her mind – some lifestyle, something she wanted to do, something she felt compelled to do – that had been there for a while. All that thought needed was the right opportunity to trigger her into action. Somehow, that opportunity might have presented itself down there and it ignited her thought processes into action. And perhaps she knew that it might be possible, and that's why she withdrew the five thousand from her savings account. Now I'm not a psychologist but I've had to reason through so many situations on other cases that this is what I've come up with for now. But that doesn't stop everything right here. Let's walk this through slowly and rationally and see if you find something that you don't think is right. I don't mind if you find any flaws in my logic – after all, you've known Sarah all her life."

"So what you're saying is that there was some switch in her brain that was ready to be flipped, and the right circumstances came along and flipped it? Is that it?"

"Essentially, that's it, Robert. Using the term 'flipped' doesn't mean that she flipped out or that there is any psychological problem with her. Something presented itself to her, some situation that put the pieces of the puzzle together for her – making the complete picture. And when she saw the complete picture she was ready to act. Let's don't dwell too much on that for now. Let me tell you a little more how I came to my conclusions."

"Remember when we looked at the contents of the bag that came home under Mary's name? Did you see her toothbrush, a hair brush, or any other personal items? Most people pack those items in their checked bag. Sarah didn't – she needed them. You told me that she flew down there in slacks and a sweater; those items were in the checked bag. She was wearing jeans, a top, and tennis shoes – comfortable clothes, but not her normal travel clothes. But the most telling item was her cell phone. Why would she pack her cell phone in her checked bag? The charger? Of course; but not the phone. If she had the phone with her, she might be tempted to use it; and all calls could be traced."

Stan stopped talking to let that sink in. Everything else could've been explained away, but not packing the cell phone in the checked bag – the bag that had been checked in under Mary's name so that it <u>would</u> be on the flight back to Seattle.

"The cell phone in her checked bag, combined with people saying they'd seen her there in San José a few weeks ago – all of that tells me that she did this voluntarily and intentionally, and that she was not abducted." Stan paused again.

Tina started crying as the reality that her daughter would want to run away was becoming more and more clear – and definite, and possibly final. "But why?" she wailed.

"I don't have an answer for that question." Stan wanted to provide more answers, but he just didn't have all of them.

"Why?" she cried again, tears flowing uncontrollably down her cheeks. She grabbed more tissues and buried her face in them.

Robert pulled the handkerchief out of his back pocket. He wiped the tears from his face and then blew his nose. He leaned back in his chair and let out a big sigh – it was becoming all too real to him.

Stan let them have a little quiet time; waiting another minute or two was not going to change anything. So why not just take a short break?

Robert and Tina just looked at each other across the table, although it's hard to know what they could see through the tears. Stan could see the questioning look on their faces. Why would she want to run away? What did we do wrong as parents? Will we ever see her again? Why? Why!

Stan felt it was time to break the silence. "I know you two have lots of questions, and they're probably questions I don't have the answers to. The first question most parents ask is what did they do wrong – you've done nothing wrong. Everything I've heard tells me that Sarah was happy. If she'd wanted to run away a long time ago, she could have. She had access to the money; she had a passport; she knew how to travel; she was self-sufficient. She could have escaped if that's what she felt she had to do. That's not it."

"No one seemed to be following her or forcing her to do anything. I've been to every shop in the area, and there's a lot more than I thought. I asked every person I talked with to contact the manager at the hotel; he has my card so he can give out my address. I feel we'll hear something; someone must know something more about her."

"What about the priest down there? What did you find out from him?" Robert asked.

"Unfortunately, that's a touchy situation. He told me to my face that he hadn't personally seen her, but that someone else there at the church said they had. When I pressed him for more information, he said that he couldn't say anything more. He said he was bound by church rules."

"But she's our daughter!" Robert exclaimed.

"I told him that. I said I just wanted information and that I wasn't trying to kidnap her and take her back home. He also reminded me that the rules in Mexico are different from the rules here. I pleaded with him to tell me more, but he wouldn't. I went to the church this past Sunday, and no one would talk to me. Obviously the word had been spread around. In a way I understand, and I'm sure there've been cases where people used any information they got to harm people rather than to help them."

"Would it help if we went down there? Do you think he would listen to her parents?"

"Robert, I don't think so. At this point, I think someone would tell Sarah – that is if she's still there and someone at the church knew where she was. That would only drive her farther away, both physically and mentally."

"So what now?" Tina managed as she regained some strength. "What do we do now?"

"I don't see that there is anything else we can do right now. Did you remove the freeze from her savings account?" he asked Robert.

"Yes," Robert replied.

"Have you checked the balance to see if she's taken any more out?"

"No, I didn't think about that."

"Here's what I want you to do. Sarah will know what the balance is, right?" Stan asked.

"Right," Robert answered.

"Wasn't it over seven thousand or something like that?"

"Yes, something over seven thousand sounds right."

"Okay. Find out the exact balance and put enough in to make the balance a little over eight thousand."

"What?" Robert yelled. "Why would I put MORE money in the account? Why don't I just take most of it out?"

"Robert, here's the reason. By putting in more money and the balance goes over eight thousand, that tells Sarah that you want her to use the money if she needs it. If you take money out, that's just one more thing that could drive her away. And if you don't do anything, she might think that you haven't even seen the statements or know that she hasn't taken any more out since before the trip. Putting more in, and making the balance over eight thousand, will tell her that you do still care about her."

"Robert, we have to do what Stan says. What's a little money when it means our daughter?" Robert might have the business sense in the family, but it was Tina who brought common sense into the discussion.

"Okay, I'll do it Monday," Robert conceded.

"Also, talk to the bank; remove the freeze on her credit card but ask them to lower the limit to five hundred dollars. That way she can use it if she needs it, but no one can steal it and run up a huge bill."

"Okay, I'll do that, too. Anything else?" Robert felt he was being run over by a steamroller.

"No, just call me if she does take any more money out or if she uses the credit card. Otherwise, there isn't a whole lot more we can do for now. Maybe you'll hear from her, or someone will contact me. She's been gone for five weeks now, and if she wants to stay hidden, she's shown she can do it. We need to ease up and just wait." Stan never liked to tell parents that. They were used to seeing the TV shows where the investigator always had the answers – and he would find the missing person at five minutes before the show ended. But this wasn't a TV show; this was real life.

"There's nothing else we can do?" Tina's question was more of a statement, resigned to the terrible fact that she might never see her daughter again.

"No," Stan said. They could hire someone else, but that wouldn't help; it might even make things worse.

"And you'll let us know if you hear something?" she asked.

"Of course I will. It may take a while, but there are lots of people down there who know that we're looking for Sarah. We'll hear something; I know that." Stan was confident in his last statement, both in the words and in the delivery.

Robert let out a big sigh. "Okay, Stan. Thanks for all you've done. We'll pray that we hear something soon. And I'll get to the bank on Monday and do what you've said."

Stan stood up in synch with Robert and the two shook hands. Tina walked around behind Stan and stood next to her husband. Stan extended his hand to her; she grasped it and then leaned against Stan for support, physically and emotionally.

The three of them walked in silence to the front door. As he walked out, Stan said, "Your yard looks really nice."

"Thanks," Robert replied.

Stan continued on to his car and drove home. It was a long drive, not the distance, but the emotional time span.

Twenty-nine/Veintinueve
Seattle, Washington
Friday, May 9th

información (ĭn'·fŏr mă'·cē ōn) – information. *Yo tengo algo de información muy importante para usted.* I have some very important information for you.

Mid-Spring iss a great time in Seattle. The flowers are blooming, and the trees are green and beginning to bud. Most of the locals have prepared their yards for the summer heat that will be coming soon. But for now, the weather's great. It's not too hot, and most of the people have already forgotten about the chilly and damp winter that's just gone by. The Spring Quarter at the University of Washington is about half over. Life's good.

Private Investigator Stan Walkorski had been enjoying a brief respite from work as the demand for his services had slowed slightly. That was fine with Stan as he was ready for a break from the emotional stresses that were involved with most of the cases he handled. He had just completed one that involved an unfaithful wife. He really didn't like that type of case because there were typically three unhappy people when he was done. This case was not any different – three unhappy people and at least two ruined lives. What a shame!

As he drove home from the final session at the court house, Stan breathed a sigh of relief as he pulled into his driveway. The case was over, and he would have about ten days until he was to do some routine investigative work for the local police. He was planning to use the free time to trim the trees, paint the living room, and start reading one of the many books that had piled up on his bed stand. He pushed the button for his garage door opener and the door opened, but the light did not come on. "Sure why not," he said out loud and somewhat sarcastically. "Oh well, at least changing the light bulb is a simple fix." He parked the car in the driveway so he would have access to the light in the garage. He grabbed his briefcase from the passenger seat and walked into the garage, and pushed the button to close the door. Once the door was closed, he realized that he hadn't turned on the overhead garage light; he normally didn't have to do that because the light on the garage door would provide enough light for him to unlock the door. But with that light not working, he needed to flip the light switch. *Ah, the things you take for granted.*

Once he was inside the house, he went to the front door to retrieve the day's mail that had been put through the mail slot. There were some last-minute Mother's Day flyers and catalogs, coupons for the local pizza joint, his credit card bill, and one white square envelope with his name neatly printed on the front. He didn't recognize the stamp, but then the Post Office issued so many new stamps each year that it was too hard to keep up with all of them. He carried the stack of mail into the kitchen, set it on the counter, and turned on the light switch. He opened the refrigerator and pulled out a diet soda and popped it open. That was refreshing. It was nice to be finished with that infidelity case. The pay was good, but even he felt some of the agony. He wasn't sure who came out on the worst end of it, or who suffered the most. Stan certainly suffered some from it.

He remembered the letter and picked it back up. Now with more light he could see the stamp better. It was a stamp from Mexico – was Carmelita sending him a letter? They had spoken not long ago, so it would seem odd for her to mail a letter to him. The envelope was postmarked April 30th, and there wasn't a return address on it. Stan took a knife from the knife block, slit open the envelope, and pulled out the two sheets. He noticed that there was a soft fragrance from the pages. *Hmmm, that's nice.* He took his soda and the letter and sat at the kitchen table. He opened the single-folded hand-printed sheets and began to read:

April 29th

Dear Mr. Walkorski,

You don't know me, but I got your address from Hotel El Nuevo here in San José del Cabo. The man at the desk was very nice when I told him that I wanted to get in touch with the man who was looking for information about Sarah. He asked me a couple of questions and then he wrote your name and address down on a piece of paper for me. He may have already contacted you since he had your business card; so you might have been expecting my letter. But as you can tell, the mail from Mexico is not very fast.

I'm sorry that it has taken me so long to write to you. This has been a very difficult decision for me. I think Sarah's doing the right thing, but I can also imagine the pain that her parents must be feeling not knowing where she is or why she didn't go home. Please tell them that their daughter is okay; at least she was the last time I saw her two weeks ago.

I can't tell you my name, but I will tell you that I'm also American and my parents don't have any idea where I am. I could probably trust you, but I can't take that chance right now. All I will tell you about me is that I work in one of the shops where you came in asking about the girl. After you were gone my manager asked me if I knew anything about her and I said "No." That was a lie, but I don't feel bad about it. What I am telling you now is the truth. I promise.

If you want to possibly find her, here is what you do:

1. Call Hotel El Nuevo (you should have their number) and tell them who you are, that you received my letter, and that you are coming back down here.

2. They will know how to contact me, or leave a signal that I understand, telling me that you are coming back down.

3. Once I see that you are coming back down, I will leave a letter for you. Please follow the instructions very carefully.

That's all that I can tell you right now. Please don't try to play any games and try to trick me. If you want to find Sarah, you'll do what I've said – I don't mean this as a threat; I just have to be careful. You seem to be a smart man, so I think you'll understand.

Sarah's Friend

p.s. Please don't tell her parents about the specifics of this letter. They've been calling down here, and if they keep doing it, you might never be able to find her. I'm going to trust you on this one.

Stan had received lots of odd letters in the past, but this one topped them all. Was he supposed to trust this person or could it be just some kook playing games with him? He decided to think about it while he fixed an early dinner. He could call down to San José, but what would that tell him? Someone playing a joke on him could have it all set for the hotel to tell him everything that sounded legitimate. No, he would have to rely on his instincts, and right now his instincts were not convinced.

He put his dinner plate on a tray and took the tray outside to the patio. The fresh air was a welcome change from the stuffy court room. This letter had to show up just when he thought he was going to be able to relax for a while. *If it means finding Sarah, I'll do it.* He took one bite of his dinner and realized it might be his last home-cooked meal for a while. He opened up the letter again and re-read it to see if there were any clues he could find. The only clues were the scent of the paper and the printing; both appeared to be feminine, but it could be a guy doing it just to add further disguise. For now, however, Stan pictured the letter writer as a young female in a similar situation as Sarah. Even if he was wrong it helped him to assess the situation by having this picture in his mind.

Stan finished his dinner, put the dishes in the dishwasher, and started it even though it was only half full. He didn't want to have to think about starting it if he were leaving town soon. As he went to brush his teeth Stan started thinking about the person who sent him the letter. *Is she someone I saw down there? Is it possible I spoke with her even though she said it was her manager I spoke with? What's her situation?* He went back to the bedroom and pulled out his suitcase and started packing. He normally wouldn't pack until the client said "Yes," but he wanted to be ready to leave right away if the Johnsons wanted him to start back on the case.

After the suitcase was packed, he went to his office, sat down at the desk, and pulled the card for the hotel out of his briefcase. "Oh, hi, Miguel. This is Stan Walkorski."

"Yes, I'm fine. Thank you very much. How are you?"

"That's great. I just received a letter today, and it looks like it was written by a young woman who says she has some information about Sarah. Do you know anything about it?"

"Is that so? Okay, well I'm going to call the family to see if they want me to go back down to San José."

"I would try to get a flight tomorrow; is that a problem?"

"Miguel, you are very nice. That's okay if the same room isn't available; all the rooms that I've seen look great. I'll call you tomorrow if I'm not coming down. Okay?"

"Right. Thanks again, Miguel. Hasta mañana."

"You, too. Gracias."

Stan disconnected the line, picked up the card with the Johnsons' number on it, and pushed the Speaker button. The speaker blared the monotonous dial tone until he started dialing the Johnson's number.

Thirty/Treinta
Seattle – Redmond, Washington
That evening, May 9th

desesperado (dā·sĕs' pĕr·ă' dō) – desperate. *El hombre está hambriento y desesperado.* The man is hungry and desperate.

The phone started ringing as Robert and Tina were just walking through the kitchen toward the door to the garage. Robert kept walking, but Tina stopped. "Don't answer it," he said. "That's why we have an answering machine."

"But it might be an important call," his wife replied.

The phone rang again.

"Maybe important for them," he began, "but not for us. We have a dinner date. Let's go."

The phone rang for the third time.

"But," Tina started. "What if it's Sarah?"

"She wouldn't call on a Friday night; she knows we usually go out then."

And it rang for the fourth time.

Tina couldn't bear the thought that their daughter might be calling them and they just stood there and let the call go to the answering machine. She walked over to the counter and picked up the handset. "Hello?" she said with anticipation.

"Hello, Tina," Stan began. "This is Stan Walkorski calling. Did I catch you at a bad time?"

"No, of course not. Just a minute." She put her hand over the phone and whispered to her husband, "It's Stan; get on the other line."

"If Robert's there, he should hear this also." Stan then heard the faint click of a second phone being picked up.

"Hi Stan, it's Robert. How are you?"

"I'm quite well, thank you. Do you two have a few minutes to talk?"

"Sure," Robert replied.

"I just received a letter today from San José del Cabo, and I think we've just received that break we'd been waiting for."

"What kind of break?" Robert asked.

"There's someone down there who has some information about Sarah for me, but I have to go down there to get it," Stan replied.

"What all does the letter say?" Tina asked.

"Unfortunately, this person asked me, or should I say she told me, that I wasn't to reveal the contents of the letter to anyone."

"Why not?" Robert asked.

Stan hesitated a bit before he continued. "At the end of the letter she added a 'p.s.' that says, 'Please don't tell her parents about the specifics of this letter. They've been calling down here, and if they keep doing it, you might never be able to find her. I'm going to trust you on this one.'"

"Who's been calling down there?" Robert exclaimed in surprise. "Tina, have you been calling down there?" he questioned his wife over the phone.

Silence. Stan then heard one phone receiver being slammed down. The sound of loud footsteps got closer and closer to the other phone in the Johnsons' residence.

"But, Robert, she's our baby!" Tina cried out.

"And I told you not to call down there. Stan's the investigator, not you." Stan could hear Robert's voice as clearly as if he were the one holding the phone instead of Tina.

Robert took the phone from Tina and said, "Stan, are you at home?"

"Yes, I am."

"I'll call you back in a few minutes. Tina and I need to have a little discussion, and you really don't want to hear it. Sorry about that."

"That's okay, Robert. I'll be here."

"Call you in a little bit. Bye." Robert hung up the phone as Tina was crying, crying because she thought she was doing the right thing in trying to find their daughter.

"How many times have you called down there?" he yelled.

"She's our daughter; I just want to find her," Tina sobbed.

"That's not your job; that's why we hired Stan."

"But we still don't have our Sarah back."

"And did you hear what Stan said was in the letter – if you keep it up, we'll never find her. How come you won't listen to me?"

"Robert, I want to find her," Tina was crying in full force now. "I want her back here; I want her in my arms. Don't you understand that?"

"Yes, I understand that. But I also understand that Sarah's extremely bright and if she wants to stay hidden from us, I know she could do it. I want her back here, also. But if she doesn't want that, then we can't force her. Do you want <u>any</u> chance of ever seeing her again?"

"You know I do," she replied.

"Then you must promise me that you won't call down there ever again. Ever! Promise?"

"But, Robert," she began.

"No buts. It has to be that way. Whoever wrote that letter to Stan must know about Sarah, and this is probably our last chance to find out anything about her. Also, things work differently down there. If that person says we might never find her if you keep on calling, then listen up! Now, what's it going to be?" Robert was quite a bit harsher than he needed to be, but he had to make sure that Tina understood the seriousness. This could be their last hope of ever knowing anything more about Sarah or of ever seeing her again.

"I'm sorry," she wailed. "I just want to see our Sarah. Is that so wrong?" She grabbed another handful of tissues for her eyes and her nose. "Is that wrong?"

"No, that's not wrong," Robert said calmly as he went to his wife and put his right arm around her shoulders. "I want to see her, too," he said in a softer voice. "But we just have to do it the right way. We need to let Stan do it. Okay? Will you just let Stan do the work? If anyone can find her, he will. Trust me, he'll find her." He leaned down and pressed his right cheek to her left cheek; it was soaked with tears.

"Do you still love me?" she said as she tearfully looked at him.

"I've always loved you, and I'll never stop loving you," he said and then he kissed her lips.

Tina thrust her arms around her husband and held him tightly. She didn't want to let him go, both figuratively and literally.

Robert held on to the embrace as he knew she needed the comfort and support. "Let me call Stan so he can get back on the case," he whispered into her ear.

Tina reluctantly released her grip and let her arms fall loosely. "I love you," she said softly.

Robert gave her a reassuring kiss on the lips and then went into his home office to make the call – he wanted to allow Tina some quiet time alone.

Stan's phone began to ring. "Hello, this is Stan."

"Hi Stan, this is Robert. What should we do now?"

"I'd like to go back down to Los Cabos right away and follow up on the letter. I did call the hotel before I called you, and the Front Desk manager confirmed that someone who knew about Sarah had asked about me and wanted my address. He thinks it's genuine, and so do I."

"Okay, go ahead and go back down there. Stay for as long as you need to. Call me as soon as you find something or if you need us to come down there." Robert paused. "We trust you, Stan. We know that you have our best interests in mind. Tina says she's sorry for interfering, but hopes you'll understand."

"Thanks, and I do. I'll call you as soon as I know something. I know it might sound silly, but I want the two of you to focus on positive thoughts, okay?"

"And one more thing," Stan began. "Please get rid of that St. Jude statue on the front porch if it's still there. And I don't mean just move it to the garage – throw it away. As long as it's out there, you two will always think that finding Sarah is a lost cause."

There was a pause as Stan waited for Robert to respond, and he did.

"All right, thanks. I'll call you. Bye." Stan was looking forward to returning to San José – for a couple of reasons – as he hung up the phone. He took his Alaska Airlines Mileage Plan card out of his wallet, turned it over, and began to call the toll-free reservations number.

Thirty-uno/Treinta y uno
Seattle to San José del Cabo
Saturday, May 10th

interesante (ĭn·tĕr' ă·săn' tā) – interesting. *Este es un libro
interesante.* This is an interesting book.

The flight from Seattle's SEA-TAC Airport to Los Cabos was not quite
as enjoyable as the other two flights that Stan had taken. When he'd called
Alaska Airlines he naturally first inquired about the non-stop flight. The
reservations agent told him that there were only a few seats left on the flight,
and Stan joked that he wasn't overweight and so he just needed one seat. His
attempt at humor was not met with any return laughter. He then asked about
flights with one connection. There were plenty of seats on the LAX-SJD
flight, but the flight down to Los Angeles that would allow him to connect
to Los Cabos was sold out. His only choice was the almost-sold-out non-
stop flight. That's why he got middle seat 22B. *Did I need to be in such a
rush to get down there? Maybe I could have waited a day or two.*

But he knew he had to get there as quickly as possible. The letter he
was re-reading on the plane indicated a sense of urgency, one that he was
acknowledging by flying down there just as soon as he could, not when it
was more convenient. He typically would have more solid information when
he'd made such a quick decision, but his instincts told him that he wasn't
going to have any solid information on this case – he had to act now! He
pulled out his notes and then realized there were two reasons why he didn't
need to look at them: he knew it all by heart, and the person sitting in 22A
had eyes that were looking at everything Stan was reading. He put the notes
back in his briefcase and pulled the airline magazine out of the seatback
pocket in front of him, found the crossword puzzle, and began to work on it
in pen.

The clue to 18 Across was "Lady, in Spanish." *Señora; how hard is
that?* Stan wondered. That immediately struck him; he wondered what his
lady friend in Los Cabos was doing. The last time he spoke with her she was
still there; had she flown back to Seattle and not let him know of her return
to the States? That would be something if she was now in Seattle just as he
was heading back to San José. Everything had been in such a blur that he

didn't even think about trying to call her – either at her home in Seattle or at her brother's house in San José.

Leaning back in his seat, although it wouldn't go back very far, Stan closed his eyes and tried to envision what this mysterious letter writer looked like. What caused her to take a sudden interest in letting Sarah's parents know about her? What was her link with Sarah?

"Excuse me, please." Stan was rudely jerked from his reverie. The passenger in 22A, the one with the wandering eyes, wanted to get by. The beer that he drank had worked its way through his system.

Stan unbuckled his seat belt, and looked over to the lady in 22C, the aisle seat. "Excuse me. He needs to get out," Stan said.

"Sure," she said as she stepped out into the aisle. Stan followed her, and Stan was then followed by 22A. Stan stepped back toward his seat once the other fellow got by and headed to the back of the airplane.

"You might as well stay out here," said the lady in 22C. "You'll just have to get back out once he returns."

"You travel often, right?" Stan said.

"A little too much," she replied. "And you?"

"Not a whole lot. But when it pops up, it's quick with no notice." Stan noticed that she was well-dressed and her jewelry seemed to complement her clothing. "I like your earrings." Stan had learned a long time ago that a man earned more points by saying something nice about a woman's earrings than almost anything else he could say. "Are they from Cabo?"

"No," she replied. "Actually they're from Albuquerque; I was on a train trip and we stopped there for an hour. There were all sorts of vendors right there on the platform between the tracks; I saw these, and I really liked them."

"Well, they go nicely with your outfit," Stan said as he saw 22A returning.

"Oh, thanks," she said as she extended her right hand to him. "Sara," she said just as 22A got there. "But no 'h' at the end," she added.

Stan was stunned – the name Sarah had previously only meant the nineteen year-old he was trying to find. Now 'Sara' was also a lady sitting right next to him on the plane.

"Excuse me," 22A said as he approached Stan who was standing in his way to get into the row of seats.

"Sorry," Stan said as he took one step forward to let 22A into the row. Taking that one step forward also meant that Stan had moved one step closer to Sara who had not moved; her face developed a light smile – Stan noticed that.

"Do you know about how much more time we have?" Stan asked.

"An hour and a half or so," Sara replied.

Stan stepped back as he felt somewhat uncomfortable standing so close to her in such a public place; it didn't bother her at all. "Well then," he began. "My treat for a drink?"

"Sure," she said.

Stan looked around for the flight attendants who had somehow managed to disappear from view.

"They're sitting in the back reading magazines," 22A said, apparently overhearing Stan's conversation.

"Oh, thanks," Stan said, not overly excited that 22A knew what he was saying.

"No problem."

Stan hated that phrase. *What happened to 'You're Welcome'?* He tried to quickly obscure any thought of 22A from his brain as he turned back toward Sara. "What would you like?"

"A Bloody Mary would be great, thanks."

"I don't know your name," she then said in a much softer voice.

"I'm sorry; it's Stan. Nice to meet you," he whispered as he put his hand back out to her even though they'd exchanged a handshake just moments earlier. "I'll be right back," he said as he walked to the back of the plane to find the flight attendants.

A few minutes later Stan returned with two drinks in his hands. Sara stepped out into the aisle and held out her hands to hold the drinks while Stan sat down. He stepped in, pushed the seat belt connections to the sides of the seat, and sat down. He quickly lowered the tray from the seat back in front of him and held out his hands to take the drinks from Sara.

"Thanks," she said as she handed the drinks to him.

She sat down gracefully and lowered her tray table as a sign that she would keep her drink in front of her. Stan set her drink on her table, picked his up, and hoisted it in the manner of a drinking toast. "Cheers," he said softly.

"Cheers," she replied as she hoisted her drink and the two of them touched their plastic cups together, not that they made any noise.

Stan took a slow sip from his drink as his eyes stayed fixed on hers as she savored the flavor of the Bloody Mary. Her blue eyes seemed to sparkle as the reddish liquid flowed down her throat.

"Thank you," she said as she set her drink on the table.

"You're welcome," Stan replied. "Go to Cabo often?" he asked.

"No, it's my first time, a business trip."

"Gee, tough business trip, right?" Stan tried to find a soft approach to the conversation.

"I know it looks crazy, but I won't have any time to enjoy any of the beaches while I'm there. I was just looking over our schedule; we're booked solid every day we're there. We might as well have stayed in Seattle." She took a long sip of her drink.

"It is something, isn't it? People schedule business meetings in nice places, but they somehow forget to pencil in the time to enjoy the area. What are they thinking?"

"That assumes they're thinking," Sara retorted.

"That's true," Stan said. "Cheers."

"Cheers," she replied as she hoisted her almost-empty plastic cup.

"Where are you staying?" Stan asked.

"El Mirador, wherever that is. Do you know?"

"No, I haven't heard of it. This is only my third time down there. My guess is that it's somewhere along the Corridor between San José and Cabo."

"I thought we were going to Cabo," Sara said.

"That's what I thought my first time down there. The overall area is known as Los Cabos, and the two main towns are San José del Cabo and Cabo San Lucas. The first one is just known as San José and the other one as Cabo. It does make it easier once you've figured it out. Is there a shuttle or a hotel bus to pick you up at the airport?"

"There's supposed to be a car and a driver waiting for me; they'll have a sign with my name on it. How confusing is it to get through the airport?"

"It won't be a problem once you get through Customs. That's still a little backwards, but I'll help you through."

"Thanks," she said as she took her left hand and gave a little tap on Stan's right hand as it was resting on his tray table.

"You're welcome," he said somewhat awkwardly. "What does your company do?"

Sara pulled her left hand back as she replied, "We manufacture fittings for hoses and other garden items. Not all that glamorous, is it?"

"If you don't make them, then my flowers won't be happy," Stan said in his attempt to be humorous.

"No, we have several competitors out there, so you'll still be able to water your flowers."

She didn't get his humor.

"And what do you do," Stan started. "Are you the boss's secretary?"

"No, I'm corporate counsel for the company."

Oops!

"I'm sorry," Stan said. "I guess that was uncalled for."

"Don't worry about it; I'm used to it. I don't wear a sign that says 'I graduated Magna Cum Laude from Stanford Law School,' so I don't expect people to know what I do." Sara was extremely polite in her handling of a situation that is toxic for other people.

"I know, but I shouldn't have stereotyped you."

Just then – and she couldn't have come by any sooner to help Stan – one of the flight attendants stopped at row 22. "More drinks?"

"Sure," Sara said quickly.

Stan was planning to have only one drink, but he couldn't say 'No' now that Sara had already said 'Yes.' "Yes, please," he said as he reached for his wallet.

"My treat," Sara said. "Actually, my company's going to pay for these, so how about two for each of us?" she said as she handed the flight attendant two twenty-dollar bills.

"I'll be right back," the flight attendant said.

"And what do you do?" Sara asked Stan.

"I'm a private investigator," Stan replied in a soft voice as he knew that he wasn't much of a match for the lady to his right, and he didn't like to broadcast what he did too loudly.

"Are you on vacation or on a case?" she asked.

"Actually, counselor, I'd prefer not to answer that."

"Got it," she replied. "So what do you do for fun?"

Stan was about to come up with an answer when the flight attendant reappeared with their drinks – two for each of them. "Here's your change," she said as she set a stack of bills on Sara's tray table.

"Thank you," Sara said as the flight attendant continued moving toward the front of the cabin. "Cheers," she said as she lifted one of the cups that were on her tray.

"Cheers," Stan replied. He'd heard that there was a lot of partying that went on at law schools; perhaps what he'd heard was right. He took a sip of his new drink; it tasted strong.

Sara took a big gulp. She looked to her left and smiled at Stan; he forced a grin back at her. "You have a card?" she asked.

"Sure," he replied as he pulled out his wallet and opened it.

"Ladies and gentlemen, this is the captain speaking. We're about ninety-five miles from Los Cabos International Airport, and I'll be turning the seat belt sign back on in about ten minutes. So if you need to stretch your legs or use the facilities before we land, please do so now. Once the seat belt sign is turned on, you must stay in your seat for the remainder of the flight. Latest weather in Los Cabos is eighty-six degrees with light winds from the southwest. On behalf of all of us at Alaska Airlines I want to thank you for flying with us today, and I hope you have an enjoyable stay in Los Cabos."

"Excuse me," Stan said. "I'd better go back there now while I can."

"Sure," Sara said as she stepped out into the aisle. Other passengers were starting to get out of their seats, but row 22 was near the back of the plane, so its one advantage was being closer to the restrooms.

"Thanks," Stan said as he clumsily climbed out of his seat and into the aisle. He smiled at Sara and then turned to the back of the plane.

When Stan returned to row 22, Sara had already finished the first drink and was now working on the next one, her third of the flight. As she stood up to let Stan in, she grabbed his arm with her right hand to steady herself. "Sorry," she said. "It's a good drink. Maybe I'd better go back there, too."

"Good idea," Stan replied. "It'll take a while once we land to get through Customs." Stan watched her as she made her way to the restrooms, and he wasn't the only one who was watching her.

Stan sat back down in his seat and took another sip of his drink; he still had a full one left sitting on the tray table. *Even if nothing else comes of this trip, sitting in the middle seat was pretty good after all.* He buckled his seat belt in anticipation of the descent to the airport. He reached over to her seat and straightened the seat belt ends so Sara wouldn't be sitting on them when she returned.

"Oh, thanks," Sara said as she got to row 22 just as Stan had moved the belt ends.

"You're welcome. So, how long are you here?" he asked.

"My flight home's next Friday; what about you?"

"I don't know; it depends on how the case goes."

"Ah ha, so you <u>are</u> here on business," Sara said.

"Oops, you caught me," Stan said. "Yes, I am. Are you sure you don't have any free time in your schedule?"

"Let me see," she said as she bent over to pick up her satchel that was under the seat in front of her. As she sat back up, she pulled out a folder and opened it. "Oh, I forgot about this. We do have Monday morning free until after lunch."

Stan decided to take the lead. "There's a great little Art District in San José, and it's easy to walk through in an hour or two max. What would you say if I picked you up at nine, we walk through the Art District, have some lunch, and I'll get you back by one?"

"It's a deal," Sara said as she put her right hand out for Stan so they could shake on the 'deal.' "Here's my card so you can call me on my cell phone if something else comes up."

"Good, my number's on the card I gave you. Let me write down the name of your resort and its location and phone so I can find you on Monday morning." Stan pulled out his pocket notebook and wrote down the address of El Mirador Resort; its address was KM19 on the Carratera Transpeninsular. He was right; it was on the Corridor. He pulled out another of his cards and wrote 'Hotel El Nuevo' on it; he had to look up their phone number, and then he added that below the hotel name. "Here's another card with the name and phone for the hotel where I am staying in San José."

"Ladies and Gentlemen, this is the captain again. We've begun our descent into Los Cabos International Airport, and at this time you should be seated in your seats with your seat belts fastened." The seat belt light above each seat became lit as the captain made the announcement.

One of the flight attendants walked by as Sara was fastening her seat belt. "Just a couple more minutes and I'll have to pick up the drinks," she said in a less than pleasant tone.

"Bottoms up," Sara said as she raised her drink cup and slowly drank it all.

Stan picked up his second drink and took some sips, but he also paused between each one. He was glad that he hadn't planned on doing any work at the hotel. "Thanks again," he said as he set his cup down for the last time.

"You're welcome," Sara said. "Thanks for making the flight a whole lot more enjoyable. And I'm looking forward to going through the Art District on Monday. I've put it on my calendar so nothing else can interfere with it."

"The Art District has about fifteen to twenty galleries, and they're fun to go through. And each one has different types of art. They're not Seattle, New York, or San Francisco, but sometimes I like going through the smaller ones anyway. Oh," Stan started, "we have to fill out the Customs forms before we land." He moved his drink cup to the left side of his tray table and pulled out the forms from the seat back pocket in front of him.

Sara got her forms out and set them on her tray table where moisture from the drink cups had accumulated. "Shoot," she said. "Do they have extra forms?"

"They usually do," Stan said, "but don't worry. You can actually get them in the Customs hall; I'll help you when we get there."

"Thanks."

Stan completed his forms except for his passport information; it was in his briefcase, and he couldn't reach it right now with the tray table still opened.

The landing was smooth and they went out the rear door of the plane, joining the trail of people walking toward the Customs hall. Stan showed Sara where she could get new forms, and he stood there with her as she completed them. After they went through Customs and retrieved their luggage, Stan commented to her, "Now is the interesting part. You put your luggage on a belt for the X-Ray machine. Once it comes out, you push a button. If a green light appears, you are free to go. But if a red light appears, they'll search your bags."

"So what's the logic behind green light or red light?" she asked.

"None that I can tell," Stan replied.

"You're right; that is interesting. Let's hope for a green light."

The two of them continued to walk through as a couple; it seemed that no couples got the red light, only some of the singles. As they took their luggage to head out of the airport, Sara asked, "How are you getting to your hotel?"

"I just take a shuttle; it's only ten dollars." Stan said.

"Come with me," Sara said. "I'll just have the driver drop you off first."

"That's okay; you don't need to do that."

"I insist; after all, I bought the last round of drinks. I know there's no logic there, but this way I might be able to see a little more of the area. Okay?" she said as her eyes sparkled, either from the bright ceiling lights or from the Bloody Mary drinks.

They kept walking through the hall until they got outside. Sara scanned the array of drivers, and there were about fifty or sixty of them. She finally noticed one of them with a sign that said SARA SEIGEL. "There he is," she said as she headed off to her right. Stan followed in step with her. "Hi, I'm Sara Seigel," she said as she approached the driver.

"Welcome to Los Cabos. Is he also going to El Mirador?" the driver asked.

"Actually no. Can you drop him off at his hotel on the way?" Sara replied.

"What hotel?"

"Hotel El Nuevo in San José," Stan responded.

Twenty-five minutes later the driver slowed the car on Boulevard Mijares as he reached Hotel El Nuevo. "Here we are, señor, Hotel El Nuevo." There weren't any open parking spots, so he just stopped in the road; there was enough space for other cars to get by. The driver got out of the car, opened Stan's door and then went to the rear of the car to get Stan's bags out of the trunk.

Stan looked over at Sara. "I'll see you on Monday morning," he said.

"I'm looking forward to it," she said as she extended her right hand to Stan. They shook hands as she said, "See you on Monday."

"Bye," Stan said as he straightened up and swung his legs to the left to get out of the car door. He walked to the rear of the car just as the driver was closing the trunk; he had taken Stan's bags out and lifted up the handles.

"Here you are, señor," the driver said.

Stan then realized that he should give the driver a tip. He pulled his wallet out, opened it, and took out a hundred pesos bill and gave it to the driver. "Gracias."

"Thank you, señor," the driver said as he accepted the folded note and put it in his pocket. He checked the traffic and then returned to the car to take Sara to El Mirador.

As Stan walked past the car to the sidewalk, Sara opened her window. "Don't forget Monday," she said.

"It's on my calendar," he said to mirror her comment.

Sara smiled at him.

Just as Stan reached the sidewalk, Miguel came running out of the hotel toward him. "Welcome back, Señor Stan. It's good to see you. Here, let me take your bags," he said as he reached for the luggage handles.

"Thank you, Miguel. It's good to see you, too."

"The same lady who asked for your address said she would drop off a note for you in the morning," Miguel said excitedly as they entered the hotel lobby.

"Good. Maybe she has some new information," Stan replied as he walked with Miguel.

Thirty-two/Treinta y dos
San José del Cabo
Sunday, May 11th

sabor (să·bōr') – flavor. *Yo quiero el sabor del alimento.* I like the flavor of the food.

Waking up to the sound of an alarm clock was not something that Stan was fond of, especially on a Sunday morning, which was probably why it took him a couple pushes of the snooze button before he finally got up. He didn't set the alarm because of a pressing appointment that he had to get to; there wasn't a whole lot happening early on Sunday morning in Los Cabos. He'd set the alarm because he was expecting a note from the person who'd mailed that mysterious letter to him. He didn't think there would be any deadlines that to meet, but he still wanted to get up early just to get the note – that's if it was delivered as early as Miguel said it might be.

An envelope <u>had</u> been pushed under his door. *I wonder what time it got here.* It was a white square envelope just like the one he'd received in Seattle.

The alarm was set for seven-thirty, and he'd left the card for breakfast [*desayuno*] on his door asking for delivery at eight. He ordered a large pot of coffee, a fruit plate, and some pastries. He decided that he should lay off the Huevos Rancheros for a while (not that the pastries were free of calories). He grabbed the robe that was in the closet and put it on over his pajamas.

The alarm clock showed 7:58 when Stan heard the knock on the door. "Room Service," the server announced from the hall. Stan went to the door and opened it. "Buenos días, señor," the server said as the door was opened.

"Buenos días," Stan replied.

"Is the table okay, señor?" the server asked as he walked toward the round table near the windows.

"That's perfect," Stan said as he followed him – the smell of the coffee was enticing. *Maybe I'm beginning to see why coffee is such a hit in Seattle.* "The bill?" Stan said as the server turned and started to walk to the door.

"It's compliments of the hotel, señor. Thank you for coming back here."

"Thank you," Stan said as he then had to get his wallet to give the server the tip that he would've normally just written on the room charge.

"Gracias, señor," the server said as Stan handed him twenty pesos.

"De nada," Stan replied, anxious to get to his coffee <u>and</u> to the envelope. He held the door open as the server walked out and headed down the hall. Stan promptly but quietly closed the door.

He carried the envelope with him to the table near the windows and poured a cup of coffee. He sat down, took the knife from the tray and slit open the envelope. He noticed that it had the same distinctive smell as the one in Seattle. He took a slow sip of the robust coffee. *Okay, I'm ready now.*

May 10th

Dear Mr. Walkorski,

The man at your hotel made the appropriate sign to tell me that you were returning. I will be delivering this letter to the hotel on Sunday morning; I hope that is when you get it.

Here is what I want you to do. Go to one of the nearby shops and buy a solid blue shirt and a red baseball cap (if you don't have them with you). Then wear them as you go to La Playita bar at 6:30 tonight (Sunday) and order a strawberry margarita.

This is all I can tell you for now; you will receive more instructions from me later. Please follow these instructions carefully and do not do any more asking in town about Sarah.

Her Friend

He read the one-page letter again – *she is either quite a super spy or she's taking this secret stuff just a little too far.* But for now, she was the one with the information, and Stan had every intention of following her instructions exactly. The coffee in his cup had cooled down enough for him to take a big drink of it. Perhaps he needed something even stronger than coffee right now, but it was too early for that. He set the coffee cup down on the tray, looked at the letter and the envelope for any obvious signs of anything that would help him, and then he put them back down. He wouldn't be able to tell anything else about the envelope or the letter without the aid of some FBI-type equipment. That wasn't available so he was on his own, just as he had been in the very beginning of this case. And not a whole lot had changed in that regard.

The shops that sold caps and shirts wouldn't be open until ten o'clock at the earliest, so there wasn't much else to do but to relax, enjoy his breakfast, and then head out to the shops later. But even once he'd bought his shirt and cap, the letter instructed him to not do any more prying about Sarah. Was this "friend" of Sarah really going to know if he resumed his investigation after the three-month break from February to May? Stan thought about that for a moment as he ate some of the fruit and one of the pastries, washing them down with the coffee.

Stan thought that perhaps there was indeed an underground information network that would let her know if he started asking around about Sarah. But even if he were discreet enough on where he asked, did he really think that he would find out anything more than what he'd found out before – especially after an additional three months went by? He decided it was better if he played by her rules for a while. If nothing surfaced, then he would take charge and re-start the process on his own. But for now, she was in charge, although he certainly wouldn't tell that to anyone.

The one thing that he thought he could do without violating the letter's instructions would be to call Carmelita to re-connect with her; maybe she'd heard something, an unlikely scenario but still a possibility. He just assumed that she was still in San José; she was the last time he'd heard from her.

As Stan left his room and walked through the lobby, he stopped at the front desk; Miguel wasn't there, and he didn't know the person behind the desk. He figured he would ask anyway.

"Buenos días, señor. May I help you?" was the polite greeting he received.

"Yes, Buenos días. A note was left under my door this morning. Did you see the person who left it for me?"

"What is your name, señor?"

"Stan Walkorski."

"Sorry, señor. I didn't see the person who left it. I was away from my desk for a few minutes, and when I returned it was sitting right here," the man said as he pointed to a spot in the center of the counter.

"Do you remember what time that was?" Stan asked.

"Sí, señor. It was about four o'clock in the morning. It is usually very quiet at that time, so I remembered it because it was unusual. Is there anything wrong, señor?"

"Nothing wrong," Stan said. "I was," Stan cut himself off mid-sentence. There was no point in saying that he didn't know who the note was from. "Gracias, señor," Stan added as he walked out of the lobby, turned right to the plaza, and then left to the church.

Stan walked out of the church feeling as if he'd been to a foreign movie; he hadn't understood a single word that was said except for "Amen." No one had approached him to talk to him; the Padre hadn't even made any indication that the two had spoken several times just a few months ago. He was a young man; his memory couldn't be that bad. That told Stan that there had to be a link between the church and Sarah – *another piece of the puzzle.* How would he figure out what the connection was? And how would he do it without asking too many questions? That was the big mystery.

It wouldn't seem that hard to find a blue shirt and a red cap in a tourist town. But it took Stan almost two hours of walking from one shop to another; many of them were closed. He finally found them – in two separate shops – and took them back to the hotel.

"Hola. Any messages for me?" he asked as he approached the front desk. The same man was there.

"No, señor. No more messages for you."

"Gracias," Stan said as he continued walking to the stairs, and then up to his room. He put the shirt on a hanger and hung it on the shower rod as he ran hot water to steam some of the wrinkles out of the shirt. He turned the faucet off and closed the bathroom door. He set the cap on the bed and thought about heading out to the plaza to watch people; he wasn't quite hungry enough for lunch. He was about ready to walk out of the room when he remembered that he hadn't called Carmelita yet.

He wished Miguel were on duty because he would ask him to make the call. He'd called once before on his own; he could do it again. As Stan dialed her brother's number, he had mixed feelings. What seemed like a possible relationship had turned cold – whose fault was it? Did that even matter? In what seemed like a relief, no one answered the phone at her brother's house. *Oh well, at least I tried to call her.*

Thirty-three/Treinta y tres
San José del Cabo
That afternoon and evening – Sunday, May 11th

camisa (kă·mē'·să) – shirt. *¿Tiene usted una camisa azul?*
Do you have a blue shirt?

Walking back to the hotel after having lunch in the plaza, Stan remembered that he had to rent a car to be able to pick up Sara tomorrow morning. *I hope the rental car agency is open today.* He still thought it was quite odd that he would meet a 'Sara' as he was looking for Sarah. He wasn't a math major, but he figured that those odds must be pretty large.

Stan had to force himself to keep walking straight down Boulevard Mijares when he reached his hotel; his natural instinct was to turn left into the hotel lobby. But he did keep walking this time. The sidewalk was quite crowded with tourists going into the various shops as they made their way to the plaza. He felt more like a local now as this was his third time here, and he'd stayed at the same hotel each time.

"What do you think of this sombrero?" one of the tourists asked.

"Maybe with your next wife," was the reply from the woman who obviously didn't like her husband's taste in touristy headwear. Stan would've agreed agree with her; it was a bit too much. But then he thought that wearing his blue shirt and red cap tonight might also fit into that category.

He was relieved when he made it down to the Quality Rent-A-Car office. The door was closed, but the sign hanging in the window said ABIERTO. He was glad to know it was open. Stan opened the door and felt the blast of cold air – the door was closed because the air conditioner was running.

"Hello, señor. Please come in," was the greeting from the agent.

As Stan stepped toward the agent's desk, he saw that it was the same agent, Alfredo, who'd rented him the car back in January when he drove up to the Tropic of Cancer Monument. Stan didn't feel that there would be anything to gain by saying that he'd rented from him before; in fact, it would probably extend what he already anticipated to be a long process.

"Hi," Stan began. "I would like to rent a car for tomorrow morning."

After going through the same routine as he did in January, Stan finally had the keys in his hand. He wasn't planning to use the car today so he just left it right there in front of the office. It was probably safer there than parked by the hotel. He put the keys in his pocket and headed back to the hotel; he still had a few hours before he needed to head to La Playita bar. He had some time to relax.

And he did relax. He went to his room, closed the blinds, took off his shoes, and lay on the bed. Stan normally didn't take a nap, but it just seemed like the right thing to do today. He'd gotten up early, and there really wasn't anything more he had to do until about six o'clock – so why not take a nap?

Awakening refreshed, Stan picked up the letter and re-read it. He folded the letter a couple times and put it into this pocket; he just might need to have it with him. He was faced with a decision: when and where would he eat dinner? He would just have to see how things played out and then he would decide. He looked at the clock and saw that he saw that it was about time to head downstairs to get a taxi to the bar. He could drive the rental car, but he felt better by taking a taxi both ways.

The taxi driver was a friendly younger driver. Stan asked him what "La Playita" meant.

"*La Playa* means the beach in Spanish, and so La Playita means the little beach. But the bar La Playita isn't on a little beach, but it's a cute name for the bar." The taxi driver was definitely engaging.

"So if it's not on a little beach," Stan began, "where is it?"

"It's at the new marina," the driver said. "It's a great spot for young people to meet. Are you meeting someone there?"

Stan didn't know how to answer that question, or whether he should. "Yes," he said, knowing that any other answer could lead to more questions. "Is it easy to catch a taxi back from there?"

"Not really. You have to call for one because there aren't too many taxis that are just out there, especially on a Sunday evening." The driver paused. "I'll give you my card so you can just call me and I'll be right out there to pick you up. There's no extra charge."

"That's a good idea; thanks." Stan was happy to have an escape plan from the bar area.

"Here you are, sir," the driver said as he handed a card back to Stan.

Stan noticed that the taxi driver called him 'sir' instead of calling him 'señor.' His English was flawless and with only the smallest hint of an accent. "Where did you go to school?" Stan asked.

"I was raised in California by my aunt and uncle," the driver replied.

"Well, you had some very good teachers; your English is excellent."

"Thank you very much," he replied.

And so are his manners.

A few minutes later, at 6:26, the taxi pulled up in front of La Playita bar. The fare was one hundred pesos; Stan gave the driver a fifty pesos tip. That large of a tip should ensure that he would promptly respond to Stan's call tonight and in the future. "My name's Stan; here's my card," Stan said as he exited the taxi and handed his card to the driver.

"Thank you, Stan. My name is Felipe but you can call me Phil; that's what I went by in the States."

"Thanks, Phil. I'll probably be calling you pretty soon." Stan turned around, but he was not in a rush to enter the bar. He was a couple minutes early and he wanted to make sure that the letter writer had the opportunity to see him.

Once Phil left, Stan slowly walked into the bar; it was a nice place. He didn't want to look for the letter writer as she would obviously know who he was – the shirt and the cap were unmistakable. He took his time as he strolled to the bar; he wasn't in a big rush. It was quiet in the bar meaning that it was either too early for the action to begin, or there wasn't going to be any action on Sunday night.

"Can I bring you a drink?" he was asked as he sat on the tall bar stool.

"Sure, a margarita," Stan replied with some hesitation in his voice.

The bartender caught the hesitation. "Plain or flavored? We have mango, strawberry, or peach."

"How about a strawberry margarita, please," Stan said loud enough just in case the letter writer was listening.

"Sure."

Stan thought that his ordering the strawberry margarita might be the trigger for someone to come over to him. But it didn't happen. He was alone at the bar sitting there in his blue shirt and red cap, sipping his strawberry margarita. That picture would not be the picture of a manly man, but he didn't worry about that. He was doing what he was told to do – his main focus was finding Sarah. His appearance was immaterial. Stan looked at his watch just to make sure; it was now 6:35. He'd been sitting at the bar for five minutes now, and nothing had happened.

He finished his drink – again, nothing happened. He ordered another margarita, but this one was a regular one, not strawberry. He also asked to see the menu. *I might as well eat since I'm already out.* The shrimp scampi were good, and the regular margarita was a lot better tasting than the strawberry one.

Stan looked at his watch again; it was 7:25. He was sent out to La Playita either as a prank, or the letter writer had some other purpose in mind. Whatever the reason was, he'd had enough for the evening. He pulled Phil's card out of his pocket, and asked the bartender to call him. "He'll be here in about ten minutes."

"Thanks," Stan said as the bartender returned Phil's card.

Phil arrived at the bar in eight minutes; Stan was impressed.

Thirty-four/Treinta y cuatro
San José del Cabo
Monday, May 12th

cena (cē'·nǎ) – dinner. *¿Qué debo comer para la cena?*
What should I eat for dinner?

Stan was awake before the alarm went off, but he didn't get out of bed. It was 6:47, and he typically didn't get up that early at home. But he had to get up, shave, shower, eat breakfast, and leave the hotel by 8:30 since he was picking up Sara at 9:00. He'd set the alarm for 7:00 last night and he wasn't going to switch off the alarm now just in case he fell asleep again.

It was still somewhat dark outside and there wasn't much traffic on Boulevard Mijares yet. He sat up in bed and saw the red cap on the dresser, reminding him of last night's wasted adventure. Was he foolish to follow the instructions in the letters he'd received? That was the first time that he'd ever gotten letters like that. What should he do now? That question was swirling around in his head as he lumbered out of bed to take a shower. He saw something on the floor as he headed toward the bathroom; it was an envelope just like the previous ones he'd received. He picked it up and went to the desk and sat down. He opened the envelope and pulled out two pages.

May 12th

Dear Mr. Walkorski,

Thank you for following my instructions last night. You are very prompt, and I'm sure that your clients appreciate that trait. I hope that you enjoyed your meal at La Playita. You might not know it, but I <u>did</u> see you.

Please don't think that I'm playing games with you; I'm not doing that at all. I asked you to wear the blue shirt and red cap, and go to the bar at 6:30 because I wanted to make sure that you were sincere about finding out more information about Sarah. Because of what you did last night, I know that you are sincere.

Here is what I want you to do today; again, please don't question or try to second guess me. I want you to buy a yellow cap and a green shirt. The pants don't matter, but I'm guessing that you have a khaki pair with you; those would be nice. You are going to another restaurant tonight, and you are going to follow a specific path to get there. Remember, I have my reasons. Here is the path <u>and</u> the time you are to be at certain places. I have timed the walk, so I know how long it should take you.

—   6:15 – leave your hotel and walk on Blvd Mijares to Calle Coronado, then go to the intersection of Calle Coronado and Calle Hidalgo.

—   6:25 – leave the intersection of Coronado and Hidalgo and go right (north) to Manuel Doblado; turn left and go one block to Morelos.

—   6:35 – leave that intersection and go right (north) to Zaragoza, turn right and head toward the plaza; turn left at Hidalgo and pass between the church and the plaza, stopping at Obregon.

—   6:50 go left (west) on Obregon one block to El Armario at the corner of Obregon and Morelos; turn right and go to Baja Brewing Company – that's where you will have dinner (don't worry, it's good there). You should arrive there by 7:00.

It's very important that you follow these instructions carefully, especially paying attention to the times. Thank you for caring about Sarah.

Her Friend

Stan showered, dressed, and then walked out the door heading downstairs for breakfast. Perhaps Miguel had seen her when she left the envelope for him; he hadn't. She had once again entered the lobby without anyone seeing her. *Maybe I should hire her to work for me.* Stan was really baffled – why was she going through so much effort to help him without just telling him what he needed to know? The only conclusion Stan could come to was that she wanted to help him find Sarah, but there was some reason why she had to be secretive about it; *that's why the outfits, the maze, and the times for tonight.*

Stan needed to relax so that he could enjoy the few hours he was going to have with Sara. He didn't know where this outing would lead, or if he would see her again – but he knew that he wanted to make the best of the time they did have together. *I'm going to think nothing more about these crazy clothes and times until after one o'clock.* Stan was getting stressed, something he normally didn't do. He closed his eyes and exhaled a big breath.

His eyes were still closed when he smelled the delicious breakfast that was being placed in front of him. He opened his eyes as he saw the waiter walking away from his table. Stan thought again of Sarah – she had so much, why would she give it up? What was she looking for or going after? Maybe he'd find that out tonight. For now, he was going to enjoy his breakfast; it smelled good and he knew it was going to taste great.

After breakfast, Stan went back up to his room. He'd told himself that he wasn't going to re-read the letter or think about it until the afternoon, but he just couldn't get it out of his mind. Why did she want him to go on this meandering route? He knew where the restaurant was; he'd seen it while going through the Art District. The restaurant itself couldn't be the most important part of the maze. If it were, she could just say 'Be at Baja Brewing Company at 7 PM.' There was more to it than that. There had to be; it couldn't be anything else. Or was there something that he just wasn't seeing?

Stan looked at his watch; it was 8:20. He needed to get going to make sure he was at El Mirador by 9:00. He didn't know how prompt Sara was, but he wasn't going to be late. He picked up the rental agreement and the car keys off the night stand and headed out of the room. The alarm clock showed 8:21.

As he walked down the stairs, Stan started to think of the possible problems: the car could've been stolen; a tire might be slashed; someone could've siphoned all the gas out of it. Stan was working himself into such a frenzy that he didn't even hear Miguel wish him a "Good Day" as he walked through the lobby. He caught himself wanting to turn right at the sidewalk. No, the car rental is to the left, about a block and a half south of the hotel.

The car was there, parked in front of Quality Rent-a-Car, just as it was yesterday when he rented it from Alfredo. He put the key into the door lock and unlocked it. He got in and started the engine. He was relieved to hear its sound; it wasn't the quietest of engines, but it was running. Stan put the car into Reverse and backed out onto the quiet street. He headed up to Manuel Doblado, turned left and drove to Federal Highway 1. When the light turned green, he made a left turn – he was on his way to the Corridor, and to Sara.

Thirty-five/Treinta y cinco
San José del Cabo Art District
Monday, May 12th

edificio (ĕ·dĭ·fĭ·sē·ō) – building. *Veo el edificio.* I see the building.

Stan arrived at El Mirador faster than he thought he would; once again he'd forgotten about the conversion from kilometers to miles, so he didn't have as far to go as he thought. Oh well, *it's better to be early than late.* As he made the left turn at Kilometer 19, he saw that the long entrance road went through a massive array of flowering cacti. Arriving at the main entrance, he saw Sara standing near the bell stand. He slowed the car as she waved to him. He pulled over, and the bellman opened the car door as Stan stopped.

"Hi," she said as she got in the car. "I see you found the place."

"Good morning," Stan said as he was really happy to see someone he knew. "The places along here have an easy address – yours is Kilometer 19, and they're marked on the road. Well, how's it been so far?"

"Company business, what else can I say?"

"Oh, yeah. I forgot." Stan waited for Sara to buckle her seatbelt before he pulled away from the curb.

"How's it going with you?" she asked excitedly.

"Let's not go there," Stan replied. "I feel as if I'm being led on some wild goose chase. I have to buy certain color shirts and caps, and be at a certain restaurant at a given time. Tonight's the last night I'll put up with that it. Have they at least been serving you some good food?" Stan really did want to change the subject; it wasn't just a matter of being nice.

"The food's fine, but I work with these people everyday. I'd rather be eating with someone I would <u>like</u> to be with, not someone I <u>have</u> to be with."

Stan took that remark to be a positive statement about the time – short, though – that the two of them would have together today. "Did you have breakfast?" he asked.

"Yes, I ordered room service; at least I was able to eat in the peace and quiet of my own room. It was nice, plus I didn't have to put on my makeup and everything before going downstairs. That can be a real hassle."

"Well, how are the rooms? It looks like a nice place." Stan was sincere about that; the entrance to the resort gave the indication of being a top-notch place. "I guess if you have to be somewhere for a business meeting, you might as well be at a nice resort along the tip of Baja California."

"Oh it's a nice place, but as you say; it's still work. And work is a four-letter word." Sara was cordial, but it was clear that she didn't want to talk about work; that was definitely okay with Stan.

"Well, we have a little extra time because the art galleries don't start opening until about ten, some maybe a little later. And it didn't take me as long to get here as I thought it might." Stan didn't mind having some extra time with Sara, but he was a little uncomfortable because he'd planned to go right from the resort to the Art District in San José. It was like asking someone out for a first date and not knowing where to go or what to do. "Is there someplace you'd like to go or see?"

"Nothing in particular; all of us are going into Cabo San Lucas tomorrow night, so I guess I'll see whatever is there then. Is there anything else to see in San José?" Sara was clearly tossing both the responsibility to Stan as well as the choice of what to do.

"Okay, I've got an idea," he said as they were heading back through the rows of cactus lining the road back to the main highway. "Let's head back to San José and then go along the beach area at Playa Azul; we might even see some surfers there."

"That sounds good to me. I didn't know there'd be any surfing along this area; I thought the only surfing was on the Pacific Ocean side."

"That does seem logical, but the waves and the undertow are actually too strong along the Pacific side down in Cabo to do any surfing. The local joke is that if you go in the water on the Pacific side, the undertow is so strong that you'll come back out in Japan." Stan's attempt at humor didn't draw a response.

"Being from California, I just remember the surf contests in Southern California."

"I'm sure there are some good surf beaches in Baja; just not too many of them here at the tip." Stan turned right when he reached the highway.

Traffic seemed a little light for Monday morning. "I'm surprised that there's not more traffic, although I'm not complaining."

"Do you think that it could be because yesterday was Mother's Day, or at least it was in the States? I don't know if they celebrate it down here on the same day as we do."

"Oh, no. I forgot all about Mother's Day. I'd better call Mom tonight. But in Mexico they celebrate Mother's Day on May 10th - it's always on May 10th, unlike the way we do it on the second Sunday in May. The light traffic could be because of that; that would just be one more thing I haven't figured out yet down here."

Sara seized the opportunity. "So what have you figured out down here? I can't imagine that the resort I'm at is all that typical."

"Probably not," Stan began as he eased the car up to speed. "It's no secret that Mexico isn't one of the wealthiest nations, although there are certainly some very rich people. I would say that the one thing I have found that is so opposite the stereotype is how industrious the people are. The standard work week is six days, and the work day is not just eight to five. Many of them work ten hours, maybe even twelve hours a day. And everyone always seems so friendly; I think they truly appreciate tourists and they want you to feel welcomed and comfortable. I might not want to come stumbling out of the bars at 2 AM, but otherwise it's a nice place."

As they continued the short drive to San José, Stan pointed out a few of the other resorts and other highlights along the way. He didn't want to bore Sara, but they didn't really know each other all that well, and he felt a little uncomfortable with the silence. Stan slowed down and turned into an overlook just past The One and Only Palmilla Resort. "There's a great view here," he said as he found a place to park.

He got out of the car and walked over to the passenger side and opened the door for Sara. "Thank you," she said as she extended her right hand to him as a gesture to help her step out of the car.

Stan clasped her hand with his left hand and she got out of the car. "You're welcome," he replied as he then released her hand. He didn't want to assume that her gesture meant any more than a courteous way of getting out.

"It _is_ pretty," Sara said as she walked to the guardrail at the edge of a steep drop-off to the water below.

"It sure is," Stan agreed. "I can see why so many people want to buy timeshares down here. Just look at those waves; and the water is so blue, it almost makes you want to jump in it." Stan just stood and looked out at the water; it was entrancing.

"Seattle is nice, but there certainly isn't anything like this up there, is there?"

"No," Stan replied. "And it's nice like this even when we're in the middle of winter up there."

"So you've been here in the winter?" Sara asked.

"Yes, I was down here in January and early February. It wasn't as warm as it is now, but the weather was still very nice. It was mid-seventies – sure beat the heck out of the thirties, forties, and the rain we were having up there."

"Give me a call the next time you're coming down here in the winter and I just might come down here with you," Sara said.

"I just might call you, so have your shorts and sandals ready," Stan replied to see what her reaction would be.

"It's a deal," she said as she put out her right hand.

"Deal," Stan replied as he shook her hand and continued to hold on to it. He looked into her eyes and saw 'happiness.'

Sara's lips pursed upwards into a grin, she squeezed his hand, and then she gently pulled it back. "So what's this case you're working on? Is it something you can tell me about, or is it a top secret deal?"

Stan paused; the question took him by surprise. "Believe it or not, I'm trying to find a missing girl by the name of Sarah – how odd is that? But she spells her name with an 'h' at the end. When you told me your name was Sara, I was a little surprised and I wondered if there was something mysterious going on."

As they stood near the edge and listened to the waves crashing against the rocks below, Stan told Sara the whole story.

"Wow, that is strange," Sara said. "I bet her parents are really hurting."

"They are, especially her mom. Sarah's their only child, and so she's really feeling an emptiness with Sarah being missing."

"And what were you saying about having to buy shirts and caps and go to some restaurant. What's that all about?" Lawyer Sara was getting more and more interested in the details.

"I'd run out of leads that led to anything productive, so I went back to Seattle. Then last week I received this letter from someone down here saying that she knew I was looking for Sarah." Stan then filled her in on the specifics of the first letter as well as some highlights of the ones that had been slipped under his hotel door.

"Why do you assume it's a female sending you these notes?"

"The handwriting, although it's actually printing, look's female, and just the way they're written. You're right, it could be a guy, but I don't think so. Plus a manager at the hotel referred to a young lady when I checked in the other day."

"I'll go along with that. What does she have you doing tonight?" Sara asked.

Stan gave her the details of the maze he was to go through, as well as the requirement to be at specific spots at certain times.

Sara shook her head in amazement. "You're definitely dealing with one smart cookie. I'd like to find her and arrange an interview at Stanford for her. She knows what she's doing, and she's being very careful about it. I think her biggest concern is trust, but I'm guessing that you've earned that by now." Sara stopped to see Stan's reaction – he was just looking at her and waiting to hear more. "You're right about going in a roundabout manner to get to a certain restaurant at a given time. It's not the restaurant; it's something that you will see along the way or as you get there."

"I believe you're right, Counselor," Stan said as he just stared at Sara. "But why wouldn't she just say, *'Be at this place at this time'?*" That was the question that was really bugging Stan.

"Come on, Stan. You know that women don't want to make it easy for men. Part of her pleasure is to make you suffer through the agony of trying to figure it all out. Have you ever had the solution to any case just handed to you – all wrapped up with a bow on top?"

"No," was Stan's simple reply.

"And so you think that a complete stranger is going to be the first one to do it for you?" Sara was demonstrating her logic and courtroom prowess, but not in a mean way.

"I know you're right, but I just want the answers!" Stan exclaimed. Others around them at the lookout point looked over at them as if they were a couple who were having an argument.

"You know better than that, Stan," Sara said in a beautiful soft voice. "You'll find her; I just wish I could go with you tonight, but I can't."

"And if she saw you with me that might mess things up." Stan had missed the subtle point in Sara's statement.

"Just take it easy; you know it'll work out." Sara looked at her watch. "Should we start heading to the galleries?"

Stan looked at his watch. "Sure, let's go," he replied. They walked hand-in-hand to the car, and when they got there Stan squeezed her hand and let it go. "Thanks," he said.

"For what?"

"For lots of things, but especially right now for forcing me to see this clearly. I really want to find Sarah; not just to close the case, but primarily for her parents."

"You will," Sara said as she put her right hand up to his left cheek and gave it a gentle stroke. "You'll find her. The reason she ran away might not be what you think or her parents think, but you'll find her." Sara's words were reassuring to Stan.

Stan didn't say anything but he slowly nodded his head in agreement with what Sara had said. He'd always felt that way, but aside from the Johnsons, he didn't have anyone else to share those thoughts with. And the Johnsons, of course, had more of a vested interest in the case than did Sara.

They rode in silence for a few minutes as they got back on the highway and continued to San José. The silence this time, however, was much more comfortable than the earlier drive. The time and their conversation at the lookout point had created a connection between the two of them, so talking wasn't necessary right now.

Once they got into San José, Stan took the same route that her driver had taken when he'd dropped Stan off at his hotel; Stan did this for her familiarity and so he could tell Sara a little about the area. "There's my hotel on the right," he said as they headed north on Boulevard Mijares approaching the plaza.

"No cactus and palm trees in front, I see," Sara said somewhat facetiously, but with a wry smile on her face.

"No," Stan replied in a matching voice. "I'm on an expense account. And I also don't have a view of the water out my window unless you want to count the water tank on top of building next door." He knew Sara was kidding – he was never one to be concerned about staying at fancy resorts. He liked them, but it didn't bother him to stay at a regular hotel.

As they turned left on Manuel Doblado, Stan pointed to the plaza. "That's the main plaza in town; it's called Plaza Mijares, the same Mijares as the boulevard we were just on. I haven't figured out a whole lot about him, but obviously he was an important figure in the establishment of the area. If we have time, we'll walk through the plaza; maybe they'll have the dancing waters on in the fountains."

Stan went three blocks and turned right on Calle Vicente Guerrero. "Hey, we're lucky; here's a parking spot and we're right at the edge of the Art District. Are you ready to walk?"

"I sure am; let's go," Sara said with a spark in her voice. She got out of the car before Stan could get to her side.

Stan had his Art District brochure with him, which he handed to Sara as they started walking. "Let's turn here," he said at Calle Ignacio Zaragoza. "We'll go counter-clockwise around the area, and that way we'll end up back here at the car." As they approached the plaza, Sara noticed the church on the left.

"Do we have time to go in there?" she asked.

"Sure, let's go up these stairs here," he said pointing to a small set of stairs along Zaragoza near the rear of the church. They crossed the street and walked up to the area around the church. "I met the padre and we had a couple discussions about Sarah. I think he knows something about her, but he just won't tell me.

"Well, that's a tough one and it doesn't surprise me," Sara said. "I don't know how it is down here, but the privacy in churches in the States is pretty huge. Some of it is good, of course, but then there are so many other things that go on that you wish you could find out more information about them."

"I know; it's somewhat of a Catch-22 at times, isn't it?"

"Most definitely," she replied. "What would you say about getting on with the art tour?"

"I'd say it's a good idea," Stan said. "That corner," Stan began as he looked back to the corner of Zaragoza and Hidalgo, "is essentially the southwest corner of the four-square block area of the Art District. La Dolce Art Gallery right over there," Stan was now pointing over to the northern edge of Plaza Mijares, "is also part of the Art District, and I'm sure that the district's boundaries will expand as more and more galleries flourish."

"I don't see a gallery over there," Sara said in reference to La Dolce. "I see La Dolce Restaurante, but I don't see the gallery."

"That one's a bit tricky. You do have to go in through the restaurant to get to the art gallery. But be careful, the smells coming from the food are heavenly. You might forget about the art and just want to sit down to eat." Stan was familiar enough with the area that he was beginning to sound like a tour guide.

"Speaking of food, are we still on for lunch?"

"Of course," Stan replied. "You don't think I'd promise it and then back out on my promise, do you?" Stan tried to sound hurt, but he wasn't terribly convincing.

"Just checking," Sara said as she ignored Stan's pitiful attempt for seeking pity.

They continued walking north to the next street, Obregon, the east-west bisector of the Art District. "There are a couple galleries on the next street down there," Stan said in reference to Arte-Plaza Paulina and the Frank Arnold Gallery on Comonfort. "We'll get over to them from the next street up if we have time. But let's turn here," he said as they turned left onto Obregon.

"So are we going to go into any art galleries or are you just going to tell me where they are? I'm beginning to think you just tricked me into leaving that wonderful time I was having with all the people I see every day of the week." Sara's sarcasm was quite thick and it was definitely not lost on Stan.

"Okay," Stan began with his attempt to be equally sarcastic. "You caught me. The truth is that your boss arranged for me to sit in the seat next to you on the plane, plan this entire charade, and get you away from the resort – he did all of that just so you would get a break from work. And because he is such a nice and caring guy, he's even paying for lunch."

"I might have believed it," Sara began, "but not the lunch. He's too cheap for that."

"Okay, that was all a lie," Stan said as they continued to walk. "Across the street is a gallery with some really great stuff; it's Shona Art from Zimbabwe."

"I think I've actually heard of that. Isn't that where they sculpt stone and then put the piece into a fire?"

"That's what I know of it," Stan replied. "Not only are the pieces somewhat amazing, the story of the Shona artists is also. Plus part of the proceeds is used to help combat malaria."

"Let's go take a look," Sara said.

"Okay," Stan said. "But we have to keep track of the time. I don't want my car to turn into a pumpkin if I don't get you back on time. AND, we have to find a place for lunch."

"I know," Sara replied. She was enjoying the day even though it was the first art gallery they'd been in. She wished she could spend the whole day strolling along the streets and going through the galleries. Of course it would be more fun; it wasn't work.

From there they went next door to the Arenas Gallery, across the street to another one, and then up to the corner. Sara commented on the 'Distrito del Arte' billboard above the second story apartment. "I like the sign up there," she said. "The sign itself has kind of an artsy look to it," she continued. Then she added, "Aren't we in the middle of the Art District? Wouldn't it be better to have the sign at the most prominent corner?"

"I'm not a marketing genius," Stan said. "But I think it's in the middle of the Art District for that very reason – we are standing right in the middle of the district."

"That makes sense. And don't worry; I didn't major in Marketing either." Sara thought about Stan's answer and realized that it did make sense. "That place looks cute; do we have time to go in?"

"Of course we can go in," Stan said. So they went into El Aramario, named "The Cutest Shop in Town." One step in the store showed why it had that name – it was cute, and so was the merchandise. No other description could apply.

"I just love this stuff," Sara said quietly to Stan. She was looking at a table of brightly colored wooden animals. "I used to collect turtles when I was a little girl; I've got to have this one," she said as she picked up a turtle that had about five different colors on it. "How much is this?" Sara asked as the owner came over.

"Fifteen dollars," came the reply.

"Cuánto cuesta en pesos?" [How much does it cost in pesos?] Stan asked.

"Cien pesos, señor." [One hundred pesos, sir.] was the reply.

"Gracias," Stan said to the shop owner. He opened his wallet and pulled out a red one hundred pesos bill and handed it to her.

The shop owner took the note and the turtle and walked over to the counter. She carefully wrapped the turtle in white tissue paper, applied a piece of tape, and put it all into a small bag. She then wrote a proper receipt and handed that to Stan. "Muchas gracias, señor," she said in Spanish although her English was likewise excellent.

"De nada," Stan replied; his Spanish was limited, but getting better all the time.

Stan and Sara walked out the door, turned right, and then turned right again to continue their way up Obregon. Half way up the block they came to Galleria Cruz. Sara looked at Stan and he nodded 'yes.' As they walked into the spacious gallery, a sandwich board sign standing on the floor caught Sara's eyes. She grabbed Stan's arm. "Look," she said. "They're going to have a Russian art exhibit here from the fifteenth to the thirtieth."

"Really? How'd you figure that?"

"The sign; it says Драгоценности Царей, which translates to Jewels of the Czars. And you can probably recognize the dates – 15 мая до 30 мая. That says 15 May to 30 May."

Stan was impressed on the plane when she said she'd graduated Magna Cum Laude from Stanford Law School. But he would have never thought that she spoke Russian. "You obviously speak Russian?" he asked.

"'Asked and answered' is how they say that in court. But yes, I do speak Russian, which is said as Я говорю на русскй."

"Are you fluent in it?" Stan asked.

"Yes, I have actually worked as a translator for some big-name companies."

"Maybe I'll give you a call the next time I need a Russian translator," Stan said.

"That's two now," Sara said. "You're going to call me the next time you come back down here, and you're also going to call me when you need help with Russian. I suppose you say those lines to all the ladies?"

"First of all," Stan started, "there are no other ladies. Second, if there were any other ladies, none of them could possibly match your charms and intelligence. And finally, you wouldn't be jealous, would you?"

"Well, obviously there's nothing to be jealous about since you just said there aren't any others. Gee, Stan, you don't get out much do you?"

Ouch, that one hurt.

"No, I don't. I work too much, but I sure would like to change that bad habit. Since we're getting personal now, what about you? Dating? Seeing someone?"

"The only guy I ever see, besides my Dad, is my computer," she answered.

"You call your computer a guy?"

"Sure, why not? The stupid thing is slow and it stops working whenever it feels like it. You think I would call it a woman?"

"No, I don't think you would," Stan agreed.

Sara picked up a flyer about the Russian art exhibition and showed it to Stan. "Want to come back here for this?"

"Sure, why not?" Stan answered, mimicking Sara's earlier response.

"Okay, let's go see some more," she said as she grabbed Stan's elbow.

"We've got to get moving," Stan said as he looked at the watch on his left arm. "We can visit one or maybe two more, and then we have to grab some lunch."

"Well then, which ones do you suggest?"

"Around the corner up there are two nice ones, and then we're close to the car."

They walked up the street to Vicente Guerrero, the same street that the car was parked on, and turned left. They first went into Galeria de Ida Victoria, and then they went next door to Casa Don Pablo. Sara resisted the temptation to buy something in Casa Don Pablo; she really liked some of the plates that looked like Pablo Picasso pieces. "Maybe next time," she said.

Stan looked at his watch and realized they didn't have enough time for a sit-down lunch if he was going to get Sara back to the resort by one o'clock. He was lucky; he saw a small food stand on the other side of the road. "Shall we?" he said as her grabbed her hand to take her across the street.

"You really are on an expense account," Sara said as she saw where she was being taken for lunch.

"We're out of time for much else. If I get you back late, your boss might not pay me for treating you to such a great time."

"I've enjoyed it. I never expected to see Shona Art here; I got a great little turtle to add to my collection, plus I can't wait to see the Russian exhibition. This is a great day. Thanks," she said as she leaned in and gave Stan a kiss on the cheek.

"You're welcome," he said. "What would you like for lunch?" They didn't have much of a selection to choose from, but they enjoyed the garlic-ladened shrimp tacos. "I'm sorry I forgot the breath mints," Stan said as they finished eating.

"That's okay," Sara said. "I'm not planning to kiss any of them when I get back." She paused and then added, "But your breath is just like mine."

They went to the car and Stan drove Sara back to El Mirador. Before she got out of the car, she undid her seatbelt, leaned to her left and gave Stan a big warm kiss – on the lips, garlic smell and all.

Thirty-six/Treinta y seis
San José del Cabo
That evening – Monday, May 12th

menú (mĕ·nū') – menu. *¿Me permite un menú por favor?*
May I please have a menu?

As he drove back into town after dropping Sara off at El Mirador – they were even a couple minutes early; she walked into her lobby at 12:58 – Stan wasn't sure what to think. He didn't think that she was trying to come on to him. She was obviously a highly educated person who wouldn't have to be subtle or coy about her intentions. *Maybe the kiss was just her very friendly of saying 'Thank you' for a great time together.* Stan wasn't going to worry about it; he certainly had enough to think about with what he had to do this evening – dress in yellow and green and follow a pre-defined path with specific time requirements. *This has to be the last time I follow her instructions.*

He wasn't going to worry about it, but he did enjoy thinking about the kiss. Sure, they'd held hands a couple of times, but it was mostly out of convenience or his leading the way. He didn't think there was any romance going on, although he wouldn't say 'No' to its possibility. They were going to try to get together later in the week for the Russian art exhibition; he'd see then how things were going to go between them.

Stan returned the car to the agency, and he went to the plaza to sit and do some people watching. The sun was warm, and it was nice to just sit and relax. He tried to block out his dislike for what he had to do that evening, but he couldn't. And he also found that he couldn't relax, so he went back to the hotel.

He was dressed and ready to go by six o'clock, but his instructions were for him to leave the hotel at a quarter past six. Stan was antsy; he wanted to get going. He was also getting hungry; *there better be some really good food at that restaurant.* Stan looked over the letters again even though he knew he wouldn't find anything new in them

6:10 – he could now leave the hotel. He was wearing his new green shirt plus the khaki pants he'd brought on the trip. He picked up his instructions, grabbed the yellow hat, and walked out of his room to go down the stairs and out the lobby. Five minutes would be plenty of time.

6:15 – Stan put on the yellow cap and walked out of the hotel lobby. He was tempted to look around to see if he could spot anyone he'd seen previously; would he be able to find a clue as to who the letter sender was? He didn't see anyone that he thought could be that person. He turned right and walked up to Calle Coronado and turned left. He was now walking against the one-way traffic, but he stayed on the sidewalk for the one-block trek to Calle Hidalgo. He looked at his watch; he had a few minutes to spare. That gave him an idea of the pace he needed.

6:25 – He left the intersection of Coronado and Hidalgo and walked the two short blocks north to Manuel Doblado. Now that he knew the pace, he did look around a little as he was walking. He tried to make it look casual but he wasn't on one of the main shopping streets so there weren't many store windows to look into. Stan saw a few people but they looked as if they belonged there; none of them looked like the letter writer. He turned left on Manuel Doblado, walked one block to Morelos, and then stopped at that corner. He checked his watch again; he could slow his pace even a little more if he wanted to.

6:35 – Stan started walking on Morelos toward Zaragoza and the Art District. He noticed that a few of the people looked at him in a slightly different way. *I'm sure the yellow cap and green shirt make me look a little odd.* He kept going; he was determined to follow through with all of the instructions. He saw the place where he'd parked the car that morning as he and Sara started out on their tour of the Art District. That thought brought back the pleasant memory of her departing kiss; how sweet that was, garlic and all. He kept walking, turned right on Zaragoza, and walked down the gentle slope toward the plaza. As he turned left on Hidalgo, he was once again walking against the traffic, but the sidewalk next to the church was quite wide. As he reached the steps leading up to the church he heard youthful laughter coming from the alleyway that led back to the Padre's office. As he reached that narrow alley, that laughter became clearer. He looked to the left and saw a small group of young women walking around in some rhythmic pattern. He didn't pay much attention to them until he noticed their clothing, their uniforms. All of the young women were wearing a yellow blouse and a green skirt. *Is that the same group I saw before?* Stan kept walking; he needed to get to the next block. He reached the corner of Hidalgo and Obregon with two minutes to spare.

6:50 – Stan turned left on Obregon; this was the same path he and Sara had taken that morning. As he walked past the art galleries, he noticed that they were closed for the evening. *That's right; they're all open on Thursday evenings for their Thursday night Art Walk.* He kept walking up the street and turned right at the next corner and went to the designated restaurant – Baja Brewing Company. He was supposed to arrive by 7:00; it was now 6:59. He was on time.

The letter writer had said she'd timed the walk, and her timing was pretty good. Her shorter stride might have made the times a little longer for her, or perhaps she was just adding in a little extra time as a buffer. Anyway, Stan had followed her instructions quite exactingly, and there was nothing else he was supposed to do tonight, except have dinner there at the restaurant. He was certainly hungry, so finally relaxing and enjoying a good dinner wouldn't be that hard to do.

Stan took off the cap; he felt he was done with the games for the evening. It wasn't that busy inside the restaurant, and that was a good thing – a quieter environment would make it a little easier for him to relax and to think.

"Good evening, sir," was the greeting from the employee who approached Stan. "Dinner or just drinks at the bar?"

"Dinner, please," Stan replied. *How odd – a young American girl working here.*

"Of course; please follow me," the greeter said as she took a menu from the rack and led Stan into the dining room. "Will this table be okay?" she asked once they reached a table against the wall, but not in a corner. It was a square table for four that was angled with a corner pointed at the wall.

"This is fine, thank you," Stan said as he sat in a chair so he could face toward the front entrance. It felt good to sit down and not have to follow specific instructions. He placed the yellow cap – he didn't want to think of it as his cap – on the chair next to him.

"Your waiter will be right out," she said as she placed the menu on the table. "Nice cap," she said. "Is it for something specific?"

"No, not really," Stan lied. What was he going to tell this total stranger? Was he going to tell her that someone he never met was telling him – a seasoned investigator – what to wear and what to do? No, he wouldn't do that. "Do you want it? It's practically brand new."

"No thanks," the greeter replied. "I don't wear them; I just thought it was a nice color."

"Yes it is, isn't it?" Stan lied again. He thought it was hideous and he couldn't wait to get rid of it. Maybe he'd just accidentally leave it in the chair, forgetting that he had it with him. With the way things were going for him, however, it would be just his luck that he would get one more letter telling him to wear that yellow cap again.

"Oh, here comes your waiter now," she said as she turned and walked away.

She can't be much older than nineteen or twenty – just about Sarah's age.

A muscular macho man approached Stan's table. If there were a typical Mexican man image, this waiter would fit it. He had bushy eyebrows and a very full moustache. "Good evening, señor. Welcome to Baja Brewing Company. Would you like one of our own hand-crafted micro brews? We make them right here."

"That sounds good; do you have a Pale Ale?" Stan wasn't much of a beer drinker, but he thought he would give it a try. Beer seemed to be the popular drink down here, just as coffee was the drink in Seattle. Somehow, Stan didn't really fit into either mold.

"You'll like our Pale Ale, señor. I'll be right back with it." The waiter turned and left the table and walked to the bar area. As he went by the front of the restaurant, the young American greeter used her right index finger to motion the waiter over to her. She said something to him, and the waiter nodded his head up and down.

A couple minutes later he reappeared at Stan's table with a tall frosted glass filled with a light golden brew. "Here you are, señor, Baja's finest Pale Ale. Have you had a chance to look at the menu yet?"

"No, not yet," Stan replied.

"I'll be back in a few minutes unless you have any questions about the menu."

"No questions, thanks," Stan said. He took a slow sip of the beer; it did taste good. Being the one to over-analyze things, Stan wondered if the waiter meant the best Pale Ale made in Baja California, or the best one made at Baja Brewing Company. All he said was 'Baja's finest.' Oh well, it tasted good and that was all that really mattered right now. He looked at the menu and saw that it was a bit different than what he expected. The one thing that did catch his eye was the selection of brick oven pizzas. That's what he'd order when the waiter returned – a supreme pizza.

As he took another sip on his beer, Stan thought about the path he'd just walked tonight. Sara might be right that the restaurant itself couldn't mean anything or he could have just come straight here. It had to be the path, and the specific times played a key role. The letter writer – *darn I wish I knew her name* – wanted Stan to see something, or be seen. Why else would he have to wear the yellow cap and green shirt and leave the intersections at exact times?

Stan thought more about it; if someone was supposed to see him, then how would this person know who Stan was, unless it was the yellow cap and green shirt that would identify him? But then how and where and when would this person contact Stan? There seemed to be too many loose ends for this to be the reason.

His mind went back to what Sara said earlier in the day at the lookout – it's not the restaurant that was important; it had to be the path and something he was to see. That's why the specific times – to be sure that Stan was at a certain place at a certain time – that's the only way the letter writer could make sure that Stan saw it. *But what is it? What was I supposed to see? Or what did I see?*

The smell of the pizza preceded its way out to Stan's table. Not only did it smell good, it looked like a work of art. The restaurant was in the Art District, so it made sense that the food might was artistically prepared. "The plate and the pizza are very hot, señor. I suggest that you let them cool a little so you don't burn yourself. How's the beer? Do you like it?"

"The beer's very good, thank you. I'm just not a big beer drinker, but I do like it."

"I'm glad you like it, señor. I'll check back with you a little later once you've had time to taste the pizza."

"That's fine, thanks," Stan said. He was more concerned right now with trying to figure out the puzzle he was working on – what was he supposed to see? Did he see it? He must have; the letter writer had been so detailed, she had to know exactly what she was doing.

He ran the sequence of events through his brain, from the moment he walked out of the hotel until he arrived at the restaurant. It couldn't have been anything to do with the traffic and the one-way streets. There was too much of it and he wouldn't have been able to focus on any one thing that quickly. There wasn't anything in any windows that he could see, not that he was looking into many of them anyway. He saw the young women at the church, but he'd seen groups there before. The art galleries were closed, so there wasn't anything to see there. What was it? *What did I miss?*

The smell of the pizza finally got to Stan's senses; it had to be cool enough to eat now. He took the large paper napkin from the under the fork and placed it in his lap. As he did, he knocked the fork off the table, and it made a clanging sound as it hit the tiled floor. Reaching down to retrieve the fork, Stan saw the yellow cap. Yellow – the young women were wearing yellow. And their skirts were green; he was wearing a green shirt. Could that be it?

Just then the young greeter came to his table; the waiter was out of sight. "Did something fall to the floor, sir?" she asked.

"Yes, I dropped my fork, but I can wipe it with my napkin," Stan said.

"No sir, let me get you a new one," she said as she hustled off to get a clean fork for Stan. She returned promptly and set the fork down on the left side of Stan's plate.

"Thank you," Stan said as he handed her the dropped one.

"You're welcome, sir. Enjoy your pizza."

"I'm sure I will; thanks," Stan replied. He used his knife and new fork to cut some bite-sized pieces of the pizza. His mind went back to yellow and green. Was that just a coincidence or was it part of the plan? The women were wearing a yellow blouse and a green skirt, while Stan was wearing a yellow cap and a green shirt. If they were to match, why wasn't Stan wearing a yellow shirt and green pants? That would seem to make more sense, wouldn't it?

Stan took a few bites of his pizza as he was forcing his brain to figure it out. He was close; he was fairly certain of that. Just then the waiter returned.

"How's the pizza, señor?" he asked.

"It's very good, thanks," Stan replied.

"How about the beer? Would you like another one?"

"No thanks, I'll just finish this one. But I'd like a glass of water."

"Certainly, señor. I'll be right back." The waiter said as he walked away from Stan's table.

Stan felt he was so close to solving the current puzzle, but he was constantly being interrupted – he was sorry now that he'd asked for the water. The waiter returned with the glass right away. "Thanks," Stan said without even looking up.

The waiter understood the body language and just quietly stepped away; Stan was now alone with his pizza, glass of water, remaining beer, and his thoughts.

He went over the picture once again in his head, but it wasn't coming together for him. Stan was a visual person, so he decided to use his napkin; it wasn't too greasy. He sketched a stick figure of a girl, and then he wrote 'yellow blouse' and 'green skirt' in the appropriate locations on his rough rendering. He then drew a male stick figure wearing a cap, and labeled it with 'yellow cap' and 'green shirt.'

Stan looked up from his drawing, certainly not an artistic creation, to have another bite of his pizza when he thought he saw the greeter looking over at him. Why would she be looking at him? He ate the pizza and took another sip of the beer; it was beginning to get a little warm, but it was still okay. Stan was not a beer purist, so the proper temperature was not a requirement for him.

As he looked at his sketch again, one thing was clear (not counting his lack of drawing ability) – it was yellow above green on both the female and the male. But the colors didn't match – it was yellow blouse, yellow cap and green skirt, green shirt. As he said this silently to himself, he thought he caught something. If 'green skirt, green shirt' meant something, then how come the yellows didn't match or rhyme? He repeated it again: yellow blouse, yellow cap; green skirt, green shirt. Yellow blouse, yellow cap.

What was another word for blouse that would sound like 'cap'? He couldn't think of a rhyming word, but he did come up with 'top.' Yellow top, yellow cap – that sounded better. And a cap is worn on the top of your head. That's it, he thought. THAT'S IT! The young women he saw at the church were wearing a yellow top and he was wearing yellow on top of his head. They were wearing a green skirt, and he wore a green shirt. That had to be it. The letter writer was leading him to see these young women at church in their yellow and green uniforms. *WHY couldn't she just tell me that? Why did we have to go through these games?* Stan wanted to yell, but he didn't.

Stan quickly finished his pizza and gulped down the rest of his beer; so much for the glass of water. He folded his napkin and put it into his pocket; he wasn't going to leave any clues for her. If she was smart enough to lead him in this manner and make him figure out what it was that she was doing, then she was certainly smart enough to do something else. He saw the waiter and motioned for him to come over.

"La cuenta, por favor," Stan said as the waiter got within reasonable hearing range. Stan was excited; he felt he was making progress again.

"Was everything okay, señor?" the waiter asked as he set the bill on the table.

"Perfect," Stan replied

"Gracias, señor."

Stan looked at the bill and left enough cash on the table to cover the bill and a nice tip. He didn't want any change – he was back in charge and he was on a mission. Reluctantly, he picked up the yellow cap off the seat and headed to the front entrance.

"Good night, sir," the young female greeter said as Stan approached.

Stan looked at her and replied, "Good night; are you sure you don't want the cap?"

"No thanks," She replied.

Stan walked out the door with cap in hand, wondering if the young women were still at the church.

Thirty-seven/Treinta y siete
San José del Cabo
That same evening – Monday, May 12th

progreso (prō·grĕ'·sō) – progress. *Él progresó bien el diá de hoy.* He made good progress today.

Stan wanted to run, but his self-esteem wouldn't let him do it. He settled for walking at a rather brisk pace. The letter writer could have cut her transit times in half if she'd walked that fast. He was hoping that the young women in the yellow and green uniforms were still there at the church. But what would he do if they <u>were</u> there? Would he approach them? What would he say to them? What about the Padre who'd already told him that he couldn't say anything; what if he came out while Stan was there? Like many situations that Stan had been in, he would figure out the answer once he was faced with the question.

He walked in the street as he went down Obregón; the sidewalk was too uneven and he didn't want to risk a fall especially as he was walking quickly. He turned right as he got to Hidalgo and listened intently – did he hear any voices? He did, but they were the voices of some youngsters running around and playing in the plaza. He was half-way up the block when he looked into the alley way where he'd seen the young women earlier; no one was there. And all indications were that everyone had already left the area – there weren't any lights on in any of the windows. Stan thought about walking back toward the Padre's office, but he didn't have a good answer if someone asked him why he was back there. He certainly couldn't say that he was back there looking for the young women he'd seen earlier. That would most likely warrant a quick call to La Policia.

I'm sure she knew that they wouldn't be here when I came back by; darn she's smart!

Stan walked a little more up the street and then went up the thirteen steps toward the church – maybe they're inside for choir practice. He walked to the main door; it was locked, and he couldn't hear anything inside. He wanted to feel frustrated, but he'd made a lot of progress tonight so he knew he really should feel happy about that. And he did, but he wanted more, especially after all the frustration that he'd had. Stan realized that he did need to put it all into perspective – his frustration compared to the Johnsons'? His didn't even come close to theirs.

He turned around and headed back through the plaza, and then to the hotel. It had been a busy day already, and now he had some pressing work to do.

"Good evening, Señor Stan," Miguel said to Stan as he headed straight through the lobby to the stairs – his focus was single-minded right now.

"Hello, Miguel. Sorry, but I'm in a rush right now. I've got some work to do."

Stan continued his fast gait to the stairs and then up them two at a time. As he went up the stairs, he was trying to remember what colors he and Carmelita had seen at the church a few months back when they were in the plaza. It seemed like they were green and yellow, but was it green blouse and yellow skirt or yellow blouse and green skirt. He knew that no matter what answer he decided on, he couldn't be one hundred percent positive of his answer. And even if he were absolutely sure, he didn't recall what that group was called.

He got to his room, unlocked the door, and then closed it behind him. He wanted to throw the yellow cap away, but it had helped him get closer to finding Sarah – or at least that's what he thought. He had more information than he started out the day with, but he still needed more. Stan opened the lid on his laptop computer and pressed the Power button; it would take a couple minutes to come on. He went into the bathroom and brushed his teeth. He liked the dinner of pizza and beer, but he didn't want them on his breath while he was trying to focus on hopefully finding out more about where Sarah might be.

He returned to his computer and logged on to the local wireless connection; the signal wasn't the strongest but he wasn't planning to upload or download any files. Stan opened his web browser and then went to Google. He typed *yellow green uniforms* into the search box and selected the Search button. The search returned 674,000 hits. He didn't want to do the math, but he knew it would take a mighty long time to go through all those hits. He put the cursor back in the search box and put quotes around "yellow and green uniforms" and also added Mexico as a search term. He then pressed the Search button and was more pleased to see only 228 results, and some of them were for the Green Bay Packers of the National Football League. He would skip across those right away.

Each page of results showed ten links that contained the phrase "yellow and green uniforms" plus the word "Mexico" on the site. He went through several pages of results until he came across one that jumped right out at him. He clicked on the link and started to read the translated page as it appeared on his screen:

> The Holy Order of Saint Christine in Guadalajara, Mexico, is a sacred gathering of young Catholic women who have chosen to give their lives to our Lord and Savior Jesus Christ. These women are selected from a large group of women who have submitted a formal application to the Holy Order. Upon their initial acceptance and entry into the Holy Order, these women wear yellow and green uniforms signifying their longing for new life. Once they have proven their worthiness,

Stan didn't need to read any more – he saw what he needed to see. He grabbed his notebook and wrote down "Holy Order of Saint Christine" and "Guadalajara." He went back to Google and typed "Holy Order of Saint Christine" plus "Guadalajara" in the search box and hit Enter. He was surprised to find more results for this search than for the previous one. He scanned through the results and found the one he was looking for.

> Welcome to the Holy Order of Saint Christine located in Guadalajara, Mexico. Some people have called us an exclusive group because we are not able to allow everyone to become a chosen follower. We prefer to think of ourselves as an inclusive gathering because we choose to include young women from all walks of life, regardless of their sinful pasts.
>
> We are not a secretive group; rather we are a collective group who have all chosen to become faithful followers of The One who will bring us true joy and salvation when we begin our eternal life in Heaven. While we are located at numerous Catholic churches throughout Mexico, all the young women who first enter into the Holy Order begin their formal indoctrination at the Saint Christine Cathedral in Guadalajara, Mexico.

There are two groups of women in the Holy Order of Saint Christine: the first group younger women who wish to devote their lives to Jesus Christ wear a green blouse and yellow skirt as they prepare to become a nun; the second group – pregnant unwed women who are devoted to the Church and who agree to put up their babies for adoption at birth – wear a yellow blouse and a green skirt.

Stan stopped reading the screen; his mind raced with questions. *Does that mean that Sarah's pregnant? Or did the letter writer know I wouldn't be able to find a green cap and a yellow shirt? Which group does Sarah belong to?*

Stan re-focused on the computer screen and scrolled down a few pages to find the street address of Saint Christine Cathedral in Guadalajara. He wrote that address down in his notebook.

He got out of the chair and went to the bed and lay down on it. Stan wasn't tired; he was elated. He closed his eyes and thought, 'Have I just found out where Sarah is?' He knew that Robert and Tina would be so excited to hear the news, but he had to be careful. He'd thought several times earlier that he was close to finding her, but those didn't materialize. He knew he had to move swiftly, but be cautious with the information that he gave to the Johnsons.

Stan got back off the bed; he needed to call the Johnsons. They had an agreement that if he were going somewhere else that he would call them and let them know. That way they wouldn't be surprised when their bill included another airline charge. Stan opened his cell phone and pressed *6 – the speed dial number on his phone for the Johnsons.

"Hello," the male voice answered the phone.

"Hi, Robert. This is Stan Walkorski calling."

"Hi Stan. How are you?"

"I'm quite well, thank you. I have some good news that I would like to share with both you and Tina. Is she there?"

"Sure, just a minute," he replied.

Stan could hear Robert in the background: "Tina, it's Stan. He says he has some good news to tell us. Pick up the phone."

"Hello," Tina said as she picked up the phone extension.

"Hi, Tina," Stan began. "As I told Robert, I have some good news to tell you. Robert, are you there?"

"I'm here," he replied into the phone.

"I won't go into all the details right now because they're not the most important thing. I'll tell you all of it later when I'm back in Seattle." Stan paused to see if they were going to say anything. The Johnsons were in a listening mode, not a talking mode. "Okay," he resumed, "I think I have found out where Sarah is."

"No!" Tina screamed. "Please tell me she's okay."

"I can't guarantee that right now, Tina, but from what I have found out, I'm sure she is. The main reason I called is that I am going to fly to Guadalajara tomorrow; I think she's there." Stan was hoping to keep the call short because he knew it would be very difficult to try to explain everything over the phone to the high anxiety parents.

"What's in Guadalajara?" Robert asked.

"Let me build up to that," Stan began. "Remember that letter I told you about? I've had a couple more of them, and tonight I figured out what they were all about."

"What do you mean?" Robert asked.

"For the last two nights I've been led on some different crazy routes where I was told what to wear. Tonight's included specific times to be at specific places. I finally figured out during dinner tonight that I was being led to see that Sarah has joined a Catholic group of young women. It's kind of like a convent, but they're not ready for that yet."

"So she's there in San José del Cabo?" Tina asked.

"I don't think so," Stan replied. "I found a website for a Holy Order, and it's based in Guadalajara. That's why I am going there tomorrow."

"Have you talked with anyone down there who's seen here recently?" Robert asked.

Stan paused before answering. "No, I haven't, Robert. I feel good about this information, however. I can't tell you everything over the phone; there'd just be too much to tell you right now. Once all of us are back in Seattle, I'll tell you everything. But the main reason for my call it to tell you that I'm going to Guadalajara tomorrow, and for you to be ready for a call from me."

"Got it," Robert said.

"What do you mean?" Tina asked. "Why would we need to be ready for a call from you?"

"I'm not exactly sure what I'm going to find out in Guadalajara," Stan said. "I'm hoping that I will find Sarah and that I'll be able to talk with her, but that might not happen. I just want you to be mentally prepared in case I call you and strongly suggest that you both get on a plane and go down there. I don't know any more than that right now. I just want you to be ready so if I do call, you aren't taken by surprise. Does that make sense?"

"Perfectly," Robert said.

"Um, I guess so," Tina hesitantly replied, although she was still quite unsure what she was agreeing to. "Stan, are you saying that Sarah's in trouble?"

"No, Tina, I'm not saying that at all. Sarah's a very strong young lady, and I'm quite confident that she's in total control of whatever it is she's doing. I just want you to be ready to fly down to Mexico if I call you. That's all."

"Okay," she said quite meekly.

"Do you have any questions, Robert?" Stan asked.

"No, I don't, Stan. Thanks for keeping us informed."

"You're welcome. I'll call you as soon as I know something more. Okay?"

"Okay," Robert responded. "Talk to you soon."

"Bye," Stan said as he closed his phone. Stan really worried about Tina. She seemed extremely fragile; he hoped she wouldn't fall apart if something bad had happened to Sarah.

Stan was used to flying in the States. If he needed to go somewhere, he would just go to Alaska Airlines' website or United's, and he would find the flight information he was looking for. But he wasn't in the States right now; how would he get flight information for flights from Los Cabos to Guadalajara? He thought about going to Google and look for flights. He then remembered that Miguel was down at the front desk.

Stan picked up his notebook and headed downstairs.

"Hello, Señor Stan. Are you okay? You were in such a hurry before."

"I'm fine, Miguel. Yes, I was in a rush before. My apologies."

"That's okay, I was just afraid that maybe you weren't feeling okay."

"Thank you for your concern, Miguel," Stan said. "I was wondering," he continued, "if you could help me with a flight reservation."

"Of course I will help you. What do you need?" Miguel was a better administrative assistant than any that Stan had known.

"I need to fly to Guadalajara tomorrow, but I don't have any idea of what airlines fly there. And even if I did, I don't think I could make my way through their websites or their phone systems. Also, if anyone comes asking for me, please don't tell them that I am gone. Just take a message."

"Of course. Interjet is probably the best way to get there. What time do you want to go there tomorrow? The flight takes about two hours."

"Any time in the morning is fine," Stan said.

"Is it okay if I check online, or do you want me to call them?"

"Whatever is the easiest is okay," Stan replied. "If you check online then I could go ahead and fill in my credit card information."

"Okay," Miguel said. "Why don't you come around the counter and let's see what I can find for you."

"Gracias, Miguel," Stan said.

"De nada, señor."

Stan walked around behind the counter as Miguel was getting to InterJet's website. He found a morning flight that left Los Cabos at 11:30 and got into Guadalajara at 1:45 – they're on different time zones so the actual flight time was only an hour and fifteen minutes. Stan typed in his credit card information for the one-way flight; he didn't know when he would be returning.

Miguel printed the flight and confirmation information for Stan. "Is there anything else I can help you with, Señor Stan?"

"Actually, yes there is, Miguel. I'll need a hotel that is near this address." Stan opened his notebook and showed Miguel the address for the Saint Christine Cathedral.

"Let's see what's near there and how much they are," Miguel said as he opened a new browser window and typed in an address for hotels in Guadalajara. He came up with fourteen hotels in the vicinity of the Saint Christine Cathedral.

"How close are they and what is the price range?" Stan asked.

Miguel selected a button to sort first by distance, and then he sorted by price. "There are two of them that are less than one kilometer, that's about a half a mile, but there are many of them within a few kilometers from the cathedral. A taxi ride would not be very expensive from the hotel."

"Okay," Stan said. "Let me see the hotels that are within let's say five kilometers."

Miguel showed Stan the list of the hotels.

"Let's pick this one; at least I know the name, so I'm sure that it will be okay. I don't mean anything bad about the others; I just haven't heard of them."

"I agree with you, señor. I might be able to stay at some of the cheaper ones because I am Mexican and they won't try to take advantage of me. I hate to say it, but some hotels do take advantage of Americans because they can't speak our language. Let me call the hotel and see what best rate I can get for you as a good customer of our hotel."

"Thank you, Miguel," Stan said as Miguel picked up the phone and began to call the hotel in Guadalajara. Stan didn't understand very much of what Miguel was saying. He picked up a single word here and there, but that wasn't enough to understand the gist of the animated conversation. He knew his name – *Stan Walkorski* is the same in English as it is in Spanish – so he knew that Miguel was getting close to securing a reservation for him.

"Sí, sí," Miguel said several times to the person on the other end of the line. "Gracias." Miguel then hung up the phone. "You have a room there for as long as you need it. It's a very nice hotel and I'm sure that you will like it."

Stan was beginning to worry about the cost when he heard Miguel say those things.

"The rate online for your room was 1,750 pesos per night –that's about $150 U.S. Dollars. But he gave you a good rate because you're a special customer here. Your rate is 990 pesos per night; that's about $85 per night. I hope that's okay, Señor Stan. It should be a very nice room, and it includes breakfast every morning."

"Gracias, Miguel. That is very good. Do you know how far the hotel is from the airport?"

"Sí, señor. The hotel is about 40 kilometers from the airport; that's about 25 miles. You will need to take a taxi from the airport to the hotel. I will give you something to give your taxi driver. It will be in Spanish, so the taxi driver won't have any excuse not to get you to your hotel. Señor Stan, why don't you go to your room and pack? I will print out everything that you will need tomorrow and when you get to Guadalajara. I will also have a taxi here for you at ten in the morning."

"Miguel, I don't know how to thank you. You are so good to me."

"I am happy to be able to assist you, Señor Stan. Did you ever hear back from your lady friend here in San José?"

"No I haven't. I've called a couple times, but I don't get an answer. I left a message saying I was coming down here and staying at this hotel. Maybe she'll call while I'm gone; will you let her know I'm in Guadalajara but I'll be coming back here?"

"Of course I'll let her know that. I hope she does call."

Stan didn't know what to say. "Thanks, Miguel," was the best he could come up with.

"Are you taking all your things with you, or do you want to leave some of them here?"

"Can I leave some things here so I only have to take a small bag with me?"

"Of course," Miguel said. "You can leave the things in your room, but I won't charge you for the room. We're not very busy right now, so I don't need to rent your room. Leave the clothes on the bed that you want washed, and they'll be ready for you when you return."

"That's very nice, Miguel. You certainly know how to make a guest feel very much at home."

"We have a saying in Mexico *'Mi casa es su casa,'* and it means 'My house is your house.' So if you are staying here at my hotel, it's the same as if you were staying at my house. And if it's my house, I want you to feel as comfortable as if it's your own house."

"Well, thank you, Miguel, because I do feel very comfortable here at your house."

"You need to go pack, señor. You are going to have a very busy day tomorrow." Miguel had no idea that he was foretelling the day for Stan that was to become a very hectic day indeed.

Thirty-eight/Treinta y ocho
Over the Sea of Cortez (Mar de Cortés)
Tuesday, May 13th

fácil (fă'·sĭl) – easy. *Esta es una lección fácil.* This is an easy lesson.

Stan didn't need an alarm clock to awaken him as he was energized at the thought of going to Guadalajara and hopefully finding Sarah. True to his word, Miguel had a packet of papers ready for Stan: his flight information; the hotel reservation; instructions to the taxi driver with the address of the hotel, and a list of some emergency phone numbers in case he encountered any problems there. Miguel knew that Stan was very comfortable in San José, but Guadalajara was a much bigger city. With over seven million people in its metropolitan area, Guadalajara could present some of the same issues as anyone going to Los Angeles, Chicago, or New York City for the first time.

"Thank you, Miguel. I don't know when I'll return, but it should be within a week or two. Do you still have my card in case you need to contact me?"

"Sí, señor, I still have your card, and I can always call your hotel there in Guadalajara. Your taxi will be here in about five minutes."

"I did leave some clothes on the bed as you told me to do. The clothes in the closet and in the dresser are fine as they are. If you would ask housekeeping to just clean the ones on the bed, I'd appreciate it." Stan was glad he wasn't taking a large suitcase with him; the smaller bag held enough clothes for a short stay. He wasn't taking the yellow cap and green shirt with him (nor the red cap and blue shirt) – they'd already served their purpose.

"We'll take care of them. If you need to call here, just ask them at your hotel there to call me; here's my card." Miguel heard a car horn outside and he looked to see if it was Stan's taxi; it was. "Your taxi is here, Señor Stan. *Buena suerte y vaya con Dios.* That means 'good luck and go with God.'"

"Gracias, Miguel. I hope to see you soon," Stan said as he extended his hand to Miguel. The two men shook hands and then Stan walked out of the lobby to the waiting taxi. Just as he had the last time that he'd arranged a taxi ride for Stan, Miguel spoke with the driver to make sure he would take Stan directly to the airport.

"Sí, señor," the taxi driver said. "Sí," he said again as Miguel stepped back from the driver's door.

Miguel then went to the other side where Stan was just getting into the taxi. "He knows he is to take you directly to the airport without any stops. The fare is two hundred pesos, so don't let him try to charge you any more than that."

"¿Dos cientos pesos, sí?" Stan asked the driver who was shocked to hear his American passenger confirm the price in Spanish.

"Sí, señor, dos cientos pesos," the driver responded.

"Excelente," Stan said to the driver as he smiled to Miguel.

"Safe travels," Miguel said.

"Thanks."

The taxi ride to the airport was uneventful. Tuesday mid-morning was a quiet time on the roads so there was no need for the driver to take the toll road; it would have probably taken him longer because he would have had to actually drive two kilometers back toward Cabo San Lucas. As they veered to the right to take the overpass to the airport at Kilometer 43, Stan pulled a couple pictures of Sarah out of his pocket. *This is why I am doing this,* he reminded himself.

A few minutes later, the taxi driver pulled up to Terminal 1 and stopped the car. Stan handed the driver the two hundred pesos as agreed on plus a fifty pesos tip. "Muchas gracias, señor," the driver said with a genuine smile. *"Buen vuelo."* [good flight]

"Gracias," Stan replied as he opened his door and stepped out. The driver got out of the taxi and opened the trunk to hand Stan his suitcase.

"Adios, señor," the driver said as Stan took the suitcase and turned toward the sliding glass doors into the terminal.

"Adios," Stan replied. He went inside and saw a long line at the U.S. Airways counter. He was relieved to see only a short line at InterJet's. He walked to the line and realized that he was the only American in line. That didn't concern him, but his Spanish wasn't that good in case there was some question. When he reached the front of the line, he was motioned to approach the counter.

"Buenos días," he said to the young agent at the counter as he handed the confirmation page that Miguel had printed out for him last night.

"Buenos días, señor," she replied along with something else that Stan didn't understand. But he could tell by the inflection in her voice that it was a question.

"English?" he said apologetically.

"Do you have your identification, señor?"

"Sure," Stan replied as he pulled his passport from his shirt pocket and handed it to her. She looked at the small picture and then looked up at Stan; she was satisfied.

"Are you checking any bags?" she then asked.

"Yes, this one bag," Stan said as he set his bag on the scale – 15 kilograms it recorded. Stan did the math in his head; that was close to 34 pounds.

"Thank you, señor," the agent said as she stapled his luggage tag to the boarding pass.

"Gracias," Stan said as he walked away from the counter. He was used to a lot more rigor when flying, but then he remembered that he was not on an international flight; he was just flying from one state in Mexico to another state in Mexico. Stan looked at his watch; it was 10:30. He left the hotel only thirty minutes ago, and he'd already checked in and received his boarding pass. *That's efficiency.* Going through the Security checkpoint was also quick and easy. He hadn't been in Terminal 1 before so he looked around to gain some familiarity with it. He saw that InterJet used Boarding Gate *[Puerta de Abordar]* 1, which was at the far right-hand side of the terminal.

Stan walked to Gate 1. He felt more comfortable once he saw they had an electronic board, so at least he would be able to see when his flight to Guadalajara was boarding. They were currently showing a flight to Mexico City. Stan wasn't a sitter; he had to keep moving, so he just wandered around. The artisans' shop was close to Gate 1 so he went over to look at a few of the items. He wondered how people got those items home; most of them would have to be shipped. He heard some Spanish being spoken over the loudspeaker, but he didn't pay much attention to it because he didn't understand. But then he heard a word that he did understand, 'Guadalajara.'

It was pronounced a little differently than how most Americans said it – the initial 'G' was pronounced like a 'W' as in 'wad.'

Stan immediately turned around and headed to Puerta de Abordar 1. The overhead sign was showing that his flight was now ready to board. He got in line; it was a short line. Apparently it wasn't going to be a very full flight, and that was fine with him. He watched to see what other passengers were doing so he would know what to do when he got to the front of the line. He showed his boarding pass and kept on walking, just like the others in front of him had done. He then followed the line through the door leading out to the planes. They didn't use any jet-ways in this terminal; the passengers walked outside to the planes and then up the boarding stairs.

Stan's seat was 9A so he used the front stairs to board the plane. As he got to the top and stepped into the plane, he was greeted with a warm "Buenos días, señor." He reciprocated with the same greeting and walked to his window seat. He didn't see any rows that were full; it <u>was</u> going to be an empty flight. It also meant that as soon as the passengers were on board that the plane would be pushed out for taxiing and take-off.

He put his briefcase under seat 8A, buckled his seatbelt and relaxed. He pulled Sarah's pictures out of his pocket again as another reminder of why he had followed the letter writer's very explicit instructions. He took a deep breath, leaned back in the seat, and closed his eyes. He tried to visualize the three Johnsons being reunited. The mental picture wasn't very clear; he wanted to see it, but it just wasn't there yet. Stan felt the pressurization as the two cabin doors were closed. He then heard an announcement in Spanish. He didn't understand it, but he knew essentially what was being said. His seat belt was fastened and his seat was upright; he was ready to go.

An empty row, how nice. Stan was the only passenger in row 9. If it were a long flight he could lift the arm rests and lie down, but the flight was just a little over an hour. He would still enjoy the quiet time along with the view out the window. The plane was pushed back, and then he heard the engines rev up as the plane began to move forward, turn a little to the left and then taxi out to the one runway. It looked like the pilot was going to use runway 16 (a heading of 160°). *I just hope for the best.* Stan didn't know, of course, what would come out of this trip. All he could hope for was a peaceful conclusion to a mysterious disappearance.

He felt the thrust of the two engines as the plane began its take-off. The sound of the engines was soothing and Stan once again leaned back in his seat and closed his eyes. He was absorbing the power and the feel of the airplane as it was leaving the comfort of the ground and heading into the uncertainties of the sky. Stan could recognize some of San José as the pilot continued on the heading of 160°, almost due South. He'd looked at a map and saw that Guadalajara was somewhat southeast of San José, so he expected the pilot to continue on the heading for a while and then turn slightly to the left to set up the approach into Guadalajara.

The landing and deplaning at Guadalajara were both very smooth. Stan was expecting to have to go through some sort of Customs or Immigration until he remembered that he had flown within Mexico; it was just the same as flying from city to city in the States. He picked up his suitcase at baggage claim and walked outside – the air didn't seem as clean as it was in San José. That made sense given that Guadalajara was a much bigger industrialized city that had some mountains surrounding it, trapping the air over the city.

It still was a nice day, though. Stan saw a line of taxi cabs and he walked over to them. He stopped to take out the page that Miguel had written for him with the directions to the hotel and the request for a price before he got in. He went to the first taxi and showed him the paper.

"No, señor, too far," the driver replied. He probably wouldn't mind taking Stan out to the hotel, but then he would have to drive all the way back here without a fare.

"Gracias," Stan said. He went to the next driver and handed him the paper.

"Sí, señor, six hundred pesos," the driver willingly said.

Stan had learned that almost everything was negotiable in Mexico. "Four hundred pesos, señor," he said.

The driver countered with "Five hundred pesos."

"Okay," Stan said and the driver got out of the taxi to put Stan's suitcase into the trunk. Stan let himself into the backseat of the taxi and fastened the seat belt.

The driver looked again at the directions to the hotel. "First time here, señor?"

Stan had been told to never appear that you were a first-timer anywhere; you would then be an easy target for rip-offs and scams. "No, my third," he said with a convincing lie.

"Welcome back, señor," the driver said as he pulled out into the traffic lane and headed to the airport exit. Stan was glad he had his seatbelt on, and they were still at the airport!

The driver was very professional as he drove to the hotel. He did drive a little fast, but then so were the other drivers. Forty minutes later, the driver pulled up into the hotel driveway and stopped. He turned around and returned the hotel directions to Stan.

"Gracias," Stan said as he unfastened his seat belt. The hotel bellman was at the taxi right away and he opened Stan's door. "Gracias," Stan said to the bellman as he stepped out.

Stan started to walk to retrieve his suitcase, when the bellman said in perfect English, "I'll get your suitcase for you." Stan continued toward the rear of the vehicle, however, as he was taking his wallet out of his back pocket. He opened the wallet and pulled out a purplish *quinientos* [five hundred] pesos note and handed it to the driver. Knowing that the driver had gone out his way, Stan also gave him an additional fifty pesos.

"Muchas gracias, señor," the driver said.

"De nada," Stan replied as he turned back to the hotel entrance. The bellman followed Stan inside and waited patiently as he checked in. Everything was in order, just as Miguel had told him. *Perhaps our hotels in the U.S. can learn something from these guys.*

The desk clerk handed the room key to the bellman and now it was Stan's turn to follow him into the elevator and up to his room. Miguel was right again; it was a very nice room. Stan handed a tip to the bellman who excused himself, and Stan proceeded to put his things away.

Thirty-nine/Treinta y nueve
Guadalajara, Mexico
That afternoon – Tuesday, May 13th

Impresionante (ĭm·prĕ'·sē·ō·năn·tā) – impressive. *Es un edificio impresionanate.* It is an impressive building.

Stan didn't really have much of a plan for what he would do once he got to Guadalajara. Now it was more of trying things, see what resulted, and then making adjustments. Investigations didn't always go in a straight line or follow strict scientific rules. Stan had relied on many hunches in the past, and he didn't have a whole lot more than that to go on right now. He only had two things to go on: the Holy Order of Saint Christine, and the yellow and green uniforms that the women wore. Stan still wondered which group Sarah was in – the green blouse and yellow skirt group who were preparing for a life in a convent, or the yellow blouse and green skirt group of unwed pregnant women who were giving up their babies for adoption. His plan was to go to Saint Christine Cathedral and look for Sarah. It wasn't much to go on, but that was all he had.

He hung his shirts and pants and jacket in the closet, put the rest of his clothes in the drawers, and then set out his shaving items on the bathroom sink. Stan liked to make his hotel rooms as much like home as possible. He was a creature of habit, but that's just the way he was. One advantage of doing the same things the same way each time was that it gave him a comfort level and it was one more thing he didn't have to think about. Everything was put away, including the suitcase – he didn't like having the suitcase in the bedroom because it would be a reminder that he was transient.

Stan left his room and headed down the hall to the elevators. As he stepped inside the open door, his stomach growled to remind him that he hadn't eaten lunch. Looking at the oversized restaurant posters in the elevator didn't help much either, but at least they did tell him that there were several restaurants in the hotel.

As he stepped out of the elevator he went to the front desk because the clerk there had spoken English with Stan when he checked in earlier. "Any of the restaurants open now for lunch?" Stan asked.

"Sí, señor. The one right behind you is open," the clerk said as he gestured with his right hand in a pointing motion over Stan's shoulder.

Stan looked around and saw where the clerk was pointing.

"Thank you," Stan said. It wasn't natural for Stan to switch between English and Spanish very easily. If someone was speaking to him in Spanish, it was easy for him to say 'gracias' or a few other phrases in Spanish. But when the other person was speaking in English, Stan always responded in English – even in Mexico. Stan knew he wasn't bi-lingual; he wished he were, but he wasn't and didn't think he ever would be.

Stan turned around and walked toward the restaurant. He was glad that he asked because he probably wouldn't have found it on his own. The entrance was cleverly disguised as an atrium garden. He made his way through the greenery, and the waiter took him to a table. Stan asked for a bottle of water while he looked at the menu. He drank the local water in Cabo and San José, but he'd been told that asking for a sealed bottle of water would be a good thing to do in Guadalajara.

The waiter returned with the sealed bottle of water and an empty glass – he had also been told to avoid the ice. Stan ordered his meal and handed the menu back to the waiter. He twisted the cap and heard it snap as the seal broke. He poured some into the glass and took a big drink of it. It was cool and refreshing, just what he needed. He looked at the pictures of Sarah and said a silent prayer that he would find her and that she was okay. Stan wasn't a very religious man, but he still felt that there was a higher power, and it wouldn't hurt to ask for some help at this point.

His plate of food was brought out on a tray and the waiter held the tray in one hand while removing the plate with the other hand. The food looked and smelled really good plus Stan was quite hungry. That was a combination that led to an empty plate and a full stomach. Stan charged the meal to his room and got up from the table and left the restaurant, weaving his way back through the greenery.

As Stan walked through the revolving glass door to the outside of the hotel, the bellman immediately came over to him. "Taxi, señor?"

"Sí gracias," Stan replied.

"Where are you going?" the bellman asked.

"Saint Christine Cathedral," Stan replied.

"That's easy, señor, and the fare is seventy pesos. I will make sure the driver is a good driver for you."

"Gracias," Stan said.

The bellman blew a whistle two times and a black taxi drove up right in front. Stan had seen both black taxis and yellow taxis. As the bellman opened the door of the black taxi, Stan knew that this one was a higher class taxi than the one he'd taken in from the airport. But the airport driver had been courteous and his taxi was clean, so Stan didn't really have any complaints about it.

The bellman went to the driver's side, told the driver where Stan wanted to go and apparently a few more things. Just like the taxi driver in San José, this one also said 'Sí, sí' after the bellman was done talking with him. "He knows to take you directly to Saint Christine Cathedral and that the fare is seventy pesos, including tip. Here's a card to give to the taxi driver when you are ready to come back to the hotel. You should only take the black taxis."

"Gracias," Stan said as he handed the bellman a tip.

"De nada, señor. Gracias," the bellman said in reply.

Stan wondered why he hadn't seen any of the black taxis at the airport; perhaps their higher fare was hard to explain or justify to tourists. Or perhaps there would have to be a line for black taxis and one for the others. It wasn't worth worrying about. The driver pulled away from the hotel and had to make only two turns until he was pulling in front of Saint Christine Cathedral; *it certainly is impressive from the outside.* Stan paid the driver and stepped out to the sidewalk.

As Stan looked at the front entrance of the cathedral, the sun was over his right shoulder, meaning that he was facing to the East. Most of the streets he had seen were perpendicular to each other, running north-south and east-west. His knowledge of architecture helped him with the inside layout even before he'd opened the massive outside doors. Standard Western ecclesiastical architectural design had the façade and main entrance on the west end of the building, and the liturgical areas (altar, apse, choir area, and others) at the east end. Not every cathedral was constructed that way due to the shape of the land and other reasons. The east end was typically the liturgical end for symbolic religious reasons.

Stan grabbed the large metallic ring on the right-hand door and pulled on it to open the door. It was not very easy to open. He had been to some cathedrals where they'd installed counter-levers that made opening a five-hundred pound door as easy as opening a regular house door. Apparently, Saint Christine Cathedral was more interested in tradition than in making it easy. As he walked into the entry way, Stan could smell burning wax and lit matches. It was cool inside and he figured it was due to the structure of the cathedral: thick block combined with tall ceilings that would collect and dissipate the warm air. Given the history and importance of the cathedral, Stan didn't think that they would have installed an air conditioning system – he was right.

The sound of a pipe organ was muted as it came from the main area. Stan approached the doors into the Nave and put twenty pesos into the Poor Box. He opened the doors and the full organ sound greeted him as he walked in quietly; he thought maybe there was a service going on right now. But it was just a practice. He walked down the center aisle a few pews and stepped in and sat down. He loved organ music, especially when it was played on a pipe organ; it was such a rich sound.

As he listened intently to the beautiful music that was seemingly coming down from the heavens, Stan thought of his one trip to Paris, France. He was staying in the Eight District and he visited the highly impressive La Madeleine Church, within walking distance of both the Louvre and the Eiffel Tower. He picked up a brochure about the church during his visit and read about its magnificent pipe organ. In the 160 years since its installation, there had only been ten organists, and two of them were renowned composers: Camille Saint-Saëns and Gabriel Fauré.

Stan continued to listen to the music when the pipe organ suddenly stopped as a group of young women filed in from the southern transept (the offshoots from the main part that resembled the arms of the cross). They were wearing green robes with a yellow stole! Had he struck it rich or was this just some similarity that would not lead to anything substantial? His research said that the Holy Order of Saint Christine wore yellow and green uniforms. Could it be that they also wore yellow and green as choir 'uniforms'? He was a little tired from the short plane flight, but seeing these women in yellow and green awakened him to a state of full alertness. He waited to see where they were going. They walked to the choir area on the northern side and filed into their rows so they faced out to the middle.

Once they were in their positions, Stan felt comfortable in moving to a closer pew. There were a lot of people inside, so his movement didn't make him stand out. He stayed on the right side so he could get the best view of their faces. The conductor raised his hands as an indication that they should be ready to begin. He then began to conduct them in a musical piece. They sang a capella; there was no musical accompaniment. Their voices were beautiful; the music was angelic. Stan didn't understand the words; he didn't know if they were singing in Latin or in Spanish. He also didn't really care; the sound was beautiful. His main interest, however was to find Sarah.

He took the pictures out of his pocket and looked at them slowly, one at a time. He cropped each picture with his hands so he would only see her face. She could have changed her hair length or colored it, so he didn't want to get confused by that. As he scanned down each of the three rows, he could bypass most of them immediately. This was one time when his subject's skin color was an advantage to him. Most of the young women were Hispanic, and there were a few who appeared to be Asian. So he didn't have too many Caucasian women to pick from. He finally saw one that he thought was Sarah, but she was standing near the far end of the middle row. That position made it difficult for him to get a really good look at her. There was one time that she turned her head about forty-five degrees to the right, giving him his best view of her.

That looked like her, but Stan knew that he couldn't say with certainty that it was Sarah because she was seventy-five to one hundred feet away. He stayed there and listened to the choir, but he was mostly watching the one who might be Sarah. But how would he know for sure?

Stan ran several scenarios through his head, but he quickly discarded all of them. If the Padre in San José wouldn't tell him anything, Stan really didn't think that anyone here in Guadalajara would tell him anything about her, even if he provided her full name, date of birth, etc. No, he'd have to come up with something else.

The choir practiced several pieces and then filed back out just as they had entered, orderly and quietly. He was impressed. He just wished they sang more pieces; he wanted to observe 'Sarah' some more. He would have to come back when they practiced again, but when was that?

Stan stepped out of the row, walked to the back of the cathedral and went through the doors into the entryway. He saw an elderly woman on the left side who was apparently selling post cards and candles. "English?" he said as he walked up to her

"No, señor," she replied. So much for that brilliant idea. There wasn't anyone else he could ask, so he walked out through the same massive door through which he'd entered. He was quite pleased, however; he saw someone who looked like Sarah. It was a lucky break, but he would take it; it had been a long time in coming.

Stan went to the sidewalk to get a taxi back to the hotel. He pulled the card out of his pocket and waited until he saw a black taxi. He motioned with his right hand and the driver pulled over to the curb. Rather than just climbing into the back seat, Stan opened the front door on the right side and leaned in. He handed the card to the driver who quickly scanned it; he'd seen cards like this before.

"Sí, señor, I'll take you to your hotel. The fare is seventy pesos," the driver said as he handed the card back to Stan.

"Gracias," Stan said as he took his card, stepped back out of the front seat, and got into the back seat. He buckled the seatbelt and thought about what he'd just experienced. Was he actually getting close to finding Sarah? He hoped so, but he wasn't going to call the Johnsons just yet. Would he tell them that she might be pregnant? Stan knew that luck played a part in all investigations, and he hoped that luck was now presenting him with the opportunity and the information that he needed to solve the case. Solving the case was important to him, but it wasn't as essential to him as it was to the Johnsons. It was crucial to them, and he fully understood why. Stan didn't have any children, but he was sure he would be as devastated as they were if he had a child who was missing; especially one who was missing in Mexico.

The driver arrived at Stan's hotel in what seemed like only a couple minutes. Stan paid the driver as the bellman opened his door. "Welcome back, señor," the bellman said as Stan stepped out.

"Thank you," Stan said – he replied in English once again even though he knew he was in Mexico.

Stan went up to his room and thought about what he would do now that it appeared that he'd seen Sarah. What could he do to be sure it was her? Or what if it wasn't her? What would he then tell the Johnsons?

Forty/Cuarenta
Guadalajara
Wednesday, May 14th

mirar (mĭ·dăr') – to watch. *Vine a mirar los niños.* I came
to watch the children.

Stan turned on his cell phone as he awakened. It would take a minute
or so to find a global network, so he went into the bathroom and washed his
face. He saw the tip of a newspaper under his door, and he opened the door
and picked up his copy of the international version of *U.S.A Today.* He
looked at the phone on his desk and he was relieved that the red Message
light wasn't flashing. Reluctantly, he picked up his cell phone expecting to
see that he'd either missed a call or that there was a message. No calls or
messages.

He liked phone calls, but he didn't want to receive a call from Tina
Johnson wanting to know if he'd seen Sarah. *I'll call them once I have
definite information.* He pushed the switch on the coffee maker; he was glad
that he didn't have to get dressed and go down stairs just to get coffee in the
morning. He didn't have to have his morning fix of Starbucks, but he did
look forward to having a cup of coffee in the morning.

The smell of the brewing coffee invigorated him. He knew it would
take a few minutes for the brewing cycle to be complete, so he decided to
shower and shave. By the time the coffee was done brewing, Stan was clean,
shaved, and he was dressed; now he could enjoy that first cup of coffee. It
tasted great. He now thought of his plans for the day.

He grabbed a few things and headed down for breakfast; one of those
things was a sealed envelope that he put into his shirt pocket. He also had
his pictures of Sarah; he never went anywhere without them – she was why
he was in Mexico. Breakfast was in the same restaurant where he'd had
lunch yesterday. He asked for a table near the back of the room; he liked to
be able to see everyone. He was shown to a table and a waiter promptly
appeared at his table carrying a carafe of steaming coffee and a pitcher of
freshly squeezed orange juice.

"Coffee and juice, señor?"

"Both please, and cream for the coffee."

"Certainly," the waiter replied as he poured a steaming cup of coffee and a tall glass of orange juice. He placed the carafe on the table as he left with the pitcher of juice. He returned in less than a minute with a small serving of half and half for the coffee.

"Gracias," Stan said as the waiter reappeared with a menu in his hand.

"Señor would you like to go through the buffet for breakfast, or would you like to order from the menu?"

"What would you recommend, uh," he stuttered as he looked at the nametag on the waiter's jacket, "Carlos?" Stan had a reason for asking which he should do.

"The eggs benedict are excellent, señor, and the chef also makes an excellent Belgian Waffle with fresh strawberries."

"Carlos," Stan began. "I can only eat one of them today. How about if you and the chef decide what I should have; I trust you."

"Of course, señor," Carlos said as he took the menu that Stan was holding. Carlos walked swiftly and tall toward the double doors that led to the kitchen area. He felt very important. Carlos didn't know that he was being primed by Stan for some help.

The orange juice was delicious, just as it had been in San José. The coffee was extremely robust and full of life; Stan wondered if they ground the beans in the kitchen. The coffee tasted too fresh to use commercial coffee grounds.

Stan looked up and saw Carlos walking toward him with a plate – it was filled with fresh fruit. "Compliments of the chef, señor." Carlos said as he displayed the fruit to Stan.

"It looks excellent, Carlos. Please tell the chef 'Thank you' for me," Stan said as the waiter was setting the plate in front of Stan.

"My pleasure, señor."

"Oh, Carlos," Stan said as the waiter was walking from the table. He turned and returned immediately to the table. "Do you think you could ask your restaurant manager to stop by my table, please? There's nothing wrong," he added to assure the waiter that he wasn't going to complain about anything.

"Of course, señor," the waiter replied as he headed toward a door that neatly blended into the wall – Stan hadn't noticed that door before. How clever.

Stan was enjoying the fruit plate when a distinguished looking man in a suit with a crisp white shirt and stunning tie approached his table. "Good morning, sir," he began. "I am the restaurant manager, Jorgé Ramirez; how may I help you?"

Stan pushed his chair back, stood up, and extended his right hand to shake hands with him. "Good morning, Señor Ramirez. My name is Stan Walkorski, and I'm staying in room 917." Stan then gestured to the seat to his right. "If you have a few minutes, would you mind having a seat so we could talk? Coffee?"

"Thank you," the restaurant manager replied as he sat down and poured himself a cup of coffee. "Is your breakfast okay so far?"

"It's excellent, thank you. And so is the service. I live in Seattle, Washington, and our city is known for its coffee, but yours is excellent. It tastes so fresh; do you grind your own beans back in the kitchen?" Stan was starting with small talk before he got to the real reason for asking him to sit down.

The restaurant manager smiled. "Not any more. We used to, but we found that it was not very efficient. So we found a coffee roaster who could deliver freshly roasted and ground coffee to us every four hours, twenty-four hours a day, seven days a week. Do you like the coffee?"

"It's very good," Stan replied. "I could taste the fresh flavor that you only get from freshly ground beans."

"If you don't mind my asking, señor, what is your work? Are you in the restaurant business?" Señor Ramirez was wondering if he'd given a competitor some information that was not widely known in the area.

"No," Stan replied. "I am not in the food business. I like to eat good food, but that's not what I do." Stan paused as he looked around to add a bit of intrigue to what he was about to say. "I am an investigator, and I need your help."

"Are you with the police?"

"No, I'm not police. I don't have a gun and I don't carry a badge. I am a private investigator who helps individuals. Do you think you could arrange a private meeting for me with your hotel manager sometime this morning?"

"Is there some problem with the hotel, señor?" The restaurant manager was starting to look worried. He took a big drink of the coffee.

"Not at all. The main reason I'm staying here is that the hotel manager in Los Cabos recommended your hotel as <u>the</u> best place to stay in this area." Stan stretched the truth a bit, but it wasn't an overt lie. Stan showed him his identification and handed him one of his cards. "I would be very grateful if you could arrange that for me, please."

"Let me see what I can do." The restaurant manager took a final sip of the coffee, stood up from the table, and promptly walked away.

There's the first piece to complete this puzzle.

Stan continued to work on the fruit plate as Carlos appeared with a combination plate that had never before been served in the restaurant. It had a single egg benedict and two halves of a Belgian waffle piled high with sliced strawberries and topped with fresh whipped cream. "The chef wanted you to try both of his specialties, so he made a special plate for you, señor," Carlos said as he placed the plate in front of Stan as soon as Stan had moved the fruit plate to the side.

"It looks marvelous", Stan said. "Tell the chef that he should add this to the menu – it's great for people like me who can't decide which one they want."

"Buen provecho," [Enjoy (the meal)] Carlos said as he stepped back from the table and returned to his station.

Stan knew he was going to enjoy the waffle; it looked too delicious to not enjoy. As he took a bite of the egg benedict, he tasted a Hollandaise sauce that he'd never had before. The flavors were distinct and fresh; there was a reason why it took some extra time for it to be prepared. Stan was very impressed with his breakfast. *I must remember to thank Miguel for booking this hotel.*

Stan couldn't eat all of the second half-waffle; he was full. He pushed his chair back just a little when he saw Señor Ramirez walking toward him. Stan took the napkin from his lap, wiped his lips, and then set the napkin to the left of his plate. Stan started to stand when the manager reached the table.

"Please stay seated, señor. I can't stay. But I just spoke with our hotel manager, Señor Carrillo, and he said he would be able to talk with you at ten-thirty this morning. Here is his card, and all you have to do is go to the front desk and tell them you have an appointment with him. Is there anything else I can do for you today?'

"Actually, yes," Stan said. "Please extend my compliments to the chef for the best tasting breakfast I've had in a very long time."

"It will be my pleasure to tell him. I hope you have a good day." The manager excused himself and walked away without shaking Stan's hand.

Stan looked at his watch; it was 9:15. He saw Carlos, and he signaled for him to bring the check, which he signed to his room. The second piece of the puzzle was now in place; Stan just needed to make sure that the hotel manager was willing to help him.

Stan left his room at 10:15 to head down to the lobby. "I have an appointment with Señor Carrillo at 10:30. I'm in room 917."

"Just one minute please, señor," the clerk at the front desk said. The clerk didn't normally have much interaction with the hotel manager or his secretary. He picked up the phone, punched in an extension, and began talking.

The only thing that Stan understood was "Gracias" as the clerk hung up the phone.

"Señor," the clerk began, "if you will please have a seat over there," he said as he gestured to a grouping of four plush chairs surrounding a polished wood square table.

"Thank you," Stan said as he walked over to the designated area by the windows. There were no magazines on the table; Stan wouldn't have been able to read them anyway if they were in Spanish. To look important and busy, Stan opened his briefcase and pulled out his notebook. He read a few pages, and then jotted down some notes.

Stan didn't notice the attractive woman who'd walked up to the table – he was the only one in the lobby who didn't. "Señor Carrillo will see you now. Won't you please come with me?"

"Thank you," Stan said as he stood and went with her through a door, to the right, and down the hall to the large office. She discreetly disappeared as Stan entered the hotel manager's office. Stan was impressed with the office and the decorations. There were plenty of pictures of Señor Carrillo with beautiful women and handsome men. It was apparent that he didn't get to his current level just by being a good accountant or an operations manager. Who you knew also helped.

The two men exchanged pleasantries for a few minutes before Stan told him precisely why he was in Guadalajara and what help he needed. Stan thanked Señor Carrillo for his help and he walked out of the manager's office at 10:55 with a half-page listing of times when the Holy Order of Saint Christine choir would be practicing in the cathedral in the next few days. The one thing he wasn't able to get was any information about a specific person in the Order – that request received a quick 'No' without any discussion. *Piece three was now in place.* Stan went up to his room; he had some time until the 12:40 choir practice.

Stan spent the next two days in the cathedral listening to the various music groups, but primarily observing the young women practicing their choral numbers in their green robes with a yellow stole. Sometimes there were a lot of people sitting in the pews, and so he was able to pull out his miniature binoculars to get a better look at the one he thought was Sarah. That had to be her. He didn't have a camera that he could use; the signs out front said 'NO PHOTOGRAPHY ALLOWED' in several languages, and he didn't want to draw any attention to himself. Now that he knew the choir's departure route, and they appeared to follow the same routine each time, Stan positioned himself so that they would walk right by him. He would be only a few feet from Sarah as she walked by. He watched her from close distance three times, each time holding a different picture of her cupped in his hand. She didn't even notice him, but he knew she was indeed Sarah. The large flowing robes hid any signs of pregnancy in the women – that's if these women were from that second group.

The puzzle was almost complete.

Forty-one/Cuarenta y uno
Guadalajara
Friday, May 16th

ocupado (ō·kū·pǎ'·dō) – busy. *Él está muy ocupado en el trabajo.* He is very busy at work.

Stan set his alarm for 7:00 so he could call the Johnsons before Robert left for work. He did have an advantage because Guadalajara was in the Central Time Zone, two hours' ahead of the Johnsons in Seattle. He'd called the Johnsons the previous night at a time when he thought they would be home, but all he got was the answering machine. The news that Stan had to tell them was not something he wanted to leave on an answering machine. He didn't leave any message at all; even saying who was calling might have caused Tina to have a panic attack.

He began with his normal morning routine: he started the coffee maker; took a shower; shaved; got dressed; then determined what to do for breakfast. This morning he decided to call downstairs and order breakfast to be sent up to his room. Stan needed to stay in the environment where he was in control and where there wouldn't be any surprises. He was also trying to figure out the exact time to place his call to Seattle. He knew that Robert would still be home at 7:00 Seattle time, meaning he could call them at 9:00 in Guadalajara. He still had plenty of time.

Room service was prompt, and the meal was as good as any of the meals that he'd eaten in the restaurants downstairs. Even the coffee from the carafe burst out in flavor; the food service at the hotel was certainly deserving of a five-star rating. Stan finished his breakfast and set the tray out in the hall, having first opened the cloth napkin to spread it out to cover the tray's contents. He brushed his teeth and then sat down at the glass-topped desk – he was ready to go to work. It was 8:56.

Stan took a deep breath; he knew this phone call, although it was going to be one of good news, was going to be an emotion-filled call. He took the pictures of Sarah, the ones he'd been carrying with him all the time, and spread them out on the desk. He pushed the Speaker button on the phone so his hands would be free to take notes. After punching in the numbers for international dialing, the U.S.A country code, and the Johnsons' phone number, he finally heard the first ring. The phone rang again – maybe they were out of town for the weekend. That would explain why he wasn't able to reach them last night. The phone rang for the third time.

"Hello," was the cautious answer. The Johnsons did not typically receive many phone calls that early in the morning.

"Good morning, Robert. It's Stan Walkorski calling. I hope it's not too early, but I wanted to catch you before you left for work." Stan exuded a voice of confidence and control; the latter could become very important.

"Oh, hi, Stan. How are you?"

"I'm doing well, Robert. How are you, and how's Tina?"

"Well, we're both doing as well as we can. Did you find her?"

"Robert, I have some good news that I want both of you to hear. Is Tina available to come to the phone?"

Robert didn't answer Stan's question. Instead, Stan heard the phone being set down as Robert went to tell his wife to get on the phone – *Stan had good news.*

"Stan, you've found her? Is she okay?" Tina's excited and anxious voice displayed the emotions that any mother would have in the same situation.

"Good morning, Tina," Stan said in his calm voice. "Let me just wait until Robert is back on the line. Okay?"

"I'm here, Stan," Robert said.

"Yes, I've found Sarah, and she looks perfectly fine."

"Oh my God! Oh my God!" Tina screamed amid tears of joy. "Did you say anything to her? Did she say why she ran away?"

"I haven't said anything to her, and she doesn't even know who I am. She's in a choir at a large cathedral, and I've been able to watch the choir practice several times a day. As I told you before, the churches down here are extremely protective about any information. So for now, I haven't even attempted to talk with any of the people in charge at the cathedral. I didn't want to cause any alarm or even frighten her; the last thing we want right now is for them to hide her or for her to run away to some other place." Stan knew the Johnsons wanted more information, but there wasn't going to be much more that he would be able to give them today. And he wasn't about to tell them that she might be pregnant – that would come later.

"If you haven't talked to them, then what do we do?" Robert asked.

"Here's what I want you to do," Stan began. "Book a flight down here to Guadalajara tomorrow, and then call me on my cell phone with your flight information. I'll meet you at the airport and I'll get a room for you here at the hotel where I am."

"Why don't we come down there today so we can see her right away?" Sarah's mom asked. She was, of course, excited and anxious to see her daughter.

"Tina," Robert began. "As much as I want to see her as soon as possible, one more day really won't matter, and we need to do what Stan suggests. Stan, I'll call the airline from the office, and then call you with the flight information. You're absolutely sure it's her?"

"Yes, I am," Stan replied. "One of the good things is that she's one of the very few Americans, so it's a lot easier to focus on her. I know this has been a long, hard time for you. Just hang in there and relax. Do you have any questions?"

"When will we be able to see her?" Tina asked.

Stan expected that question, but he'd hoped they wouldn't ask it. "Sunday," he said.

"Thanks, Stan. I'm sure we haven't been your easiest clients to work with, but we do appreciate your genuine interest in finding Sarah for us. I don't know how we can ever thank you enough." Stan could tell that stoic Robert's voice was breaking as all the emotion was settling in.

"You just did, Robert. Give me a call once you have the flight information." Stan wanted to cut this call; it had served its purpose. There would be plenty of time once they got to Guadalajara to talk and hug and cry.

"I will. Thanks again, Stan. Bye."

"Good bye for now. Bye, Tina."

Tina couldn't talk, so she didn't answer Stan. She just hung up the phone.

Stan pushed the Speaker button again, this time to disconnect the line. Now he had one more thing he needed to do to complete the puzzle – *this will be the hardest piece.*

Stan took the hotel manager's card out of his wallet and placed it on the desk. He picked up the handset and dialed the extension for Señor Carrillo.

The line was quickly answered, but the only thing he understood was "Buenos días."

"Buenos días," Stan began. "My name is Stan Walkorski in room 917."

"Yes sir, good morning. How may I help you?" was the female response.

"Señor Carrillo was kind enough to meet with me on Wednesday. I have one more – I'm not sure how to say it – one more request to ask him. Is it possible to meet with him today?" Stan wasn't sure if he'd already worn out his welcome with the hotel manager, but it wasn't going to hurt to try.

"I know that he's very busy today; Friday's always the busiest day before the weekend. May I put you on hold while I see if I can ask him?"

"Thank you," Stan replied. As he waited, Stan thought about the possible answers she might come back with. The worst answer was that he wasn't available today (or tomorrow); the next would be that he came on the phone and flatly turned down Stan's request; the best hope was that Stan would be able to meet with him today.

"Hello, sir? Are you in the hotel right now?"

"Yes, I am."

"Señor Carrillo said that he could see you for about ten minutes if you come down here to his office right away. Is that possible?"

"Yes, it is. I'm on my way right now. Thank you," Stan hung up the phone, gathered the items from the desk and put them into his notebook and headed out the door. The elevator responded right away and Stan was soon inside it on its way down to the main floor. He composed his thoughts, and said a quick silent prayer.

The elevator door opened and Stan strode confidently to the front desk, where the hotel manager's secretary was waiting for him. "Please come with me," she said as Stan approached.

"Thank you for arranging this," Stan said as the two walked the same path as they had two days earlier.

"My pleasure," she said as they reached Señor Carrillo's office; the door was open.

"Come on in, please," the manager said as he saw Stan at the door. The secretary closed the door behind him. "How is your stay at the hotel? I've heard that you've paid some very nice compliments to our food and beverage staff. They appreciate it, and of course, I use those comments when I give them their review each six months. But I'm guessing that you didn't want to come down here to talk about that."

"You're right, I didn't. But I do want to say that my stay here has been great. I don't know how the manager in Los Cabos knew about your hotel, but he certainly picked the best one for me to stay at."

"What is his name? I would like to send him a nice note," the manager said as he picked up a pen to write down Miguel's name at Hotel El Nuevo in San José. "So how can I help you today?"

Well, here goes. Stan began to tell him about Sarah and the Johnsons. The manager's eyes flinched as he saw the pictures of Sarah; *maybe he has a daughter.* They're flying down tomorrow; is there <u>any</u> way he could arrange for a meeting with Sarah?

"That is very difficult as I've explained to you before. The Holy Order of Saint Christine is very particular and protective of its young women." Señor Carrillo was telling Stan things he already knew.

Stan took the sealed envelope from his jacket pocket and set it on the desk. "It would give me great pleasure," Stan began, "if you would give this generous donation in your name to the Holy Order. This girl is their only daughter and they're devastated. Anything that you could help with would be so greatly appreciated not only by the parents but also by me." Stan then stood up and extended his hand to the manager. "Thank you for your time, Señor Carrillo. You have been very kind for even making time in your busy day for me. Thank you again."

The men shook hands and Stan turned to walk out of the office. The manager lifted a standing photo frame on his desk and set the envelope under it. The photos were of his wife and daughter who'd both been killed in a horrific car crash two years ago. He certainly knew the pain that the Johnsons were feeling.

Stan walked out of the hotel to clear his head. He wasn't sure what would happen next, but he'd done all he could. Stan had seen a small park close to the hotel, and so he went walking in the direction where he thought it was. He was about to cross the street to the park when his cell phone rang; would Robert be calling back already?

He looked at the caller ID, it was area code 206 – he thought Robert was going to be calling later. "Hello, this is Stan."

"Hi, Stan. Remember me?" the female voice asked.

"If I don't then I should be shot," Stan replied. He <u>didn't</u> know who it was; he was trying to run the voice through his brain – nothing came up. It wasn't Tina, and it certainly wasn't Robert.

"So do I shoot you now, or do I put you on the spot to call me by my name?"

His mind still drew a blank. "I'm very sorry, but do I get to order my last meal before you shoot me?" Stan couldn't recall any time that he was in this situation.

"Would you like borscht soup and vodka?" she asked.

"Nyet," he replied hoping that he picked up on the Russian hint and that it was Sara. "How's your business meeting, Sara?" He emphasized her name as he said it.

"How about boring with a capital B. How are you?"

Stan had completely forgotten to call her to say he was going to Guadalajara. What would he tell her now, *'Gee I can't make lunch because I'm across the Sea of Cortez'*? No, that wouldn't work. "I'm fine, thanks." Stan wanted to sound upbeat but he didn't know what to say.

"Well," Sara said. "I was waiting for your call so we could go to the Russian Art Exhibition, but I guess you found another petrushka to go with."

"Not really," Stan said. "I've been quite busy." At least <u>that</u> was the truth; he had been busy, just not in Los Cabos.

"Okay, I guess I'll believe you." Stan couldn't tell if Sara was actually pouting or if she was just playing a game. "Bad news from the exciting world at El Mirador," she said.

"What's that?" Stan said.

"At our breakfast meeting today, the boss said he was cutting our meeting short, and that we're all flying back today." Sara now sounded genuinely disappointed.

"You're kidding?" he asked. Stan wasn't sure if he'd rather hear that she was kidding (what would he do then?) of if she wasn't. He didn't have to wait long to find out.

"Not kidding; I could have thrown my glass of juice at him. What a jerk; he could've at least let us stay down here through the weekend. I was hoping to see you again."

"That is too bad," Stan said. He meant it, but he was also glad to not be caught in an untenable situation. "How about if I call you when I get to Seattle?"

"I'd like that," Sara said. "Oh, by the way. Have you found her yet?"

"I'd rather not say on the phone right now. How about if I tell you when we go out for dinner along Pike Place Market?" Stan wanted to switch the subject to the future and to Washington rather than the present time in Mexico, especially since they were hundreds of miles apart – something she didn't know.

"If that's an invitation, I'll accept it," Sara said. "Call me soon, okay?" She asked. Her voice was sounding happier.

"It's a deal," Stan said. "Have a safe flight home. I'll call you."

"All right. Bye."

"Bye," Stan said as he closed his phone. He'd dodged a bullet.

Stan was sitting in the park, which was actually a relatively quiet place given its location in the middle of a big city. His cell phone rang again. This time it <u>was</u> Robert with the information for their flight. Stan wrote down the flight number and times, and told him that he would meet them just as they came out of Customs.

He didn't know where Customs was; he didn't have to go through it when he flew in from Los Cabos. Oh well, he'd figure out where to meet them.

Stan stopped at a local restaurant for lunch; it reminded him of Lupita's in San José – small and friendly where everyone knew everyone else. Except for Stan; he didn't know anyone and no one knew him. But that didn't matter; he received great service as if he were a regular there.

Walking back to the hotel, a taxi sped through the red light and almost hit Stan as he was walking in the crosswalk. *I guess I'd better pay more attention.*

Stan's heart was beating a little faster as he walked back to the hotel. He took the elevator up to the fifth floor, the seventh floor, and finally to the ninth floor. Some kids had pushed the buttons just as they got off as he was getting on. As Stan opened the door to room 917, he saw an envelope on the floor. He picked it up and carried it to the desk.

Forty-two/Cuarenta y dos
Guadalajara International Airport
Saturday, May 17th

completa (cōm·plā'·tă) – complete. *¿Cuándo se completará la casa?* When will the house be completed?

Stan had more than enough excitement on Friday. He'd met with the hotel manager, Señor Carrillo, asking for his help to arrange a meeting with Sarah. He'd had a phone call from Sara, whose call reminded him of the Russian Art Exhibit in San José that he'd forgotten about; she had to go back to Seattle right away. *I wonder where and why she learned to read and speak Russian.* He almost got ran over by a speeding cab even though he was in the crosswalk and the light was green in his direction. An envelope was slid under his door; the return address was "Sr. Ernesto Carrillo, Hotel Manager" along with the name and address of the hotel. Stan had received a reply from the meeting yesterday with the hotel manager.

The sealed envelope still lay on the desk in Stan's room. He didn't open it on Friday because he wouldn't have been able to do anything about its contents. If the hotel manager had good news for Stan; there was no one he could tell. And if the letter said No to his request, well then he would be frustrated for the rest of the evening. He didn't want that. So Stan decided to wait until Saturday morning to open the letter, but not until after breakfast.

After his morning ritual of coffee pot, shower, shave, dress, Stan slid the envelope under the phone on the desk and went downstairs for breakfast. It was just like every other meal he'd eaten at the hotel – excellent! The restaurant was quieter than it had been during the week; perhaps there weren't as many business people there on the weekend. He didn't mind the quiet; it allowed him some time to think about the day.

The Johnsons would be boarding their plane at SEA-TAC in about an hour. He knew that Robert would be getting on the plane in an "I do this every day" fashion. Tina, however, would be a complete nervous wreck. Would she be able to see and talk to "her baby"? What should she say to her? What should she ask her? Robert would think about buying a drink or two for Tina to calm her down, but he knew the drinks might have a residual effect once they landed in Guadalajara. Robert was clearly the rock of the family; he would now need to be extremely comforting to his wife in her greatest time of need.

As Stan walked through the lobby on his way to the elevator his path was intersecting with that of the hotel manager. "Buenos días, Señor Carrillo," Stan said as the two men shook hands.

"Ah, Buenos días, señor," he replied. "I trust you received my reply."

"Yes, thank you."

"And I trust you are satisfied with the contents?"

Stan wasn't exactly sure what to say – he hadn't actually looked at the manager's reply yet. *But I can't tell him that.* "Yes, thank you. I'm very grateful for what you've been able to do." Stan phrased his response so it would be appropriate regardless of what the letter actually said. *I guess I'd better go read it.*

"You're welcome," the manager said. "I'm glad I've been able to be of service to you. I wish you a good day," he said as he prepared to continue on his way.

"And you, too," Stan replied.

Returning to the ninth floor after breakfast, Stan put the "Do Not Disturb" sign on the door knob so he could have some privacy as he got mentally prepared for the day. He sat down at the desk, lifted the phone, and retrieved the envelope. He gently loosened the flap and as he pulled out the contents of the envelope, and a business card fell out onto the desk. Stan unfolded the two pages and read them. He then re-folded the two pages and put them and the card back into the envelope. Stan put the envelope on the desk, closed his eyes, and thought of the Johnsons – all three of them.

The puzzle was now complete.

It was now time to go to the airport to pick up the Johnsons.

Stan had asked the concierge to make arrangements for him to be able to go to the airport and pick up the Johnsons. Stan said he wanted something bigger than a normal taxi, but he didn't want a limousine. The van that arrived was perfect. It was large enough for the three of them plus the Johnsons' luggage. The concierge went with Stan to meet the driver and to make sure that there weren't any misunderstandings. The driver was to take Stan to the airport, specifically to the International terminal to meet the Johnsons; the driver would wait there for Stan and the Johnsons, and then he would drive the three of them back to the hotel. Only then would he be paid, and it was a flat amount that had already been agreed upon.

"He's my brother-in-law," the concierge told Stan. "He will take good care of you; I guarantee it."

"Thank you very much," Stan said as he tipped the concierge and then stepped into the van. The inside was spotless and smoke-free; great service once again.

As the van pulled up to the airport terminal, the driver told Stan where to go inside to meet the Johnsons as they came out of Customs. "I will be parked right over there," the driver said as he pointed to an area where the limousines waited for their passengers.

"Thank you," Stan said as he got out of the van. The outside of the terminal looked calm; the inside was hectic. Mid-afternoon on a Saturday meant the arrival of thousands of tourists, some of them coming to Mexico for the first time. The first-timers were easy to spot as they exited Customs and came through the frosted glass doors – the sandals and the bright shirts or tank tops, plus some of them had already started their partying on the plane. *Bienvenidos a México.*

The Johnsons were also easy to spot. Stan knew them, so of course he would recognize them. But the Johnsons also had a "business trip" look about them – they weren't there to party. Each of them was pulling a large roller bag; Tina also had her purse, and Robert had his briefcase. *Do they think they will be here that long?* It was easier for Stan to spot them than for them to spot him, so he approached them through the crowd.

"Hello, Robert. Hi, Tina," Stan said as he shook Robert's hand. "Looks like the flight had some people on it ready to party." Stan wanted to keep the conversation light for a while; he didn't want to jump right into the "Sarah discussion" immediately.

"Oh, yes," Robert said. "There were a couple of groups who appeared to be traveling together, and I think their goal was to have the plane land with the most empty liquor bottles. I don't know what the record is, but they sure gave it their best shot."

"Have you seen Sarah today?" Tina asked. "Does she know that we're here?"

"No and no," Stan replied. "Let's go outside where it's a little quieter," he said as he led them out of the terminal building.

It was indeed quieter outside and there weren't as many people smoking as there had been in the congested terminal. The three of them walked in the direction of the van, and then Stan stopped. "There's a van to take us to the hotel, but let me tell you the situation first. I'll give you all the details once we get there, but I just want you to know the main things right now."

Stan paused and then continued. "I told you yesterday that I've seen her several times at the cathedral. I've looked at her through my binoculars, and I've been able to stand where the choir walks out. I was as close to her as you are to me right now."

"How does she look? She was always so full of life and energy. Is she okay?"

"She looks fine, Tina. All I can really see is her head, but she looks fine." Stan then told them about the Holy Order of Saint Christine, at least what he'd been able to find online plus what a few people locally were willing to tell him. Stan was surprised how secretive the people in town seemed to be when the discussion turned to the Order.

"You said we'd be able to see her tomorrow, right?" Tina asked.

"Yes, that's what we're planning to do," Stan said. He wanted to set the tone that he was in charge. They were paying him, but he had to be the decision-maker and the leader.

"Are they practicing today? Why can't we go watch that?"

"Tina," Robert said. "Stan said we would see her tomorrow."

"I'm afraid what she might do if she sees you at choir practice today. She doesn't know me, so my being there isn't a threat to her. Let's go back to the hotel and have a late lunch. We can sit down there and I'll tell you everything that's happened ever since I came back down. Okay?"

"Sure," they replied.

The drive back to the hotel was smooth and uneventful, something that helped to calm Tina down a bit. Stan got the Johnsons checked into their room on the ninth floor, and then the three of them went downstairs to the nearly empty restaurant. They were shown to a table in the corner, but Stan asked for one away from the wall and near the center of the room. "Most people," Stan began as they sat down, "think that the table in the corner is the best place for a quiet conversation. It might be quiet for them, but the acoustics of the corner and the ceiling will push their conversation out to the center of the room. If you want to talk in private, the center of the room is the best place, except, of course, for your own private room."

"I've seen that on TV," Robert said. "At Grand Central Station in New York, you can whisper in one corner of the big room, and someone at the opposite corner can hear you."

"Right," Stan said. "I don't have any real secrets to keep from others, but there's also no reason for them to know what's going on. Now here's our plan for tomorrow." Just then the waiter arrived with their drink order.

"Have you decided yet?" the waiter asked.

The Johnsons were hungry, so they ordered large meals; Stan ordered a salad. The waiter walked away.

"Tomorrow," Stan began, "we'll go to the nine o'clock Mass where her choir will be singing. So you'll be able to see her there, but we'll sit where she won't see you. Here's what we'll do after the service." Stan lowered his voice to indicate that what he was about to say was not for everyone else to hear. "I've arranged for us to meet with her after Mass. That may not sound like much, but it's not easy to have direct contact with them once they've joined the Order. So we have to respect the rules. I know she's your daughter, but that fact really means nothing to them. Can you do that?" Stan looked intently both at Robert and at Tina.

"Yes, we can," Robert replied. "Well, if it's that hard, then how did you arrange it?"

"Most people genuinely do want to help other people. I made a contact down here whom I knew would feel sympathetic to you in terms of being able to see Sarah and talk with her. You see, his wife and daughter were killed a couple years ago, but he doesn't know that I knew that. I told him your situation and how this has really left you feeling empty. I just asked him that if there were anything he could do, that I knew you would be very grateful. And I left it at that."

The waiter reappeared with the meals for the three of them. *"Mas café, por favor."*

"You're beginning to sound like a local," Robert said as Stan asked for more coffee.

"I don't know a whole lot more than that. I try some of the basics, and it just helps if I try at least a little bit."

"What'd he say?" Tina asked, referring to the man who'd helped Stan arrange the meeting.

"He didn't say anything. I was in his office and I just stood up and left. Here's his response," Stan said as he pulled out the envelope. "He has called a friend to arrange a meeting for us tomorrow, and he also included a letter of introduction that's essentially our invitation to get in." Stan opened the envelope and pulled out the pages; he was careful to not let the business card fall into the food. He handed the two sheets to Robert who just nodded his head up and down as he read the first page. The second page was in Spanish, so he wasn't able to read it.

Robert handed the pages to Tina who started sobbing as she read the first page; Robert reached to take the pages back from her. "So what happens after we meet with her?" Robert asked.

"That I don't know," Stan replied. "I would say that's really up to Sarah. But for now, let's just take one step at a time." Stan refolded the letter with the card, and put them back into the envelope – he would need them tomorrow. He decided that he wouldn't tell them that Sarah might be pregnant; he'd leave that up to her.

The three ate their meals in relative silence; there was some small talk, but nothing more than that. They agreed to meet in the lobby at 8:15 in the morning.

Forty-three/Cuarenta y tres
Saint Christine Cathedral – Guadalajara
Sunday, May 18th

nervioso (nĕr·vē·ō'·sō) – nervous. *El hombre está muy nervioso.* The man is very nervous.

The early morning sun was bright as it poured through Stan's window. Today could be a hot day, in more ways than just the outside temperature. Stan knew it was going to be a very emotional day for everyone, perhaps everyone except the guardian who would be with Sarah at their meeting after Mass. Room service brought breakfast to room 917 promptly at 7 AM. Stan wanted time to enjoy the breakfast before he made his preparations for the morning.

Heading downstairs at a few minutes past eight, Stan wanted to be in the lobby early so the Johnsons wouldn't have to wait for him. They came out of the restaurant right at quarter past eight. Stan walked over to greet them; it was time for him to once again be in charge. "Good morning," he said to both of them forcefully but politely. Stan didn't have a suit with him, but he was wearing a dress shirt, tie, slacks, and a sport coat.

Robert had on a dark suit and Tina's dress was pale blue with a short sleeve coat that matched. They looked very distinguished, but they also looked tired. Stan was not going to ask them if they slept well because it looked as if they didn't get any sleep at all.

"Good morning, Stan," Robert said as they shook hands.

"Good morning," Tina offered.

"What'd you have for breakfast? I had the waffle one morning, and it was great." Stan decided to try a lighter subject.

"I had the Mexican eggs, and Tina had cereal and yogurt. Are we going now?"

"Yes, let's go," Stan said. As the three of them walked out of the hotel, the bellman whistled for a black taxi. Stan had learned that the bellman had two whistles, each with a distinctive sound. One was for the regular taxis and the other was for the black ones. The bellman knew Stan by now and so he automatically called for the better taxi. Stan tipped the man as the Johnsons got into the back seat and he sat in the front seat.

"Saint Christine Cathedral," Stan said to the driver.

"Buenos días, everyone," the driver said as he pulled away from the hotel. "It looks like a very nice day today."

"Yes, it does," replied Stan. Robert and Tina were quiet in the back seat.

They arrived at the cathedral and Tina said "Wow" at her first glimpse of the impressive building.

"The service will be in Spanish or some parts will be in Latin," Stan said. "They do have an English service but it's at noon and the choir doesn't sing at that service."

"That's okay," Robert said. "We're not really here for the service itself, you know."

Stan hoped he'd timed it right so they could sit on the right side not too far back but not too close to the front. He didn't want Sarah to see them as the choir walked out, and he also didn't want Tina to be close enough that she might call Sarah's name or do something else to cause an issue. Stan felt as if he were "parent sitting" – he thought he could trust Robert to not do or say anything, but he wasn't sure about Tina.

The big entry doors were standing open as they walked up the steps. They walked on in and then went through the other doors into the main sanctuary. Tina just stopped and gazed in amazement. "Where will she be?" she whispered to Stan.

Stan didn't answer the question, but instead he led them down the main aisle to the row where he'd sat a few times to observe Sarah. "Let's sit in here on the right," he said in a soft voice. Tina walked in, followed by Robert and then Stan. They were early enough so no one else was already in that pew. The sanctuary began to fill as the 9:00 Mass was a popular time for the parishioners to attend. That is also why Stan picked this service; more people in the pews would allow Robert and Tina to blend in more. Sarah would not think to look out there for them as she'd not yet been told of the meeting; that was also intentional.

Fidgety Tina kept looking at her watch; when would the choir come in? What if they decided not to sing today? Tina had all sorts of questions running around inside her head, but she was doing what any mother would do. Her left hand reached over to hold Robert's right hand; grab and clutch was more like it. She was holding on to him as if she were in danger of falling off a building; she was not going to let go. Robert turned to the right to give her a reassuring look, but her eyes were locked straight ahead. She was not going to look anywhere else or at anything else because she might miss seeing Sarah. Robert leaned over and gave Tina a light kiss on her left cheek; that should reassure her.

The pipe organ began to play a processional, and all the people around them stood up. The three of them also stood up not only because everyone else did, but also so they could see. Stan knew the choir would come in from the right, so he nudged Robert and looked to the right at a thirty degree angle; Robert got the hint. He looked over there and saw the first pairs of young women in their green robes and yellow stoles. Tina was paying attention to what Robert was doing, and so she too looked over to see the choir begin to enter. It was harder for her to see between the people in front of them, but she managed to see them walk in. She squeezed Robert's hand even harder; she was a strong woman!

Stan saw Sarah; he leaned toward Robert. "There she is," he said.

"I see her," he replied softly. "There's Sarah," Robert whispered to Tina. He tried to hold back his emotion, but tears formed in the corner of each eye.

Tina gasped at the sight of her daughter, and she sat back down. She'd let go of Robert's hand, but he sat down beside her and put his right arm around her to comfort her.

"It's okay," he said to his wife. "She looks fine, and we'll see her later. I love you."

"I love you, too," she said through tears and sniffles. She was drained emotionally. It had been over four and a half months since she'd seen Sarah. She didn't know what she was to think or to feel.

The choir took their position. The priest and a few members of the clergy continued their procession to the altar area; their robes and the stately entrance were very impressive. Stan had told Robert and Tina about the Mass he'd attended in San José – he didn't understand anything but "Amen." He stood when they stood, and he sat down when they sat down. That's what they would do during this service; it was just like playing a game of follow the leader.

Stan handed his mini-binoculars to Robert so he and Tina could look at Sarah. Her face was angelic and it showed no signs of care or concern.

When the choir stood and sang, Tina sat at the edge of the pew. Her eyes were so focused on her daughter that it was like shooting a laser beam from one person to another. She once again grabbed for Robert's hand, but this time he managed to turn his hand so they actually held hands. She squeezed and he squeezed back.

When the choir finished their piece and sat down, Tina sat back in the pew and rested her head against Robert's shoulder. Her breathing was heaving, and she occasionally sniffled. Robert felt the pull of energy from his body to Tina's; she needed any she could get. Stan wasn't unaffected by all of this. His empathy for the Johnsons raised his emotion level even though he thought he'd be immune from it. He'd seen Sarah several times during her choir practice, and he thought that his professionalism would be a safeguard for him. But it wasn't. And that seemed to be okay.

The service ended with a final hymn sung by everyone; everyone except Stan, Robert, and Tina. They were all standing for the hymn and the organ piece that resounded throughout the majestic cathedral. The choir left the sanctuary in the same direction from where it had entered, and the three of them focused their attention once more on Sarah.

"I wonder what she's thinking about right now," Robert whispered to Stan. "Do you think she has any idea of how worried we were and how torn up we are?"

"Teenagers think differently than we do," Stan replied softly. "They aren't always thinking about others or how their actions can affect them. But that doesn't mean that they don't care. It's just not the highest priority for them."

"Tina's been an absolute wreck," Robert continued. "I almost had to have her committed because she's so torn up by this."

"I'm sorry," Stan said as he put his arm around Robert.

"Thanks."

The congregation began to file out of the sanctuary, an obvious sign that the service was over. Stan, Robert, and Tina sat down; they weren't in a rush to leave; not just yet anyway. "What now?" Robert asked.

Forty-four/Cuarenta y cuatro
Saint Christine Cathedral – Guadalajara
That same morning – Sunday, May 18th

seguridad (sā·gŭr'·ē·dăd') – safety. *La seguridad es muy importante.* Safety is very important.

Stan was still seated with the Johnsons in the sanctuary as the rest of the parishioners had filed out of the cathedral. He pulled an envelope out of his jacket pocket, the envelope that hotel manager Sr. Ernesto Carrillo had sent to his hotel room. "What we do now," Stan read from the note so he could answer Robert's question, "is to move to the third pew from the front and wait for someone to come get us."

"This seems a little spooky, doesn't it?" Robert asked.

"They are somewhat secretive, there's no question about that," Stan replied as he stood so he could move forward to the third pew; Robert and Tina followed him. They were sitting in the third pew for about five minutes when Stan saw a man of the cloth walk up the side aisle toward them.

"Hello," the man said. "Do you have a letter for me?"

"Yes, I do," Stan replied as he handed the second page to him.

The man of the cloth read the letter and seemed satisfied with it. "And do you also have a card for me?"

"Yes, I do," Stan said as he pulled Sr. Carrillo's card out of the envelope. "Here it is."

"Thank you," the man said. "Who are you?" he asked Stan.

"I'm Stan Walkorski; I am the investigator from the States and I was hired by the Johnsons here to find their daughter Sarah."

"Do you have identification?" the man asked.

"Yes, I do," Stan said as he pulled out both his driver's license and his Investigator's Identification card. The man looked at both of them and handed them back to Stan.

"Who are you?" the man now asked Robert.

"I'm Sarah's dad, Robert Johnson," he replied as he reached to his back pocket to pull out his wallet. He then took his driver's license from the wallet and handed it to the man. Seeing what was happening, Tina opened her purse to get her license. The man looked at Robert's ID and handed it back to him.

"And who are you?" he asked Tina.

"I'm her mother," Tina sobbed. "Why are you doing this to us? She's our daughter!" She started crying uncontrollably and Robert put his arm around her and pulled her to him.

"May I see your identification?" the man asked without any emotion.

Robert took the license from her hand and handed it him.

"Thank you," he said, and he handed it back to Robert. "First of all you must understand that Sarah came to us voluntarily; we did not seek her or approach her to join the Holy Order of Saint Christine. The second thing is that you are being allowed to have a short meeting with her only because of the request that we received from a very special person. Your introduction from Señor Carrillo is important and necessary, and without his special request, you would not be allowed to be with her. Third, we have rules that you must agree to before I can take you to the meeting area." The man stopped talking to allow everything he said to sink in.

"What are these rules?" Stan asked.

"You are limited to thirty minutes maximum, and there will be a guardian in the room with her all the time. You're not allowed to have any physical contact with her, and she may leave any time that she wants. You're not allowed to ask any questions about the Holy Order, nor does Sarah have to answer any of your questions. Do you all understand these rules, and will you abide by them?"

"Yes, we will," Stan answered.

"That's not enough," the man said. "I need to hear from everyone."

"What is this, some kind of a prison? This is ridiculous." Robert was beginning to lose his cool; Stan turned to him and placed his hand on his shoulder.

"If you don't want to see her, that's your decision," said the man of cloth.

"Do you not have any emotion?" Robert continued. "This is not some robot we're talking about; this is our daughter, our only child. Don't you see that?" he asked as he clinched his fist in a demonstration of his frustration.

The man just stood there absent of emotion or response.

"Robert," Stan began. "I don't like the rules either. But let's agree to them so we can have some time with Sarah. I'm willing to stay out of the room if you want me to. This is our only chance for now to be with her; this is what we've been working for since January. Okay?" He paused. "Do it for Tina," he added as a whisper.

Robert shook his head as he reluctantly said, "I agree."

The man looked at Tina who was now in a fog; she had no idea what was happening. Why couldn't she see Sarah; why did there have to be all these stupid rules? Why are there rules just to see your own child? "Okay," she managed to say. Tina was so worn down that she would agree to anything, even if someone said that the moon is out during the day and the sun at night.

"One last thing," the man began again. "You will be going through a metal detector. If you have anything you would like to put in this safe box now, you may."

"Nothing," Stan said. Robert and Tina both indicated 'No.'

"Okay, follow me."

The three of them followed the man who made it sound like someone had committed a crime. Robert was beginning to wonder if this Holy Order were somehow connected to the mafia or some other crime family. He would never get an answer to that thought.

They wandered down halls and through doors until they came to 'the' door. "I will be standing out here in case there is any problem inside," the robed man said as he opened the door and stepped inside to force them to their side of the table, which had been pushed against the far wall. Stan stepped aside to let the Johnsons go in first.

Sarah was sitting in a chair next to her guardian; they were both wearing full-length black outfits. She didn't say anything as her parents entered the room. Stan followed the Johnsons in and he sat down first; he looked at his watch to keep track of the time.

"Sarah!" Tina cried out loud. "Sarah, we miss you. Why? Please tell us why." Tina broke down in uncontrollable sobs as she placed her head in her arms on the table. Sarah just sat there, alternating her looks between each parent. She would occasionally look at Stan as if she recognized him.

"Sarah, honey," her dad began. "We're so happy to see you. Are you okay?" He too had a hard time holding back his emotions.

"Hi, Dad. Hi, Mom," she said with minimal emotion. "I'm fine."

"Honey, can you tell us why you left without saying anything to us or to Mary? We were so worried about you." Robert wanted to ask more, but he just wanted to hear her talk.

"You shouldn't have worried about me; you know I've always been able to take care of myself. And nothing's really wrong with me; I'm fine, in a way."

"Why couldn't you have told us something? You could've sent a card, called us, anything." Robert continued without any success.

"You wouldn't understand," she replied.

"But," Robert began, and then Stan put his hand on Robert's arm. The questioning wasn't going anywhere, and the time was running out.

Tina sat up; her eyes were red and full of tears. She sniffled and Robert handed his handkerchief to her; it was already out of his pocket. "Sarah, honey, I love you. I'll always love you. Are you coming home?" She could hardly say it all before her eyes welled up with tears again.

"This is my home for now," Sarah said rather hesitantly.

"You disappeared so suddenly, were you kidnapped by anyone?" Robert asked.

The guardian once again put her hand on Sarah's arm, but Sarah ignored her. "I'm here because I want to be here." Sarah paused and then continued. "I'm pregnant and I didn't want my pregnancy to be a distraction or an embarrassment to you."

Tina gasped. "You're pregnant?" she asked in a non-believing voice.

"Yes, I am. I'm sorry, but I felt it was better if I came here where I could be nurtured and loved and taken care of." Sarah was being quite matter-of-fact with her parents. Sensing their next questions, she continued. "I'm about seven months pregnant, and they'll put the baby up for adoption when it's born. I'll have to stay here for a little while after that, but then I can either go home or stay here in the other part of the Order."

"I'll explain that to you later," Stan whispered to Robert.

"I'm sorry if I've disappointed you," Sarah continued. "This isn't what I wanted either, but it's the best for the current situation."

Robert was about to say something when the door opened; the man of the cloth looked into the room. Stan looked at his watch. "Your time is up," the man said.

"No!" bawled Tina. "Robert," she continued. "I can't leave her here. Isn't there anything we can do? She's my baby."

Robert put his arm around Tina and held her up so they could walk out of the room. Sarah said nothing as they left. She and her guardian stayed seated; Sarah had said more than she was supposed to say.

The man of the cloth led them back through the maze of hallways until they reached a side door to the outside. He opened the door and said, "Do not try to have any further contact with her." He then shut the door. They were in a little garden area with benches. Robert and Tina sat down on a bench under a bushy tree.

"I'll leave you two alone for a few minutes. Don't worry, I won't leave you here; I'll be back in a while," Stan said as he started to walk down a path leading to some roses.

Robert and Tina sat on the bench with arms wrapped around each other, for emotional support and for physical support. They both felt as if their hearts had been snatched from them, and they had no energy left at all. They didn't talk; they couldn't.

Forty-five/Cuarenta y cinco
Guadalajara International Airport
Monday, May 19th

volver (vōl·vĕr') – to return. *Espero volver pronto.* I hope
to return soon.

Robert said that he and Tina didn't feel like going out for dinner on
Sunday night; they were still too emotional over their visit with Sarah. Her
pregnancy really took them by surprise, but even more surprising to them
was that Sarah didn't think that they would understand, not that they would.
Stan tried to counsel them about Sarah's decision, but they just didn't want
to hear it. He then told them about the two groups within the Holy Order of
Saint Christine, and that he didn't know that Sarah was pregnant – it was a
surprise to him, too.

They agreed to have breakfast together in the morning before going to
the airport. Stan met them downstairs even though their room was right
down the hall from his. Meeting them downstairs gave them the privacy and
the time they needed. Robert and Tina emerged from the elevator and
walked slowly toward Stan; their movements were slow and deliberate.

"Hi," Stan said as they approached. "I hope you got some sleep."

"We did, thanks." Robert replied. "A locomotive could've come
through our room, and I don't think we would've heard it."

"Stan," Tina said as she leaned against him and put her arms around
him. "I know you did everything you could. You did find her, and we do
thank you for that. Why she's down here now couldn't have been stopped by
us. We don't know what she'll decide to do, but we hope she'll come back
home and get back into school. Thanks," she said as she stepped up on her
toes and gave Stan a kiss on the right cheek.

"You're welcome," Stan said. "She's alive and that <u>is</u> the most
important thing."

The three of them stood there in awkward silence for a minute before
Robert said, "Let's go eat; there's nothing else we can do." Robert and Tina
devoured their breakfasts; they must not have gone out for dinner last night
– eating was returning some life to their faces.

"When are you coming back to Seattle?" Robert asked Stan.

"I have to go to San José first because I still have some things there and I need to personally thank the two people who helped me the most to locate Sarah. I'll be there a day or two before I head home." *That's two people if I can find who she was.*

Well, we'd like to take you out for dinner when you do get back," Tina said.

"I'll certainly let you know; it should only be a couple days." Stan looked at his watch and realized that they needed to get going to the airport.

They went back to their rooms to clean up, finish packing, and head back downstairs. Stan was the first one to the lobby. He paid his bill, and left a sealed envelope for Sr. Ernesto Carrillo. He walked over to the concierge and gave him a tip.

"My brother-in-law is waiting outside for you. I'll get someone to put the bags in the van."

The Johnsons exited the elevator without any hint of the extreme disappointment they had suffered, and would continue to suffer even after they got home. They were dressed for travel, looking very sharp. Robert paid the bill as Tina approached Stan. Somehow her face didn't show the signs of her crying and anguish from the past twenty-four hours. *Perhaps she is much stronger than I thought she was.*

The bellman gathered their bags and followed them out to the waiting van. Stan's flight to Los Cabos was two hours after the Johnsons' flight, but it made sense for them to all go at the same time. Plus this gave them more time to talk – at the airport, not in the van.

Stan paid for the taxi while the Johnsons were getting their luggage. The three of them walked into the International terminal and saw that Alaska Airlines was to the right; Stan would have to go to the Domestic terminal for his flight to Los Cabos. But since he had more time he waited for them as they got their boarding passes and checked their luggage. The three of them went to a small area where they could talk.

"Bring us the final bill when you get back to Seattle," Robert said. "But we don't want to see any receipts, just the final amount. It's going to take us a while to get used to the fact that Sarah is gone for now, and she might not come back. Maybe we'll see her again; maybe we won't. But there's nothing we can do about it; we know that although it's still hard to accept. We love her; we miss her; we'd give anything to have her back home. Just like baby birds leave the nest when they learn how to fly, our baby bird has grown her wings and is going to new places."

"Thank you, Stan." Tina was able to talk without crying. "I know I wasn't easy to deal with, and I thank you with all my heart for never giving up. Sarah didn't want to be found, but you found her. I don't know how you did it, but I'm glad you did." Tina stood up and went over to Stan, who was still sitting, and she kissed him on both cheeks.

Stan's face had the look of embarrassment, being kissed by a woman whose husband was sitting right there. Robert said, "That's okay. I'd do it too but I'm not man enough." He shook Stan's hand.

"The thought's good enough for me," Stan said as he got up.

Robert and Tina had a plane to catch. When they got home, they would start living a life that was different than what it used to be. It wouldn't be easy to make the change, but it was a change they knew they had to accept. They missed Sarah, and there would always be a place in their hearts, and in their home, for her. She would always be their daughter.

Stan waved as the Johnsons headed down the concourse. As he started the slow walk to his plane, he wondered how many of the children he saw laughing and playing would someday feel the need to fly from their nest.

Forty-six/Cuarenta y seis
San José del Cabo
Tuesday, May 20th

casi (kă'·sē) – almost. *Él casi gana la carrera.* He almost won the race.

Stan's flight in from Guadalajara Monday had been canceled, so he had to get a hotel room at the airport and fly back to San José the next afternoon. He wasn't able to get on an earlier flight; he hadn't yet learned the ways of flying within Mexico. His flight was quite crowded, but comfort was not his top priority at the moment. It probably wasn't even in the top ten. It was only a ninety minute flight, and Stan knew he could put up with almost anything for ninety minutes. The thing he was most grateful for was that he didn't have to go through Customs because it was a Mexico-to-Mexico flight.

He took a shuttle from the airport to Hotel El Nuevo and asked about Miguel when he got there. "Miguel will be here in the morning, señor. Is there anything I can do for you this evening?"

"Gracias, no," Stan replied. He went up the stairs to his room; the clothes he'd left out had all been cleaned and put away. Even the shirts that were hanging in the closet – the ones that he said didn't need to be washed – had been starched and pressed for him.

Stan was hungry. He'd eaten breakfast at the airport hotel in Guadalajara, but then he didn't eat lunch at the airport. *Maybe I should have had that Burrito Grande.* He knew what he would do – he would see if he could accomplish two things at once. He washed up, changed his shirt, and headed out the door.

It was nice to walk through Plaza Mijares again. He hadn't realized how much he missed it until he saw the fountains and the children running around. This was the one place that made him feel like he was at home in San José. The fountains were dancing to some music that he couldn't hear very well. As he walked toward the church, his thoughts turned once again to Sarah. He wondered what she would've done if they hadn't gone to San José for Christmas; would she have found some other place to go to have her baby? He knew it didn't do any good to think of the what ifs – there were too many of them, and he couldn't change the past anyway.

He continued his walk to Baja Brewing Company. The restaurant had been his destination a week ago when he was given the directions and times to follow before he ended up there. His reasoning was that the real purpose of the maze he was on was to see the yellow and green uniforms at the church. And it was those yellow and green uniforms – the same colors he was wearing that night – that actually led him to finding Sarah in Guadalajara. The letter writer could've had him end up anywhere after she had him see those uniforms. So why was he then led to Baja Brewing Company for dinner when there were other restaurants that are closer?

Stan remembered that the hostess at Baja Brewing seemed to pay special attention to him; she'd even made a comment about his yellow hat. Could she be the letter writer? He entered the restaurant and found a young man at the front stand. "One for dinner, señor?" he asked.

"Yes, but I have a question. I was in here last week, and there was a young American girl here who seated me. Is she here tonight?" Stan knew he had to be careful; he didn't want to sound too forward – after all he was old enough to be her father.

"You mean Tammy? She only works on Monday," the host replied.

"Do you have her address?" Stan re-thought what he just said. "What I mean is that I would like to get a note to her. If I gave you a note, could you get it to her?"

"We don't have her address. She works on Monday night and is paid at the end of her shift. Is this table okay?"

"It's fine," Stan said; he was frustrated. Perhaps it was Tammy who sent him the letters, but he didn't have any way of contacting her. What would he do now? He really couldn't justify staying in town for six more days just on the possibility that it was her. He decided that he would write a note at the hotel, seal it in an envelope, and bring it back to the restaurant. *If yesterday's flight hadn't been cancelled, I could've been here last night. And she was here!* Now he was really frustrated!

Stan ordered a beer, ate his dinner, and then ordered another beer. He was feeling a little better now. There weren't as many people in the plaza as he walked back to the hotel.

His job down here was almost done; he could go home tomorrow.

Forty-seven/Cuarenta y siete
Hotel El Nuevo – San José del Cabo
Wednesday, May 21st

flores (flō·rās') – flowers. *Estas son flores bonitas.* Those
are pretty flowers.

Stan woke without the need for the alarm clock. He'd slept well, and he
felt relaxed. It would've been nice if Sarah decided to leave the Order and
go back with the Johnsons, but life doesn't always go the path that the
parents want. He did his job, and he was pleased with the results.

He went downstairs for breakfast – it was good as it always – and then
he returned to his room to do his final packing. Everything was ready, so he
got his bags and briefcase and headed back downstairs. He went to the front
desk and saw Miguel. "Buenos días, Miguel!" he said to the man who'd
really helped him, both in San José and in Guadalajara.

"Señor Stan! It's good to see you. I saw that you got back yesterday.
How did it go?" Miguel asked in a tentative voice. He didn't want to pry; he
was just being courteous.

"It went as well as it could. The parents flew down and we had a
meeting with her. She's part of a Holy Order down there, so there's not
much else the parents could do." Stan didn't feel it was necessary to reveal
any other information; after all, it was confidential. "But they were happy to
see her and know that she's okay – it's been a long four and a half months
for them not knowing what had happened to her."

"That's good; I'm happy that she's okay."

"Thank you, Miguel. And thank you for setting me up at the hotel; it
was excellent. Here you are, my friend. Thank you so much," Stan said as he
handed him a sealed envelope.

Once again, Miguel was too professional to open it. "Thank you, Señor
Stan. It's been my pleasure to have you here as my guest. I hope that you
will be able to come back down here for pleasure some time. You know I'll
always have a good room for you."

"Thank you. Oh, I have one last favor to ask of you." Stan remembered
the note that he wanted taken to the restaurant for Tammy. "Would you be
so kind as to take this note to Baja Brewing? I think she is the one who

helped me know what I needed to look for to find Sarah. But she only works on Mondays." Stan pulled the envelope out of his briefcase and handed it to Miguel.

"Of course I will," Miguel replied as Stan handed the envelope to him. "Oh, I almost forgot. Remember the señora you saw a couple times a few months back? She came by and wanted me to tell you that she's in town, and that she's moving back to San José."

"Thanks, I'll try to call her when I'm at the airport." Stan didn't really think he would call Carmelita, but he had to say something.

"I asked her," Miguel began, "if she wanted to leave a note for you with her address and phone, but she said *'No, just tell him that.'*"

"Well," Stan said awkwardly, "I guess it's time to go."

"Your taxi's waiting for you. Please, and I do mean it, let me know if I can ever help you anywhere in Mexico," Miguel said as the two men shook hands.

"I will, Miguel. And if you ever come up my way, do call me. Thank you for everything," Stan said as they continued to shake hands.

Stan went outside to get in the taxi. As he reached the sidewalk, a young lady came up to him – it was the hostess from his dinner at the Baja Brewing Company last week. "Hi," she said. "I'm glad you found her, and I hope her parents understand 'cause I know mine won't." She then turned and briskly walked away.

"Tammy?" Stan hollered for her, but the girl kept walking, and then she was gone.

Forty-eight/Cuarenta y ocho
Johnsons' home – Redmond, Washington
Saturday, September 6th

sol (sōl') – sun. *El sol está brillando.* The sun is shining.

Summer was winding down, but you couldn't tell it from the immaculate Johnson yard. Robert had gone into the house after spending most of the morning and early afternoon outside mowing, trimming, and cleaning the flower beds. He poured himself a glass of iced tea and sat down to relax when the phone rang.

"Hello," he spoke into the phone.

"Hi, Dad. It's Sarah. How are you?" Sarah's voice sounded full of life.

"We're fine, honey. It's so great to hear from you. Where are you?" he asked.

"We're at SEA-TAC; you want to come pick us up?" Sarah replied.

"Of course," he said excitedly. "Who's with you?"

"Maria," Sarah answered.

"Oh, is Maria one of the girls you met down in Guadalajara?"

"No, Dad," Sarah started. "Maria's your new granddaughter."

About the Author

Stuart Gustafson learned the love of travel at a very young age when the family moved often as his father was in the US Navy. The frequent relocations also ensured that he was able to establish new friendships as well as integrate into established ones. He was born in Southern California, and while he moved many times as a youngster, Stuart ended back up in San Diego where he met and married Darlene Smith in 1974. They have one daughter and one son.

His formal education was a BA in Mathematics from San Diego State University and an MBA from the University of San Diego. He spent twenty-nine years in high-technology endeavors, including a move from San Diego to Boise, Idaho, in 1993. He took early retirement in 2007 to devote more time to writing, traveling, and taking care of his mother, who recently passed away at the age of 94. Mom also loved to travel, and the collages on her walls showed some of her more enjoyable trips.

The Los Cabos area of Mexico's Baja California is one of Stuart's favorite places to visit, and so it was only natural that his first mystery tourism novel is set there. He went to Cabo numerous times to ensure the authenticity of many of the book's descriptions and locations. In addition to novels, he writes travel articles and posts pictures of great travel places he's visited. He has Million-Mile Flier status on a major air carrier and he's been to 32 different countries, thus it's easy to see why he has the trademarked name *America's International Travel Expert*®. For more travel information, and to read about Stuart's other books and speaking opportunities, visit **www.stuartgustafson.com**.